SAFE AS HOUSES

Carlin, very best wishes

[signature]

By the same author:

The Angel Within

Cornflakes and Candlelight (2006)

Janet Wade

SAFE AS HOUSES

Williams Publications

First published in 2005
By Williams Publications.

Copyright © Janet Wade 2005

The moral right of the author has been asserted.

All characters in this publication are fictitious
and any resemblance to real persons, living or dead is purely
coincidental.

All rights reserved. No part of this publication may be reproduced, stored in a retrieval system, or transmitted, in any form or by any means, without the prior permission in writing of the publisher, nor be otherwise circulated in any form of binding or cover other than that in which it is published and without a similar condition including this condition being imposed on the subsequent purchaser.

A CIP catalogue record for this book is available from the British Library

ISBN   0-9548598-1-2

Printed in England by Intype Libra, Wimbledon SW19 4HE

Marketing and Sales:
Williams Publications
8 Ranulph Way
Hatfield Peverel
Essex CM3 2RN
Tel. 01245 381064

PART ONE
CHAPTER ONE

The child, wrapped warmly in a calf length coat, both to guard against the biting wind and to accommodate next year's growth, walked serenely beside the short stocky figure of her father, towards Grandmother's house, two long streets away from her own. Her fingers were clasped within his broad hand as he gently measured and timed his steps to spare her the necessity to hurry.

She knew every cracked paving slab, each scrubbed front doorstep and polished brass knocker of the street where she lived, for pride and poverty coexisted in the centre of the Midlands town of her birth. There was, in the two long streets separating the home of her father and that of his mother, evidence that poverty had triumphed, and the struggle to maintain appearances, abandoned. Limp unwashed curtains framing grimy windows hung faded and degenerate, whilst alleys allowing access to backyards now and then spewed rubbish onto the pavement.

The deep brown of the child's strikingly large eyes was accentuated by her wan face, suggesting she lived on a diet of more chimney smoke than fresh air. She was not aware of this, or indeed any other deprivation, and the delight at being alone in her father's company was unmistakable to those who passed by, though both were oblivious to others who trod the same path. The man said little, but smiled often, squeezing as he did so, the tiny hand enclosed in his own.

They tapped the sash window, and a slight movement of the curtain acknowledged their presence. Routinely the child lifted the latch of the back door whilst her father stooped into the shed to chop firewood sufficient for his mother's needs until he returned next evening. The old lady laid an arthritic hand on her grand daughter's head as she moved the kettle to the centre of the range, and they sat in the dimness of the parlour watching the flames in the grate until the sound of wood chippings being swept was audible.

SAFE AS HOUSES

"Dad's finished Gran. Shall I get the cups?"

"They're on the tray, child. I haven't a biscuit tonight. Tomorrow maybe."

"It's alright Gran. I'm not hungry."

She was, but had inherited from the two whose company she now shared, the grace that enabled her to take generous account of the feelings of others. The Grandmother beckoned to her son in the doorway as he hung his cap.

"Come to the fire Alex."

There was no physical demonstration of the profound affection between them, but the chemistry of it enveloped all three, and the child imbibed it; felt it's warmth, and wished only that it could last forever. But she needed no more than the fact of her Grandmother's white hair and frail physique to understand that this could not be so.

Dad had been the last of seven children and the only son. Her grandfather she could barely remember, save that he always wore a polka dot handkerchief in his breast pocket, and required that she should remain silent, and sit straight-backed in her chair at mealtimes, whenever she visited. They no longer came for meals: the preparation now being too much for Gran who nodded in the direction of the sideboard. "The box is yours when I go Alex. And my ring is for the child - you'll see to it?"

Her father smiled, refraining from solicitous clichés, which pleased the old lady, for not being given to many words, she preferred the sentiments she did express to be taken seriously. "And there's enough money in my bank book to put me away when the time comes."

They drank tea from the precious china cups she had treasured since her wedding day, Kate fingering the delicate gold leaf pattern whilst Alex talked with his mother, keeping her involved with their family life, and he with hers. She rarely left the house now, and listened avidly to the wireless, thus able to communicate newscasts her son missed during the daytime.

"Their Majesties seem determined to stay in London despite the bombing." And then, as if the mention of royalty reminded her of her life in service, she touched her granddaughter's arm and remonstrated gently, "Don't throw back your head to drain your cup dear."

She had touched marginally on the one area that might have created tension had not both been equally averse to confrontation.

"We aren't in the best circles, Ma. We're in the parlour having a cup of tea together. She enjoyed every drop, and you wouldn't want her to waste any would you?"

"No indeed. We never had enough to waste. But she looked so like the mistress' girl sitting there, I could hear her ladyship speaking." Reminiscing on years past, she was able now from the comfort of her high backed chair, to forget the exhaustion of running up and downstairs with jugs of hot water for the family ablutions, black leading grates and carrying in wood and coal. She tapped the table beside her as if to bring herself back to the present. "You'll want to be on your way now - Lucy will be needing you. Another mouth to feed soon."

"We'll manage. No need for you to worry. I'll walk you down the yard afore we go."

He handed her her stick and withdrew the wooden stool he had made, from beneath her feet. With slow and graceful dignity she rose from her chair, leaning barely perceptibly on his arm, drawing her shawl around her shoulders. Sensing her lack of confidence once outside, he escorted her to the door of the privy, and then returned to the child until the old lady's re-emergence indicated the need for him again.

This was the part she hated. But rather her son to witness the loss of independence than anyone else. Except the child. But the child was not old enough yet. She reflected on the fact of having six daughters, including Eve who lived with her, at least shared the same address, but as she came home after midnight and slept in late, they saw little of each other. The others visited sporadically when the fancy took them.

Safely ensconced in her chair again, she returned her son's smile as he noted the dainty feet could no longer reach the ground. "I'll put a sliver of wood on that stool when I come tomorrow. You're shrinking Ma."

"No doubt," she agreed, wasting no further words on what was an obvious fact. "God bless you both."

They drew the bolt on the kitchen door, kissed her 'goodnight', and then left by the front door. Kate looked enviously at Grandmother's front door that opened directly onto the street, wishing their house had been similarly designed, and not as it was, with visitors access half way down a narrow alley, where facing it at only one yard's distance was an identical door to the Orfield's house. At the end of the alley, two gates each set at an angle, offered access to their respective backyards. People who knocked at Grandmother's house could be clearly seen, whereas those calling on Kate's family stood in the gloom of the unlit alley, and if strangers, appeared menacing to a six year old sent to see 'who was knocking'. Even the rent-man came round the back. He always tweaked her ear; perhaps from a natural affability, or likely because Kate's parents were the rarity who had

SAFE AS HOUSES

cash ready on the windowsill each Friday night.

"What's in Gran's box?" Kate asked. A little of the magic was disappearing now, but it would return tomorrow. It always did.

"Just the Family Bible and Grandpa's watch."

"Why doesn't she give it to you instead of reminding you every evening?"

"That wouldn't be right Kate."

She didn't question his statement. If her father said it wouldn't be right, that must be the case. "Gran won't die until my finger fits her ring will she?"

He smiled at his daughter. "We don't decide when we go pal."

"I think Gran will."

This time it was he who did not challenge. "Aye, her will is bigger than she is, I'll give you that."

How alike they were, he thought; the two people he loved so effortlessly. It wasn't that his love for Lucy had grown cold, but rather that he saw her only in the context of his mother in law who lived with them in their back-to-back Victorian house. There was so little time to talk, and when they finally retreated to their bedroom it was with exhaustion; he having driven a coal lorry from pit head to factories since early morning, and she from working in the factory in the street that ran parallel to their own.

Being wartime, many a night's sleep was lost as the wail of the sirens summoned them to the shelter in Freeman Street. With practised efficiency, Alex would lift Kate from her bed whilst Lucy tucked her blue dressing gown around her before joining the scuffle to get underground before the bombing began. Not appreciating the implications of war, Kate enjoyed the night excursions to the security of the shelter where camaraderie abounded and mugs of cocoa were shared magnanimously. If it was dawn before the all clear sounded, then Kate was the only one to go back to bed. Big Grandma trudged to the cigar factory, Alex through the cobbled streets to where the lorry was garaged, and Lucy, without breakfast, went straight onto the early shift.

At only six it was not viewed seriously if she caught up on sleep before reporting to school. Indeed she, and others who did were fortunate, for many emerged from the shelter to find their homes obliterated. Miss Dixon turned a blind eye as tired heads drooped onto folded arms. After lunch and the routine dose of orange juice and cod liver oil, they could all legitimately curl up on oval rush mats, whilst she read a story to those capable of concentration.

Most days Kate walked home with her classmate Chrissie Biggs. The girl was worldly, less needful of the affection essential to her companion. Her father was away in the army - a situation that appeared to trouble Mrs. Briggs not at all. Relieved, but feeling guilty he had not been conscripted due the essential nature of his work, Alex duplicated whatever he made for Kate, though Chrissie appeared indifferent, and Lucy, to whom gratitude was essential, would grumble, "I don't know why you bother."

"Maybe she resents her Dad being away."

"Her ma finds plenty of substitutes." Big Grandma's acerbic tone was sceptical, if unsurprised, at the information gained from her nightly visit to the Jug and Bottle department of the Feathers Arms. The time it took to drink two halves of light and bitter - and she was expert at making them last if the company were congenial - provided not only companionship, but an opportunity for Lucy and Alex to have time to themselves. But Alex was such a reticent chap she suspected rightly that he'd need a month without her, to come out of his shell. Not her type at all. She preferred the bawdy, loquacious, leather-belted men whose jokes kept the evening crackling until she left with her nightcap jug of frothing ale. But he was a good husband to her girl: after her own life with Joseph, it was almost beyond her to comprehend such caring. Occasionally she suspected Lucy was just a little bored, but knew exactly why his gentle manner and quiet strength had captivated her at fifteen until at twenty-one she became his bride.

Joe was dead by then; the drink finally took him. And though Lucy had retained an inexplicable affection for her errant father, Ruth herself could only be mightily relieved. He'd made their lives a living hell ever since her two sons Jack and David had left home, she and Lucy having more than once crouched silently in terror behind a locked door to escape the vehement consequences of his drunkenness. The debts he left meant she couldn't manage a place of her own out of wages from rolling cigars, so when Alex and Lucy were married, the three moved into 168 Courtney Street. There, she shared a room with Kate whom she idolised, yet failed to get close to, something she envied the other Grandmother, for it did not escape her that Kate could not wait to visit each evening.

She hadn't seen Alex' mother since Joe's funeral. Even were the old lady not practically housebound they would hardly have chanced to meet in any of the local hostelries, for evidently she disapproved of drink.

'Not that we haven't both 'ad cause to,' Ruth pondered. 'By all accounts her chap led her a pretty dance often enough. And as for that daughter who lived with her - brazen blonde hussy – she'd been carried home a time or two. Hostess at the Business Men's Club: that was a laugh.'

Of ample figure and gregarious personality, it was to Big Grandma that the residents of the street turned to manage their annual outing to Blackpool, their Penny Savings Bank and their Sick Club. Her sharp brain and natural facility for organisation indicated that had she been born in a different bed, she would have gone far. But the cigar factory was her horizon by day with The Feathers providing her evening venue. The pub was only a stone's throw away, and whenever Kate had cause to pass it on an errand, she did so by hugging the wall and creeping low beneath the window for if Grandma chanced to notice her she would call her inside, indecorously showing her off to her companions.

"She's a real picture Ruth," Bella Pearce would comply, belching uninhibitedly.

"Beautiful brown eyes, ain't yer darlin'?" Bill Creasey invariably seized on the opportunity to kiss the child, breathing ale into her nostrils, whilst from the crowded bar would be tossed a reminder intended to puncture Grandma's pride. "Can't hide that Jewish blood though, can you Ruthie?"

"It's in the background where it can stop," Ruth would retort, unabashed. And then beaming at the child, "Off you go now Kate," as if she had only been summoned for a special treat which must be rationed.

"What's Jewish blood?" Kate once asked her father as she sat on the cellar steps watching him fashion a strut for the kitchen chair.

"Nothing you need worry about," he had replied without raising his eyes. "Sit on your cushion - step's cold."

Eager to see the article take shape, she had edged along the step to where she had an unimpeded view. Dad kept their feet warm by putting plenty of sawdust on the concrete floor and if he worked beyond dusk, two candles reflected in a mirror provided all the light he needed.

The cellar was his retreat from coal dust, factory smoke and mother-in-law. It wasn't that he disliked her for she was remarkably benevolent: but just that she was there. Nearly all the time she was there, if not in person, then in influence or effect. The moment they were alone, Lucy would open a conversation with 'Ma was saying'... or 'Ma brought this or that home today.' In her absence, her overall hanging on the kitchen door substituted for her actual presence, whilst her capacious bag occupied a stool 'so it shouldn't trip anyone over,' for there was inadequate room for generations forced to live together in these old back-to-backs.

To his chagrin, he minded that Lucy became more animated when talking to her mother. He couldn't blame her for he lacked the parlance to communicate facilely, and was rendered tongue tied as others effortlessly exchanged inconsequential detail. He failed to understand it; after all a man thought in words didn't he? And then he wasn't sure whether it would actually be an advantage to articulate, for might it not prove that the state of needing no words to be spoken that he enjoyed with his mother and young Kate, was beyond them? He blew onto the piece of wood he had sandpapered and Kate, observing there was now nothing to be spoiled by interruption, moved closer toward him.

"Dad, you said the baby was our secret, and now Chrissie knows. I didn't tell her."

"Did she say so?"

"She shouted it down the street. Jimmy said they'd known a long time."

"Babies don't stay secret for long pal - don't worry about it. We'll have to make the cradle soon; Mam's already started the bedding." He paused. "Kate, you know that Jimmy's Ma is very ill?"

"No. Jimmy usually tells me everything."

"Mam will make them a pie tomorrow."

"I like Jimmy - George too, but not their Dad. He gets drunk a lot. I've seen him."

"In the Feathers?"

"Sometimes. But the other day he was in the entry and was sick. I couldn't get past him to the back gate so I banged on the front door and Big Grandma let me in."

"Did she see him? What did she do?" he asked in sharper tones than she was accustomed to hearing.

"She thumped on their door and told George to drag their Dad inside."

He smiled wryly. That sounded true to form. Lucy's Ma wouldn't bandy words or trouble with refinements as she made her demand.

How he wished he had the means to give Lucy the house and life she deserved, for she worked harder than anyone he knew and yet so little was hers in return. Neither new clothes nor Sunday roast could he afford for her but somehow she found ways to manage so that they were all comfortable. He vowed she could put money on elastic for an occasional length of fabric from the man who wheeled his barrow round on Thursdays was all she needed to keep them respectably dressed.

Her nimble fingers and culinary skills ensured that whenever there was a wedding in the street, it was to Lucy the bride came for both cake and gown. Her customers being neighbours, she rarely charged sufficient to cover the long hours of labour. In any case it was a labour she loved and compared to the drudgery of the factory, the sheer artistry set her spirit free. She turned to Alex at every stage to ask his opinion, which he gave knowing that whatever he said she would follow her own instinct. If his view confirmed her own, it was a bonus, and if not it required only that she proved the accuracy of her decision.

Watching her graceful movements as she worked he thought that worse than not providing for her so she could give all her time to her creations instead of toiling in the sweat shop, was that he couldn't take her dancing; an activity she adored. Whilst he was devoid of all sense of rhythm, her feet were as nimble as her fingers. Not since they met fifteen years ago had she gone dancing at the Palais though her brother David and wife Laura had won numerous trophies for their ballroom dancing.

He had wanted to urge, 'Go on, have a dance - I don't mind.' But truth was that he did, for within the gentle nature lay a concealed but passionately jealous streak, not just for Lucy, but Kate and his mother too. As long as none threatened the love that bound them, the potential tempest would be harnessed. Lucy was not the only one to recognise it, for the apparent easy going temperament that might initially be interpreted as weakness, was never actually challenged. She understood, and despite being the Piper, well knew on whose strength she depended to provide the tune.

An honest man in all his dealings, he would, and did, break his strictly held code of ethics if the alternative caused his family to suffer. At dusk, on his way to garage the lorry he would now and then hump a sack of coal down the alley to the back yard. Lucy and little Kate must be warm, and that was something he *could* make happen. He did not go unseen but there was an understanding in the street; a man was allowed to look after his own and his manner of doing it his own business. 'We didn't see' was the philosophy adults taught their young, and the young understood.

Kate, at six, knew that Jimmy and George had found a way to deplete the gas meter; that Chrissie's mother smuggled cardigans out of the factory to sell to her relatives, and never got into trouble because she did the foreman favours. Here her knowledge ended for she had no notion what the favours could be, nor was she greatly interested. Although a perceptive child, her observations rarely impinged on her own life that was made secure by the love that surrounded her. Though love was all she had in abundance, its manifestation - in shoes Alex polished until they shone, clothes contrived from left over pieces of fabric and her rag doll dressed identically, bore testimony to the midnight oil burned for love of her. She did not voice the longing for a china doll whose limbs could be moved and whose eyes opened and closed, feeling that if the expected baby were not a fact, she might have had one this coming Christmas, but Mam was right; a live doll that she could help to bath would be much better.

She enjoyed Friday nights when Dad built up a huge fire, and carried in the long tin bathtub from the hook on the wall dividing their yard from the Thorntons who were their other neighbours. He put the tub alongside the hearth and Mam filled it with a pan from the copper boiler. As soon as Kate had been scrubbed clean and wrapped in a warm towel, Dad would add another pan of scalding water ready for Lucy and then disappear to the cellar whilst Kate went up to double bed she shared with Big Grandma. The flock mattress had been duly rolled and smoothed at morning bed making, and if Kate didn't wriggle too much, it might just be comfortable when Grandma returned from The Feathers. In any case, the effect of the beer caused her to worry less about the state of the bed at night than she did each morning.

Dad was the last to have his bath - Grandma went to the slipper baths near to her factory to have hers. Another shovel of coal on the fire, two more pans of water in the tub, and the grime and dust of his coal truck oozed blissfully from his body, whilst Lucy made cocoa for the three of them.

Their sitting on her bed with Friday night cocoa was as nice as being at Little Gran's. Though the room was not as genteel, Mam had time to be with them, and just for a while didn't appear as if she were already thinking what job must be done next. The steaming bath having smoothed away her tiredness, her flushed cheeks almost making her young again, she the more closely resembled the sepia photograph Dad had on his dressing table, in which she wore a Charleston dress and long beads, and her bobbed hair waved in the Eugene fashion.

"Dance for us Mam," Kate would plead excitedly. And sensing her mother weaken she would seize the moment. "Hurry Dad. Wind the gramophone."

"Draw the curtains then," Lucy instructed, "so them at the back can't see." She referred to the row of houses backing onto theirs - the next street in fact, but less than thirty yards away. Kate was in seventh heaven and bounced up and down on the bed in time to the music. "You clap Dad!"
Her father grinned shyly. "I can't even do that pal. The music doesn't get

inside me as it does your Mam."

Lucy's feet shot out; her fingers crossed her knees, her weariness dispelled as she performed her favourite Charleston. Kate hugged them in turn. "I like it here," she gulped emotionally. "I don't like other Mams and Dads."

"Well that's alright then, cos we're the folks you're stuck with. What's brought this on Sunshine?"

She was too young to explain. She only knew she hadn't liked what Jimmy's Dad had done when she had tried to get past him in the alley again today. Confused too, feeling it was wrong not to like it because he had smiled so kindly at her as he'd put his hand beneath her dress and urged her to nurse him 'here where it feels sore.' But if it was sore, why did he want her to press hard on the heavy cloth of his trousers? His fingers had fumbled to get inside her knickers, but she was outgrowing them, and the tight elastic prevented his progress.

"What a nice little bottom. Our Kate from next door."

She was frightened but he was still smiling, still sprawled across the width of the alley. His eyes were red, though his demeanour was not unhappy, but he must be if Jimmy's Mam were dying. And then George appeared from the street, whistling as he turned into the entry. He stopped as if paralysed.

"You bloody fool. Her Dad'll kill you!" He wrenched his father's arm from the child. "You go in Kate. My Dad wasn't feeling so good - no need to tell your Mam."

"Shall I not tell her to bring a bandage?"

She liked George; he climbed up to the guttering when she and Jimmy threw the sorbo ball too high.

"Bandage?" George appeared confused.

"Your Dad says he's sore and it hurts."

"I'll see it bloody hurts." George muttered under his breath, and then, "It's alright Kate, we've got some bandages inside."

Kate was surprised. They didn't often have the things they needed at home, and Jimmy was always being sent round to borrow this or that.

"So whose parents don't you like,?" Lucy and Alex gazed at her intently. But she couldn't say, because George had said her Dad would kill Mr. Orfield, and that would mean the boys would be all alone, and she didn't want that. Looking up into the adoring grey eyes of her father, she couldn't imagine him killing anyone but instinct made her feel George's statement had not been totally inaccurate.

"We'll be having that one out again soon," Lucy said happily. "Your

Uncle David's coming home on leave next week - we'll put on a party for him. Just forty-eight hours. That's all before going to the Front, but we'll give him a night to remember."

"I like Uncle David."

"And he loves you - wishes you were his."

"Why hasn't he got a boy or girl?"

"He'd like to know the answer to that one," her father replied. "One thing I do know, it'll be mighty special when it does decide to put in an appearance - all the waiting they've done."

The bad thoughts about this afternoon were receding. "I'm going to sleep now," she sighed. "I wish it was bath night every night."

"You think I'm Popeye lifting that old bath in more than once a week?" Alex joked. "Night pal. Sleep tight."

It was quite a party one way or another. Uncle David had arrived in his RAF Sergeant's uniform bearing Aunt Laura proudly on his arm. She had a natural dress sense and the favourite sage green she wore added an air of sophistication. Jack came too with his wife Rose, a buxom, earthier character who eyed Aunt Laura furtively, Kate noticed. Jack smoked and coughed a great deal and each time an opportunity presented itself, tried to persuade Alex to join his haulage business.

"I've no capital to invest," she heard her father declare repeatedly, resisting the lure of a larger pay packet. "I'll help you out at a weekend, but that's all."

"Never did any good mixing family and business," he maintained later, choosing not to tell Lucy of his discovery Jack was often involved with dubious acquaintances.

Three of Dad's sisters, Emma, Connie and Amy came with their families. Aunt Eve had taken the night off, and sang to the tunes Great Aunt Lisa thumped out on the piano. Everyone had contributed a few of their precious ration tokens, and Lucy had woken early to make plate loads of potted beef and haslet sandwiches.

Kate sat on her stool, tired legs dangling inches above the floor, quietly mesmerised by the general conviviality. They didn't seem to be quite the same people somehow. Looking the same, yet behaving differently. They would put their arms on each other's shoulders but she couldn't be certain whether to demonstrate affection or for the physical support afforded by so doing. They smiled a great deal as glasses were refilled, and she didn't seem to know them so well and wished they'd go back to being themselves, especially Uncle David. She wondered where the place called The Front was but felt too sleepy to ask and everyone seemed happily engaged in conversation, patting her head now and then as they passed.

Uncle David was beckoning to her now. "Before I go," he said, suddenly conscious that he did not feel as steady as he might. "Before I go I have something for my little sweetheart to remember me by."

Some were confused, and looked first at Laura, before following his gaze towards Kate.

"Luce, pass me the box I left in your kitchen - side of the wash tub. Thanks Sis."

He took out a china doll in a long white dress, whose generous eyebrows tilted as Kate, wide eyed, opened her arms to receive it. Struggling to express her thanks, tears of joy streamed down her face. "Uncle David, - is she really mine?" Holding the doll close, she yielded herself, and it, to her Uncle's fierce embrace,

"I'll come back to you little Kate. Yes I'm weeping too now." The drink released his emotion, and Kate was bewildered. Even invulnerable Big Grandma was wrestling to withhold tears. Lucy put on a record, and pulled Alex into the centre of the room.

"I can't dance," he protested, "You know I can't dance!"

"Don't matter. Just until everybody gets going again."

"Do the Charleston Mam!" begged her daughter. Lucy dancing, a baby doll in her arms, and Dad looking very content now that Mam had released him from the purgatory of trying to move rhythmically to music. Everything perfect. And yet that was not what she was feeling. It was all so confusing. She moved her stool into a corner the more easily to admire her gift unobserved, but the tiredness and heat were overwhelming. Lucy's hand was on her shoulder.

"Time for Dreamland." she was saying, "and you've plenty to dream about tonight."

Kate opened the door at the very moment Jack reappeared after going outside to give vent to one of the coughing fits that plagued him. Entering the smoke filled room, he immediately felt another attack coming on and swiftly brought up his hand to stifle it, unaware of the child crossing his path. The abrupt action caught Kate off guard, and the doll's fall to the floor drew a general gasp and immediate silence. A disfiguring crack appeared across its forehead, and Kate grew white with disbelief.

"Christ I'm sorry kid," Jack spluttered. "Wouldn't have done that for the world."

"Clumsy bugger." Eve snorted.

In desperate pleading Kate's eyes sought her adored Uncle David whose only reaction had been to toss back a large whisky.

"And that's just how it'll be when it comes," he panicked. "God this bloody war!"

Her father's arms were lifting her and the doll to which she clung, and together they went upstairs. He tucked her into bed, and sat silently beside her. In an instant, grief had replaced such joy. Tiredness had dulled her reactions and the price was enormous. Eventually her hand sought his. "Will you be able to mend her Dad? Make her as good as new?"

"No. But good enough for you to love her Kate. We'll get some extra hair and yer Mam can fix her a fringe. Glue and a bit o patience and no one'll know."

"I'll know - and remember she was perfect, but for such a little time. I let her get spoiled. Will Uncle David forgive me?"

"He already has. Nothing he wouldn't forgive you. It wasn't your fault."

"Yes it was. It looked as if Uncle Jack knocked me, but I dropped her when he made me jump."

"It was terrible bad luck but my Kate's big enough to get over it." He lifted her chin. "Eh?"

She nodded. Nothing would make her disappoint him, but when the door was closed, she wept silently into her pillow. She had glimpsed such beauty, allowed it to escape, and the ache and yearning would be to no avail.

CHAPTER TWO

For several days now, her parents had talked in hushed tones whenever she was within earshot and she supposed it was to do with Uncle Jack, for evidently he had become seriously ill and was soon to go into the Sanatorium.

Tonight she had gone out as usual to meet her father, and as she rushed towards him, he swung her upwards, planting a smutty kiss on her cheek -a kiss that was normally reserved for later, when, standing at the kitchen sink, braces hanging down over his trousers, he had removed the day's coal dust. He studied the grime he had transferred to her white blouse and grinned.

"Your Mam'll not be pleased about that."

Hand in his she escorted him proudly homeward into their community, her poised little body seeming to announce to the world, "This is my Dad." Strangely, tonight he didn't ask her what she had done at school, but gripped her hand tightly, remaining silent.

He washed and sat down to his dinner, his girl on the low stool beside him, for Lucy and Kate had already eaten their main meal at noon with Grandma, satisfying themselves with bread and dripping for tea. But Kate knew that if she sat quietly Dad would hold out his fork to her now and then with a piece of sausage meat or fried potato. He cleaned his plate with a thick wedge of bread, and then brought Lucy up to date with the day's events. But tonight their conversation was artificial and Kate looked from one to the other for explanation of that which she only sensed.

"We had to go into the shelters again today at school," she said to break the awkward silence, "for a long time." Unwittingly she had given them their cue, Lucy knowing that Alex would leave her to pick it up.

"Kate, Dad and me have been thinking a lot about something. The party ... it wasn't just for Uncle David. It was for all of us....the family. You see the sirens are wailing a lot these days, and we'll feel better if you're somewhere safe... in the country."

Startled, Kate stared at her father. "I'm alright here. It's only London children who are leaving their homes."

Taking her hands in his, Dad said, "Not any longer Kate. Lots of children are having a spell away from the bombing."

"We've had some near misses," Lucy continued. "Grandma's factory was hit last night - that's why she didn't go to work today. And Aunt Laura knows a lady with a place in the country."

"But I don't want to be safe in the country without you and Dad. Please don't send me away. Please."

Alex lifted her on his knee. "It's best this way Kate. I'll come and see you at weekends. You'll like Miss Smith - there's a plum tree by the kitchen door, and a shed full plant pots and things."

Kate was mystified beyond bearing. How could they imagine their presence could be replaced by such insignificant trivia. Whose idea had it been and why hadn't they asked her? Dad had said the lady knew Aunt Laura. Was Aunt Laura jealous of the doll Uncle David had given her, or was she punishing her for breaking it? And if Mam and Dad were going to die how could they believe she would want to go on living without them? What was Mam doing having a baby if she was going to be killed. Oh why couldn't they just talk to her and explain? Pulling away, she rushed outside to where Jimmy, when not in the street, could always be found in his yard.

"It smells better out here," he said, "Mam being queer, and Dad full of booze." He listened enrapt as she unfolded her tale.

"You lucky beggar," he whistled enviously,

"But I don't want to go. You're the lucky one."

"For staying here?" Jimmy exploded in disgust, aiming a stone at a rat scampering behind the uncovered dustbin. "Yea it feels lucky, alright."

"But my backyard's not like this. Dad and I play catchball on the path where he's planted London Pride .... and put red geraniums on the wall...."

But young Jim did not hear. "Fields to play in," he dreamed aloud. "Maybe a river and farms. Go back and ask yer Dad if I can stay with this 'ere Miss Smith instead then."

"But you don't know her."

"Don't matter as long as she can cook. You gonna 'ave a room to yerself an all?"

Kate's spirits lifted momentarily. She would like that immensely. But nothing else. She wandered back through her own yard. Mam and Dad would be miserable, and she had made them feel worse by her ingratitude. She saw they had not moved from their seats, but were tight lipped and drawn, all colour drained from their faces.

"It really is best Kate," Lucy began desperately.

"I know. Jimmy said so."

In such a short space of time she had lost the doll, and now it seemed her home. Was this what growing up was about - getting to love something and then losing it?

She was still awake when Grandma came up to bed and stood her jug of beer on the dressing table. Just for a moment Kate wondered if it had been her idea so that she could have the bedroom all to herself, but the notion quickly passed. She knew that Grandma would miss her, for being alone held no appeal for the sociable old lady.

"You not asleep yet love? Here, sit up then and help me unlace these devils."

Kate grimaced with distaste at the bulges of fat overhanging the grimy pink corsets before nimbly unhooking the restraining laces, revealing as she did so a home-made pocket stitched to the garment in which were concealed several crumpled pound notes. Grandma expelled an immense sigh of relief, and promptly reached for the chamber pot under her side of the bed.

Kate was suddenly filled with a new courage. "Why don't you go down the yard?" she asked, protesting more than posing a question.

"Too ruddy cold. 'Ere what are you getting so high and mighty about?"

"I'm sorry. 'Night Grandma." She paid in penitence for the uncharacteristic bravado, and plunging her fingers in her ears and head under the blanket, diminished her awareness of Grandma's ablutions.

"G'night little 'un. Bit upset about going away are yer? I can understand that. I'd miss the old street as well."

Kate stiffened. Was the street all that she thought could be missed? She had no idea! The joy of setting out to meet Dad each evening, the walk to Little Gran's - watching Mam make a wedding cake and helping to fold a bridal gown so that it shouldn't crease.... Imprisoned tears of frustration burned her eyes. They shared the same bed, but inhabited different worlds and it was not only age that separated them.

Kate having been sent on an errand to the corner shop, Little Gran shot an accusing glance at her son. "Six sisters and you still haven't learned to put your foot down!"

Alex sat down in the chair opposite, acknowledging her need for explanation. "Kate must have fresh air and farm food, Mother. The school doctor says she's far from well - malnutrition he called it. Do you think I could bear to be without her if I were not convinced she'll get what I can't provide. It's this, or risk having her taken away from us for a while. By going into the country she's doing what dozens of others are doing and won't arouse suspicion."

"I'm not certain it wouldn't have been better to tell her the truth, but I respect your right to decide what's best."

"You were right anyway," he conceded readily, "It was Lucy who had to tell her."

"You wouldn't have let her if you thought she was wrong." Painfully she reached up to the shelf for her purse and took out a half crown piece. "That will pay for Lucy to go with you to take the child." Before he could protest his mother added firmly, "I can afford it, and wish to do it. Please don't deprive me of the pleasure."

He accepted the coin, appreciative of the fact that sensitive to his proud nature, she had offered it whilst they were alone. She had done so much more than provide an extra bus fare, for now the anguish of parting from his girl would be lessened with Lucy there to do and say the right things to Miss Smith. His mother, observing him closely, wondered at his lack of self-esteem. She smiled as Kate entered. "Your Dad has been telling me about this long holiday you are to have. I envy you for I was raised in the country and would love to return. Come and see me the minute you are back. I'll be eager to hear your news."

It mattered a great deal that Little Gran thought it was a good idea and seemed to have no doubt at all she would be here when Kate returned. And if she were still alive, surely Mam and Dad would be too.

On Saturday they walked a half hour's distance to the coach station and boarded the Midland Red Bus. Once out of town Kate sat entranced by the vista of picture book cottages, green fields and Tudor pubs as they meandered through villages.

"It's so pretty," she said, as wedged between her parents, she looked at each in turn. "I didn't know the world was like this."

Lucy tweaked her cheek. "You wait until the war's over and we go to Blackpool and see the lights!"

If the unknown remotely resembled what she saw from the window - and given that Mam and Dad were not going to be killed, which seemed unlikely if they were planning a trip to Blackpool, then her protracted stay in the country was surely something pleasant. Hadn't Dad said there was a plum tree in the garden? That could only mean that he had been to check everything was alright - but why hadn't he said? Sometimes she thought words were a greater challenge to him than Mr. Hitler's war. What kind of a world was locked inside him; what made him feel others had no interest in what he had to say?

Lucy interrupted her thoughts. "We're nearly there. Put your coat on."

Alex lifted her bag from the luggage rack and took Kate's hand.

"Which way?" she asked as the bus pulled away.

"No way," her Dad smiled. "There's Miss Smith at her gate."

Kate, facing a mediaeval church and seemingly enrapt at what she beheld, turned about to see a lady slightly younger than Little Gran, yet so similar in dress and demeanour, that she ran towards her eagerly, stopping short only feet away when the realisation she was approaching a total stranger made it's impact. Her hand crept toward Alex' jacket as he and Lucy held out their hands in greeting.

"How do y'do," Alex began, and Miss Smith smiled at the similarity between father and daughter. Relief was added to her smile too, Lucy observed, which meant she liked Kate with that glorious instantaneous chemistry that occasionally sparks between people. Thank God, her girl would be well looked after here.

"Kettle's coming to the boil - come in all of you."

The branches of the plum tree bore down upon them as they went in, and an inviting smell of apple pie came from the kitchen range. Kate decided that if this were not Heaven itself, it was as near as she wanted to get to it. As the grown ups drank tea she gravitated towards the window to where she could see the church again, this time noticing a pub close by, and standing outside it, a sight that made her heart leap.

"That will be Ernie's pony and trap." Miss Smith said, following her gaze. "I expect he'll call to take you for a ride before your parents return."

Kate's eyes were on fire. Even Jimmy's wildest imaginings hadn't verbalised being taken like a lady through the countryside, and she could already hear his 'Didn't I tell you so!' Her host was suggesting she showed Mam and Dad her room. "There won't be space for me to come as well," she laughed, "It's the one on the left of the stairs. Mine's to the right."

Kate took Alex' hand, but was forced to release it immediately, for Dad's shoulders touched either side of the spiral stairway. There were no doors to the bedrooms and just inside Miss Smith's room she saw a washstand, with jug and bowl sprigged with pink rosebuds. Lucy squeezed past Alex. A single bed with patchwork quilt, a wash stand again, and the smallest of cupboards set into the wall, all set her mind at rest.

But it was the view that drew Kate to the minute dormer window where branches tapped on the four tiny panes, beckoning to her to look below into a garden crammed with thriving vegetables. Currant bushes filled every nook and cranny, whilst roses clambered unchecked over a red brick-wall, and rockery plants peeped from every available crevice.

Alex, eager to see what had captivated her, peered over her head. "Oh Kate." was all he could murmur, his eyes saying the rest.

"Everything alright?" Miss Smith called, and in a tell tale choked voice Lucy thanked her for it being perfect.

"Come and eat then. I've packed a basket of veg to take back with you."

Kate glanced at her mother. How she would love to see her installed in a home like this, making her wedding gowns in such surroundings. She pictured the sewing machine in the parlour, and the activity surrounding the wedding cakes in the kitchen. Surely Dad could find work repairing fences and gates, or was everyone in the country self-sufficient? It would take courage of a new kind to leave the familiar ways of earning a living, and both parents were disinclined to take risks that might affect those they loved. She had momentarily forgotten her two Grandmothers - and the new baby. Perhaps such a tiny cottage wouldn't adequately house them all.

"Here's Ernie now," their host announced. "He'll show you the village." And Kate didn't believe it was possible to be any happier.

"It's all in her eyes," Miss Smith noted. "She doesn't express it, but I'll bet her head's not short of words. A very private little family." she judged. "All the bolts hard tight."

She introduced Ernie who told them he and his wife had a girl from London staying. "Given us a new lease of life, not 'avin any of our own see."

All aboard, he set the pony off at a trot indicating the various landmarks but Kate barely heard, despite his rich baritone voice and hearty laugh, for she was too occupied being a princess in her own carriage. "Isn't it the best thing that ever happened Dad," she whispered, and Lucy conceded she would be sorry when the day ended.

"I wish you didn't have to go. Will you be safe?" Kate craved assurance.

"Safe as houses." And immediately Alex regretted the analogy in view of the blitzed areas they had passed on the way out of the city.

SAFE AS HOUSES

They were deposited at the cottage as affably as they had been collected, and their gratitude expressed, it was only a matter of a last cup of tea before the bus was due.

"Don't worry dear," Miss Smith said. "The driver knows you're here - he'll hoot."

How comfortingly different was village life. And though she wondered how they could bear to leave, so also Kate yearned to go with them. She waved them out of sight and returned to the parlour with Miss Smith, who in the course of the next few minutes became Aunt Polly.

"If we're going to become friends, as I know we are, then we can't remain on formal terms," she smiled. "And we'll put some colour in those cheeks by the time your father comes to visit."

"He will come?" Kate felt free now to surrender to gnawing anxiety.

"Do you trust him?"

"Yes."

"Then you know he will. So now you can enjoy the days up to the weekend."

Kate stole a moment to assess such practical confidence. "Do people you trust never let you down then?"

"Only if the trust is misplaced, or the person is under such stress that they cannot be themselves." Deciding that was a great deal for one so young to absorb, she resorted to more mundane matters. "Put your jacket on and we'll go for water." Kate appeared perplexed and she added quickly, "I don't have it on tap as you do at home. You see the town does have some advantages over the country!"

The two walked the few steps to the green and Kate noticed the pump near where the bus had stopped. Signalling to her to lever the handle, Aunt Polly asked what was so fascinating about the church on which again Kate's attention was focussed, and received a prompt reply. "The grey is so pretty with all the green around it. I never saw a church in a field before." At which Aunt Polly put her hands on her hips and laughed aloud. "We'll tell Walter the churchyard looks like a field - that should generate him into taking a hold of his scythe!"

The child had an eye for beauty; more than that, it was important to her.

"Do you go inside the church, Miss Smith?" Kate asked diffidently, incapable of asking both a personal question and using the familiar name.

"I frequent neither church nor public house," was the frank response, "though you'll notice both are accessible. I suspect they satisfy the same

need for different people." Then surmising the reason for the question, "You'd like to see inside, wouldn't you? We'll go tomorrow when the morning light is on the windows."
She took one pail in her left hand, the other being carried between them, and once in the kitchen refilled the huge kettle that sat permanently on the range.
"We'll make a drink before bed. Do you like cocoa? I've plenty of fresh milk."
Cocoa made with milk was a luxury Kate had never had, and eagerly agreed to try, though the mention of it had suggested bedtime was imminent.
"Do you go to bed early Aunt Polly?" she asked.
"In summer I go when dusk falls, but in winter I light the lamp in the evening."
Kate glanced around and observed there were no electric light switches.
"You must take a candle up to bed with you tonight - leave it lit if you feel strange in your new surroundings."
She was assured there was no need. For a child brought up in street where petty thieving was a way of life, Kate felt instinctively that danger was a million miles away from this cottage. Slowly sipping her cocoa to make it last, she watched, fascinated, as Aunt Polly prepared bread for the morrow, then placed the tin by the range for the dough to rise overnight. Tomorrow she would show Kate how to make soft cheese that must be hung in the net for several days until the whey was all discarded.
"Do you make everything you eat?" she was asked.
"Practically. The farm and garden produce most of what we need to survive."
"Will I learn to do everything too?"
"That depends how long you stay. But I think you've learned enough for one day!"
Aunt Polly poured hot water into a jug she carried up to Kate's room. After washing, the child curled between the crisp clean sheets, tracing the patterns of the patchwork quilt with fingers that moved appreciatively over its surface. Lifting her hand she found she could touch the sloping ceiling, and several times got out of bed to peep through the rosebud curtains at the hazy moonlit scene across the green. The church was silent, but moving grey shapes indicated activity at The Three Horseshoes. It was with a mixture of guilt and consternation that she realised she was feeling more at home here than in the house in which she had been born. Houses she felt were like people - some you got on with immediately whilst others needed time. And

sometimes, however well you knew them, you could never make the magic of easy familiarity happen.

Succumbing to sleep, she pondered wistfully the possibility of her parents living here, but though Lucy had loved the cottage, Kate knew her mother would need the bustle and stimulus of many lives around her; Lucy could make her own beauty whilst switching off the ugliness of her surroundings. She liked people more than places.

CHAPTER THREE

A sound she did not expect to hear disturbed her slumber and the damp stillness of the night. An aircraft was not far away: surely the war had not followed her here. Her immediate thought, almost one of panic, was that she would be returned to the city without ever getting to know Aunt Polly; that she would be forced to leave the pretty room with the starched linen and rosebud curtains. Suddenly it was all too precious to lose, and in fear she cried out. The old lady was soon beside her.

"Don't be afraid. I expect the plane woke you.

"Will I have to go away?"

"Indeed not. There's a small aerodrome nearby and pilots fly across the channel from there. Some of them keep their bicycles in my shed. You'll see them in the morning."

"Why is it safe to come here if the war is so near?"

"Hitler doesn't know our aerodrome exists. He's more interested in big cities."

"Big Grandma's factory was bombed last week. That's why she's changing her job – she's going to work in a café now."

Aunt Polly's voice was soft and comforting. Soon they heard the latch of the shed door, and Kate, unused to the silence, or the crisper sounds it enabled, was startled. Her host breathed an audible sigh of relief. "One plane safely back. Say a prayer for the others Kate."

The child was perplexed. "What others? And you want me to say a prayer *before* we go to church?"

Polly Smith had no wish to create confusion. "Why then I'll do it for both of us. You don't believe God is locked in a building do you my dear?" And with no further ado she dropped to her knees beside Kate's bed and asked the Almighty to ensure the safe return of more than half a dozen young men, whom she named individually.

Kate gazed earnestly at the petite figure, hands clasped and head bowed. The grey hair that by day had been swept into a neat bun was now plaited and secured with a ribbon half way down her back. She was pleading gently but yet so fervently that Kate could not imagine how God could ever refuse such a request - assuming He could hear her of course. In any case Aunt Polly seemed very sure about not needing to wait until they were in church, which Kate had heard described as God's house. She remained motionless for as long as the prayer continued and was beginning to feel that God must be a familiar neighbour in these parts when there was a short pause in what felt more like a conversation than a prayer. Aunt Polly said finally, "And Lord help me to make my little guest feel safe and at home with me. Amen." At which point Kate asked, "Can God really hear you?"

Miss Smith took the child's hand and their eyes met. "Is your Dad coming on Sunday?"

"Trust?"

Nodding her delight at Kate's crisp response, Polly Smith realised that in one short day she had already grown to love this little girl.

Plainly Kate's slumbers would not easily be resumed. "Put your dressing gown on and come and meet whoever is in the kitchen," Miss Smith invited.

"It could be a burglar."

"It will be the pilots. I always leave pie on the table for when they return." Kate scrambled out of bed, fascinated and absorbed by this novel way of life, but her natural shyness blunted the desire to encounter a stranger. She carried her candle behind Aunt Polly, and together they went downstairs.

A tall, dishevelled young man barely into his twenties was lighting the oil lamp as they entered the kitchen. Nervous exhaustion made his hands tremble as he held match to wick, and only as the flame grew could Kate see clearly the blue, but oh such tired eyes.

"Miss Smith." The young pilot moved to greet her, though his legs seemed almost incapable of following the outstretched hand. "Are we the first?" As Polly Smith's eyes framed a question, he added, "John and Phil have stayed back at base."

Polly Smith nodded. "Sit down Oliver. I'll make you a hot drink." She turned to Kate. "You too dear. Oliver this is the visitor I told you was coming to stay with me."

He held out his hand and Kate shook it tentatively. It was the first time she had been greeted thus, and the adult, civilised act pleased her. She was intrigued too that anyone could have thought her sufficiently important to discuss her before she actually arrived.

"Hello Kate. Miss Smith told me she was expecting you."

"I heard you go to the shed and thought you were a burglar."

"I was putting the bike in there ready to go back to base. We always come here for pie after a raid." He smiled warmly at his host. "Then we know we're really home."

Kate fixed her eyes on Oliver, pensive and observant, whilst he and Aunt Polly exchanged news and disguised anxious glances. Several times she noticed him place his wrist in such a position as to be able to look at his watch without seeming to do so. Eventually he made a conscious effort to transfer his concentration to the newcomer, who, had she been more selfishly demanding of attention, would have made it easier. He was drawn to the deep stillness in her; a balm to the mental anguish that sapped him.

"Those big brown eyes are going to break someone's heart one day, little Kate. I'm sorry I was careless and didn't ask where you've come from."

"I don't think you're careless, but you are very tired. Your eyes are all scratched. I've come from my home in the city because of the bombing."

"And I've just come from a city in Germany. So we are at Miss Smith's cottage for the same reason - except that you're luckier because you'll stay."

"Won't *you*?"

"I come here after each duty - so my scratched eyes can get better."

She cast him a quizzical glance, and was so aware of the effort it cost him to be flippant, she could only be serious.

"Later you'll meet T." He stopped short and substituted 'some of the other chaps.'

"Are you afraid they might be killed?" Kate asked, and her perception shocked him.

"It happens. The waiting's hard when you're the first plane home."

He had not attempted a soft option to her enquiry and his head-on response dispelled any imminent homesickness on her own part as she was sucked into another world of inconceivably deeper significance. Until tonight the only aeroplanes of which she had been aware were German ones that destroyed the houses around her. Now here she was in the presence of the pilot of an aircraft who was sent across the channel to safeguard the lives of millions of people like her. Were German pilots, equally young, as anxious as Oliver about their friends?

At first he attempted small talk but elicited little response from the child for whom comments without substance were an unfamiliar challenge to which she felt neither desire nor ability to rise. Too tired to persist he could contain his fear no longer.

"God, where are they?" he murmured.

His words barely audible, the child sprang to life. "I expect they've just got a bit lost 'cos you went ahead too fast, but if they've been killed I'll hold your hand 'til you stop crying."

The barriers between strangers, age and experience, were toppled and the lack of her understanding of war was important to neither. What she had not yet experienced was compensated for by intuitive recognition of his need to voice his anxiety, for had not her life been spent amongst adults who fought constantly against adversity?

He found her a comfortable recipient of his fatigued apprehensions, and Polly Smith, knowing that that the flow of words was washing away some of the poison, did not interrupt. In another context she would have deemed the child too young, but the weary pilot had been pitched into the horrors of war whilst little more than a child himself. Tonight, his need was greatest. And though somewhat early in her life, his arrival had enabled Kate to reach out beyond those things she had been accustomed to think of as reality.

Polly Smith marvelled at the instant rapport between the two and had grown wise enough to accept one did not fracture serenity by a need to know. For a long time he seemed to express his thoughts aloud rather than address Kate directly, which made her feel at ease - valued in a strange way that she didn't understand. Eventually, aware of drooping eyelids despite a stubborn effort to resist, Aunt Polly relit Kate's candle from the lamp. Whether due the activity of walking upstairs or the slight chill of leaving the armchair into which she had curled like a dormouse, she did not close her eyes for a long time, listening instead for T. Had Oliver begun to say Tim or Tom or Ted? All had been included in Aunt Polly's prayer.

Aware of their muffled voices below, she knew they too were waiting. And then somewhere in the mist that separated tiredness from actual sleep, she heard at intervals, the sound of aircraft throbbing home. Heard too an unrestrained whoop of joy from Oliver and imagined him lifting Aunt Polly from the ground as fear gave way to relief. And she longed to be part of that joy despite the fact that forty-eight hours ago their names had meant nothing to her. But this was their private time to release the anxiety they had shared for young men she had yet to meet. She would deny the urge to tumble downstairs to join them because for sure she would not waste moments lighting a candle. Oliver's eyes would be different now.

The early morning sun shrouded her as she pulled first the rosebud, then the blackout curtains apart and breathed in the pungent smell of honeysuckle. It seemed proper to wait until she heard activity in the kitchen before going downstairs but Miss Smith was still abed despite the clock having chimed eight. And then she remembered Oliver, and presumed the likelihood of their having talked late. It was only when pouring water from jug to bowl, she thought of Mam and Dad and Big Grandma, and it shocked her to realise they had not been constantly on her mind when only yesterday she had been distraught at the prospect of leaving them. Stepping down the one step onto the tiny landing and almost immediately up an identical one into the opposite bedroom, she saw Miss Smith sit up and shake her head.

"I'm sorry Aunt Polly. I didn't mean to wake you. I'll put the kettle on and bring you some tea."

"You've forgotten Kate - we've no electricity here. I'll come as soon as I've dressed and show you how to move the kettle to bring it to the boil."

"I know how to do it. I watched you last night. And I'll open the flue before I put more wood on the stove." She paused but the question for which she needed an answer was too important to be delayed by discretion. "Did Oliver's friends come back?"

"One crew - not long after you went to bed, and another before dawn."
The question had not been fully answered, but experience had taught her not to press the point; patience would ultimately yield the omissions. If she were not here the old lady would probably sleep in but she wasn't sure how to express her thought tactfully and said merely, "I could have my breakfast late - with no school."

"And get it all muddled up with dinner. No indeed - we'll have it directly, and fetch water from the pump; something I normally do first to blow away the cobwebs."

Polly Smith became increasingly aware of the child's powers of observation, despite a reluctance to ask questions. Maybe shyness was the obstacle, or lack of curiosity; a conjecture that somehow lacked credibility. But of one thing she was confident - Kate would not become known to her until absolute trust was established. A pity, for being intrigued by the child she was eager to know her.

By the time Aunt Polly was washed and dressed, the ashes had been raked, the embers glowed healthily, and the kettle ready to fill the teapot. They ate, and then collected water from the pump. Covering each of the pails with a circular net cap Aunt Polly asked if she would she would like to walk as far as the aerodrome. Assuming the probability of meeting with Oliver, Kate readily accepted and was disappointed there was so little to see for the planes were carefully concealed in converted barns and the pilots obviously snatching a few hours sleep before further missions.

"Not the sort of place to attract attention Kate," Miss Smith reminded her, and aware of the disappointment, decided to call briefly on Ernie and his wife Julia.

"Need to put roses in them cheeks young Madam," Aunt Julia bugled. "Janet was just the same when she arrived."

Ernie's wife reminded Kate of Big Grandma who expressed kind thoughts, but so loudly the whole world could hear. She was rescued by Aunt Polly saying they had left soup on the range and must go; a move which served to strengthen the bond that was already set to grow between them.

"Anyone would think you had the responsibility of the country on your shoulders Polly Smith - never time to stay and gossip," Julia complained as they closed her gate.

"Would you like to visit again Kate when we have more time?"

"If you would," was the reply that caused Miss Smith to laugh and declare that the two of them would get along just fine.

"But Julia's right - I don't socialise a great deal. I'm too happy in my cottage, and there's no problem about filling the hours for there simply aren't enough of them. But you'll need a playmate..."

"I'm happy with you," Kate interrupted. And indeed she was, for without doubt she had found a kindred spirit.

In the ensuing days they saw little of Oliver but two of his friends called and enjoyed broth and apple pie with them. They proved more gregarious than he and teased with their light-hearted banter. Kate, too young to recognise it as a release from the tension of war, accepted it at face value.

"When the war's over," Tim declared, "I shall have ten children and bring them all to eat with Miss Smith!"

"Make it eleven and you'll have yourself a cricket team," Aunt Polly countered dryly instead of protesting about all the cooking.

"We're going to have a baby soon," Kate announced.

"That's what Aunt Polly should have done," David laughed. "An awful lot of chaps must have gone around with their eyes shut when she was young!" Draining his mug he asked provocatively, "So why did you never marry, Miss Smith?"

"Because the right man never asked me. And now it's too late if he did, so I'll have no more personal questions young man if you don't mind."

"But they're the only interesting ones!" her guest persisted, and Kate wondered if the right man had asked someone else, or that he never actually met Aunt Polly.

It was quiet when they left, but not a lonely quiet. She curled into the smaller of the two old chintz covered chairs, whilst Miss Smith mended her lisle stockings. Both utterly content, they talked from time to time, each observing the other without the necessity to conceal the fact.

"She watches and paints pictures in her mind, without judging. Is it that she already accepts folk for what and who they are, or does she feel she has no right to make demands?" Polly Smith mused, before asking, "Do you keep a diary Kate?"

"No, but I write stories at school for my teacher. Sometimes she asks me to read them in Assembly."

"You only write at school?"

"Yes."

She waited for qualification but none came. "Would you like to write a diary here?"

"Yes please."

Polly Smith drew out several sheets of notepaper from her bureau, and folding them into a booklet handed them to Kate and was somewhat mystified by the uncertain reaction.

"I can do it now?"

"Of course - whenever you wish. Sit at the table - it's easier."

No sooner was a pencil in her hand than words spilled onto the blank sheets. Often Miss Smith's fingers remained still, her gaze fixed on the child who said so little, yet had so much to express. For over an hour she was totally absorbed, her eyes alight with inspiration. The light began to fade, and Aunt Polly said, "I'd no idea an author had come to stay with me!"

No other words could have evoked such spontaneous pleasure, and for the first time since her arrival, little Kate Benson laughed. She liked Aunt Polly's jokes - fancy saying she was an author!

"Would you do me the honour of reading it to me?"

Kate stopped laughing, becoming instantly withdrawn. "Please can I read it when it's finished - I might need to alter some bits."

It was inconceivable that a child could write at length and not want to exhibit the result, but Polly replied softly, "Of course. Whenever you are ready."

"And then I'll read it to Oliver?"

So it was Oliver who, in such a short time, had communicated a special quality that had made her feel emotionally safe.

"I'm sure he will consider himself privileged. And only when he has approved, shall I consent to hear it."

"Sorry Aunt Polly, you should be first - it was your idea."

Was there no limit to the child's sense of duty? "When you've read it to Oliver you'll have overcome stage fright, and it will sound even better when it's my turn!"

Kate warmed appreciatively to such understanding, and yielded momentarily to a wish to stay here forever. Truth was she had endeavoured to imagine and commit to paper Oliver's fear and apprehension as he flew over the Channel towards enemy territory and unless her concept were accurate she had no right to communicate it to another. When he did come, she was shocked to see him using a stick and limping.

"The war hurt you!" she cried, rushing towards him.

"Goodness me no, little Kate. Just a torn muscle that's all. Certainly not enough to keep me away from two of the nicest ladies I know!"

"Aunt Polly's a lady but I'm not."

"Uh uh. Maybe just a little one, but definitely a lady! What do you say Miss Smith?"

"And not just a lady, Oliver, but an authoress, no less!"

"Really? May I look forward to being read to, this afternoon?"

Kate rushed to turn face downward the last page of her writing. "Oh no .... not yet, I want to make it exactly right. Please when you've finished speaking with Aunt Polly, will you describe something to me?"

"Talk to Oliver right now whilst I make the tea," Polly Smith instructed.

When she returned to the parlour they were involved in such intense conversation, Kate's expression one of avid concentration as Oliver answered her queries. He refused to be patronising in his response to her questions and only as her eyes grew wider with disbelief did he modify his anecdotes, for unwittingly she was acting as therapist in releasing those experiences that would forever torment him.

"But this is your diary, Kate," he said. "Shan't I get to hear how you feel about living here in the country with Aunt Polly and the things that are special for you?"

"They're all in the diary," Kate assured him. "I've written about my bedroom, the pretty things in it, the rides with Uncle Ernie, and my Dad coming on a Sunday and everything. It's just that when I'm in bed at night and I can hear the planes, I wonder what you're thinking. I wish I could come with you. Would anyone mind?"

"Most certainly young lady!"

"But I wouldn't take up much room."

Miss Smith smiled. "Kate, give Oliver a photograph, then he'd have your company."

"But I don't have one."

"I do. Your parents sent one when they asked if you could stay here."

"Good idea Miss Smith," Oliver colluded. "It won't help Kate with her diary, but it will help me. Now a cup of tea, a piece of your delicious pie, and I must go back."

It was no hardship to keep his word to call as often as he could, for Polly Smith had created a second home for these young men who may never see the end of a war that had wrenched them so precipitously from their families. But Oliver was the special one, not least because of the bond that had grown between him and the child without whom Polly Smith was beginning to have difficulty imagining her own future.

Dad came to see her each Sunday, and Ernie Carter who was disposed to this quiet man from the city, called after Sunday lunch to take them for a ride in the trap.

"Take the reins," he insisted one day. "It'll be a change for me to be a passenger."

"The reins. Me?" her father repeated. "Yes Ernie, I will and thank you."

The sound of the pony's hooves on a lane overhung with greenery, the riot of colour in the cottage gardens, and the balmy air of a late summer afternoon filled Kate with ecstasy.

"Quiet young 'un, your girl." She was aware of Mr. Carter's voice.

"She don't say much," her father felt obliged to agree, feeling somehow disloyal because the comment appeared critical as if he were disappointed in her. He struggled but failed, to find the words to explain that discussion was superfluous when feelings told you all you needed to know.

"She could move in with us if y' thinks it would bring her out of herself."

Ice-cold trepidation gripped Kate, which instantly communicated itself to Alex whose paternal instinct suffered from no inhibiting shyness.

"Thank you, no. She's fair taken with the old lady and besides, she might not be here much longer. She'll come home when the new baby arrives."

"You missin' her?"

"I can't wait to have her back."

Poor Dad. She'd been so happy with Aunt Polly - more than that - her vocabulary did not extend to 'serene' - she hadn't really considered the impact of an imminent baby for weeks now. Nor had she appreciated that Dad would be as lonely without her as she would undoubtedly have been without him had not Aunt Polly miraculously filled her life with new experiences, and opportunities to write about them. No longer could the glow in her cheeks be attributed solely to the country air. Why couldn't all the people she loved - for yes, she loved Aunt Polly too - be altogether in one place?

"I'll come home whenever you say Dad," she whispered, as hand in his, they waited for his bus.

"Love you Kate. See you next week pal."

After he had gone, she realised she had not told him anything about the diary, or her writing desk outside; perhaps because it was a special link with this part of her life away from home. Mam would have laughed dismissively and said, 'You and your books', and Big Grandma would have grumbled that the dishes could have been wiped in the time she took to chew a pencil.

She hoped when he read it, Oliver would approve of the entries as he had done when she had described her feelings on looking out of the window each morning - how she feared that one day she would wake to find the little grey church a heap of ruins; that 'The Three Horseshoes' had turned into 'The Feathers' and litter had replaced the roses and sweet scented jasmine. Each morning when it was all waiting for her she hugged herself with sweet relief, and wanted to cry out for joy, not knowing how delighted Aunt Polly would have been, had such a rapturous shout met her ears.

So strong was her inclination to return to the cottage whenever they were out walking that it could not be ignored, though no actual request was ever voiced. Eventually Aunt Polly suggested they move an old chair and rickety table from the shed into the garden, so that she could write outside whenever it wasn't damp. Kate was ecstatic; she had been given Paradise and now it was being even more sharply defined. Miss Smith shook her head at the jumble that evoked such joy.

"T'ain't right," Uncle Ernie scoffed one day. "Child that age should be out playing. I told her Dad she should have moved in with us where she'd 'ave a playmate. What in 'eaven's name does she find to write about?"

SAFE AS HOUSES

"The things you and I take for granted and have stopped noticing Ernie. This village where nothing ever happens, is a new and exciting world for her."

But he was not persuaded. "T'ain't natural," he insisted.

One evening some weeks later, snug in her dressing gown and curled into an armchair, Kate clutched her diary as if it were the crown jewels. Now and then she put it down casually as if to convince herself that it was indeed only a bundle of papers, but at the least sound that might have heralded Oliver's approach, it was in her grasp again. She felt certain he would be coming this evening, for though Aunt Polly had not actually said so, neither had she yet suggested Kate went to bed. How deliciously uninhibited it all was. When sensible routine served good purpose, it was adhered to, but recognition that some things were too important to be ruled by clocks and conventions was an innovation to her life that thrilled her.

Aware that Aunt Polly was glancing at the clock more frequently and the studied attempt to conceal any hint of anxiety less convincing, Kate refused to drowse, and her fingers tightened their hold, for never again would fatigue cause her to lose that which was precious.

"Go to bed Kate," Aunt Polly urged. "I'll wake you when Oliver comes." She lit candle and handed it to the child who needed no further assurance than that she had heard 'when' and not 'if'. She finally yielded to sleep, well knowing that war did not adhere to a timetable, and confident Miss Smith would keep her word.

In the event, she was not woken, because Oliver did not return. It was the blackbird that invited her to open her eyes and glimpse the sunlight squeezing in past the edges of the blind, and falling onto the diary on her chair. Aunt Polly was making the porridge and Kate's innate perception foiled any attempt to disguise the desolation. Weary red eyes bore testimony to forlorn hope after long hours of futile waiting. No words were forthcoming, nor did Kate press for any, but they clasped hands and stirred the porridge together. In the absence of appetite they removed it from the range and put a token amount into two bowls.

"He need not be dead .... missing perhaps."

But the child with life ahead, and an old lady nearing the end of hers, knew with that eerie certainty of instinct that they would not see Oliver again. Though their contact had been short, it had for each of them, been intense.

"He feels like he was your son Aunt Polly," Kate began, "but I know he wasn't."

"Yes." Miss Smith whispered, but then no words would come. Some minutes later and unaware of the intervening time, she said, "I think I did steal him for awhile - just a while. And for you Kate .. what was he for you .... an older brother perhaps?."

"Yes.... And he was like Uncle David. He used to read the stories I wrote when I stayed at weekends. I kept them specially for him 'cos he said they were important."

"You don't read your stories at home dear?"

"No, Mam and Dad are so busy you see. And Big Grandma says scribbling isn't any good when there's jobs to be done." There was no resentment in her tone; she had merely stated the facts. And then, "I think I loved Oliver like I love Uncle David. But that's not possible is it Aunt Polly ... I mean he wasn't my family."

"Oh it's entirely possible Kate. What do you think a funny old stick like me would do when I have no family in the proper sense? And believe you me, families don't have a monopoly when it comes to love."

"All the pilots feel like your family. But Oliver was special, wasn't he?"

"Yes. And Kate, you and I aren't related." She stopped short of voicing the words she longed to say.

"But I love you Aunt Polly. I love you so much. You and me and Oliver were a family - the best kind - weren't we?"

The child buried her face in Miss Smith's apron, and together, and in silence, they felt the full, unremitting force of being bereft.

Afterwards Kate stayed only another month at the cottage. With the war continuing, she wasn't sure whether she was to go home because her cheeks were now the required shade of pink, or because the new baby had arrived.

"Your mother has written to say there is less bombing now," Aunt Polly read from a letter one day. Having been persuaded to her complicity in Kate's convalescence, she endeavoured to be convincing, but her heart was heavy with impending loss.

Kate hadn't known how to give Aunt Polly the diary on the last evening without making her feel second best. Then Uncle Ernie had arrived and stayed until her bedtime and when later Miss Smith tiptoed into her room, Kate had been drowsy, and whispered, "It was for Oliver, but...."

"Absolutely right. So even though Oliver has lost his life, he still has your diary. He'll be pleased about that. Goodnight Kate."

Kate recognised a confusion that ought to exist in Aunt Polly's statement but warmed to the refusal to allow death to be an obstacle or barrier to the fulfilment of plans.

"Yes he will. And he has my photograph. Do you think he did talk to me before...."

"Without a doubt Kate. It.. you... will have been very precious to him."

Dad collected her next morning and there seemed no means of doing other than to say goodbye briefly and so inadequately to the person who had done no less than change her world.

"Bus is here Kate," Dad said gently, sensitive to the existence of a bond of which on this occasion he was not part, but nonetheless loathe to fracture. As the driver tooted his horn Kate accepted the inevitability of relinquishing that which being abstract could not be transported. She turned to look for the last time at that which *was* tangible; the little grey church, and the cottage that was like nowhere else in the world. "I love you Aunt Polly," she whispered. "Always."

Miss Smith's hand gripped her own. "Kate."

The diary was suddenly thrust into the old lady's grasp. "You keep it for him. You tell him about it. I don't know how."

Dad was mystified, feeling as if he were being given back a daughter who wasn't quite the same Kate he had brought here some months ago. From now on there would be a part of her that did not belong to him; something that had developed as a result of living here in this tiny cottage.

The bus pulled away and Polly Smith lifted the latch of her garden gate and bent forlornly to pick up plums that had fallen by the kitchen door. Somehow she must make a pie for those who would return safely tonight.

"Oh Oliver, what you might have unlocked for that little girl. And now I shall never know, for you are both gone from me."

CHAPTER FOUR

Mam was in bed in the front room, for it was customary to bring the bed downstairs when a birth was due so that the district nurse had hot water from the kitchen stove, and mother and baby shared a warmth so blatantly absent in the bedrooms. There were sufficient contents left from its days as the Sunday best parlour to make it feel special. Despite their cramped conditions, the family rarely came into this room, spending all their time when not at work in the aptly named living room, as the cost of keeping two parlours warm would have been prohibitive. Only when relatives came on an occasional Sunday did they take tea in the living room and then adjourn to the 'front', which boasted a brown vinyl suite and square of carpet instead of peg rugs. Dad's bike, normally stored in it, was put in the backyard when visitors came. He kept it chromed and polished and if he had to go to the doctor's or see one of his sisters, it was ready. Now, covered in an old raincoat, it was propped against the white washed wall with the geraniums.

The three of them chatted, engulfed in the warmth thrown out by a blazing fire. Of course there were four of them really, but the baby seemed insignificant having made no sound since Kate's arrival an hour ago.

"Babies sleep a lot," Mam explained. She looked very tired and there were dark rings under her eyes and her cheekbones more prominent.

"Are you going to be better soon Mam?" Kate asked anxiously.

"I'm not ill ducky. When you have a baby you stay in bed to let everything heal."

Kate was contemplating what awfulness was hidden beneath the bedclothes, when they heard the back door being opened.

"It'll be our Eve." Dad reckoned. "Said she'd drop by."

Kate smiled as the familiar heady perfume preceded her Aunt into the room.

"So what have yer called her?" She bent down over the cot and without waiting for a reply announced, "Polly Six Hairs! She's almost bald."

"Is she Polly?" Kate asked. Surely the name could only belong to Miss Smith.

"Only joking, sweetheart. Polly's an old name." She sat down heavily on the bed and Kate moved to make room for her. "What about you - we've missed yer."

"I've missed you too," she replied dutifully, realising as she did so that she was not exactly telling the truth.

"Bet y' glad to be back in the town where things are happening?"

And Kate had no wish to explain that just as much, if not more, happened in the country, and that she liked what happened there.

"I see Bill Orchard's got six months for the pub burglary." Her Aunt's comment only served to confirm her thoughts. Nevertheless she liked Dad's colourful, reprobate sister and was sorry when she had to go.

"Another day, another dollar," Eve called cheerily, "or rather another night!"

"Aye and you be careful 'ow you earn it." There was no jest in Alex' tone.

Her Aunt had had a rapid wartime romance and was married only three weeks to a naval officer before his ship went down, sunk by German torpedoes, She was finding solace in her own gregarious way and whatever that was, Kate knew her Dad didn't approve.

"However she came to marry an officer I'll never understand," he murmured, shaking his head.

"She's beautiful... well turned out. It might not have lasted. But who's to know? People are different in wartime," Lucy said.

Baby Gillian was sitting up in her pram before Kate had adjusted to being home again. The reality, but not the memory of Aunt Polly, was at last receding Only the distinctive noise of aircraft would not leave her. She had a new class teacher who though fiery and easily angered, Kate liked, for she had recognised the child's love of language and encouraged her to write. Her talent with words was brought to the attention of the Headmaster who took a keen interest in her progress. 'Read all you can girlie,' he had urged, unaware of how difficult that was, for Lucy, within months, was pregnant again, and Kate's reading and scribbling only irritated for there was no time for leisure.

"Feed Gillian for me luv, then I can hem this skirt." She had extended her bridal work to general dressmaking, the latter being a more continuous trade. But the old sewing machine seemed in constant need of attention and came the morning when it resisted all persuasion, whilst a dress urgently needed for the weekend lay in pieces on the table. There was nothing for it but to buy one on credit, and if one had to be bought why not an electric model? She drove herself unremittingly so that an hour before Alex came home the outfit was virtually complete.

Though not strong on intellect, he was keenly observant. "New machine?"
"I had to. The other's beyond repair."
"You gave me no time to look at it."
"You've mended it a hundred times Alex. I need it to be reliable."
"Paid for?"
"No, but with what I earn....." She made no effort to finish the sentence.

He hung his jacket on the door and unlaced his boots. Kate as always, fetched his slippers, aware of a silent wrath she had never before encountered. He placed a hand gently on her head as she bent down, indicating it was not for her he harboured anger, so instead of remaining by his side, she moved to a space between the two.

"We'll have no tick in this house. Take it back tomorrow. If it's an electric one you want, I'll get a motor fixed to your other one."
He didn't raise his voice; only the taut lips revealed a frustration that was not really aimed at Lucy, but at himself for failing to bring in a decent wage.

"Kate, you'll have to have the morning off school tomorrow," her mother announced acidly. "I can't carry the machine and baby to town." And as she bent to get his supper from the range, added, "And I'd hate to waste the bus fare."

Tomorrow Kate was to have read her story in Assembly and the disappointment was not lost on her mother who immediately tried to compensate. "I'll pick up that piece of sheet music Miss Grey wants you to play. Tell her I can't go any more."

"I can afford that," Alex retorted. "And off course you'll go on the bus."
For over a year before she went to the country, Kate and her mother had walked through the back streets to Miss Grey's house. She was not a registered teacher, but could pass on the basics that were as far as most stayed the course.

"Mam, you're much better than me. You have the lesson and I'll do the cleaning."

"No Kate. You don't get much in the way of fun. Sides you need it for your education."

SAFE AS HOUSES

Was there an edge of jealousy in her tone or had Kate imagined it? But the child was right. Notes that lurched awkwardly from her fingers, flowed with ease as her mother took her place at the piano. And as for being fun, why the metronome was the very devil. The more she slipped out of rhythm, the more frequently her knuckles were tapped with the short cane. Whilst Lucy seized the moment to practise, Kate prolonged the agony. And now because her mother could no longer spare the time, the lesson for Kate was deemed a privilege.

"I'm sorry about your machine," Kate sympathised next morning as she spooned Gillian's porridge.

But Lucy had already donned her coat. "That's alright, I had another idea in the night that'll mebbe pay better than dressmaking But take the morning off anyway ducky – I might need to talk to someone." She was excited, radiated by challenge. "Peel the potatoes, there's a luv."

The request irritated Kate. She would have peeled them anyway.

Once 9.30 had passed Kate rose above her disappointment knowing that Assembly was now over. She performed the household chores as adeptly as her mother and as dinnertime neared, put potatoes on to boil. She peeked inside the pot and forked the flesh of the rabbit; it would be tender by the time Lucy came back. When she did, it was with a parcel under each arm, and an air of total satisfaction.

"I've been to the warehouse," she said removing her coat and immediately ladling stew and potatoes. "I've got sheets, towels and four tablecloths."

"Mam, have you come into a fortune! Now what will Dad say?"

"Not for us Kate - to sell. I'll clear out half the sideboard and when the word gets around that folks can save themselves the walk to town and get what they need at less than shop prices we won't know what's hit us. I only spent what I made on the last wedding dress. And it'll be a darned sight easier than sewing half the night." And as Kate began to clear the plates, "Oh good girl...and don't tell anyone at school yet. I'll just mention it to a few at first. I don't want trouble with the rent man."

If Kate hurried she would catch Mrs. Broomwade before she left the staff room and explain why she had had to let her down this morning, She knocked tentatively and overheard a conversation. "Another Noel Coward play next Saturday too... don't miss it. Home Service, 8 o'clock." She tapped again and asked for her teacher.

"I looked after Gill while Mam went to the doctor's," she lied, knowing that a visit to the surgery would be a more acceptable reason for absence.

"We missed you Kate. Run along now... needlework isn't it?"

Kate nodded, uncertain whether she had been believed. She feared the sewing teacher, not because she had the least problem with a needle and thread, but the embittered spinster constantly made reference to 'the likes of parents who would doubtless return a Labour Government when the war ended, not knowing what was good for them.'

It was a simple matter to discern that she despised those living in the environs of the school, which Kate could understand to a degree, for she too hated the walk home through the less than salubrious streets. And unlike storybook versions, poor people were not always kind, gentle and deferential to their betters. Often their lifestyle, their language and their habits were ugly. But for Kate, because she was one of them, it was not the people, but the ugliness that was distasteful; a distinction Miss Dunton had failed to make. Kate was therefore the more forgiving of her than others who, when she had her back to them, were emboldened to gesture rudely in her direction.

"Ignorant cow," Jimmy sniped. "Who does she think she is?"

She would ask Dad to set the wireless on the Home Service when he and Mam had their night out on Saturday. Lucy offered no resistance for this meant that Gillian didn't have to sleep in the pram. And Kate could read with no guilt attached for this was the time her parents also took for leisure.

"Ave the Light programme." urged Big Grandma. "It's livelier. A play could be one o' them murders, frighten ye to death on yer own."

"I'll bring a bag o' crisps home." Her father tweaked her ear and would have chosen to listen with her, but going to the pub on a Saturday night was the way of things, and it was not in his nature to change patterns laid down for him since boyhood.

On Sundays, a walk to little Gran's and then home to Yorkshire pudding and a bottle of dandelion and burdock had made Sunday special for as long as she could remember. There was almost a festive feeling about the day with Kate in her Sunday-best frilled pinafore and Dad wearing a stiff collar attached to his shirt with studs that he would unfasten only after dinner before his Sunday nap. Unlike on their evening visits to Gran, Aunt Eve would be there too, elaborately preparing for work. Whilst Dad talked with Little Gran, Kate would sit on the edge of her Aunt's bed fascinated by the extravagant amount of jewellery, perfume and pancake makeup. Cupid lips clearly defined, Eve would throw her fox fur around her shoulders, slip into elbow length gloves and then clasping her diamante purse, depart the house on black patent three-inch heels. It was a performance that entranced young Kate as she marvelled at her aunt's joie de vivre in the face of war, rationing and blackout.

"See you sunshine," Eve breezed, as drop-ear rings swinging defiantly, she stepped into a waiting taxi befitting a naval war widow.

"More money than sense." Alex shook his head.

"You like her Dad though, don't you?"

"Aye."

To no-one's surprise Lucy's venture did well.

"Will you be able to have your piano lesson now then?" Kate asked her.

"No time ducky. Can't be out when the customers come knocking can I?" She was embarked on a new project, and there would be no half measures. Every hour of the day was utilised to maximum efficiency, the adrenalin of success providing all the energy she needed to walk in and out of the city centre several times a week.

"Why don't you buy in bulk and save your legs," Mr. Johnson asked repeatedly. "I can give you credit."

"No thanks. I'll just buy what I've money for. Every penny goes back into the business so I should soon only have two trips each week."

"Whatever you say Madam. You're the client," her supplier smiled, silently admiring Lucy's determination and wishing she were available to work for him. She would run rings around anyone currently employed at the warehouse. "Jewish background somewhere," he murmured, slipping an extra hand towel into the parcel. "Slight reject amongst that lot," he lied. "There's an extra one to compensate." Music to Lucy's ears, that gave buoyancy to her step. She would soon be making as much as she had earned at the factory, which was just as well with yet another pregnancy confirmed. She had railed only briefly. After all, having babies was what being married was all about for most folks. If only David who had miraculously survived the war for five years now, and could afford half a dozen, could have his first. Life could be so damnably contrary.

The state of Alex legs troubled her a great deal too these days for they were constantly ulcerating and for the first time in his life, he had recently taken time off work. Thank Heaven for the Sick Club - they'd paid sixpence a week now for some years, and with Ma as the secretary, there had been no delay in getting the benefits.

"Doctor's going to call later," Nurse said as she eased the blood stained bandages.

"Oh aye. And what's that all about?"

"He'll probably suggest you change your job. The coal dust is playing havoc with those open sores."

"Can't you cover them up?"

"Dust penetrates."

He absorbed her words in silence. Collecting coal from the pits was deemed essential work and the reason for his not having been called up. Once off the coal lorries he'd get his papers and with legs like these, fail the medical. Listed as an invalid there'd be precious little hope of a job.

"Thank him, but tell him not to bother," he said brusquely..

"You're being obstructive, Mr. Benson. It's imperative you take care of yourself."

"And I've to take care of this family. Do you have proof it's the coal dust?"

"We have to eliminate the possibilities."

"Mebbe. But not at the expense of my livelihood."

"I can't spare the time to come every day - and that's what's needed if you continue to get them so dirty," she explained.

"But I could do it," Lucy offered immediately, "If you let us have the stuff and bandages here... you wouldn't need to come hardly at all."

And so it was agreed. Nurse was already doing the work of two and in the air raids was often on her feet all night.

"If you're sure you can manage, Lucy... it's not pleasant with open sores."

"He's my man." was the curt reply. There seemed nothing more to be said.

CHAPTER FIVE

Kate was nine when hostilities came to an end, by which time she had another sister, Beth. How contrary was human nature in that an unborn baby could be so devastating and yet be rapturously received the moment it became a reality.

"She's a somebody now, that's why," Mam said. "We didn't know her before."

Spirits were too high to be daunted by the weather, and Bill Buckley magnanimously threw open his storage sheds to house the trestle tables decorated in red white and blue, laden with jellies made from crystals and cakes from powdered eggs. As the rain continued to fall in torrents, the jollification continued into the night. Beer flowed as men and women across the nation gave vent to joy and relief. Morning would be soon enough to face the enormous problems that lay ahead. Intrigued, Kate watched adults who hitherto seemed only to work and rear children, throw themselves into the Lambeth Walk and Hokey Cokey, congering over the cobblestones, kissing each other's wives and drowning the years of tension in a steady flow of brown ale.

She noticed George return several times to his house and finally signal his young brother to leave the gathering, not, as Jimmy suspected because he had been sipping ale, but to say goodbye to his Mam, who mercifully died before her husband returned, too inebriated to notice.

No more frantic trips to the air raid shelters, for the wail of the sirens had been silenced. Hitler was dead, and gas masks returned at last to their boxes to gather dust. Better not throw them away just yet though: six years had been a long time. Uncle David returned from the war physically unscathed, as did Dad's friend Harry, and Cousin Steve. Two distant relatives whom Kate had never met, and Uncle John, Aunt Eve's husband were the family's casualties. Life could, and would, go on.

With the war over, Uncle David came often to take her to the house he had purchased - a mansion to Kate - in a pleasant avenue with gardens with a stream running along its boundary at the back. A perfectionist by nature, he had soon turned house and garden into a showpiece, whilst a responsible job as floor manager in a factory supplying one of Britain's quality stores, had helped him to adjust quicker than most to life in peacetime.

"You like being here Kate?" She nodded, smiling her pleasure. "You could live here always if you wanted."

"I couldn't leave Mam and Dad."

She could never be his, and the likelihood of his having a child of his own was becoming ever more remote. "We'll go to London for a day soon. How would you like that?"

She would, and did. Despite the devastation Hitler had wrought, the sheer size and magnificent defiance of the buildings that had resisted him, rendered Kate awe-struck.

"You enjoyed being with Aunt Polly," David said, "but I can see more in the town than in the country. The line and shape of the buildings against the sky... even the bombed parts can be pictures."

They paused to watch a pavement artist and Kate was aware that her uncle was in a reverie of his own. She put a ha'penny from her dress pocket into the man's Oxo tin, and he smiled up at her. "Thanks littl'un."

"That's what my Dad calls me," she told him happily, and David was reminded that much as she loved his company, he could never compete with Alex for her affection.

"He draws just like you do," she said and was surprised to see him so tight lipped.

"Kate I only wish I had the guts to do what he's doing... to throw up my job and create pictures. Look at the peace and contentment in his eyes."

"Are you sad? You paint pictures when I come and stay."

"He may not be happy... it's not the same. But he's at peace with himself.... exchanging the days of his life for something that satisfies him. He can cope with the poverty that almost drove me insane. I spent years fighting to get out of the hell you live in Kate, just as you will. And the only thing I really want to do would toss me back there. Nothing is worth that."

"Can't you stay in your nice house and paint?"

"I'd need to come to the city to be noticed, like this chap... waiting and hoping. And that house is mine because I'm a factory floor manager, not a pavement artist. I detest poverty too much to take the risk. Vanity or not, I'm staying out of that particular pit."

She was shaken by his vehemence and glad to move on through Marble Arch and walk to the Palace. They stopped to buy a postcard, and suddenly

SAFE AS HOUSES

- perhaps his passion directed her thoughts - she wondered if he would mention the doll she had allowed to fall. But dolls weren't important to a man whose soul was on fire, which is what coming to London had done for him. He'd be calmer when they were back on the train.

She told Mam of how Uncle David had watched the pavement artist for a long time.

"It's a wonder that brother of mine didn't get down on the pavement with him," Lucy said. "He painted like you scribble Kate. Always at it. Draw anybody he could."

"Where's Dad?" Kate asked. "I bought you both a postcard."

"On the bed love. His legs are pretty bad tonight. Let him rest up for half an hour."

"He's goin' to have to do as he's told afore long," Big Grandma announced, thumbing through the London paper Kate had given her, fascinated by the pictures of the city no more at war, but which would suffer the after effects for years to come. "With 'is stubbornness I'll give him no more'n six months afore he's crippled. By God, I'd like to have seen my Joe as eager to go to work."

In fact she underestimated his stubbornness that continued beyond Kate's tenth birthday. But a sudden onset of influenza brought him to a low ebb, and though far from convinced that the coal dust was to blame, he yielded to persuasion to accept a sick certificate, knowing as he did so that his employer's tolerance of the situation would be short lived, as indeed proved to be the case.

"We'll ask for outdoor work from the factory," Big Grandma announced, immediately taking control. "When I get home we can do a bundle of jumpers each – Kate'll have to learn. It's only finishing off the cuff seams - you'll soon get the hang of it. Your Dad can keep the darners threaded, and count the bundles as we finish."

And so the tiny house bulged with knitwear. It occupied every available chair and surface until at 10am each morning Alex carried the finished work round to the factory, and brought home more to be done. Each learned to live with fatigue and the necessity to stretch every penny, managed by Grandma who decisively cut her visit to The Feathers down to fifteen minutes just prior to closing time. Lucy's nimble fingers made light work of the tedious monotony and Kate was not far behind. They listened to the wireless as they worked - Donald Peers, The Man in Black, the Boxing commentaries for Dad, and the News, always the News that extended Dad's world and provided an escape from the claustrophobic circumstances in which they were determined to survive.

Each evening Mrs Thornton passed her evening paper over the wall so that Alex could scan the Situations Vacant column.

"Chap here needs a chauffeur," he said one night. "Can't get cleaner work than that. Give me a hand with the spelling pal, and we'll make a start. Wonder if he has a Rolls?"

"Then you'd have to wear a cap Dad."

"As long as I can shed these bandages Sunshine, I don't care if I wear a busby."

"I've got a pencil right here Dad."

"When did you not have a pencil 'right here', our Kate? Lucy shook her head and smiled phlegmatically. "Whatever do you think of to keep writing about?"

And Kate longed for her mother to see what she had written - to be interested as Aunt Polly and Oliver had been. But of course Aunt Polly didn't have three children to look after, or the need to work in the factory by day, and for it by night. Within this tight little circle intent on survival, the only way to earn praise was to extract 60 seconds of work from each unforgiving minute. Food for soul only merited Grandma's derision, and as her influence was paramount, Mam and Dad had adopted the same principles.

The prospect of putting pen to paper was daunting and Alex delayed by glancing through the 'hatched, matched and despatched' before applying himself. "No!" he suddenly exclaimed.

"Who is it Alex? Somebody we know?"

"Someone we all know." Alex put an arm around Kate. "It's Miss Smith - though I'm not sure they'll be any relatives left to see it."

Kate's face whitened. "My Miss Smith Dad? Aunt Polly?"

"Aye Kate. There's no mistakin' the address. "Sorry pal. You liked her a lot I know. But you knew she was old – 'appens to us all one day."

The darning needle quivered in her hand and wouldn't go into the right hole and a tight feeling in her throat made her choke.

"Come on Kate," Grandma said. "I'm getting ahead of you."

"I need to get something," she stammered. "I won't be long."

"What's the matter with 'er," Grandma commented irritably. "Polly Smith wasn't close - not family even. And Kate was only there a matter of months. We 'ain't got time for prima donna outbursts. Too much to do."

Alex went upstairs to where Kate was hunched on the landing, and they sat in silence for some minutes.

"I loved her Dad. I think about her every day. I wish we lived near so I could have gone to see her on my own."

"I should have taken you over there pal. Just never seems to be time or cash." He should have recognised Kate's need to have remained in contact; heaven knows it was obvious enough.

"Is it wrong that I loved her more than Big Grandma, Dad?"

"I understand luv." He was glad she hadn't said 'more than Little Gran.' "What say we get the bus on Saturday and stand in her garden and say cheerio?"

She curled into his arm. "Please. But what about the work?"

"I'll get up at the crack o' dawn, and get a head start. When we come back you and I can listen to the wireless while we bundle the cardigans."

She took the paper from his grasp and he knew that she needed the few minutes it would take to return it, to regain her composure. He had underestimated the bond that had taken hold while she had been in Polly Smith's care and was ashamed. He had witnessed the chemistry, recognised the ideals that bound them and yes, had wanted her home before the love could grow stronger. And that was *his* lack of self-esteem, for no one could have deposed him in her affections.

Within a week, Alex was in the employ of Frederick Charlesworth, owner of a substantial business and impressive mansion, who had made his money out of the hosiery trade. He missed his workmates on the coal runs from pitheads more than he admitted but could not deny that his legs at long last appeared to be healing. And though he sometimes feared he would go mad with the gentility of it all - for nothing physical was ever demanded of those broad shoulders, he was again able to support his adored family. Indeed he found satisfaction, and strangely almost a companionship that persisted, despite the social strata that must prevent its expression, in driving Mr. Charlesworth.

"One day," he murmured resolutely, "I'll drive a car of my own and take Ma and Kate for a drive in the country - drink tea in a cottage garden. Oh they'll like that."

Lucy's business was thriving too and had, in tandem with the mending, provided for them during the weeks Alex was without work. Whilst he drove to business and social functions, Lucy and Kate sat together of an evening discussing the baby that was at last almost due for David and Laura. Unlike Lucy's offspring, their son Jonathan was born in a private ward of the City Hospital and proudly escorted home by taxi.

"They'll give him the earth," Lucy had murmured, "And our Kate will be the loser."

And so the members of the Benson family, each with private dreams - unexpressed in case they should signify dissatisfaction with their shared lot, - worked hard and played little. To squeeze the most from each hour was Lucy's maxim; a mode of life quickly absorbed by her daughter.

CHAPTER SIX

Education was again the focus of school life: survival no longer all that mattered. Teachers bemoaned undue absence, shoddy work and untidy handwriting, and attributed to each, or so it seemed to their charges, the importance only recently attached to the task of staying alive. All of which increased Kate's dilemma.

Mrs. Broomwade was mystified when she was frequently late for school and even more bewildered when warnings had no effect. Eventually, the boardman was notified. Mr. Fellowes, her headmaster, placed a protective hand on Kate's shoulder as he instructed her to answer the visitor's questions. 'No, it wasn't Mam's fault: she always had her breakfast in time. But her Little Gran was ill, and she needed to go each morning. She was extremely sorry for 'being bad' and would do her sums at home.'

"But would she promise not to be late again?" she was asked. And of course she could give no such guarantee because they must understand that Dad had to go off to work before daylight and Mam had two younger ones to care for, and who else was there to make Gran a cup of tea and plump her pillows? Patiently she explained a second time, and as she did so the attendance officer cursed the red tape that now entwined her, but wheels had been set in motion and her parents must be sent for.

"Doesn't he believe my Gran's ill?" she asked her teacher. "Doesn't he understand?"

They all did of course, but she must not miss school; it was against the law.

And so she sat in the Headmaster's office with Lucy and Alex on either side of her, and it was pointed out that tending to Little Gran's needs was not Kate's responsibility.

"But we don't give her that responsibility," Lucy protested. "We'd no idea she was visiting each morning. She's there every bloomin' evenin' as it is."

"So, Luce," Alex thought, "your anger is not because Kate has missed school, but because she wanted to go to her Gran. Ma's never said a word to hurt you, never interfered in our lives." But he knew that had he voiced such sentiments, Lucy would have countered with the fact that 'she had to do without him whilst he checked on his Ma each evening - she hadn't time to do more'. He had long ago learned that she could contrive to win any argument, particularly concerning his mother. He wasn't certain at what point he had actually decided to keep his love for them separate but it hurt nonetheless that Lucy never suggested having her ma in law round for a cuppa, and would have asserted that 'family shouldn't need invitations ... and if his mother wasn't interested enough to call, then it was her loss'. But someone with Ma's sensitivity needed to *feel* welcome before imposing her presence and Lucy knew it. And now here was Kate in trouble for giving Gran her time.

"Kate why did you tell me an untruth - that you *had* to visit your Gran?" Mr Fellowes asked and she fought back the tears of shame at being thus questioned.

"I didn't," she insisted, and he detected a hint of stubborn pride. "I wasn't *told* to visit. I went 'cos *I* had to - for me. If Gran is ill then I *have* to go. It was the truth."

"My sister is there," Dad intervened.

"What do you say to that Kate?" Mr. Fellowes asked.

She was in no doubt what she had to say. Dad had given her no option. It was obvious they were all reaching the false conclusion that the fact of a body in the house must mean that the body could perform a required function: in this case, make a cup of tea.

"Aunt Eve gets home after midnight, so she doesn't always wake up when Gran needs her tea. And often her head is so bad she *can't* make a cup of tea next morning."

Mr Fellowes hid a smile at the child's frank acceptance of life as she saw it until he noticed with sympathy Alex' embarrassment that his sister's failings should become public knowledge.

"It won't 'appen again," Lucy assured him, and Alex knew that Eve would shortly be on the receiving end of some plain speaking.

Glancing at Kate, her Headmaster was not so certain. She may not have inherited her mother's strong personality but that silent willpower was not to be underestimated.

Kate returned to class to consider her problem. Could the household chores be done the night before, she wondered, thus allowing time to visit Gran *and* be at school on time, for it seemed mightily important to all the adults present this morning that she was at school promptly. Aunt Polly would certainly not have made such unreasonable demands, knowing very surely where the priorities lay. The trouble was that chores at that time of day pertained to the family breakfast - the dishes, and laying the table for lunchtime. Feeding the hens was essential. There was also the daily visit to the shop to collect a loaf of bread to take home at lunchtime. Urgent reorganisation was called for.

By mid morning she had a solution. She would ask Jimmy to feed the hens in return for the pennyworth of sweets Dad bought her each Friday night. Mam would be too busy with the girls and getting herself ready for work to notice him slip through the back gate. But the visit to the shop must be rescheduled. On occasions she was served in a flash, but most often she queued behind customers for whom a gossip with Mrs.Merrill was the highlight of the day, wasting ten or so of Kate's precious minutes. There was nothing for it but to slip out of school at mid-morning break and hope her disappearance went undetected. She would also have to offload her staff-tea job but any number of girls would be happy to do that for it provided an excuse not to go out in cold weather.

Getting someone to drink her compulsory bottle of milk was more difficult; moreover someone who wouldn't tell. Jimmy again, she decided. Though close as a brother having grown up next door, he would nonetheless exact his price. Survival had been the name of the game all his life, for he had none of the love showered on Kate. The price could be worked out later; he trusted her.

Problem resolved she was able at last to concentrate on the essay she was to write. Flustered on seeing how little time remained, the child jerked pen to paper, failing to notice that the nib had picked up a scrap of blotting paper lodged in the bottom of the inkwell. The blot settled menacingly on the top of her page. It was all too much and the tears she had held back in the Headmaster's office trickled down her face. She refused to be seen snivelling, and hurriedly pulled her sleeve across her eyes, but not before a salty tear had added itself to the blot. Head bent, she requested another sheet of paper.

"Kate you know that paper is still very strictly rationed. I can only give you one sheet." The child was distraught, and taking the pen into her own hand, Mrs. Broomwade drew forth the shape of a butterfly from the blot.

"We can often make something worthwhile out of a mistake," she said gently. "That's not so bad, is it? Write a story about a butterfly!"

Her story, though grammatically perfect, lacked the poignancy that had characterised previous ones.

SAFE AS HOUSES

Jimmy settled for the Friday sweets but extracted an agreement to queue up at the fish and chip van on Wednesday nights to 'compensate' for drinking her milk. Kate grimaced for it was no hardship for him.

"Remember to put lots o' salt and vinegar on me Dad's," he warned, "or he'll beat the living daylights out o' me."

It was now only a matter of waiting for the duty teacher to turn her head whilst she slipped behind the coalsheds to where a bar was missing from the railings.

"Funny time for you Kate," Mrs. Merrill remarked, but business was business and who cared as long as the till rattled. "That'll be fourpence - going up to fourpence farthing next week, tell yer Mam."

For days her plans remained undetected. And then after that she didn't care. It was almost ten o'clock when she reported to class one Friday morning.

"Come to my office, Kate," Mr. Fellowes instructed, looking gravely at the white face, due he assumed, to the predicament in which she now found herself. "Kate, your Gran obviously means a great deal to you. Yesterday I saw you in the street. Today you are very late. You must let me help you."

"Thank you," she interrupted almost inaudibly, "but you don't need to. My Gran's dead. It was when I gave her her tea. I've woken Aunt Eve."

He saw her lips tremble as she folded her arms around herself to provide the comfort she so desperately needed. And then the fragile little body crumpled in a heap on the floor. Lifting her gently onto the bed in the medical room, he covered her with a blanket. Frightened and shocked, she was utterly drained by the self-imposed responsibility. Sleep would heal her a little, and meanwhile he would visit the factory where her mother worked. But Aunt Eve was there ahead of him.

"I did all I could for the old dear," Eve wept volubly and Lucy refrained from harsh words in front of Mr. Fellowes who explained that Kate would be sleeping for as long as was needed. He promised to use the school telephone to contact Mr. Charlesworth.

Kate had imagined that only she and Dad would be at the funeral for she had not known Little Gran in any other context than the three of them tightly together in a world that seemed separate from the greater world outside. It would not have seemed strange if Aunt Eve had been at work, and Mam at home with Beth and Gillian, and Dad's other sisters with their own families. But they were all there, looking smart in black hats and Sunday best. She slid her hand into Dad's and pulled gently on his sleeve.

"Why can people come now, when they couldn't visit Gran before?"

SAFE AS HOUSES

Eyes damp and lips tightly drawn he swallowed hard. "It's called hypocrisy Kate. Pretend it's just you and me."
She knew that he was unaware how hard he was gripping her hand and was glad to be feeling some of his pain. Afterwards she would tell him that if Aunt Polly had been right - and she had not the slightest doubt of it - then Gran would be with Oliver now. He would look after her; he was that kind of person and would love Gran just as he had loved Aunt Polly, because of their gentleness and because they were special.

That had all been a year ago. And now, at his request, Kate was tapping at Mr. Fellowe's door.

"Kate come in!" He was waving a piece of paper. "Congratulations."
Kate looked up at him questioningly. "Sir?"

"You've done it Kate. You've done it! A scholarship to Brierley. Oh this is a red letter day indeed." He beckoned to her to sit down. "Aren't you pleased?"

"Well yes, if you are Sir. I don't rightly know where Brierley Hall is."

He slapped his thigh delightedly. "Well I daresay we shall find it," he declared. "Kate the world lies at your feet. Who knows what the future holds. I always felt you had a chance, but a full scholarship...why that's really something! It means Kate that your tuition, books, games equipment are all paid for."

"Good." she nodded seriously, and his eyebrows raised questioningly. "Well Sir, if they weren't I wouldn't be going. As it is, I don't know whether Mam and Dad will like the idea."

"Kate what are you saying? They'll be delighted. You *must* go."

This he had not foreseen. The child *had* to take up the place offered; surely they would not deny her the chance. "Kate, ask your parents to come and see me tomorrow."

"I don't suppose my Dad will get time off, Sir, and Mam has her job and the girls to look after. I 'spect I'll just bring a message, if you please. Mam is on piece work - they don't pay her for talking, you know."

He placed his hands on her shoulders and looked hard into the pale wistful face. "Kate, listen carefully. You will never get such an opportunity again. It can change your whole life. You must not throw it away."

She smiled having no wish to displease him. Nor indeed would she if Mam said yes. She supposed it was perhaps that it was because he wasn't married

SAFE AS HOUSES

that he failed to comprehend the practicalities. You couldn't just wish away two little sisters because your headmaster wanted you to go to a different school. Besides she could already write stories and would be an author one day just like Aunt Polly had said, wherever she passed the intervening years.

"Perhaps I should come and have a word with your parents tonight."

"Oh no Sir. If you please I don't think that would be a good idea." Thursday night was cleaning night, a job made almost self-defeating by the ravages of damp and decay, though every corner would be swept and dusted meticulously. Mam would have her hair in a turban, Dad battling with the range, and she herself black leading the grate. No, it would not do for Mr. Fellowes to call tonight.

He sensed her unease. "Very well Kate, but promise to tell them how important it is."

"I will Mr Fellowes," she assured him. "I'm glad you're happy. It'll make up for my upsetting you last year when my Gran was ill."

Happy! How could he make her realise the implications of the award. All through her years in his school, successive teachers had brought her work to him and voiced their hopes. He recollected how after an air raid he had gone back into the shelter to find her.

"You shouldn't have worried about me," she'd said. "It always takes a long time for the whole school to get out and I had an idea for the ending of my story, so I just took a minute to write it down."

And now he was imagining his school without her: the scrubbed, diminutive little figure who skipped down the corridor to fetch 'staff-tea.' With a wisdom beyond her years, and at eleven years old having had so little childhood, self esteem was non existent. Certainly not for lack of affection for her father's love of her though silent, was almost fierce; her mother's total, even if combined with an expectation that her girl should be already almost adult. The deep-set eyes were looking up at him as if for confirmation of what he had told her. Perhaps elation was not in fact appropriate. Public school alongside girls who lacked for nothing would be no picnic for her - maybe she wouldn't cope. And then he recalled her determination to be with her Gran as she lay dying. "She'll cope," he decided. "But she'll have one hell of a battle."

Mr.Fellowes had seemed to think highly of this chance she had. Standards were very high - many of the pupils went on to Oxford and Cambridge he had said, as if these places were prestigious, in a way she did not yet know. Tonight she would put the idea to Mam and Dad.

SAFE AS HOUSES

She was drying the dishes when the opportunity arose. "Remember that exam I took," she said, surprised to be feeling some of her headmaster's enthusiasm. "Mr. Fellowes reckons I've passed."

"That right, love?" Lucy was more pleased than Kate had expected.

"Another clever one in the family," sighed Big Grandma. "Your mam did too. But we couldn't afford it, so she had to forget it in a hurry."

Kate shot a glance at her mother, seeing instantly what a difference it could have made. Enough to change a whole life, Mr Fellowes had said.

"If Kate's passed, she'll go," Lucy asserted. But Big Grandma was not to be outdone.

"You just stop and think for a minute my girl. If Kate goes to grammar school she'll be sixteen afore she's put owt into the 'ousekeeping."

Lucy flushed. "If we can keep her 'til she's fifteen, we can manage another year. She's going." Kate, incredulous at the exchange, wished after all that Mr. Fellowes had come to visit this evening.

"You'll rue the day." Grandma hung her overall on the kitchen door. "Pass my jug, Kate and talk some sense into your Mam. She was just the same when her teacher told her." She eased herself past the piano and the back door closed decisively behind her.

"Did you want to go very badly, Mam?"

"I had a dream of working in an office instead of a factory, and wearing a smart dress and my hair in a bob."

And they saw that the dream was still there.

"Did you pass as well Dad?"

Her father affected to be engrossed in lifting the cinders from the range.

"Not me Kate. There's no brain inside this head."

She hugged him, sensing his feeling of inadequacy yet failing to understand why it should be so, for wasn't he the epitome of all men?

"Anyway, it's not me we're discussing. You're the star tonight. You'll have a fair walk each morning if it's the school on Harrison Way."

"Well there's a bit more I haven't told you. Mr Fellowes says it's a special sort of place. Lots of girls live there in term time, but I'd just go each day." Intercepting their glances of alarm she added quickly. "He wrote the name on this paper and he wants to talk to you about it. It won't cost anything."

Alex whistled out a deep breath. "Well beat that. That's where Charlesworth's lass is. And a pretty penny it costs too by all accounts."

"You're sure you have it right Kate," Lucy demanded, now totally perplexed. "This isn't something out of your imagination?"

SAFE AS HOUSES

"Mr. Fellowes says it's important to go." Until now it had hardly seemed a matter of urgency, but the exchanges had channelled her into a decision.

"It won't be easy young 'un." Dad continued. "They're not our kind of people."

Kate knew now that she had to go. The news had first elated then drained them. When Lucy finally filled a bowl for the pans, Kate was by her side, dish towel in hand.

"Will you be alright with the girls, Mam? I'll be a bit later home from this school. Who'll collect Gill from Infants...and Beth from Mrs. Liddle?"

Lucy didn't reply, and in the silence that followed both Kate and Alex noticed her brow crease painfully, and hands shake a little in the bowl.

"I'll be here to look after them Kate." Her voice was scarcely more than a whisper. "I won't be going to the factory when you start your new school."

Worn out with never ending work, she clung to them both in turn and the fear she had kept hidden for two months now, was released. And as if by changing her own plans so newly formulated, she could also change events, Kate said, "I won't go to the school. It'll be much easier for us if I'm at Gypsy Road."

"Over my dead body," Lucy wept. "No. I've spoken with Mr. Jeps and I can do the mending at home again. I've got the sideboard shop, and Dad's with Mr. Charlesworth. We'll manage Kate. I promise."

Though emotionally torn to ribbons, health of mind and body so nearly crushed, the relentless business of living must continue. Washing, sweeping, meal after meal to find in order to sustain the strength to wake to another day. Alex put a protective arm around her, panic stricken as he contemplated where the new baby would sleep. In their room for a time he supposed...and afterwards? He was devastated. A quiet unassuming man who did not make undue demands of his wife, yet it seemed he only had to breathe on her.

And now Kate wanted to go to the same school as the Charlesworth girl. How could any good come of that? People should stay in their own class if they didn't want to get their fingers burned. For once he agreed with ma-in-law. Better to go with other kids in the street. But he'd be no match for Lucy if she'd set her mind on it.

When Kate left for school next morning Mam and Big Grandma were talking in hushed tones as they fed the sheets through the wringer. She was glad they had got over their difference for it was onerous and unpleasant to be the subject of an adult quarrel.

CHAPTER SEVEN

The trauma of going to 'a very special school' was bearing down heavily before term even began. Mr.Fellowes had said everything would be paid for but 'everything' hadn't included uniform, and evidently the school patronised only quality stores. Lucy's ingenuity had ensured copies of standard items and her tailoring of the grey blazer matched the professional but even so there had been painful tightening of the family belt.

"We'll manage with one blouse," Lucy had decided. "I can quickly rinse it through of an evening, and dry it by the range."

"I'm supposed to have two pairs of shoes - lace ups for outdoors and bar shoes for inside. Mam I'm sorry."

"Well I can't copy a pair of shoes, that's for sure," her mother declared.

"Never heard of such a daft idea," Grandma interrupted. "No child should have more than one pair of shoes. Both pairs will be outgrown afore they're worn out."

"One will have to do love," Lucy agreed, stepping back to admire her daughter and her heart sang. "We'll settle for the lace-ups."

"You're a real bobby-dazzler," Alex said. "You've done her proud Luce." Lucy counted the change from her purse. "There's your 2/ld dinner money- fivepence a day it said. . ... and tuppence a day for your break."

"I can manage without that Mam. I'll just take dinner money." Her mother winked conspiratorially. "It's from your Grandma."

"But."

"Take no notice of 'er." Lucy whispered. "She's proud as punch really." Kate determined to keep the tuppences for any further necessities that failed to come under 'everything provided'.

"Best get up the apples and pears now pal. Early start in the morning," Dad said, and Lucy crumpled into the chair.

"How do you think she'll make out Alex?"

"Luce I know what trouble you've gone to, but if Kate's miserable she'll come back to school in Gipsy Road. Alright?"

Lucy nodded her acquiescence. "But we had to let her try."

SAFE AS HOUSES

"I'll get you the necessary tonight - have a really 'ot bath straight away
Grandma was saying earnestly. "If that don't work, you could go round
Bessie's. I ain't sure it's worth the risk - if it doesn't come away, the bat
might be damaged, but ."

"God forbid!" Lucy was at breaking point. "What are we going to d
We can't manage another one. Why every time I get on my feet...."

Mam was very white when Kate came home - distant and troubled.
course it would be because of the pregnancy and the talk of Brierley H
last night.

"You alright Luce?" Alex whispered as he reached for a saucepan
needed from the dresser, the simple action enabling the closeness th
desperately yearned for. "I mean apart from...."

"Just a migraine." Impotent with angry misery because not even a sim
exercise like taking a bath was available to her without creating suspici
To have a bath when it wasn't Friday...laboriously to fill the copper bo
so that she could immerse herself in the necessary temperature to facili
the effect of the gin, and worse, for the family to witness her insobriety .
was all too much to bear. Tomorrow she would seek out Bessie Brigsh
and afterwards tell Alex and Kate she had miscarried. Alone she wc
take decisive action, alone would risk the consequences.

"We had to let you both try."

She smiled with the last little energy she could summon. "Don't be daft. If I hadn't gone to Gipsy Road, I wouldn't have met you."

And privately he thought, "Maybe that would have been no bad thing."

The bus transported her out of the world of back streets to one of desirable residences in avenues of copper beech. She checked the map Dad had drawn and followed the groups similarly attired who turned into a sweeping drive, at the end of which stood an impressive Georgian building where two uniformed porters stood ready to direct the new girls. Kate could only gasp in wonder. Fancy walking down a drive to school! She already had so much to tell and the day was only just beginning.

"New Miss?" enquired the porter. "Go to the side entrance on the left there. The maid is waiting to show you to your classroom."

Maid! Mam would never believe it. The woman's glance took in Kate's lack of confidence. "Please wait here. I'll take you to your room presently."

"She don't 'alf talk nice for a maid," Kate thought, whose experience of such persona was limited to the plays she had heard on Saturday Night Theatre. And then the whole marvellous new world fell apart as en route to the classroom she was instructed to change into indoor shoes. Kate's heart missed a beat and forgetting the pleasantries she had so carefully rehearsed in her bedroom, stammered, "I've only got me lace-ups," and was instantly aware of giggles being stifled.

An ample, expressionless Senior Mistress, with a multitude of dark hairs on her chin and upper lip, eyed the miscreant. "Forgotten your indoor shoes? Rather a careless start to a new term, don't you think? We expect higher standards of our girls. I'll call your mother - just this once."

"We 'aven't got a phone and I didn't forget my shoes. I've only got one pair - there just wasn't enough money you see," blurted Kate.

"But you did receive a uniform list? Call on me before going home, and I'll see that a letter is ready for your parents."

The maid was summoned and Kate escorted to her classroom where something was discreetly whispered to the class teacher. She was mortified, the more so when a seat beside the girl who had giggled in the cloakroom, was indicated. The girl smirked perceptibly to her companions who with just sufficient twitching of facial muscles left Kate in no doubt they found her embarrassment entertaining.

SAFE AS HOUSES

At lunchtime, she stared at the array of cutlery in front of her, unable to imagine what dishes could necessitate so many utensils. But she was not a scholarship girl for nothing and cast surreptitious glances in the direction of those who were familiar with such situations.

"I'll tell Mam about the napkins all starched crisp and white," she thought to herself. It was going to be painful but worth every tortuous moment if she could learn proper manners. Her error was to accept a second helping of steamed chocolate pudding whilst the rest looked on with disdain whilst she ate it.

"Typical school stodge," someone said and Kate was pleased to hear that such fare could be considered typical for she had feared that being the first day the food might be a special treat. She had savoured every delicious satisfying mouthful.

"Finished?" a voice asked. "If so, our table can go now staff have left."

She collected her letter and breathed deeply again as she walked the leafy drive. What would the kids at home say to this? Knowing exactly what they'd say, she decided to tell only the family about it. She burst into the kitchen with all her news but Lucy was struggling to retrieve the ironing Beth had pulled to the floor.

"Oh Kate thank Heavens you're home. "Just take Beth for me will you? Look at the time. Dad'll be home soon and I ain't chipped the taters yet."

"I'll do that. Come on Beth, let's wipe your face."

"Better take your uniform off love. What was it like? Gillian don't touch that! Did you have a good dinner Kate - or do I need to cook extra?"

"I had plenty Mam. I'll just have bread with you."

Changed into one of Lucy's altered skirts, she sliced the potatoes. This wasn't the moment for the letter; later when they had all eaten perhaps.

"Who the Dickens do they think they are?" Lucy exploded when she had digested the contents. "And how do I get a pair of shoes by tomorrow even if we had the cash?"

"Won't the weekend do?" Alex asked phlegmatically, for it was outside his experience to be able to draw on reserves of money to change events.

"Oh yes, the weekend will do, as long as Kate doesn't put in an appearance til then. No indoor shoes: no lessons."

Grandma refrained from uttering the words on the tip of her tongue. Corporately they were no nearer a solution when suddenly Lucy said, "Alex! Your Ma had a pair!"

"Ma? But they'll be too big."

"Not with stuffing in the toe they won't. Go to Eve now before she goes to work. Hurry."

Eve laughed. "Who'd 'ave thought the shoes Ma wore in service were just what's needed in a posh school like yours Kate. I've not done any clearing so they'll still be at the bottom of her wardrobe. Pop up and see ducky."

Alex glanced around his mother's old home. He had imagined Eve would change it beyond recognition but in fact it had remained much the same.

"I'm out most of the time," Eve read his thoughts. And then, "Reckon as 'ow Lucy will have to move the buttons if Kate's not to sprain her ankle. Not very fashion conscious, your teacher, is she Kate?"

They hurried back to put Lucy's mind at ease and she struggled to force her bodkin through the thick leather. Her sore fingers didn't trouble her; enough that the problem was solved. Kate had not mentioned until now that she had homework.

"Is this going to be every night?" Grandma asked incredulously. "Good Lord, do they think you eat, drink and sleep school?"

Her class had been asked to write about the piece of music played at morning assembly. Kate had wanted to ask what it was called, but keeping a low profile after the shoe incident had prohibited such a question. The composer had made the piano resemble a stream and words were such a joy that tiredness was no obstacle to putting pen to paper.

Big Grandma didn't go to the Feathers that night and when she too came upstairs she said that fine words wouldn't pay for shoes. She was angry at the posh school for causing Mam distress, and Kate didn't blame her. But neither did she tell her about the long leafy drive.

"You'll have to watch yerself in them shoes tomorrow," Grandma warned as she settled heavily on the bed and Kate was too young to realise the resentment hid a genuine concern for the battle the child undoubtedly had ahead of her. Nor did she understand why the shoes were so vital, but it seemed her whole world could be disastrously changed by the lack of them. She had practised walking around the living room and by scrunching her toes, her feet would accommodate all the space between sole and upper whilst the ball of newspaper took care of the superfluous length. Even so she was glad Gran had had such small feet for a grown up.

She was to discover that well-bred eleven year olds could be just as vindictive as those with whom she had shared her primary years. Joan grabbed her shoes and holding them aloft called out, "Oh look - Kate Benson's got new shoes - except they don't look exactly new. Second hand

SAFE AS HOUSES

are they Kate? Oh and what's this - they're filled with newspaper! And which newspaper I wonder. Oh dear me - the News of the World! My what quality press you do read at your house."

"Give them back!" Kate pleaded as they were passed around the giggling group.

"Say please Kate. You do know that that's polite don't you?"

The door opened and Phyllis, the maid of yesterday, demanded to know what all the noise was about.

"I think Kate has lost her newspaper," Joan announced. "Don't worry, we'll just get out of the way so that she can find it."

"And I think them that lost it should find it," retorted Phyllis, playing for time to assess the situation that now faced the girl who had been so humiliated the day before.

Her face crimson, Kate stooped to rescue the balls of newspaper and replace them in her shoes. Circumstances becoming clear, Phyllis gently took them from her. "Oh you mean the bits we put in last night when they got so wet after Mr. Drayton found them outside." She winked at Kate. "Off you go all of you and tell your teacher Kate will be along soon. I shall of course tell her myself later."

As soon as they were gone she addressed Kate urgently. "Put the paper in the bin and we'll stop by the first aid cupboard and get some cotton wool. And Kate, if you're to survive here, you'll have to keep your wits about you." Half way down the corridor Phyllis looked about her. "I'm not supposed to touch that cupboard - don't tell!"

"I won't. And thank you. Will you really explain to my teacher?"

"Wouldn't dare," Phyllis grinned. "This place is full of rules. But *they* won't know. Not a word mind! Now go in with your head up, apologise for stopping to help me carry something, wait for leave to sit down and then go to your desk."

"But.. .. Oh I see."

"Survival Kate."

Grandma didn't go to the pub for several nights, and when Kate asked her mother the reason, Lucy passed on the reply she herself had received. "She says the ale's off - that Harry has not been too particular with his cellar."

"Is that true?"

"I don't suppose so, but she'll have her reasons."

On Friday evening Grandma took a pair of bar shoes from her bag. "Try 'em on," she instructed Kate, and Lucy felt over them.

SAFE AS HOUSES

"We'll have to put that one on the stretcher."

"Albert's stall on the market," Grandma said. "They're seconds but you'd never know. I've paid 'alf a crown and told him we'll pay the rest off at a bob a week."

"So that's why you stayed home." Lucy hugged her mother. "Thanks Ma." Kate was ashamed that instead of feeling appreciative as she ought, she could only think that half the street would now know of the letter she had brought home, and wondered how many of her classmates wore shoes that had to be paid for at a bob a week, but she said, "Thanks Grandma. I'm very grateful."

She had told no one all week about the drive leading to her school. Sufficient the body should be fed; satisfying the soul was a luxury they could not afford. And anyway, Grandma would only complain that a long drive would wear out her shoes more quickly.

And so passed painful and challenging months. Her lack of social graces and faulty grammar were incessantly scrutinised and corrected, publicly by some for whom the need to correct was an irritating interruption to the flow of the lesson, whilst other, more sensitive staff took her aside to point out errors of expression or response. Ever vigilant, her wits constantly employed, she listened and adopted the speech surrounding her. Tired, but elated too, for each humiliation brought her nearer to her goal. Even Miss Turnbull's open resentment of scholarship girls lost its edge on such days, though Kate still dreaded every period spent with her.

"Kate you have paid less than eight shillings towards your needlework. We ordered best quality cambric and your mother should be delighted at 14/6d," she said in strident tones one afternoon. Kate's eyes smarted. It had not escaped her attention that the other girls had brought in their payment in one amount. Only Kate had paid her ten pence tuck money each week plus the shilling she earned for looking after a neighbour's children on Saturday mornings. Lucy would have refused them for she could run up a pair of pyjamas in an hour from the unworn sides of sheets that had become thin in the middle. Only film stars wore the best cambric!

Grimly determined, Kate struggled through her first year, keeping home and school poles apart. Her peers were aware of her personality yet not within any tangible context. Not even Emmeline knew Kate's father was chauffeur to her own. Tied tightly like a parcel, she was intriguing to staff who required dissertations, for then words were released and her essays some of the best they had read.

Learning to survive as a scholarship girl she moved on into middle school, even in her early teens steadfastly refusing to draw attention to herself, yet feeling more confident as the years passed. All proceeded without major social catastrophe until two girls with whom events caused her to form a tentative alliance, asked her to join them for a cycle ride. Committed to caring for Beth and Gillian in the school holidays, Kate made excuses that were dismissed as implausible, occasioning her to exaggerate. "We may go to France," she lied. "My father's on business."

Theresa with suspicion alerted, sought an opportunity to check Kate's address from the register. Intrigued that anyone living in the inner city could have business connections, she decided it would be amusing to investigate. To Kate's humiliation the two arrived minutes after Lucy had left for work one day. She was elbow deep in soapsuds and before she could dry her hands, Gillian had invited them in.

"We came to see if you'd changed your mind," Theresa began. "But I see you can't. Is it like this every day?"

"No.... no," Kate stammered. "My mother isn't well so I must take care of things." But fate cruelly brought Lucy back for a tablecloth that someone had ordered.

"Early visitors," she said, casting them the most peremptory glance.

"Your mother seems to be better." Theresa bristled at Lucy's attitude.
Kate, aware of their glance towards the backyard, saw the fleeting expression of distaste pass between them, and hearing Beth suddenly scream from the living room, was utterly devoid of inspiration. "I'll see you when term begins."

"Well," she heard Theresa gasp as the two wheeled their bicycles back through the alley to the street. "What do you make of that?"

"A whole lot," Kate thought, pressing her backside against the door.
It was a pity they were out of earshot as Sheila said, "Poor Kate. No wonder no one knows much about her. I think we should go back."

"And be frozen by her mother. No thanks!"
By the time Kate returned to the living room Beth's lip was bleeding profusely.

"She fell on the hearth," Gillian whimpered in the manner of one who may not have been altogether innocent, "but she didn't fall into the fire."

"Run and get some cotton wool... kitchen cupboard... quick."

SAFE AS HOUSES

"Will she die Kate? I didn't mean to push her."

"No. But I can't stop the bleeding. Better go to the factory for Mam." Seconds after Gillian left, her grip took effect and with the situation under control by the time she arrived, Lucy gave her attention to being cross. In all her young years, Kate had never incurred her mother's wrath.

"That's what comes of not keeping your eyes on the job."

"I didn't know they would invite me on a picnic," she said defensively. Lucy was unmoved. "Tell them you can go on a Saturday. Weekends are for days off." She deftly applied a dressing to Gillian's chin and declared there was nothing to be done for the lip, which though now swollen, had stopped bleeding. "I'll 'ave to make up the time from my lunch hour, so I'll be late back," she said. "C'mon, don't take it to heart. You're a good kid really."

School holidays were grey routine days of being big sister, but lacked the pain of school, where Kate rose to each challenge because there was no alternative if she were to contend with the education she was, as Miss Turnbull reminded her, 'privileged to receive'. The Senior Mistress made known her opposition to the Board's decision to offer an annual scholarship. But with Attlee's government in power it mattered little now. Even the girls in the preparatory department would have to satisfy examiners before progressing to the Lower school. Those who didn't would merely leave gaps for more urchins like young Kate here. Standards would inevitably fall.

Jane Brownlow, head gardener noticed how often Kate walked alone in the rockeries away from the main grounds where others played in groups for it had not taken long for the class to be made aware of Kate's origins; the description of her home had been colourfully explicit.

"You enjoy plants and trees?" she asked finding an opportunity to engage Kate in conversation. "Do you help with the garden at home?" A catch question, but she had become expert at parrying such enquiries. Her monosyllabic response was not a lie for she still watered the red geraniums in their baskets on the whitewashed wall. Despite the apparent resistance, Jane felt disinclined to abandon the conversation because the girl's body language suggested no desire to move on. "Suppose you introduce yourself and tell me what you enjoy doing most. Cutting the grass? The borders?"

"I'm Kate, and I don't do either of those."

"So what do you like so much about the school gardens?"

With no further need to be evasive, words cascaded; she was smiling, had come alive inside. "The trees that sway, especially those by the lake that mirrors them, and the tall poplars along the drive .... the silver birch when the bark turns speckled white. In springtime the cherry blossom is prettier than anything I've ever seen. Sometimes when I walk past the lawns I imagine royalty holding a garden party here. They are like velvet - no weeds or moss. And the two shades of green when they have just been mown are almost military, suggesting they mustn't be disturbed."

"Thank you for quite the most beautiful compliment I have ever had. It's hard work keeping them in good condition, but now I shall always remember that someone noticed, and appreciated the results." She regarded her young companion. "Would you care to help me during a lunch hour?" Kate glanced up to check there was nothing devious afoot, but the face was still warmed by an inviting smile.

"I'd enjoy that very much. Can I come tomorrow please?"

"May you come tomorrow," Miss Brownlow corrected gently. "You are asking permission - 'can I' means 'able to' in the way I might ask you if you can swim."

"Thank you," said Kate, and meant it for there was no hint of condescension or derision in Jane Brownlow's manner. "Then may I begin tomorrow please?"

They laughed at the careful articulation. For the first time in over three years she sensed she had a real friend. She told Alex about it when they cleaned the parlour whilst Lucy took Grandma's Sick Club at the Feathers.

"Latin will be easier now. Plants have Latin names so I've a reason to learn it."

"Beats me what you need Latin for. Nobody speaks it. Do they?"

"It isn't possible to get into University without it."

"Kate, you're not thinking ...... we can't."

"No Dad. But I will be going to the Christmas Ball," she said as if to reassert her right to attend something alien to their position in society. "We receive printed invitations and must reply on correspondence cards."

"Why don't they just ask if y' wants to go?" Alex was puzzled.

"So that we know how to reply to invitations in the future."

"Kate. ..." His unspoken words designated the whole exercise stupidly futile, but with just a hint of defiance she added, "I would like to know how to reply correctly."

They were quiet for some time until Alex said, "Ask Mam to make you a posh frock. She'll love it - always talking about the day she'll make you a bridal gown."

"But not for years yet!"

"You're fourteen. Won't be long now afore you have a job in an office. No cafés and factories for you eh Kate? Maybe you'll be on the post office counter when I get my postal order for the pools." He became troubled. "Fourteen's a bit young to go dancing. I don't want fellas around you yet."

"There won't be any boys Dad. It's so that we know how to behave at a proper ball when we are older." They were still discussing gardens and balls when Lucy returned.

"Ooh lovely," she enthused. "We'll go to market for a length o' taffeta, and I'll dress you like a lady. And guess what - the boss has offered to pay for all the factory hands to go to the Mario Lanza film. We'll sketch the frocks in that! I'll make you something that'll knock 'em flat."

Capable resourceful Mam; Kate would indeed go to the ball.

"I'll make the cocoa." she said, "Do you think Grandma would like one?"

"I shouldn't think so," Lucy laughed. "She's not best pleased at 'avin' a temperature and missing the pub. I'd best go and give her a report." Then exhilarated by something beautiful taking shape in her head, added, "We'll see if we can't find a few sequins as well."

No matter the financial restrictions placed on the choice of fabric, she would make magic of it. Little did the brides in the street realise that the gowns Lucy created, made those in department stores look like also-rans. Sadly she had never rated her talent, nor was she sufficiently worldly to advertise to those who could pay for it.

But when she reappeared, the excitement was lashed from her face, now ashen with shock. Apart from two days of head cold, Grandma had suffered not at all before dying painlessly in her sleep.

"I didn't even say Goodbye," Lucy wept. "All 'cos we got talking about that dress."

It seemed the whole street turned out to bid Ruth Brightman 'farewell', the landlord of the Feathers opening half an hour late as a mark of respect. Kate wasn't sure Grandma would have approved of his gesture, but Lucy said it made no odds, for what they weren't drinking inside, they were imbibing in the street with what was left of the whip-round after they had paid for the wreath.

"We'll give the old girl a good send off," Albert Jones said philosophically. "Wonder who'll run the Sick Club for us now?"

Directing his gaze at Lucy, she knew it had already been decided.

CHAPTER EIGHT

By November Lucy had saved enough to buy a length of taffeta. "We'll nip it in tight at the waist," she enthused. "You're so trim, and instead of sleeves we'll make a sort of cape, just like the star in the film. Look, I've sketched it for you."
"Oh Mam, I shall feel like a princess. I've never seen you draw before."
"Your Uncle David ain't the only one," her mother laughed.
"Then why...." Kate began.
"Waste of time. I sees it in me 'ead, so I just takes the scissors and gets on with it. I'm not good with hair though. What can we do with your plaits?"
"Could I go to the hairdressers just this once - for the Christmas ball, I mean?" She almost said 'May I' but stopped in time. It would have sounded artificial at home.
"Tell you what," Lucy said. "Have it cut. Joyce won't charge full cos you're not sixteen yet. Take my turn. We'll ask her to do it real special."
Alex listened to their excitement. "What did you marry a dumb cluck like me for?"
"Cos you were the one who whistled under me winder," Lucy retorted.
"You're brighter lately. And it's not just the dress making you bubble."
For some time now he had felt she was hatching an idea. Intrigued, he noticed too that she visited the Off License frequently, and yet came back empty handed. The Bennetts had long since indicated their wish to retire and consequently the windows were drab, the stock low and customers beginning to look elsewhere.
"Alex, it's got a real bathroom...small of course, made out of the box room. But we could manage with two bedrooms now that Ma's gone. Most of the trade is done at night when the young 'uns are in bed, and Kate could give us a hand to start with. We could get a good deal considering they haven't found anyone yet. And the factory's at the end o' the yard so I can make ham and cheese cobs and get the lunch time trade just by passing it over the wall." She stopped to draw breath, not daring to look at him.
"If the Brewery's not found anybody, how can it be such a good deal?"

"We can *make* it a good deal. We can't afford to miss it."

"And where do we get the deposit money?" he asked knowing full well what the answer would be. Lucy relaxed; he had not dismissed it out of hand and by asking the first question had started to walk along the path she had already mapped out.

"When nobody else has eyes to see is when we seize our opportunity."

"Can't take the risk." And then, "You've already told them, haven't you?"

"It only needs your signature."

He turned away from her and into the kitchen. Lucy wanted to follow him; to confront the pain of uncertainty he would be suffering, but she knew better than to obey her emotion. He needed space to come round to her thinking. And come round he surely would, for her confidence in her own instinct was magnetic.

He smoothed a hand along his bandaged leg. This was what was worrying him most - if ever he could no longer drive, which was all he knew how to do. If the ulcers resurged maybe Lucy had the solution and if the worst happened he could sit in a chair behind a counter. What an existence, selling packets of tea to prattling women. Hardly man's work. Unless of course he had a man's reason for doing it.

"We'll use the hundred pounds Ma left, and see the Brewery tomorrow."

Relief spread over her face, and she moved towards him, gently, because she didn't want him to feel he had yielded to persuasion against his will.

"Glad to see the back of that," he said. "Always bothered me Ma left it all to me."

"Hundred pound between seven of you would have done nobody any good. You're the only son and your sisters soon helped themselves to the bed linen and china."

"I wonder who had her ring. That was for Kate, though I don't suppose she's ever bothered. Wouldn't be worth much after all these years."

"You've never mentioned it before."

"Just something Ma used to say about the box and family Bible."

"No matter. If it was promised, then Kate should have had it."

"Well it's too late now, and I've not a mind to question each one."

"You're too soft by half with them."

Irked though she was, she refrained from further comment because it was important they remained united over the shop. Kate had indeed been disappointed not to have had the ring because Gran had talked of it so often, but she supposed one of her aunts had had a stronger claim.

SAFE AS HOUSES

Neither slept easily that night; Lucy due the exhilaration a new challenge presented, and Alex because he would find no peace of mind until the decision was irrevocable.

"Are you sure you'll manage in the daytime with me out at work. No point in giving up my job just yet and adding another risk."

"No, it won't support the two of us to start with. And if I can manage to go to work in a factory, make wedding dresses and cakes of a night as well as the piece work, then I can surely run a shop." She allowed herself to dream again. "Oh Alex, you'll see. When I've put all my plans into action they'll come from miles around!"

"Just as long as they come from down the street'll do me," he murmured.

"I can still sell my linens on the side."

"Now don't upset the brewery afore we've even started. It's an Off License and Grocery shop remember." Squeezing her hand in a rare demonstration of affection, he asked, "How long do you think it'll take?"

"We can be in within three months. Asked as many questions as I could think of so if you agreed there'd be fewer holdups."

"And if I hadn't?"

"We wouldn't have gone."

Nor would they. All the ideas and drive were Lucy's, but never would she take the final step without his approval.

Kate assessed they would be moving into the shop just before her exams. Christmas parties were the topic of conversation for most girls, and teachers reduced the pressure slightly, and very occasionally 'forgot' to set homework. Since there were no such functions for Kate, or brothers to collect from boarding school, she disciplined herself to maintain a fair rate of work. Though still a challenge she was finding her Latin less difficult since working with Jane Brownlow in the lunch hours. It was vital if she were to go into the Sixth form and University. But she of course she wasn't. She would leave school at sixteen and contribute to the housekeeping as had always been understood. She accepted it - academically. There are some things the heart will not accept.

Late at night she would pack another box for the move; something that could be coped with when the brain ceased function at an intellectual level.

"Jobs first, then all the other," Lucy complained and Kate knew her mother would never be convinced that 'all the other' *was* her job, for though it would have broken Lucy to admit it, jealousy of Kate's chance to wear a smart dress in an office, lingered. Alex may imagine his daughter behind the post office counter but he never set his sights high enough. Kate could be someone's personal secretary; the woman behind the dynamic entrepreneur.

"I'd need to go to Secretarial College," Kate said when Lucy verbalised her dreams.

"Course you wouldn't - you can do shorthand and typing at night school and work your way to the top. And with a lot less strain than all that Latin and stuff," she added, contemplating the difference it would make to the family budget with Kate standing on her own feet financially. "Still, I'm glad we gave you your chance." Finishing the ironing she said, "I'll fill the copper for tomorrow's boil and then we'll pin the hem of your dress."

She was visibly tired out and Kate could not bear the fatigue that sometimes seemed strong enough to threaten Mam's life.

"We can do it tomorrow."

"I might not be 'ere tomorrow," Lucy grinned, unaware of her daughter's fears, "and then it wouldn't be finished for you to go to the ball."

"If you weren't here I wouldn't want to go to the ball."

"Eh c'mon. Don't be so serious. Did I tell you I stuck the sequins on at dinner time. Meg lent me her colourless nail varnish - neater'n quicker than sewing 'em on."

"You two get the dress out. I'll fill the boiler." Alex took charge of the situation.

"No Dad, you've to be up at five in the morning."

"No matter. I can't wait till tomorrow to see you in it."

There was a voice from the stairs. "Ooh she looks like a film star. Can I have a dress like that when I'm fifteen," Gillian pleaded.

"May I," Kate admonished, feeling free to correct her sister.

"You're just posh."

"Back to bed," Alex reprimanded, "You're lucky to have a big sister to learn you."

"Teach you," Gillian giggled, and then no one could desist from mirth. And Kate laughed too because the humour was evident, but not without irony. She'd been lonely at school, and now the 'polishing' that was at last enabling her to fit in at Brierley was estranging her from her own family. She smiled at Lucy. "You should be dressing Princess Margaret Mam."

"You're our princess," her Dad said, and she knew she would do anything for him, even work in the Post Office.

Lucy, mouth full of pins, told Kate to stand on a chair. "You'll have to be careful not to get the hem dirty when you get on the bus."

SAFE AS HOUSES

"She won't be going on the bus," Alex announced. "I'm taking her."

"I can't go with Emmeline, Dad!"

"I'll drop you off before collecting her. Then you'll arrive in style too." Hoping desperately that the love of his girl wouldn't get him into trouble, Lucy said nothing. It was one of those rare times when the final word had already been spoken.

There was more than one ribald comment as Alex pulled up in the Bentley outside their house. "Bloody 'ell, the King and Queen's come to visit," Alf Corfield gasped as he emerged from the alley on his way to The Feathers.

"Quick, hop in," Lucy urged, "afore anybody else sees. Have a lovely time ducky."

"Bit of alright, eh Kate? Wish it was you and your Mam I was driving every day," Alex smiled.

"If it was me and Mam in the car," she replied, knowingly returning to her pre-Brierley mode of speech, "you'd be the owner, and someone else the chauffeur."

"Aye. And if I *owned* a Bentley I wouldn't be having the thrill I'm getting now. Just shows - nobody has it all."

As they swept into the school drive Kate was cocooned in an unfamiliar security. The father she had left behind in her family life and missed so dreadfully, was literally, physically, and metaphorically, taking charge of her here in the very surroundings in which she had fought to survive alone. He had crossed into her other world; was caring for her again and she wanted to cry with the sheer relief of it all.

The porter, utterly familiar with Rolls and Bentleys, opened the passenger door for her. "Good evening Miss." There was evidently no necessity to greet a mere chauffeur. She so desperately wanted to say, 'This is my father.' But Alex put his finger to his lips, winked, and the Bentley glided silently away.

"You're the first, Miss, but the musicians are in the main hall."

"Thank you," she replied with an affectation of confidence, and went instead to the cloakroom to wait until she heard voices in the corridor. Emmeline's was one of the first. "My dress is creased - that's because I had to sit and wait. The wretched chauffeur was five minutes late. He'd better be on time at the end."

"He will be," Kate whispered, emerging from the cloakroom.

"Wow. Some dress!" Emmeline whistled in genuine admiration, and all attention was on Kate.

"Did your Gran leave a fortune stuffed in the kitchen chair then?" Theresa, who courted Emmeline's friendship, endeavoured to impress, but the jibe was lost on Emmeline, who though arrogant, was not vindictive. She saw the hurt pass fleetingly across Kate's eyes.

"Come on," she invited, "let's get it over with. Whoever heard of a ball without the boys? The whole thing's a charade in case our respective papas fail to cough up for finishing school."

It was Theresa's turn to suffer discomfort. Her parents, though comfortably middle class, were by no means in the Charlesworth bracket.

"Will you be going, Emmeline?" Kate posed the question genuinely.

"'Fraid so. Mummy's already been out to Switzerland to find a suitable place."

"And you Theresa?" Kate smiled from a new position of strength. With everyone having been informed of her background, she had nothing to lose.

"Oh ..I," Theresa began.

"Let's go in." Kate gently touched her adversary's arm. "If we aren't going to Finishing School, we may as well enjoy the rehearsal."

"I'm sorry I've been a cat."

"I did sometimes feel the scratches!" No one would ever know how deep the wounds had been.

Senior staff received the girls formally, checking posture and handshakes. "Drop the head slightly, Kate," Miss Carey whispered, and while Emmeline bristled, Kate thrilled inside. Another social grace under her belt. Having avoided friendships and associated complications, she had expected to spend the evening watching others prove the worth of the dancing lessons they had received from the elegant, bombastic Miss Melwood who had directed their course through waltz, rumba and samba each Friday.

"Dignity, dignity! Back straight and head erect... fingers lightly on your partner's shoulder." She was not, this evening, calling out instructions, but she may as well have been, as she observed her charges from the balcony.

To Emmeline it was all a bore; for Kate, sheer joy. Possessed of a new confidence she danced all evening, the sequins in her cape catching the light as she twirled untiringly. Puberty was late for her and her desire for male company not yet awoken. It was enough to look and feel pretty; to hear music, and dream dreams. No matter if the clock should strike. For just a few short hours she had been a princess.

Her father was first in the line of cars and Emmeline climbed nonchalantly into the back of the Bentley. He glanced at Kate before going round to the driver's side, his expression saying nothing for the world to interpret, and Kate touched her purse to indicate she had the fare home.

"Not being collected?" the porter asked. "I remember that dress. . very attractive."

"I'm being met at the end of the drive." It was back to deception and survival again.

She negotiated the pitch black of the alley and one of the girls pushed up the sash window. "Come and tell us all about it Kate!"

"I heard," Lucy grinned. "Better go to them whilst I sort something out for tomorrow's dinner. Just carry this ironing up with you, love. Not all of us have been out on the razzle tonight!" The magic was gone.

She hung her dress and went downstairs. "I'll peel the potatoes for tomorrow," she offered. "Dad will be home soon. It was really lovely - and the dress was perfect."

"As long as it was worth it." And Kate wasn't sure whether Lucy meant the long hours of toil or the expense. Neither had the measure of Lucy's talent, which, had it been noticed in the right quarters, could have changed their lives. They heard footsteps, then the back door being bolted.

"You were a sight for sore eyes!" Dad hugged her as he came into the room. "The rest couldn't hold a candle to you. But you've changed already...I was hoping to see your dress just once more. And curtsies too eh? Beat that Luce."

"Sounds a bit daft to me," was his wife's tired response.

Kate kissed them. "I'll go to bed now. Thank you both - it was the best night."

"Just help me unwrap these oranges, then you can take the tissues down to the lav before you go." Lucy looked about her and saw nothing else to demand her attention. "And that'll have to do for tonight - I 'aven't stopped since you went."

Orange wrappers were softer than the newsprint she tore into squares and through which Dad threaded string when he had finished reading the News of the World. As she smoothed the tissues, she dreamed of the house she would have one day in which there would be talk of music and books and theatre.

CHAPTER NINE

Despite Lucy's determination for events to proceed rapidly, there were inevitably delays.

"No bad thing." Alex was unperturbed. "Gives us longer to save for more stock. They can't put the price up though can they?"

"No that's fixed," Lucy replied, hoping desperately she was right. "Means we go on living out of boxes - I'm not going to unpack." She looked at him earnestly. "We've *got* to get in before they know I'm expectin' again."

"It's early days. You might have got it wrong." There was a warning in the tension that followed. "If you are, even if we lose the shop, we go through with it this time."

She coloured. "You didn't tell me you knew."

"I'm not a fool. I should have had it out with you and your Ma but in any case it was too late. I don't want you in that state again. She could have killed you, as well as the baby - whoever it was. You might have stopped to think I was worth consulting."

"You'd never 'ave agreed and worried yourself sick about supporting us when your legs were bad."

There was a tacit agreement that the subject would not be raised again.

Someone knocked at the front door and negotiating Dad's bike that occupied the space between it and stairs because the front parlour was full of boxes, Kate opened it. Her blood froze as she stared into the face of her new form mistress.

"Kate, there was a call for you today - just after you left, from a Company asking about you. They'd like you to attend for interview tomorrow."

Kate longed with all her heart to say 'Do come in. Won't you sit down ..... May I introduce my parents...' But how could she.

"Kate you are going to take your exams in the summer aren't you?"

"Yes of course. Thank you so much for coming - it must have been a lot of trouble."

"Who's there Kate," Lucy called from the kitchen. "If it's the new rent man tell him to go round the back. Money'll be on the shelf on Friday."

SAFE AS HOUSES

"It's my teacher."

Miss Walker leaned over the bicycle and touched Kate's shoulder. "Think about your exams, and don't take the job if you've any doubts. Bye." Getting into her car she wondered how the girl could have survived five years at Brierley; even more intriguing was how she had arrived there in the first place. She would look up the records tomorrow.

For a moment Kate almost hated her mother. As if reading her thoughts Lucy said, "Sorry love... got so much on my mind just now....did you sort y' teacher out? Long way for 'er to come. Should 'ave made her a cup o' tea. Ne'er mind. We'll 'ave one together - just the two of us."

"I have an interview tomorrow. I'd rather stay on and take my exams in June even though I'll be sixteen in February. Perhaps they'll wait."

"Well how about that! You can borrow my white blouse and we'll give your skirt a press." Ignoring the comment about exams, Lucy lifted her daughter's chin. "You don't seem excited. Cheer up. Worried about what you 'eard me tell yer Dad are you?"

Surely Miss Walker would not talk as Theresa had done. Now in her final year she was feeling safe, able to approach people, to be a real person. Speech and manners had long ceased to be corrected and resulting confidence motivated latent ability in other areas. With the move postponed, Lucy and Alex attended her Folk Dance Festival.

"Oh Alex, ain't it grand?" his wife whispered.

"Isn't it grand," he had teased her. Though Kate had never challenged their manner of speech, they were nonetheless aware of the change in hers.

"I'll keep quiet and not let her down," Lucy promised, grinning conspiratorially,

"Then they *will* think we are a pair of morons," Alex replied ruefully, "for I can never think what to say at the best o' times."

In the event they were not given the choice, for Miss Walker, now in possession of a comprehensive background of Kate, made a point of joining them at the interval. "Kate did well. You must be very proud of her."

"We are," Lucy asserted, "even though she could have given it a bit more style. She knew the steps alright, but she didn't have that bit of extra - know what I mean?"

The younger woman had not expected to lose the initiative quite so soon, but admired Lucy's powers of detached observation, untypical of most parents.

"I thought she was the tops," Alex said quietly.

"Course you did." Lucy winked at Miss Walker. "Apple of his eye."
And Alex felt as if his attempt to prove that Lucy was not the only one who could form an opinion was immediately nullified by the implication that love had affected his judgement.

Miss Walker was determined to take control. "We've been assessing Kate's prospects for the future."

"She's had an interview already," Lucy told her "They were very keen to have her. She'll do it, she always does."

"What does she always do, Mrs. Benson?"

"Whatever she 'as to. If she needs exams, she'll get 'em."

"That sums up Kate very well. And she *does* need them so I'm glad you've agreed she will stay on until summer," she pressured, knowing Lucy had not meant school exams. "I'll see you on Speech Day next term," and lowering her tone conspiratorially, added, "She may well be nominated for the literature prize."

She had broken a rule that could have serious repercussions, but the risk was worth taking if she had sown a seed that would bring forth fruit.

Dad used the coal truck to move them, and all agreed the bathroom was worth one less bedroom. No more trips to a draughty privy on winter nights.

"We'll teach you to work the pumps Kate," Lucy said. "If you're staying on at school 'til summer, you'll have to be pulling your weight, specially when the baby's born."

"And serve beer?" Kate imagined facing Bill Creasey on his way home from the Feathers having already consumed several pints.

"Well it's not cocoa that comes out of 'em," Dad laughed.

What Kate had dreaded, in fact proved a boon, for she could sit quietly behind the counter with her books, putting them to one side each time a customer called. Dad joined her when trade picked up and then he and Lucy took over while Kate studied in the living room. They should have closed at ten, but that was when some 'Feathers' regulars called on the way home. Alex pulled down the blind but left the door on the latch, and checking the law was nowhere to be seen, filled jugs noisily placed on the counter.

"Don't want to lose the license before the paint's dry above the door," he would say, switching the light off before they left.

Measures washed, shelves restocked and the contents of the till tipped into a basin, they would retire to the living room where Kate had cocoa, bread

SAFE AS HOUSES

and cheese waiting. Alex paid the 1/4d for the Woodbines he had smoked, and Lucy for grocery items.

"Make them a part of your wage allowance," Kate had suggested. "That way you won't pay tax twice."

But all had to be just so, then they'd know exactly how things stood.

Soon there would be another baby in the house, so she must capitalise on every available moment, for only success would justify her delayed entry into the world of commerce. It would not do to tell Lucy she had stayed on after her birthday to no avail!

Alex had given the place a coat of paint and Lucy's displays transformed the window, now bright and inviting. Takings improved and a favourable impression made on the Brewery. Their representative was less confident however when in due course Lucy's condition became apparent, but over a pint of best bitter to inspect the state of his Company's draught ale, he accepted her assurances that contingency plans were in hand. He suspected Kate was the contingency, but as long as pipes and pumps were in excellent order, and the business was run efficiently, he had no complaint.

The birth of their fourth child was painfully long drawn out and Lucy, drained of her strength, was wet with perspiration. Silent with their fears, Alex and Kate listened intently to the activities above, and were on their feet as soon as Nurse called, "More hot water please. It can't be long now. The waters broke long ago, but the little mite doesn't seem to want to help itself."

Alex' normally rich voice was clipped. "Is she alright? She's not going to.." The fear refused to be articulated.

Realising she had more than one patient, Nurse took his arm. "You know Lucy won't give in. But she's no strength left to push. And she needs to, so I can't let her sleep. She could do with fresh sheets though."

Kate was already at the airing cupboard, relieved at last to be of use. Alex longed to be with his wife but this was women's work to which was still added an air of mystery.

"If you have to make a choice, I want Lucy," he whispered hoarsely.

"It won't come to that. But call Doctor and tell him I'm still here."

No sooner were the words uttered than Alex was down the stairs. "Don't let anything happen to her!" He had uttered one of the rare commands of his life, to be quickly followed by a second. "Kate, get some sleep."

SAFE AS HOUSES

Dawn broke before the first cry was heard: the faintest whimper from a baby already exhausted by the process of being born. They were on their feet in an instant. Nurse's energy renewed, she could be heard responding to the needs of mother and child. Alex met her on the stairs to be handed the now familiar newspaper parcel for the dustbin.

Lucy's eyelids were black from thirty hours of labour, and in stark contrast to the pallid face. The pillowcase changed only a few hours ago was wet and stained, and Kate took her mother's hand. "Oh Mam, I never knew it was like this." Alex' arm was around her shoulders and in their comfort of each other they did not notice the anxious looks between nurse and doctor as they placed the long awaited son into the cradle beside her.

"Get some sleep now Nurse." Dr. Bostin was fastening his bag.

"Will I not tell...?"

"Time enough when she wakes. I'll drop by on my way to surgery." And then to Alex, "You'll want a few minutes together with us out of the way." He knew they would sit silently beside her, thankful to be released from the fear of losing her. The street was waking, and word would quickly get around that all had not been well.

"Thank you for coming out Doctor." Nurse attached her bag to her bicycle. "She's always done it easily before."

Doctor threw his overcoat into the car. "Thank *you*. It may not have gone so well with someone less experienced."

Alex left for work urging Kate to rest as soon as Gillian and Beth were off to school.

"Maybe if you tell Mr. Charlesworth how things are, he'll let you come home, Dad."

But it had not been his experience that jobs could be held down by bleating about your difficulties. And with four children he needed a job, for it would be some time, if ever, before the shop could support them both. Still it would be a bit easier when Kate went to work; to have one of them standing on her own feet. His footsteps echoed through the alley and out on to the street.

Mam's breathing was shallow and she looked so very ill. Suddenly school, and wanting to go to University, belonged to another, less real world.

"I'll help you Mam. Please don't die," she whispered. "Don't leave us." She did not feel tired; the adrenalin of fear had seen to that. Tip-toeing downstairs she decided to make a broth of which Lucy was fond; perhaps she could tempt her to eat a little when she woke. But what about the baby?

SAFE AS HOUSES

Why hadn't he cried for his breakfast as Gillian and Beth had done? Surely he hadn't died. She put her finger into his tiny hand. He was warm and pink now but obviously finding sleep irresistible.

"Kate." She turned as her mother, still motionless, whispered her name.

She knelt on the floor and put her face next to Lucy's. "I love you Mam." The few tears each allowed became mixed and Lucy asked, "Did I hear Nurse say 'a boy', Kate?"

"He's in the cradle, but he doesn't seem hungry yet."

"We'll soon know when he is," Lucy smiled weakly. "It's the one thing babies don't leave you in any doubt about. I bet your Dad was pleased wasn't he?"

She didn't say that Dad had been so concerned about her that he had hardly taken any notice of the baby. "Over the moon. Now why don't you go back to sleep? Or would you like a cup of tea first?"

"Please."

"Just lie there. I'll get it."

"I'm not planning on going anywhere ducky!"

And Kate delighted in the sense of humour, absent in herself and her father under such circumstances, but which was never far from Lucy. But in the short time she took to make the tea, Lucy had fallen asleep again, and realising her own tiredness and with the broth simmering on the range, she succumbed to the comfort of Dad's armchair.

She jumped to her feet on hearing Dr.Bostin, and discovered that a neighbour had left a meat and potato pie on the table. Grateful that supper was now taken care of, she told him of Lucy's fancy for a cup of tea earlier.

"Make one for all of us Kate. I'll go and check the two of them."

As he opened the door, Lucy looked up at him from the pillow, finding it arduous to lift her head. But she said contentedly, "So it's a boy at last. I'd like to have seen Alex' face Doctor." But he seemed not to have heard her, and she said again, "Doctor.."

He jerked his head and taking her hands, said curtly, "Lucy, we've got a little Joey here. It's best you know while I'm with you - you would see when you picked him up."

"You mean he's not quite right?"

He nodded. "I'm sorry."

Lucy stared at the ceiling, too weak to remonstrate. "I don't think God likes us very much." Tears of desolation trickled onto the pillow as the tragedy engulfed her.

SAFE AS HOUSES

"Nurse will be coming back later. Talk with her when you've taken it in."

"And what good will talking do?"

"It can't change anything I know. But it helps to find a way to cope." He was feeling so totally inadequate; the ability to comfort her eluding him.

"Always having to cope. Why is it that nothing seems to be asked of them that *can't* cope?" The direction of her gaze did not alter, putting an intangible distance between them as she prepared herself for the fact that no one could help. At last she turned to him, defeat and pleading in her eyes. He drew his hand across her forehead, knowing, as she did, that defeat could only be a temporary affair.

Alex' homecoming was something else to face. All these years he had wanted a son and now she would have to tell him that she hadn't got it right. The male she had produced would remain ever dependant on the strength that by nature was hers. Kate had stood so silently that they had both forgotten her presence, and now she asked, "What does it mean?"

While Dr.Bostin searched for a more compassionate explanation than he had managed for her mother, Lucy whispered, "We've got a little Peter Pan, our Kate. He won't never grow up. A Joey, like the Doctor says." She managed a faint smile of resignation. "And we was going to call him Alan." Kate wanted to ask why it still couldn't be so, but sensed resistance. "We'll talk with Dad when he comes home."

And the doctor felt the closeness of the Benson family both tightening and excluding him. He could support, but only from outside. They would unite as they always did to tackle what life threw at them.

"You'll need a lot of rest Lucy," he warned.

"I've a shop to run," Lucy replied tartly.

"And you've a life to think of, if you want to keep it." The emphasis in his words frightened Kate, who said "I can look after the shop 'til you're well, Mam."

"Oh and what about your precious school?" Lucy's bitterness against life in general was now rushing at Kate in particular. "I've seen the way them teachers look at me. Education first, and survival next - if you can fit it in."

The doctor laid a hand on Kate's shoulder to restrain the tide of guilt. "Your mother's exhausted and very miserable," he rationalised, leading her to the kitchen. "Normally the joy of creating life is enough to renew it in the mother, but when a long labour like hers ends in disaster, the impact is enormous."

"Is he a disaster," Kate asked. "He looks very much like any other baby."

SAFE AS HOUSES

"But he won't, as he grows Kate. It's not going to be easy for her. Why don't you curl up in the armchair. I'll put a note on the shop door to say you are closed."

"No need," said Dad from the doorway. "Boss don't need me 'til tonight." Aware of tension, he looked from one to the other. "What's up?" He had been expecting the usual air of excitement that no matter what, a birth always produced, and the knowledge that at last he had a son had exhilarated him. No reply forthcoming, he said, "Well come on Kate, show me young Alan then."

"He's not an Alan Dad."

"What are you trying to tell me? Don't worry - babies are often sickly at the beginning, and Dr. Bostin will give Mam a tonic and have her on her feet in no time."

"Kate's trying not to hurt you Alex. Your baby is retarded."

Her father stared in disbelief. "He's only hours old. What are you talking about?" And again, Kate, devastated at the sight of her adored father so bowed and broken, thought how trivial were the things that bothered her at school. He sipped the tea she poured and she maintained the silence she knew he needed.

"How did Mam take it?" he asked eventually, and as Kate sought a reply, "If she's sleeping, we'll walk awhile." He didn't suggest going to see the baby first, and such avoidance troubled her. "I need a little time Kate."

Their footsteps took them as far as Little Gran's house and he sat in the chair he had always used, and she on the stool beside him as she had when they had visited each evening. He would have scoffed at the idea of imagining he was talking to Little Gran, but to Kate it was the most natural thing in the world to be doing. The memories they shared had kept Gran alive, and each drew strength from what she would have said. 'If you are given a problem not of your own making, you are also given the means of dealing with it.'

But this was his own making surely. In every sense of the word this child was his creation. And worse, it would be Lucy who would have to cope until he could get home of an evening. His fear manifested itself in the agitated tapping of his fingers, and Kate said, "We can all help with the baby, Dad. We'll manage. He doesn't seem any different from any other baby to me - except he's quieter than Gillian and Beth were."

He took her hand as he had when she was a little girl, unable to conceive of sharing these moments with anyone else. She could not know, but her words had given him immense relief, for in his mind the baby had become already a hideous monster.

"I don't want to go back, Kate."

Never before had she heard her father express a preference that did not coincide with what was expected of him, and it frightened her. She rose from the stool, and then unconscious of the reason, sat down again, but this time on Little Gran's high backed chair. "We have to go back Dad. Mam will be wanting us."

He nodded. It was the only time he had caused her to be alarmed, and it would be the last. Never again would she need to remind him of his duty. He was the man of the house and of course he would be there.

"I see Kate has told you," Nurse said, her arrival coinciding with theirs.

He nodded courteously but did not trust himself to speak. He turned the 'Closed' sign around, and smiled at Kate. "That'll please your Mam," and then to Nurse, "I'll go and see her."

He was quietly at the helm again. If only he could have taken credit for that, instead of thinking he had to chart the seas as well. Opening the door quietly, he prepared to comfort and console, and in the event found neither was welcome. Though wretched, Lucy was not one to indulge in futile regrets.

"I'm not the first it's 'appened to," she said weakly. "T'ain't the end o' the world. One day when he's older he might just be the one to 'elp stack the shelves."

She was fighting again and ready to take on the unknown. They'd be alright.

CHAPTER TEN

Expensive cars entering the main gates, gleamed in the June sunshine, their occupants dismounting at the wide curved steps with the assertive confidence of wealth. The Bentley glided to a halt and the school porter opened the nearside rear door for Mrs. Charlesworth. His leg, again badly inflamed, Alex extracted himself to open the offside door for his employer.

"Should be over in about ninety minutes - have the car ready promptly Benson. Want to get back to the factory to tie up a contract later."

"With your permission Sir, I'd appreciate attending Speech Day myself. My girl's last one, so a bit special like. I'll leave early and 'ave the car waiting for you of course."

It was out in the open at last, and Alex sighed his relief. Charlesworth's face registered at first incredulity, then a natural good humour, while his wife's eyebrows having been raised to a plane where inferiors were not so presumptuous, seemed rooted to the spot.

"You bloody dark horse Benson! You've had a daughter here and never said?"

"Aye Sir - five years now."

"Good God man, aren't you proud of her?"

In that moment it struck Alex that he had been infinitely more worried than proud; anxious lest Kate should not hold her own among those whose backgrounds he could not begin to imagine. She had come here against his judgement and in deference to her headmaster who must have known best, and Lucy because there was no point in opposing her. But he could not remember once congratulating her. Yet Fred Charlesworth seemed in no doubt about her achievement. And as if to drive the point home further – though that was by no means her intention – his wife interjected, "She must have come in on scholarship surely?"

Fred Charlesworth, who had left school at fourteen and climbed a rough and rocky road to the top, thought what a bitch he had married and was relieved her sarcasm was lost on his chauffeur, whilst Alex, flattered she should have addressed a remark to him said proudly, "Aye Ma'am, she did that!"

SAFE AS HOUSES

Shaking his head in disbelief, Charlesworth asked, "But where's your wife man?"

"Came on the bus, Sir. Probably here by now."

"Why didn't you say?" But he did not continue. He knew why no request had been made. Veronica would have resisted the preposterous idea of Lucy accompanying them, and Alex, ever conscious of rank, would not have given her the opportunity. He reflected on his own success, his beautiful if shallow partner, a daughter whose every whim was indulged to demonstrate his ability to provide, whilst the man he employed had only his stubborn pride. But a pride that was beyond even his purchasing power; a fact that gave Alex the advantage. It was a blessing to both that the advantage went unrecognised by the latter.

Mrs.Charlesworth smiled graciously at other guests as they took their seats and indicated her annoyance at her husband's fidgeting. Abruptly he exercised his will. "Won't be a moment. I'm going to get the Bensons."

"Frederick, you will do no such thing."

But he was on his feet. "You may have assigned my roots to the past Veronica, but they happen to be an integral part of what I am today. It will be the same for young Kate. Now, excuse me."

The school was seated in the main body of the hall, with guests, parents and press above in the horseshoe balcony. Kate glanced up towards the back rows assuming her parents would have slipped in at the last moment to avoid being noticed by the Charlesworths. With barely a movement of the head, eyes scanning swiftly, it was a matter of seconds to sight them overlooking the right hand stage. And surely that was Mr. Charlesworth - and his wife, elegant as always. Kate had seen her often when she collected Emmeline in the sports car, and never less than flawlessly turned out. But what had taken place for them all to be sitting together?

There was no time to wonder. Traditional speeches followed the School Hymn, scholarships to Oxford and Cambridge announced, farewells to retiring staff, and finally Lady Abingdon was asked to present the awards. Kate was convinced Lucy had erroneously understood she would be receiving a prize, from a chance compliment her teacher had paid. Since coming to the house, Miss Walker had been very kind to Kate who had spent a long sleepless night imagining the repercussions of such a visit. But her secret was safe. And Kate had chosen not to disillusion her mother because she so badly wanted her to be here today, and knew that she might not have found the time had there been no special reason to warrant her presence. Perhaps if they could be part of it all - just for an hour or so, they would understand her aspirations. Fervently she wanted them to share her pride in this place, which after a seemingly interminable struggle - often a living nightmare to gain acceptance, she was actually sad to be leaving. She wished Mr. Fellowes were here to see that she had stayed the course, for he, more than anyone, would have known what it had cost.

The school applauded her Ladyship's speech and settled back for the presentations. Kate allowed herself to imagine going to University, but she had never seriously challenged the inevitability of earning her own living at sixteen. She had had her extra year and been grateful. And then her reverie was pierced by the sound of her own name, and she stood in a haze of disbelief.

'The Abbingdon award for creative writing is awarded, exceptionally this year to a pupil who has not yet entered the sixth form - Kate Benson.'

And as taught, she walked, head erect, and mounted the dais to receive her prize. Smiling courteously at her benefactor she dropped a curtsey before leaving the rostrum - but not before stealing the swiftest of glances up at her parents who were applauding as if their very lives depended on it, whilst Mr. Charlesworth, a broad smile on his face, was slapping her father's back. There was no time to register more, which was fortunate for Veronica Charlesworth's disapproval of such demonstrative sentiment was unmistakeable. A final hymn, the School prayer and both pupils and audience prepared to leave; the former in silence and precision whilst the latter congratulated, commiserated and exchanged farewells.

"Damn fine show. Congratulations man!" Fred Charlesworth magnanimously concealed his disappointment that Emmeline had obviously not exerted herself. That was the trouble about being able to give your offspring the best - no fight in them.

"I must ask you to excuse me," Mrs Charlesworth smiled, lowering her eyelids to spare her the necessity of looking at the Bensons. "I must catch the Grahams. Delighted for you." Turning to her husband she said. " I'll confirm Thursday for drinks darling."

Instantly Lucy seized the initiative. "And I must go too. I'm expected at the Lord Mayor's parlour at four." And before Alex could ask her what the devil she was playing at, she was gone.

She was in fact waiting for Kate at the bus stop. "Come on ducky. If we 'urries we'll catch the market afore they pack up." Then glancing at the volume in Kate's hands, she shook her head. "Another book for you to get your 'ead stuck into. Did they forget you've finished your exams now?" Even so she made no attempt to conceal her satisfaction with the day's events, and added "Gold leaf pages an' all!"

Stepping out sharply, Lucy was already thinking ahead. "It'll be a bit of a rush. Mrs. Merrill's got Gill and Beth, and Bob is with the Buckleys. We'll 'ave to open up as soon as we get 'ome - you'll 'elp with the teas luv won't yer? I told them as 'ow it was a special day. They didn't mind - said your Big Grandma would have been proud."

"But were *you* proud Mam?" Kate asked diffidently, yearning for acknowledgement.

"Course we were ducky. Real smack in the eye for Mrs. Lah-di-dah eh?"

"If she's got to go to work, Benson, then I'll pay half a crown over what anyone else has offered," Charlesworth said as they drove back to the factory. "No favours mind. She'll lick stamps and make tea like any other junior starting at the bottom."

"With respect Sir," Alex said, smoothly negotiating the traffic, "if there are no favours involved why are you offering the job?"

"Dammit man, not everything's a question of which bed you're born in. I'm the one who's getting the favour. She's a fine lass."

"That's alright then Sir. I'll speak with Lucy tonight."

Fred Charlesworth hid a wry smile behind his newspaper. Woe betide anyone who insulted that steely pride! Removing his glasses he said dryly, "Kate too."

"Sir?"

"Speak with Kate as well as Lucy. She must come of her own volition." He was content that Lucy would be happy with the extra halfcrown, and young Kate's influence might not be entirely lost to Emmeline if she had the sense to remain in contact.

And so Kate began her work as office junior within a week of leaving school. She took home her seventeen shillings a week, of which she gave fourteen and sixpence to the family purse. She had left the required postcard for the school secretary to indicate pass or fail beside each of the ten subjects she had listed and one day in August, came home to find Lucy smiling broadly and nodding in the direction of the mantelpiece.

"Your Grandma would have enjoyed telling them at the Feathers our Kate!" Lucy's assertion made it appear that Grandma had been her sole sponsor in opposition to the many whose scepticism had proved misplaced.

SAFE AS HOUSES

"Did I get Maths?" Kate asked.
"And nearly everything else as well!"
"Just my Latin then?"
"And you only just missed that. Forty nine percent. You'd thought they'd 'ave given you the extra one. Still everything else is over seventy so I don't suppose fifty would have done for you." Lucy pulled her purse from her overall pocket and called for Beth. "Let's 'ave fish'n chips to celebrate."

Normally when Kate took in Mr. Charlesworth's coffee and biscuits, nothing in his manner suggested he had personally intervened in the hiring of his latest junior. This morning however he put down his file and smiled broadly. "I hear congratulations are in order. Emmeline went into school yesterday to arrange her sixth form course and saw your name high on the list." Realising he had been less than tactful, and anxious to return the limelight to Kate, he added, "She did just enough to get by as usual."
Kate who would have given much to have been arranging her own academic future, said simply, "I like Emmeline."
"Then she's more fortunate than I supposed, though I understand you didn't get to know each other well until recently, despite being in the same class for so long. After Speech Day in fact. Pity."
"That was my fault. Will there be anything else Sir?"
"No." He had understood more than she would have imagined, but it was not yet timely to pursue the point and he asked only, "What are your plans now? I assume you'll do shorthand and typing at evening class. Essential for a secretarial career."
"Yes, but I shall first retake my Latin Sir."
He waited a qualifying statement but none came. "May I ask why?"
She breathed deeply and then raised her eyes towards him and said in almost a whisper, "I don't like failure Sir."
Unable in that instant to respond in appropriate style, he drained his cup and replaced it on the tray. "May as well take this with you."
As she closed the door he felt supremely content to have two Bensons working for him. Clenching his fist, he brought it down with a satisfying thud on the table. "By God young Kate," his voice resounded. "And neither do I."
They were a compatible group into which she slotted with ease. Alwyn Turner was Charlesworth's 2 I.C. in the sales field while Brenda Forbes, his

P.A. had her finger on the pulse of both office and factory. Foreman Bill Collins was in charge of the factory hands whose cheerful banter helped to pass hours of noisy repetitive work in return for their bread and butter, and it did not escape her notice that he signalled to some to moderate their language when she collected the clocking in cards. Unaware her background was so like their own, they would have been hard put to shock her.

Intrigued by the interaction of their varied personalities, it was Pat Osborne who most fascinated her; a striking, colourful character who selected yarns used in the factory. She had trained as an actress but the rest periods had become too frequent to convince her she would get further than rep. which Kate considered a pity for she had sophistication a plenty, and a vivacious personality that could lift them all when the occasion demanded. She asked Pat when she had known it was time to accept defeat.

"Easy. When I was so much in debt that others made the decision for me!"

"So why come here?"

"Not finding a handsome fella to support me - settling for the last resort I suppose! And what about you? I don't believe you aren't hiding a few secret ambitions!"

Marvelling at her ability to be so dismissive of events that had literally changed her life, Kate only smiled in reply.

"I think there are dreams in that head of yours," Pat continued, "though maybe not enough selfishness to motivate you to go after them. Don't leave it too long to give them an airing, eh?"

Charlesworth who had overheard, reprimanded her good-naturedly. "I'd prefer to retain the services of my new junior if you've no objection Miss Osborne. Nevertheless you've summed her up accurately - it was good advice."

In six months an ad went out for Kate's replacement. "I want her to spend at least two days a week with you," Charlesworth told Brenda Forbes. "Give her a good insight into the running of the whole operation."

"Do I sense my replacement?" Brenda teased.

"No – but definitely your match! And I've been getting the impression you agree?"

"Absolutely. She's good."

As Charlesworth left the building, Alex drew alongside.

"There's your father Kate. Hop in and he can drop you off before taking me home."

SAFE AS HOUSES

She hesitated, uncomfortable in a situation that linked her in status with him in so far as they would be driven by her father as chauffeur.

"Thank you Sir, - for the promotion, and the offer of a lift. But if you don't mind I'll catch the bus." He shook his head and thinking she had given offence, she added, "Or come all the way and walk back with him."

"Come on. However you say for I'm well satisfied to have the pair of you, though not for long, more's the pity. Your father tells me he needs to be at the shop full time. I've asked him to stay on until January."

"Then I'm sure he will," she said candidly.

Obviously Dad had not told him the whole story. His legs and feet were ulcerated, making it impossible to wear the black uniform shoes without considerable pain. Had he explained to their employer, she was confident the problem would have been resolved, but Alex would have none of it.

"Can you imagine what her ladyship would say if the chauffeur turned up in carpet slippers?" he had protested and though she insisted an alternative must be available, he staunchly maintained the shop was too much for Lucy alone, given that Bobby's infancy was so prolonged. His mind was made up. As they approached, Alex opened the door and shot a questioning glance at Kate.

"I offered her a lift," Charlesworth said, intercepting it. "But she doesn't want to upstage her father."

The two men talked affably, a situation made possible by Alex' sensitivity, and the mutual respect that had grown between them.

"I'm not going anywhere this evening," Charlesworth said as Alex swept into the drive. "Take the car and pick me up at eight in the morning."

"Thank you Sir, but that would not be advisable. Better leave it where it's safe." Kate knew he would not sleep were the vehicle to be parked outside the shop all night.

"Then take it back to the factory. That will cut your walk by a mile. No opposition," he ordered. And as Alex resumed the driver's seat, "You're limping Benson - get yourself attended to."

"All in hand Sir. Thank you, and goodnight."

Truth to tell, Fred Charlesworth would have preferred to spend the evening in the company of these two people who would probably be going home to scrag end of mutton, than put his key in his own front door.

They drove in silence a while until Alex said, "We've a decent boss Kate."

"I don't have much experience but I suspect they don't come much better," she agreed. "Did Nurse bring you some more dressings today?"

SAFE AS HOUSES
"Aye. I'll bathe my legs after supper. By God they sting."

With promotion came the opportunity to widen horizons and develop her expertise. Kate and Brenda formed a strong partnership as the factory took on more staff and increased production. Her ability acknowledged, she exceeded all expectations, and over the next five years an affinity and interdependence developed between the three until both office and factory staff saw her unquestionably as part of management. Often Kate took the train northwards to visit suppliers and clients, and travelling through the Dales, the sheer unspoilt beauty made her heart sing.

So it hadn't been so bad after all, realising Mam's dream of working in an office. She had suffered none of the pangs of being out of her social depth as had been the case at school, but that was due the confidence and poise that had accrued whilst there. It would be no problem now to meet with Emmeline, but Emmeline, like her mother, never came into the factory that had been Fred Charlesworth's dream. Suffice that it provided a considerable income and position in society; taken in a vacuum it was vulgar and distasteful. And so the hope Fred Charlesworth had entertained of Kate's influence touching his daughter, came to naught.

And then one day without any warning, everything was changed. She would not have been surprised by take-overs or mergers, for the company was ripe for further expansion, but what she was ill prepared for was the culmination of events that must have been developing under her nose for months, perhaps years.

"I'm to be in overall charge with you as my P.A. Kate," Alwyn said with a perplexing lack of surprise.

"What do you mean? Where's Mr. Charlesworth? What's happened?"

"Gone north. Taken over Wilkinsons and bought a hefty share in Tyndales. Shrewd move - gotta hand it to him."

"But Brenda isn't here either."

"Dear gullible Kate. They've gone together - you must have seen."

"What must I have seen? And Mrs. Charlesworth?"

"She's still around and will be taken care of. People who are not willing to take care of themselves, usually are, haven't you noticed?"

She was stupefied, finding it impossible to conceive of reliable, solid Mr. Charlesworth going off the rails like this. She went into his office and sat in his oak chair as if trying to see life from his perspective. The few personal

SAFE AS HOUSES

things had been removed but everything else was in efficient order awaiting Alwyn's control.

Moved by the visible effect of broken trust, Alwyn sat in the client's chair opposite, only her misery obscuring the irony of their positions.

"Maybe he felt he had spent too long being reliable and respectable. He can afford to continue caring for those he sees as his responsibility without actually being with them. I think he married Veronica because she'd decided on it but I doubt he really loved her - could anyone have done? She's as hard as nails and wouldn't have stayed without his wealth. Brenda helped him build up this place - gave him hundred per cent support. If she's going to get something out of it, good luck to her I say."

"I wish he'd told me - though there's no reason he should."

"I suspect you were the one person he couldn't tell. He left this for you."

As Kate unsealed the letter, he withdrew to allow her to assimilate the changed circumstances.

'Dear Kate,' she read. 'The success I have made in financial terms is not open to question and I thank you for the part you have played in it. But there is an area that remains a failure that I cannot rectify as you did your Latin – already more than five years ago. Nor can I continue to live with it because having recognised it, I shall compound one error with another.

I have not left without immense heart searching. You, more than anyone, will understand this. The old inkstand you used to polished for me, - you thought I didn't notice – is yours, and the envelope in the safe is to use for whatever will give you pleasure. Keep fighting dear Kate, for you have much to accomplish.   F.C.'

She remained at his desk for some time, and looked out into the Town Hall Square where the trees, with the encouragement of a mild winter were already showing signs of new life. She had loved the birches; the only trees between office and home. Even on the coldest days she had, as junior, taken her sandwiches to eat beneath them.

He had written a cheque for two hundred pounds – well over half a year's salary. Yet the gift had no power to relieve the pain of his departure.

"I would rather you had talked with me," she whispered, "for I would have wished you well. And I shall do something that will give me pleasure - very much pleasure."

If the man she had admired so much could go in search of something new, then so too, could she. But what and where? There would be newspapers in the reference library... Not knowing what she was seeking, and suppressing the ambition that lingered, she was confronted by a national airline's half page ad for air stewardesses. 'A mere flight of fancy' she had heard the job described by the school's careers mistress, - 'certainly not for serious consideration.' Well maybe it was time she abandoned serious thinking: at least the application would concentrate her mind whilst she sought the way ahead.

CHAPTER ELEVEN

The job afforded little satisfaction, but one particular flight - a domestic run to Edinburgh - provided more interest. With few passengers, duties were quickly completed, and she conversed at length with an American.

"If you decide to revert to secretarial work, I'd be pleased to hear from you," he said, offering his card. "It's no minor decision to change base, but I'm sure you wouldn't regret the move. At least think about it." He shook her hand warmly. "I'm serious."

The Captain entered the cabin looking strained, and told the crew an engine fault had developed, which though minor, must be rectified. They would be booked into The George overnight. Glad of the unexpected change from the London flat, Kate entered the dining room and saw that Stan Johnson had chosen the same hotel.

"So we are not to be ships that pass in the night!" He smiled broadly. "Won't you join me? He didn't disguise his pleasure that he would not have to eat alone. "I take my wife on trips as often as I can, but with our first grandchild expected the day after I left, there was no way Winona would leave."

They talked a great deal and new vistas were opening up. "Why don't you come out to the States on short term contract, then stay if you like it enough. I'll give you a Company brochure before you leave tomorrow, - you already have my card."

"It would take the best part of a year to save the passage money but ...."

Stan Johnson laughed. "The Company would pay your passage and within three months you'll have saved enough to visit the folks back home if you feel so inclined. Do I get the impression you'll give it a try?"

Such opportunities hardly fell from the sky every day of the week. "I think I rather like the idea, Mr. Johnson."

"You do? Sure that's great. As soon as I get back my secretary can type out a contract and if you like the terms, she'll organise your visa and travel arrangements. You can book into a hotel and Win will help you find an apartment."

SAFE AS HOUSES

"So who do you know on the other side of the pond?" her flat mate asked pointedly as she handed Kate the post over breakfast coffee some three weeks later. Stan Johnson had been as good as his word.

"Probably from someone I met on a flight to Edinburgh recently," she replied, failing in an attempt to appear casual.

"Fraternising with the clients! That will never do Miss Benson. Anyway I'm going back to bed. No point in going up to town in this godawful weather. So read your letter in peace." Jen picked up her coffee and a copy of Vogue, and languidly returned to the bed she had only twenty minutes ago vacated.

'We move into new premises at the end of September,' the letter informed. 'Suggest that might be a good time to join us - assuming you are still of the same mind. And I very much hope you are.'

There was a little about the trip and its success, the new grandson, and the reassurance that Winona was looking forward to meeting her. They were both confident she would not regret the move. . . .

She signed the contract before she could change her mind, penned a letter of thanks and walked to the postbox. The decision was made. Irrevocable, because she had given her word, the enormity of it suddenly gripped her like a physical pain. She must now write to Lucy and Alex to tell them that by autumn, she would be living in New York.

Queuing the following Saturday night in the hope of a cancellation for a Margaret Rutherford performance, she shielded her face from an unseasonable gusty wind. A young man in a worn duffel coat who arrived at more or less the same moment stood behind her reading the evening paper. He whistled softly as if the contents required little or no concentration.

"So let's see what the critics have to say about it," he said to no one in particular, and Kate, thinking he had addressed her, looked up and smiled.

"They slated it."

"Good. That means I'll probably enjoy it." He surrendered to the impact of the wind, and stuffed the paper into his pocket.

"One in Row H. One only," a strident voice from the ticket voice called.

"Go on," he urged. "Your turn."

"You have it. We arrived at the same time."

He nudged her towards the booth. "Take it. See you for a drink at the interval if I get in."

SAFE AS HOUSES

Words of but a few moments; thistledown in the wind. For no accountable reason, sheer joy threatened to lift her feet from the ground. That he might not get a ticket was suddenly too agonising to contemplate as she entered the auditorium alone. Surely fate wouldn't be so cruel.

Her concentration was minimal as she rebuked the senseless hope beating inside her. Surely it was impossible for one phrase to have such an effect. Casual words from a total stranger and she had floated like a young girl.

"But I am young," she allowed herself, and wondered how she had reached twenty two without experiencing the whirling exhilaration that now made her want to dance. Chemistry that had pounced from nowhere would not be denied, and as the lights rose she excused herself as she struggled past the people in her row who seemed not to understand the hurry. She would go to the bar all the same, just in case...

"So what do you think?" a voice said from behind her in the crush. And it seemed an eternity before she could reply 'Wonderful,' realising how little she had absorbed.

"Um? Wouldn't have gone that far but I'm glad I got a ticket. She's got immense energy. Do you go to the theatre often?"

"Yes. Yes I do." It was infuriating to be so tongue-tied.

"I usually prefer films - more credible. Not restricted by the confines of a stage."

She yearned to converse, but her mind refused to function, all her concentration being needed to keep her feet on the ground.

"Here come on," he urged, "let's get near the bar. Do you drink beer?"

"No thanks," she grimaced. "I'll get a coffee."

"They're at opposite ends. Sure you won't have a drink?"

"A juice then - thank you."

"You're nice," he said abruptly, and the earlier hint of Geordie became more pronounced. "So what are you doing in the Big Smoke?"

When she told him, he whistled appreciatively. "I've never been out with an air hostess before."

She laughed, thinking what a strange thing to have said, yet overjoyed that at any moment he was going to ask her. It was all happening so very fast. In one short hour, her whole life had assumed new and exciting possibilities, had developed another dimension.

He replaced their two glasses on the bar. "See you next interval? We'll go to the coffee end next time. I'm on the other side of the wide aisle - three rows behind you."

SAFE AS HOUSES

So he had looked for her and noted where she sat. And the knowledge that he had, was heaven itself. The play now was only a means to an end. But she must concentrate in case he asked her opinion again.

"This coffee's muck - I must teach you to drink beer. Come to the Peter Sellars film in Leicester Square tomorrow?" They endeavoured to sip the innocuous liquid amidst the jostling crowd of people yet to be served, and Kate explained she was flying to Munich next day. "But I could manage Friday though."

"See you outside the tube station about 7.30 then,"

"I'll look forward to it. You do realise I don't even know your name."

He laughed loudly as if she had made a major problem out of a minor detail. "Tom. Tom Heydon. And yours?"

"Kate."

"Kate! That's not a name for an airhostess! My Grandmother's called Kate."

"For which I apologise," she said with feigned indignation. "But I do declare it's almost as glamorous a name as Tom!"

"Touché," he grinned, and then, "You will come on Friday?"

She nodded, not trusting herself to speak in case she let him know that wild horses wouldn't stop her. He walked her to the tube, and touched her shoulder as he left. "Friday then."

She turned and smiled before disappearing down the escalator, and he wondered what had attracted him to her. She was neither elegant nor beautiful in the fashionable sense - not his type at all really. Yet those wide brown eyes had radiated such an innocent delight that had made him feel more special than he was prepared to admit. "Funny little thing," he mused. "Sort of girl you took home to meet the folks."

"Boy, what happened to you?" Jennifer gasped as Kate hung up her jacket, "You look as if you had just slid down a rainbow!"

"Jen, that's exactly what it feels like. I met Tom."

"Great name. Shall I swoon now or later? Where is he? You didn't bring him back?"

"I'm seeing him on Friday - we're going to a film. Do you want some cocoa?"

"You and your cocoa. Go on - it will probably taste like champagne tonight anyway." Jennifer continued her manicure. "You haven't been around much, have you Kate?"

"Does it show?"

SAFE AS HOUSES

"Yes. Maybe that's what attracted him. Just remember all men are swines; that way you won't get hurt."

"My father isn't." There was a conviction in Kate's voice that made her flatmate think twice about challenging her.

"Then your father has created problems for you. Play them at their own game Kate, or you'll pay."

It seemed a harsh generalisation but remembering Mr. Charlesworth Kate remained silent. She boiled the milk and dreamed of Friday, the fact that within months she would be emigrating, obliterated from her mind. She woke in the night, cruelly smitten by the realisation of it.

"No!" she cried out and Jennifer grunted disinterestedly. "What?"

"Nothing, I'm sorry - go to sleep. Just a nightmare."

Contract signed, her trans Atlantic ticket would soon follow. The rosy glow and sound of violins that had followed her all the way home from the theatre were now surrendering to an all too familiar greyness again. Over reaction, she told herself. Good Heavens he'd only asked her to a film - probably had strings of girlfriends and would drop her as soon as he realised how dull she was. But the aching void remained, went to Munich and back, and only evaporated as she got ready to meet him.

"Tell me about yourself, Kate," he said, as they sat in the summer sunlight in the Square outside the Zodiac bar. And though she intended to begin at the beginning, she found herself explaining that she had accepted a job - only recently - that would take her to New York in October.

"No! So we both leave Blighty together. I'm off to Africa in November."

"Africa?"

"Ghana to be precise, I'm repping for a pharmaceutical company."

She couldn't tell which was greater - the shock of their both going away, or that of discovering that whereas she was mortified she had made the decision only a short time before meeting him, he was obviously still delighted about emigrating, despite meeting her. She said merely, " Why?"

He laughed uninhibitedly. "You don't waste many words, do you Kate! What do you mean, 'why'?"

She was relieved her one word had been misunderstood. Before she could fabricate an answer he said, "Failed medical school. This offers an alternative. Besides I think I have a flair for business."

She noted the ease with which he had dismissed failure. "Did it hurt?"

Again he was amused at her choice of phrase. "Immensely enjoyable actually. It was the price I paid for wasting my time and substance. The hurt

SAFE AS HOUSES

was telling my old lady. I'm too much like my father for him to have demanded an explanation and I shall make a success of business as he has. But Mother was looking forward to taking pictures of my graduation. Depriving her of it made me feel a swine. I'll make it up to her."

"You're very fond of her. As I am of my father. He's the gentlest, yet strongest, man I know."

"He'll miss you then?"

Having not the slightest idea how vulnerable she was to guilt, he could not know his remark had stabbed her conscience.

"I keep in touch regularly, but I needed to get away."

"Of course. Everyone does - the way Nature intended."

He had freed her again, unaware of her need to justify every thought and action; made her realise why she wanted so much to be with him. Swinging his jacket over his shoulder he took her by the hand. "Let's go to Windsor." Had he said Paradise he could not have generated more joy. It mattered not where he led, for Kate Benson was wonderfully and undeniably in love.

And the blissful weeks that followed were filled with the ecstasy of being alive, with no requirement to achieve, attain, or earn approval. Acceptable just as she was, she flew to meet him at every available moment and an ordinary, everyday world assumed an ethereal quality. Soon she would be leaving for the States and he to Africa, and with that boundary of time - itself made bearable in that it was also something shared - came an acute awareness of each precious fleeting moment. They strolled in the parks, went to theatres, concerts and galleries, and their togetherness needed no words or promises. Kate knew she would be loving this man when she was old and grey, and if the magic receded a little, it could only be because a comfortable, secure bond had grown between them that no force could sever. If a mere ocean were to separate them for a time, what could it matter compared to the ultimate joy of one day being together for all time.

And so the days, of which she could recall every joyous detail, slipped by like quicksilver. They sat one day in the window seat of an Elizabethan inn and he said, "I've to go away on Sunday evening Kate, to the training base in Wales, just a week. Seems a last minute reshuffle of arrangements."

Her eyes told him how much he would be missed before she could prevent their doing otherwise, so there was no point in being flippant. "Why don't you come and join me on your days off?"

"It might be possible," she hesitated. "I'm due for my three days between roster changes after the Amsterdam run..... I'll try."

SAFE AS HOUSES

"We could hire a car and drive to the coast - evidently it's quite dramatic - and travel back to London on the train together."

Knowing only that she would not have changed places with anyone in the realm, she must somehow disregard their imminent departure to two other continents and capture each precious moment, allowing none to be tarnished with apprehension or regret. On an ordinary night, an ordinary girl had gone to a London theatre. Her world had been spinning steadily in a humdrum sort of way, when quite suddenly that world had stopped, wobbled precariously as the voice of a stranger had entered her consciousness, and then bewilderingly, excitingly, gone into reverse before rushing onward with a fervency that had lifted her sky high.

He walked her to her train in time for her evening flight.

"Should be different," she said. "We're flying a real old granny of an aircraft to Salzburg. Pity the crew can't stay on for the whole Festival."

"Then you wouldn't be able to come to Wales."

"True. But it would be quite an alternative, you have to agree!" She made an attempt at pertness because she didn't want him to know the intensity of her longing; that she would have rejected a world tour than miss a day of the time they had left together.

Relaxing into the corner seat of the carriage, she intended to catch up on the sleep her recent timetable had denied, but the prospect of seeing Tom in just a few more hours allowed only the most pleasurable dozing. At last she saw him waving from the barrier.

"Hi - you made it." He lifted and swung her round. "C'mon I've found a place you'll love - it's on the way to the hotel - cream teas, china cups and chintz curtains!"

"You make me sound like an old lady!"

He turned her face to his and kissed her lightly. "You'll grow into such a charming old lady Kate. But you mustn't be alone, even though you'll try." It was a strange, disarming comment and one that troubled her by its implication that he wouldn't be with her. Throughout the entire journey she had travelled through the years ahead, wanting nothing more than to be a part of the life his personality would surely carve for them.

"It's very quiet here. You might miss London at first."

"No, I won't," she said with conviction. So it wasn't happening to him; this pervasive joy that would accept the Sahara as an alternative to the metropolis if that was where they could be together. From the moment he had left, London was as bereft of meaning as Stockton or Stoke.

Over tea he chatted so animatedly about the course, mimicking the mannerisms of the lecturers, that she had to let go of the sudden icy fear that she would lose him. She must have misunderstood: it had been a casual meaningless comment.

"Later we'll walk along the coast... then have supper by a log fire."

"Perfect."

"I knew you'd like it. And I'm glad you won't miss London. I did at first, but it's OK now you're here."

His words were music, and her hand in his all the bliss she could ever want. She *had* misunderstood. If only something could happen to prevent them being half a world apart before the year's end. They finished the plate of cakes and walked the short distance to the small hotel. He watched her, sharing an amused glance with the owner as Kate signed her own name in the visitor's book. She had not come as another might have done - for a brief fling with no commitment on either side, but simply because she wanted to be with him. He thought of the girls he had had as a student: there had been no shortage and yet he was not aware of stirring the depth of feeling as he had tapped in Kate. If he handled the situation insensitively he would wound, perhaps irreparably, and he had discovered that he cared about her too much to do that. Genuinely touched and not a little stunned by the strength of her affection, there was no other course than to book her a single room. The manageress whispered to Tom, "And it wouldn't have worked if you'd signed as Mr. and Mrs Smith - I can always tell!"

Strolling the coastal path overlooking a series of rocky bays, Kate called out excitedly, "Look Tom, a seal - the first I've ever seen!"

He put an arm around her shoulder. "This is beautiful. I'm glad you came."

She was troubled again. His statement implied she had had a choice and she wanted him to know that loving him had meant there could be no question. And if only he felt the same she might find the courage to break her word to Mr. Johnson, though such an idea was totally alien; barely on the periphery of her thinking.

"We'll get a car tomorrow and go up to St. Davids. Pity the world and his missus will be there at this time of year."

"We could leave early whilst the world's still asleep."

"As long as I'm allowed a siesta in the afternoon. I can't remember the last time I was awake at dawn."

SAFE AS HOUSES

As it happened, the rain fell in torrents next day, and mist hung all about them all morning.

"Let's follow the estuary, and see how things look this afternoon," Tom suggested.

Meandering along a lane, they drew into the bank to allow an oncoming car to pass, when Kate fairly lurched out of her seat.

"Tom look!"

"It's got to be nothing less than a miracle - you gave me a start."

"It *is* a miracle!"

"Kate I'm hanged if I can see anything other than a cottage."

"That's it. The cottage. Tom it's so like Aunt Polly's it could almost have been transplanted. Do let's stop."

"We have," he grinned. "OK Just a tick and I'll pull off the bend."

An elderly man, and his very short, smiling wife regarded them curiously. "You lost, Sir?"

"No," Tom said affably. "My friend here is rather taken by your cottage." Kate flushed. "I'm so sorry, but.."

The man opened the gate. "Have a look round then m'dear." He held out his hand to Tom. "Rees is the name."

"I'll go and put the kettle on. Why we didn't expect visitors. So nice." His wife was clearly delighted, and before Kate could protest, Mrs Rees hurried inside. Tom, grinning at her embarrassment, was quickly engaged in conversation by Mr. Rees. Kate followed his wife into the kitchen and was dazed by such similarity to the cottage in which she had stayed as a child that it would hardly have surprised her to find Aunt Polly too. She supposed that many tied cottages were built like this. The setting and local stone in each area would be different of course, but the rooms with their thick walls and small windows to keep the house cool in summer and warn in winter, much the same.

"It's not a very special place m'dear." Mrs. Rees interrupted her thoughts. "What made you stop? Plenty more fancy places around."

"It's so like a cottage I was happy in as a child.... just for a short time in the war."

"But it will have been people who made it special?"

"Just one. I shall never forget her."

They had tea and barabrith at the sturdy pine table in the kitchen, and the couple made them promise to call again if they were ever in the area.

"I'm sorry we have to go back to London tomorrow," Tom explained.

SAFE AS HOUSES

"But you'll be back - I just feel it." Mrs Rees smiled "One day." Their hosts waved them out of sight and they set off for the coast.

"Kate you amaze me. Two perfect strangers, and shy as you are, you went straight in and chatted as if they were your own folks!"

"I think a little bit of me expected them to be," she said simply. And she told him about Aunt Polly and Oliver and the war; the little bedroom that looked out towards the church and the pub.... And once the floodgates were unlocked, he heard about Uncle David and Little Gran, and realised how fiercely she loved and thus how vulnerable she would be to hurt.

There was no holding back the hours that seemed to be running away unchecked, and they boarded the train to London. A stillness settled over them as villages flashed past, reminding of the speed with which the weeks that were left would also disappear.

"Are you looking forward to Africa Tom?" she asked suddenly.

He took her hand, determined to answer with care. "I like the prospect of a new country Kate. Much as I love England I want to experience life elsewhere. I don't attach too much credence to the notion that travel broadens the mind but it can be restricting to stay in one place. We're both young, and it's the right time to be gaining experience. What about you?"

"I was thrilled to be offered the job," she answered, wanting so much to tell him that loving him as she did, nothing in the world other than being with him, could ever again have the same attraction.

"If you change your mind, you could come and live with me."

He was setting the record straight. In those few words, he had told her that though he enjoyed being with her - was extremely fond of her - marriage didn't feature in his immediate plans: that if she joined him, they would both remain free agents.

"Yes, its the right time to travel," she agreed, receiving his message but refusing to respond as though it had been an invitation. Was she being impossibly naïve? He was offering her the opportunity to see him every day; be with him in a precious closeness that she had only ever understood as marriage. Except that the closeness would be fragile. Someone else would come along and make his heart sing as he had made hers. And, she was forced to accept that it would be someone so much more elegant and assured than she.

He did not invade the silence that fell, as hand in hand they apparently focused on the passing scenes. Only the imminent parting inflicted its pain.

"It looks as if I shall go first," she said finally.

SAFE AS HOUSES

"I'll try to come and see you off Kate – or send flowers to the boat. It's been a great summer. But we'll fit in more theatre before then eh?"

"I love you Tom," was all she wanted to say, but the words must be silenced if the bubble were to remain intact in for the future. Feeling the closeness of his physical support, she would pretend she had had no expectations of this most special of summers.

In Wales he had understood a little of why she both yearned to, yet held back from attaching herself to others whilst there remained a risk of rejection. He had suggested she came to Africa, recognising that she wouldn't without the sort of commitment only she was capable of: a cast iron promise that he was not ready to give in return. It occurred to him that for someone who beyond a special fondness she had evoked - was nothing more to him than any other - he was acutely in tune with Kate Benson.

But Africa and adventure were beckoning. There would be other girls.

"There isn't much room, I guess." Her cabin mate was a middle-aged American. "Do you mind having the top bunk - I see you are young."

Kate nodded her acquiescence. There were no flowers, no message; only an emptiness that told her he had already forgotten. The lonely void of the cabin meant the affair was over. And now there was not even a private space in which to weep. She was an anonymous voyager now, about to relinquish all that was safe and familiar; hers one of a thousand destinies to be fulfilled. The ship's siren swamped all human sound and a lull lay over the passengers as each came to terms with the decision that had brought them thus far.

As the vessel swung out across the great ocean lying quiet and grey around them, the joy and optimism of the past weeks deserted her. Life, with both feet on the ground, was for coping again. The swell increased and a sudden queasiness determined her to sit and draw in the fresh air. She concentrated on a lone seagull offering no resistance to the elements, content to allow his immediate direction to be decided by outside forces. She could do nothing about the unknown that lay ahead. She too must trust.

PART TWO
CHAPTER TWELVE

Thirteen-year-old Bob grinned broadly at Beth as with meticulous care he cut his sandwich into small, uneven shapes. "Kate coming home," he murmured. Beth, an infinitely slighter figure than her solid younger brother, tousled his hair affectionately, wondering how much of Kate he actually remembered.

"That's right Bobby. Exciting eh?" Gillian glanced in the mirror above the fireplace, and pleased with what she saw, turned to Beth for approval.

"Stunning," Beth said, genuinely admiring her sister.

With the priority of looking her best now accomplished, Gillian switched her attention to the imminence of Kate's arrival. "I wonder what she'll be like Beth. I mean it's all changed isn't it?"

Beth having addressed the possibility herself more than once, said, "Kate doesn't have to be different just because she's married."

"But she'll be almost a visitor...it's so long since she was here." She assessed the impact of the new situation. "Did you see Dad's face when Mam read the airmail! And where will she sleep?"

"In my room of course. I'll sleep on the camp bed. And Gill, Dad's only anxious because she's told then so little about her life."

"She's written every week."

"Kate could write pages to describe the kitchen tablecloth."

Beth cleared away Bobby's plate, and Gillian, still pensive added, "Strange she's coming home alone."

"Evidently Duncan's following later. She'll explain."

"He still looks handsome - in the photo I mean."

"Why shouldn't he - thirty-five isn't ancient!" And then suddenly their closeness as sisters rendered Beth's attempts to keep the conversation on an artificial level, abortive. She sat down, dishtowel in hand and said simply, "Do you think she's happy Gill?"

"She's never said she's not."

"She wouldn't would she? Not Kate."

"Maybe not. Beth you don't think.....?"

SAFE AS HOUSES

"I don't know what I think. We'll just have to wait. I'm glad you could come home for a couple of days to see her."

"She won't escape Mam's questions."

"Mam will question all she likes but if Kate doesn't want to tell her, she won't. Oh I hope she's alright - the same I mean."

Alex polished the car – his first, and smiled positively at his handiwork. Though his hair showed no sign of receding, it had grown grey in Kate's absence, and the lines on his forehead emphasized. A noticeable loss of weight made his broad shoulders the more pronounced, and the ulcers that plagued him intermittently caused him to limp. But these were the inevitable changes of the passing years and mattered not at all now that he was to see her again. Unlike Lucy, he hadn't challenged the fact of her returning alone, taking her written explanation at face value. Even if there were undercurrents they would be of no consequence, for she could stay with them again. Beth was still at home though Gill had moved to Birmingham. Bobby would need constant support, but it was no longer a problem.

Kate had said little beyond requesting to stay until Duncan could follow, when they would get a place of their own. And mercifully Lucy had agreed not to mention how mortally wounded she had been not to have made the dress and planned the wedding she'd dreamed of for years. If they had insisted on marrying in the States, ignoring the family that had brought her up, well that would have to remain on Kate's conscience - sentiments she had made abundantly clear to her daughter six years ago. And though Kate had explained that neither family would be present; that they wanted to be married quietly with no fuss, Lucy refused to be placated.

"No fuss," she had remonstrated. "Everyone wants a fuss on a wedding day. There's something amiss if you ask me." But she could not sustain her annoyance and was soon writing her airmails again to Alex' great relief, who, having enough difficulty communicating verbally, found committing his thoughts to paper well nigh impossible. But that was all in the past now; by tomorrow night she'd be home.

"Funny there's been no sign of a family," Lucy commented sceptically. She was looking for the best Irish linen tablecloth, whilst Gillian was doing clever things with the large white napkins they had never before used.

"That's their business, Lucy. At least these days they have a choice." His wife opened her mouth to retort but he took the linen from her and handed it to Gill. "Come on now - let's be off. And don't forget what you promised."

SAFE AS HOUSES

As she emerged from the Customs Hall, Kate cut a striking figure, wearing a cloche hat of 1930 style that Lucy too had once worn to such effect. It complimented to perfection the dress of dark peacock paisley silk whose fine pleats hung gracefully from a blouson waistline. She hesitated, smiled, and concealing her shock at how much Dad had aged, continued briskly towards the barrier that separated them. Lucy hugged her excitedly as Alex waited contentedly until she put out a hand to touch his face, before holding him so tightly. "Oh Kate," was all he could say.

"Dad," she whispered, refusing to upstage him.

"Do you want some coffee love?" Lucy asked. "Though we've a long journey ahead of us."

Kate shook her head, and Alex put her cases into the boot. "Not unless you do. I'd just like to get home."

Her unguarded choice of word did not escape him. So America was not home, which suggested she had not been happy. Effortlessly he manoeuvred the car through the lanes of traffic leaving Heathrow. Lucy's banter made short work of the miles and Alex, affecting to concentrate on the drive, missed neither innuendo nor the intonation of Kate's replies.

The shop was in darkness when they arrived, but the house lights very much in evidence. The door was flung open to reveal Beth gripping Bob's hand, both squinting out into the darkness. Before their eyes had accustomed themselves, Kate had an arm around each, and tears of joy ran freely as Bobby stepped on their feet more accurately in the darkness than if he had tried in broad daylight.

"You're beautiful," Kate complimented Gillian in genuine amazement at the change the years had wrought on the schoolgirl she had left behind. "Oh it's so good to see you all again." She gasped at the table that greeted them, as indeed did Lucy, for Gillian was no mean culinary artist.

"Isn't it just perfect?" Beth was delighted for her sister at their pleasure.

"That's why she's landed a job at the new Mitre Hotel," Alex announced proudly.

"Gill that's wonderful. I'm so happy for you. When do you start?"

"Day after tomorrow. So you can have my old bed! We both got the timing right."

"And tonight you're having mine Kate," Beth said. "And before you ask, I'm still at the timber merchants office - nothing to get excited about there!"

"Running it you mean," Kate corrected her, "if my information is correct. And I'm not taking anyone's bed. An armchair will do."

"I've already made up the camp bed. How could we talk half the night with you downstairs?"

"We'll argue later. Now let's do justice to this supper."

What a credit they were, Alex thought. Each one had inherited something of their mother's talent.

"Come on now Kate, you sit here." Though Gillian raised an amused eyebrow, all succumbed to Lucy's organisation, - except Bobby who could only cope with one idea in his head at once. And at this moment, that was to sit between Kate - because he instinctively recalled how much he had loved her, - and Beth, because it was her gentleness which currently provided the secure backdrop to his life.

Alex was opposite Kate and in the glow of the candles, detected a sadness in her eyes to which her demeanour gave no credibility. She was obviously buoyed by the fact of the whole family being together, which pleased him, for her previous surroundings must have been considerably more comfortable than those to which she had returned.

Bobby surrendered to tiredness as soon as he had eaten, and well content that all those he loved so demonstrably, were together in the fold, ambled off to bed. It was late when they finished the dishes and returned everything to its rightful place.

"You go now Kate," Lucy commanded. "You're looking proper drained."

"It's just time difference Mam. I'll be fine after a night's sleep."

"Mind you don't stay talking then." And Kate wondered if she would ever feel more than ten years old in her mother's presence. "Of course, we only had the two bedrooms when you left Kate," Lucy recalled, pulling out a stool. "And then the Brewery offered to build on an extra room when we said we'd have to look for another place. Didn't want to lose us as tenants."

"I'm glad it worked out for you," Kate said, realising immediately that Lucy would not appreciate their success being attributed to mere chance.

"Not without a struggle," she was reminded firmly, and Kate smiled at the accuracy with which she could have forecast her mother's comment. "But it was better when we started making enough money for Dad to stay home too - but then he left Mr. Charlesworth before you did, so you'll remember."

"Have you heard anything of him?" Kate asked, aware that now there were just the three of them, that she must be on her guard.

"Nothing since he went north - 'ave we Dad?"

Alex shook his head, and yet to Kate, appeared uncomfortable. He took off his tie, as though indicating they ought not to be embarking on another conversation. "We can speculate on where everybody has gone to in the morning," he yawned. The exertion of will to remain alert was a strain, and she was relieved to accept Dad's cue.

The perfume of Gillian's toiletries pervaded the bathroom in which Kate had forgotten there was no shower. It would not be convenient to run a bath, so she settled for a quick wash down and tiptoed into her sisters' bedroom.

"You alright Kate?" Beth whispered,

"It's so good to be home Beth. I've missed you all." A reply, which though truthful, left Beth to answer her own question. All three now recognised that the emotional tension as yet tightly held in check, was seeking release, and too that it would best be achieved in the only privacy the room afforded; that of sleep.

"Night Beth, Night Gill. Sleep tight," She had unconsciously adopted the language of their childhood when she, as older sister, had put them to bed. And now, as then, the words signalled that the day was over; their world was safe because they were together.

She woke early to plan her reactions to questions that would inevitably arise, for Lucy had done well to discipline herself for one evening. A second would prove impossible. In the event, Bobby provided her with an opportunity to acclimatise next morning. She woke feeling an unaccustomed chill. "I've grown soft with central heating," she admitted just as Bob's ample frame appeared in the doorway.

"Walk with me Kate?"

She looked at her watch and saw that it was not yet six thirty. Signalling to him not to wake the others, she whispered, "The wind's cold. Go and put your anorak on. I'll be with you in moment."

He sought her hand as soon as they closed the door, and bowed his head against the blustery wind. He beamed despite the cold. "Like it with Kate."

"And I like it with you. Let's go and get a paper for Dad."

"I give it to him?"

"Sure." He looked up enquiringly. "I mean yes!"

A squally shower hampered their return and the wind full in their faces, combined with Bob's solidarity of stature, caused him to become breathless. Kate indicated a doorway where they stood for some moments and he grinned at the dampened newspaper, before awkwardly pushing it inside his coat. "Go home?" he asked assuming the sheltered conditions of the doorway now existed everywhere.

"Put your arm in mine," she invited. "Let's sing all the way back!"

Dad was laying the fire when they crept in the back door, and he looked up in surprise. "Hello you two! I didn't hear you get up. Overslept a bit this morning - must have been all the excitement last night."

Kate suspected he had lain awake to reflect on the evening. Not having the quickest reactions, it was his manner to let things simmer before reaching conclusions. She moved to put the kettle on, but her brother was ahead of her.

"That's Bobby's job now. And he lays the tray!"

"So what is there for me to do?"

"Nothing," Alex replied peremptorily, adding more wood to the fire. "Just sit in that chair and tell me how you are."

Lucy, she had planned for, but not Dad, who in the past had waited patiently to be told, and if the information had not been forthcoming had assumed it had not been for him to know. Only anxiety would cause him to breach this self imposed code of ethics.

"I'm fine Dad...really."

"Fine - but alone?"

"Duncan hopes to follow soon."

"Only hopes?"

"I meant hopes sooner, rather than later."

"Good."

He said no more. How could he know it was good? Lucy came into the kitchen and remarked on Bobby's rosy complexion.

"Early morning fresh air," Kate said lightly, hiding a fierce resolve to avoid causing Alex any pain.

"Yes, he could do with more," Lucy told her. "He's indoors far too much. But needing someone with him whenever he leaves the house.... you can understand Kate."

Seizing the totally unexpected opportunity, Kate said, "In that case why don't I take him to the country while the weather is still decent. There are some people I need to see and Bobby would be company for me."

Lucy was openly offended that she should suggest going away almost as soon as she had arrived, but no more surprised than Kate, who heard herself expressing the idea the moment it entered her head. Until then she had had no plan to go anywhere.

"It's some business for Duncan," she lied, to justify the suggestion and convince them that any fears they entertained were groundless. "We may as well use the trip to Bob's advantage too.

SAFE AS HOUSES

"I go with Kate? I go on holiday?" Bobby beseeched,
"He hasn't had a holiday since we stopped taking the girls," Lucy regained her natural good humour. "I suppose we can't assume an Indian summer. But if you make plans at this rate I won't keep up with you. Where do you have to go Kate?"

"A little beyond Cardiff." She couldn't recall how far, but it was a relief to have been able to respond to her mother's question with a degree of truth. Bobby's enormous beam was so infectious that all were won over, and Kate found herself with a journey ahead that half an hour ago, she had not imagined. And just why was she going, she asked herself, and was disturbed that eight years on, memories of a certain summer still held their magic.

"It will be nice for Bob," Lucy conceded. At least Kate couldn't be meeting anyone who could significantly affect her if she was taking her handicapped brother with her. But how irritatingly secret - an irritation Kate was aware of, but could do nothing about since she had been equally taken aback by her announcement.

"Rum do," Lucy complained, the moment Kate was out of earshot. "What business can Duncan have with people in Wales?"

"Not a lot I should think," Alex replied, equally perplexed. "But obviously Kate has, and I think we'll have to accept that until she's ready to tell us, it's not our affair. I'm glad it's all right for Bob to go along though, as I expect you are."

Bobby was an amenable, if silent, companion, which was fortunate since the speed with which her mind was churning would have made more garrulous company intrusive. They spent the night in Cardiff so that they should reach the coast when they were fresh, and the day still young.

"We're going to see some nice people who live in a cottage with a large garden, Bob. And when we've had a cup of tea with them, we'll go out to lunch and then to the shore."

Her brother relaxed. Having Kate home was very heaven.

For a while she found no familiar landmarks. She imagined Mr. and Mrs. Rees greyer perhaps, but still as welcoming, insisting they had been right, for she *had* come back, albeit years later. An Estate Agent's notice indicating the cottage was to be sold by auction brought her journey to an abrupt end, and deflated, she pulled on the hand brake. How could she have imagined that even in this paradise, life would stand still?

SAFE AS HOUSES

"No cup o' tea Kate? Go home again?" Life held few complexities for her brother.

"We're not going back Bob, but lunch might be later than planned." Noting the agent's address, she made straight for the nearby town. "I've called about Two Ways cottage - due for auction next Thursday," she said, explaining her wish to trace Mr. and Mrs. Rees with whom she had lost contact whilst living in America.

"Mrs. Rees died a year ago," the young woman volunteered. "Mr. Rees still lives there but he's away for a few days."

The joy of discovering that all contact was not lost, was interrupted by a discreet cough from a well groomed man in his late thirties- presumably the agent.

"I'm afraid we are not at liberty to divulge...."

"I knew Mr. and Mrs. Rees some years ago," Kate embarked on an explanation. The agent looked at Bobby and decided that if she harboured devious motive, she would hardly bring a companion who would be so easily remembered.

"If you would take a seat Mrs...?"

"Carter."

"Please sit down and I'll phone Mr. Rees to tell him of your interest.... you have recently returned from the States?" Business was slow, and he had no intention of losing another prospective client to a private sale. Kate assured him she was not currently seeking to purchase, but disappearing into a smaller office, he emerged to say that Mr. Rees would receive her tomorrow.

She booked them into a small inn near the coast, and later a deliriously content Bobby sat at the sea's edge for the waves to lap around him before gathering shells for Beth and Gillian. He walked barefoot amongst the rock pools; the day was warm and oozed a blissful timelessness and lack of urgency. He chuckled as the sand squelched between his toes, and stared awesomely at a seagull swooping across the bay.

"After we've seen Mr. Rees, we'll drive up the coast. I know a spot where we can watch the seals."

"Take a picnic?" His question evoked yet another memory.

"Would you like that? Then we will."

"You not go back to America Kate?" and she realised without the advantage of intellect he nevertheless knew intuitively how quickly happiness could be snatched away,

SAFE AS HOUSES

"No. But I might well come to Wales again!"

As dusk fell, and the sun began to disappear behind the rocky coves, the scent of sea lavender was heavy on the air. "Race you back to the car," she urged, but he was not tempted. Content and weary, he sauntered, becoming breathless as he toiled up the path.

Over breakfast, Kate entertained misgivings. Supposing Mr. Rees didn't remember her; that he had agreed with the request to call, out of loneliness. Time would have taken its toll of someone who was elderly eight years ago. But the intervening years having flown for him, he had no difficulty in recognising her. Supporting himself with a stick, an arm outstretched in greeting, he smiled warmly. "Mr.Griffiths said someone was coming to see me who called on us some years ago. I hoped it would be you but I didn't recognise the name. But where's your husband?"

Momentarily nonplussed by his question that had so abruptly revived the past, she stammered, "We weren't m.."

"No, but you did eventually, surely?" he cut in, and then, "Oh my, you must forgive an old man. I'm leaping to conclusions." Nevertheless he had noticed her wedding ring.

"Tom and I didn't marry," she said. "But I am married to someone else. My husband is abroad, so my brother has accompanied me. This is Bob."

His welcome was genuine, and uninhibited by embarrassment.

"Come and sit down boyo, and I'll put the kettle on." And then looking at Kate, "Unless you'd like to do it m'dear. You know where everything is."

He spoke as if she had visited only yesterday, and she responded to the warmth of such familiarity. Indeed everything was just as it had been when she had made tea with Mrs Rees, whilst the men had chatted in the garden.

"Biscuits are in the tin, blue one on the top shelf," he called. "I'm sure Bobby would enjoy some."

They sat comfortably together, until Mr. Rees said, "So what happened to Tom? You were so right for each other. We talked about you a lot after you left us; knew you'd come back one day. Pity it wasn't together though. No matter; you have come, and if I have to sell, why I'd rather it was to you than anyone."

"I'm terribly sorry," she began, but he wasn't listening.

"You see Kate, I can't manage such a large garden any longer, - though the meadow takes care of itself - but oh it will surely break my heart if I have to leave the old place. And I'm not so clever at managing the house either, though that's not a problem, for there's only me to notice the dust."

SAFE AS HOUSES

She smiled, warmed by the knowledge that he didn't worry about it in her presence. "Couldn't you get help?"

"Help costs money and the only money I have is locked in the cottage. So stupid.... to raise money to pay for the help I need, I must sell and go into a Home where I don't need any help! The Agent told you the price, did he? Two thousand three hundred and seventy five pounds. Seems a deuce of lot of money but he says that's the going rate."

"I haven't got that amount," she told him, feeling suddenly and uncontrollably whisked along. "I saved fifteen hundred pounds in America, but I couldn't raise... I came here not considering that either of you might not be alive. I didn't know your home was for sale until I arrived yesterday."

"You mean you don't want my cottage Kate?"

She heard herself speaking as if from a distance. "Mr. Rees I would love to have your cottage, but..."

And then the same idea occurred to both, though it was Kate who gave it expression. "Mr. Rees, supposing I bought Two Ways for the money I do have, and you carried on living here?"

"For how long?"

"As long as you want........for the rest of your life."

The colour that had drained from him only minutes ago, leaving him frail and vulnerable, returned. "Why that's a capital idea - I'd have more money than I've ever had in my life..... I could have Reggie to do the digging and a woman to dust now and then, and no need to move from the place I brought Mary as a bride." He sat forward again, asking, "But what about you? Wouldn't you want to live here?"

"One day maybe, but my work necessitates living in the city."

"You'd come for a holiday?"

So far the discussion had been beyond Bobby's comprehension, but he knew the meaning of holiday and glanced at Kate expectantly.

"Nothing would give me more pleasure," she assured them both.

They sat quite still for some minutes, each pondering the implications.

"Let's go and tell Griffiths," Mr. Rees said resolutely.

"If you're sure. Only if you're really sure."

He slapped the sides of his chair, "Why I haven't been so sure about anything since I proposed to Mary. Come on Bobby-boyo."

"But how sure are *you*?" she asked herself as she took the wheel. And both her head and her heart replied affirmatively.

SAFE AS HOUSES

"I must advise you both in the strongest terms against the course of action you propose." Griffiths' grave tones reverberated through his office next day. Then he stopped pacing and asked, "What guarantee have you that your purchaser will not have you evicted the moment the tenancy becomes inconvenient?"

"Mr. Rees will not be my tenant: no rent is chargeable." Kate stated calmly. "He will merely stay in his own home until he no longer needs it."

Ignoring her intervention, he continued, "And you Mrs. Carter, have you considered Mr. Rees may live for another ten, perhaps twenty years?"

"I do hope so," she smiled, leaving him in no doubt of her intransigence.

He puffed with indignation. "But do you know enough about each other?"

"It's not a marriage we're planning," Mr. Rees chuckled, marvelling at the complication an expert could make of a straightforward transaction. "And since you ask, I didn't know her surname until today. But I do know that I trust her, and that's all I need to know."

"Enough to let her take possession of your house for a ridiculous price?"

"That ridiculous price is a fortune, for it will buy me the right to stay where I belong. And Kate will have the place when I'm gone."

Observing that discord caused Bobby unease, Mr. Rees got up.

"Your solicitor will give you the same advice," Griffiths continued.

"Then he can save his breath," Mr. Rees grunted, his irritation exacerbated by the arrogance of the man.

Realising if he adopted a less aggressive stance he may well have the benefit of two transactions in the future, Griffiths extended his hand. "At least sleep on it," he urged.

"I shall sleep happier than in months," Mr. Rees assured him. "Good day to you Sir." Such encounters were outside his experience and the exchange had tired him.

Griffiths put a hand on Kate's shoulder. "We have many other cottages on our books... within your price range. Some require attention of course but..."

"As we've explained, I've agreed to purchase Two Ways, Mr. Griffiths." Now openly annoyed, he said, "I don't understand. Yesterday you went to great pains to convince me you were in the area for a social visit only."

"Then I thank you for disregarding what today I assumed you must have misunderstood," she flashed, and he had the grace to appear admonished.

He pushed his fingers through his hair, then seeming to sense a powerful advantage, added, "I don't know if what you propose is legally feasible."

SAFE AS HOUSES

Fatigued, patience exhausted, but with a politeness born of feeling inferior in intellect to the man he now addressed, Mr. Rees said with a strength he was far from feeling, "It is legally feasible because I will sell my cottage to whomever I please, for whatever sum I decide. If it is the loss of commission that troubles you, I suggest you address your energy to a better prospect than I, for I've never made anyone rich yet. Good day again Sir."

They drove back via Barafundle Bay and after a celebratory lunch - though Bobby hadn't the faintest idea what was being celebrated - walked over the headland to the beach. He knew only that he was part of some effervescent joy, in which stress found no place, and all around him was an exciting beauty he had never before experienced.

"Enough for one day?" Kate asked.

"I can't remember when I had such an eventful one," Mr.Rees replied, "but I could do with a nap now. To think it's taken a lifetime to learn that miracles actually happen."

She saw him inside, filled the kettle and promised to see him next morning.

"Goodbye Kate. You know, Mary was so certain you'd come back. I'm sorry she missed you. I wonder how she knew."

"I must have had a destination tag around my neck," she laughed.

She walked the coastal path with Bobby next day feeling a serenity born of conviction of having done the right thing, something that had been meant as surely as if it had been programmed in her from her very beginning. She had decided to keep St. David's for late afternoon, knowing that tea and cream scones would spell Paradise for Bob. He stopped now and then whenever he sighted a grey seal. "Nice," he grinned, pointing delightedly.

"They're a bit like you," she teased, putting an arm around his shoulder. And so they were - placid, plump, awkward on the rocks, and with such appealing eyes. "You've really enjoyed it?"

He nodded, lacking adequate language with which to tell her just how much.

"Come again Kate?"

"You bet!"

They sat for a long time over tea and Kate shed more of the tension that had held her prisoner for so long. Her cramped self began to expand and note things with a newly awakened sensibility. Soon she must not only face the future, but whatever problems the past might still throw at her. She had had the respite for which she had instinctively driven here, been calmed by it, and was returning with much more than she'd anticipated. Urgent organisation of finance was now a priority.

SAFE AS HOUSES

She reflected on the events that had brought her back to England and the rapid twist of fate that resulted in the ownership of a cottage that had seemed to halt her emotional drifting. Sensibly or intuitively she had somehow weighed anchor, and such a response to Duncan's latest angry exhortations to get out, was less tenuous than running away. But it disturbed her to discover how little destruction distance alone could inflict on a shared life. It was not ended by turning one's back, for the thread spanned the ocean she had crossed. She may have drawn it so thin that it would prove too fragile to offer strength to either of them, but that it was still there, she was in no doubt.

She wondered if he were now regretting the separation he had insisted on; whether he saw his outbursts as part of the fabric of their relationship, and the survival of them as proof of its strength. If so, then she was less strong than that which had bound them for she had been ground down by the unjust and brutal accusations that still stung. The debts he incurred and the debilitating uncertainty his spending brought to their marriage eroded her stamina; destroyed her belief in herself as a separate identity.

She had no evidence that he spent on other women; he drank, but not to excess, and his taste exceeded capacity to pay for toys that once possessed, held no further attraction. She had embarked on the irrational task of increasing her income to balance his expenditure and achieved success commensurate with containing liquid in a colander, and near exhaustion as a result. At last, with no evident realisation of the effect or consequence of his words, he had ultimately given her the freedom she could never have taken for herself, by informing her she had been superseded. Even as he uttered the words she recognised them for the sham they were, but they justified her release.

The money she would use to purchase Two Ways, was what she had transferred to England whilst earning a high salary with Mr. Johnson. Promotion to personal assistant had been rapid, and her future with his company assured, but Parkinson's disease had developed, devastating the plans he had made, and the company was sold.

It was in this context she had met Duncan who was working for the accountants handling the sale. Soon afterwards he decided to go freelance, and though she had accepted a post with a competitive company, he prevailed upon her to help him whenever she could, whilst he was becoming established. Almost imperceptibly, it became a joint enterprise. And then she was posted to Washington where for six months a significant amount of

SAFE AS HOUSES

soul searching convinced her that her mind for so long had been fixed on the man she had lost that she may well be giving too little regard to the one whose companionship she was in danger of taking for granted.

They phoned daily, and Duncan flew to Washington most weekends armed with roses, chocolates and charm, and paperwork for them to tackle together, which gave added credence to the conclusion she had reached. She missed him as soon as he had left and filled the intervening days with work until he returned, content that her social life revolved solely around him.

He was demonstrative in his admiration, readily conceding that he needed her. It was, he said, all too easy to indulge in the play-acting of being hard to get, only to discover that the object of one's affections was no longer around to be trifled with. He was certain Kate was the woman for him; why pretend otherwise? Fun to be with, he had a lively enquiring mind. Sensitivity was not strongly developed but no less than most men she had met. Openly adoring her, he filled the vacuum left by Tom, except that in her most honest moments she knew instinctively that no one could ever do that.

On her return to New York they married and Duncan naturally assumed management of their finances. They should, he decided, delay having a family until his new company was on its feet. Grateful she would not have to endure the nightmare of chance that had beset her mother's life, Kate threw herself into the fashion industry, winning the esteem of those with whom she worked or competed.

It was a chance message three years later that had caused alarm bells to ring. A secretary at one of the finance houses who, anxious to get away for the Thanksgiving weekend and having been unable to track Duncan all day, broke the procedure of speaking with the client only. There would doubtless be an explanation; he often reviewed their investments. All the same she was troubled.

In the event, he reacted to her questioning so vehemently that from that moment she was on her guard. He came as near as he ever did to an apology before they went to bed, offering workload as the cause. It was a minor detail and one he would sort out as soon as he could make contact on Monday. He agreed his outburst had been out of proportion - let this not spoil the rest of the weekend. But Kate was too much the businesswoman not to heed a warning, however tenuous, and as she delved to convince herself that trust had not been misplaced, so her concern grew. That the years had passed and she so slow to perceive their collateral was being used for other ventures now seemed incredible. Repeatedly she urged that he acquaint her with the whole situation so that together they could solve the problems he seemed intent on keeping to himself. There *were* no problems, he insisted. Only the ones she was fabricating in her own twisted mind. Why couldn't she stay on her own side of the fence, concentrate on her fashion world and leave the finance to him. He was the expert - or had she overlooked the fact? Had she any idea what it could do to be doubted by the one supposedly closest?

And so she allowed her own judgement to be overruled by Duncan's stronger character and innate authority. But not for long. He, having the measure of Kate's perception, became increasingly wary; the strain began to tell and exchanges were electric. Until he released her from the anxiety, she would, she told him, take her full share of the bills and commitments, but have her salary paid into a separate account. It was then that his fury had boiled over and she was to endure the wrath that raged inside him.

It was only a matter of time before he maintained that as she had obviously lost all trust, he could see no point in their staying together. He no longer had any affection for her; in fact loved someone else. That he had become disenchanted with her, she could accept. But she doubted the truth of his final statement for she would not have missed signs that a third party had entered the scene. She agreed to be the one to move out, privately conceding he had given her a freedom she would never have taken for herself.

And now Nature was so infuriatingly contrary as to ensure that she missed him, feeling disembodied almost in having purchased a cottage without reference to anyone. Had she really left because he had demanded her to do so, or because she desperately needed to find peace from his furious accusations? And would this be the definitive reaction or might he, as so often before, dismiss it as irrational, feminine behaviour under stress. The end, or a hiatus? She couldn't put it all together in her mind yet, but the cottage was something tangible that drew her out of the morass into the future.

She expected sleep to elude her that night, but not so. She slept soundly and woke with the conviction that all was well. Her instinct held good: there were no regrets. Tomorrow she would return and set about the awesome business of sorting out her life.

CHAPTER THIRTEEN

The exhilaration of so unexpectedly owning a cottage lifted her spirits as she drove in heavy traffic and grey, monotonous drizzle to the Midlands.

'You'd like the cottage Aunt Polly,' she mused. 'It would be so familiar to you - which is why I fell in love with it when I first saw it with Tom, as I expect you know.'

Some people, she decided, however brief their influence, make such an impact that they go on living inside, becoming an essential part of you, whilst others leave your personality untouched, remaining on the periphery of your existence, and affecting it not at all. She too had a garden now and the thought of Mr. Rees pottering in it at his leisure with Aunt Polly keeping a watchful eye on him, both amused and pleased her. The longing was almost tangible and she whispered, "I *have* missed you Polly Smith...your quiet strength.... I was too young to realise you must have been lonely too, longing to share your life with someone who would care for you in return. If only Oliver hadn't been killed, I know he would have stayed in contact with the dignified little lady who made apple pies for him. What a funny scrap I must have been then and how gentle you were...."

And as Bob snored gently, she saw as vividly as if it had been yesterday, the bedroom under the eaves with its sloping floor and scent of honeysuckle through the tiny window; the patchwork quilt and crisp white linen. People like Aunt Polly should live and influence the world for always.

Bob stirred, and smiled. "Not walk by the sea tonight Kate?"

"The sea's a long way behind now Bob, but we'll see the family soon."

"Kate stay?"

She tweaked his ear. "I'm not going back to America."

She parked the car outside the shop and Bob took the suitcases into the welcoming light of the customer entrance. She gave scant regard to the car that made her entry into the narrow back yard a tight negotiation, assuming a customer had parked hurriedly. Beth slipped into the passenger seat.

"I've been listening for you," she said. "Kate, you've got a visitor." Her tone confirmed the visitor was not a casual one.

SAFE AS HOUSES

Kate stiffened and met her sister's eyes.

"Mam can't decide whether you went away to avoid him, or that you're so out of touch with each other that you didn't know he was coming."

"Wrong on both counts," Kate smiled, "but we won't tell her."

"I might be more help to you if you could tell *me*?"

Taking her hand, Kate promised she would, but Beth shot her a barely discernible, but meaningful glance to indicate Duncan's presence in the kitchen doorway.

"Duncan," Kate smiled, noticing Mam's not so subtle presence only yards away. Her husband, indicating with a resigned expression to Beth, that he considered she had deprived him of the astonishment he might have expected, advanced to greet her warmly. Aware that all eyes were upon her, Kate responded equally.

"Flew in early this morning - thought I'd surprise you. Hired a car and was here by noon. As it was, you surprised me by not being here!"

Kate did not bite the bait. "I didn't imagine you would tie everything up so soon," she said, offering him a clue as to the line of conversation to follow.

"I wonder you didn't wait and come together Kate," Lucy interjected, and Kate knew she was fencing on two fronts.

"Duncan *is* here," she said, concentrating on tactics, "and that's all that matters. Bob and I have had a very long journey and could do with a cup of tea. You've all obviously become acquainted. I'm sorry I wasn't here to make the introductions."

"So where were you?" Duncan asked, and Lucy's censure indicated she had been less than considerate in leaving them to cope with a son-in-law they had never met.

"By the sea!" Bob was pleased to know the answer. "Holiday!"

"Had a good time Bob? Tell us about it," Beth urged, as she filled the kettle.

"Got shells for you and Gill......got them on the beach. Look!" He plummeted into his bag, Kate appreciating the part he was so innocently playing in delaying explanations. Mercifully, he had not understood the agreement she had reached with Mr. Rees, knowing only that he had been in a place and with people much to his liking. How much, if anything, should she now tell? Duncan would, were he cognisant of the facts, stifle the whole agreement before any formal contract were made, empathising unequivocally with the sentiments of the estate agent, so at this moment there was only one course of action open; that of saying absolutely nothing.

SAFE AS HOUSES

Conversation was inevitably stilted and Lucy was openly concerned about where everyone would sleep; not a problem Duncan had addressed since he would not have conceived of such a modest house. "Don't worry, I'm sure sorry to have caused inconvenience," he apologised lightly. "There must be a hotel in town. Kate and I will stay there."

Kate controlled a sudden panic. "Oh but.." Her money now committed, she could not think in terms of hotel rooms indefinitely.

"There's only one," she began but Duncan laughed, pulling her close to him. "No problem Kate. You've had a holiday with Bobby, and now you and I will have one."

"Good Lord, she's only just come home, and now she's off again," snapped Lucy. "Shouldn't you be finding somewhere to live first?"

Beth lifted her eyes to grin at Kate. "Good old Mam," they were silently agreeing. "If other people didn't know their priorities, she would certainly inform them."

"We shall do that too, Mrs.Benson." Duncan was unappreciative of what he saw as interference. "You unpack Kate, and I'll check the situation at the hotel. Perhaps you'd join us for dinner there later?"

"Very good of you Duncan, but the shop is open until ten - licensing hours you know," Alex apologised.

"You have no relief staff? Well that's too bad."

Stunned by the unanticipated arrival after a tiring drive, Kate carried the cases upstairs, and sank onto the bed.

"Want some help Kate - with the unpacking?" Beth appeared in the doorway.

"The unpacking I can handle Beth," she said wearily.

"Just the rest of your life you've got reservations about?"

"Is it that obvious?"

"No. You did well," Beth assured her. "It could easily have been travel fatigue for both of you. But I wish you'd talk."

"Maybe you should have come to Wales instead of Bob. Beth, it was so beautiful, but unreal now. What *is* real is that I'm going to upset Mam or Duncan, depending on where I sleep tonight."

Beth put a comforting arm on her sister's shoulder. "They can each cope with that kind of upset. I'm more concerned about the dilemma inside you."

"Beth I left the States, not knowing whether I'd ever see Duncan again. Part of me expected him to turn up one day, but not so soon."

"You thought he would at least try to get along without you?"

SAFE AS HOUSES

"I thought he *wanted* to get along without me."

"Then you both played it very coolly given the rapt attention of your audience!"

"It was somewhat charged, wasn't it." Kate smiled ruefully, closing her eyes in a desperate attempt to identify with the situation, and Beth busied herself until voices were heard from downstairs.

"What do you think Alex?"

"I think you didn't make him as welcome as you might have done, Lucy."

"I meant.."

"Nice enough chap. Takes time to get to know people."

Lucy snorted. "Bit of a rum do turning up so soon after Kate. And now it looks as if she's off again."

"So all those questions will have to wait eh love?"

"I'm not being nosey. I just want to know how things are."

Kate bit her bottom lip hard. "I'm not being fair to them Beth. Of course they want to know all about us."

"Then the sooner you go away with Duncan the better. You might know what it is you can tell them then. Mam will be no more pleased at your second departure than the first, but it will be for the best."

In the event there was no decision to be made. Duncan reported the hotel had been booked for a conference and that he had taken the last available room - a single one "Doesn't even have private facilities," he told them in bemused tones. "So you'll be in the bosom of the family tonight Kate, and tomorrow we'll go to the Cotswolds you've told me so much about."

How could he be so infuriatingly casual, as if the series of events that had caused her to move base from one country to another had been a figment of her imagination? In the brief moments they were alone, Kate rounded on him, more in urgency than in anger, "Duncan, don't you consider it more important to discuss matters fundamental to our marriage than to go off sightseeing?"

"Sure," he agreed, "but we obviously can't talk here with any degree of privacy, so why not combine our discussions with an opportunity to sample one of the most beautiful areas of England? Or do you prefer a less salubrious backdrop. Kate, let's not make a trauma out of it."

"But that's exactly what it has been!" His refusal to acknowledge the gravity of the situation, frustrated her.

"Only to you. You take everything so damn seriously."

"Whilst you are cannot take even our marriage seriously. It's not a game."

SAFE AS HOUSES

"It can be fun though," Duncan smiled patronisingly. "Do relax, honey."

"I don't know where I am with you." Kate was exasperated.

"Kate, I'm sorry I didn't realise how essential it is for you to feel secure. But you do give the impression of such self-sufficiency; I had no idea you harboured fears of your own. You live so fully – I assumed you wanted to. Now I suspect the immense activity is justification of the enjoyment, not a part of it." His words had gone home, but before she could comment he added, "You are uncomfortable I should have discovered that about you?"

He was right. Her privacy of thought had been her defence in the constant struggle to achieve, and now there was about her a vulnerability, as if such knowledge gave him both the power to betray her, or to set her free from the demands she made of herself. The untroubled peace she had found in Wales had gone and would not return. She felt as if she did not understand anything anymore, and that even if she would regret it tomorrow, she was somehow glad that he was here now.

"What have you decided then?" Lucy asked, and they explained about the hotel, which served as a reason for going away next day.

"You'll be able to sort things out better that way," Alex agreed, ignoring the antagonism his wife exuded.

"We'll tell you our plans once we know them ourselves," Duncan promised, which went some way towards satisfying Lucy. "I didn't expect to be able to join Kate quite so soon, so we'll rethink the situation and go from there. You couldn't join me tonight - what about lunch tomorrow?"

"Same problem Duncan," Alex explained, and Duncan laughed. "I see what is meant by a 'tied house'!" He declined Lucy's invitation to have a drink with them in the living room. "If you'll excuse me tonight, Mrs. Benson, I'm ready to hit the sack."

"Then come for a sherry before we open in the morning," Lucy instructed, and as I'm your ma in law, I don't reckon as 'ow I can be Mrs. Benson."

Alex winked at Kate. Lucy had mercifully called a truce.

"Well sure, that's fine by me. Goodnight momma!" Duncan put an arm around her shoulder. "See you tomorrow."

"Better now?" Alex grinned. Lucy chose not to reply.

"Shall I do the cash?" Kate offered, as the door closed behind her husband.

"Thanks love. Book's over by the wireless. You'll find a pencil inside."

Beth's self-appointed role of subject changer was not exercised as they all partook of the customary bread and cheese supper before retiring.

"Have you decided what to do?" she asked as they undressed.

"That's the trouble Beth. We never jointly decide anything. Duncan just ignores incidents in our lives that are inconvenient to him and then proceeds as if nothing of significance had occurred. The fact of my leaving the States has not even been mentioned except in so far as I take things too seriously. Do I Beth?"

"Some things *are* serious. As for the question in general, it's irrelevant. You're entitled to be as serious or jocular as you please - the person he chose, and whom I'm personally glad is here instead of America. Duncan's presumably given up his job as well. How long do you think it will take him to get one over here?"

"That's got to be tomorrow's problem, Beth. I can't absorb any more."

There was a muffled thump on the wall. "Night Beth and Kate."

Kate stuck out the leg she had just put into bed. "I'll go and see him."

Bobby grinned sleepily. "Nice holiday Kate. I liked the shells and the waves." He was tenaciously holding on to the idyllic days that had already slipped so far away from his eldest sister.

"So did I Bobby Boyo," she assured him, and he hunched his shoulders delightedly at her use of Mr. Rees' name for him. "Night now."

CHAPTER FOURTEEN

They sat in the Tudor lounge of the Royal Oak Hotel, ostensibly devoid of the pressures and emotional strain that had plagued their relationship, and of which Kate bore the evidence and Duncan refused to acknowledge. The separation having already blunted the edge of her resolve, she was being lured away from her new found singleness of mind and had in the silence, responded to the corresponding need in him. Held in grip of a situation she knew to be tenuous, the whole thing was in danger of starting over again.

"Kate, none of it matters. I love you. And I believe you love me, I've retained some of my equity in Washington until Charles finds another partner to buy me out. It won't be a problem to find a job over here."

"I thought you and Charles had already agreed to wind things up?"

"We had discussed the possibility. A fresh start was one option. And it may have worked had the timing been different."

"Timing? I don't understand."

"You deciding to return to England of course. I could hardly run a business in the States with a wife on the other side of the Atlantic."

"Duncan that just isn't fair. You told me I was ruining your life. I didn't decide to come to England for a change of scene; I left you to live the life you insisted you no longer wished to share with me."

"You were tired and confused. I know I'm not easy. Revenge was a tempting consolation. You didn't want to quit, we both know that."

It had taken all her stamina to leave when bidden; to insist on maintaining her stance whilst he was here to plead with her to revoke her decision, was beyond her. Her mind captive to an upbringing of loyalty and obligation, the attempt to separate was about to be aborted.

"Order coffee. We'll put some letters in today's post. The girl at the desk won't be above accepting a few bucks for typing a couple of notes in her lunch hour."

She was able to accept his assurances because she wanted to believe him and later, with a delighted young receptionist generously remunerated, Duncan joined her in the dining room.

"Now can we draw a line under the past and spend time together in these quaint little hamlets?"

He smiled, taking her hand in his, and though common sense predicted the dream would always be more valid than reality, and that another new start could last no longer than its many predecessors, she surrendered to his persuasion. To take her freedom at his expense without help, was inconceivable; she would be torn apart by a guilt which was as much a part of her as her own breathing.

The days that followed were without rancour or bitterness. Occasionally Kate made reference to the escalating hotel bill, but Duncan silenced any such overture. "My personal spending seems to have caused more than one of our problems. At least now let me indulge you."

But with a forecasted change in the weather, it seemed appropriate to plan their departure. They were packing when the telephone rang.

"Quick Kate, a pen," Duncan instructed, and then, "Thank you Susan."

"Mr. Carter. Richard Hurst, Hallerton Pharmaceuticals. Glad I've caught you. I'm in the office unexpectedly today. .... I see you're in the area – not more than forty minutes drive. Wonder if you could call on us..... say two fifteen? An informal interview of course. .... don't expect you to have your paperwork with you."

"No problem Sir. Just having a few days vacation. I look forward to meeting you." Replacing the receiver, he hugged her vehemently. "What did I tell you Kate! Everything's going to be fine."

Given an injection of hope, she needed little persuasion to postpone reality, and recognising her need for a single solid human relationship, she chose not to acknowledge that Duncan would be unlikely to provide it.

"Mr Carter. Do take a seat. Mr. Hurst is on the phone but will see you as soon as possible. A colleague is on his way down."

Duncan picked up a paper but had hardly selected an article to read when he was greeted by a man somewhat younger than himself who though immaculately turned out, gave the impression he would be decidedly more comfortable in a rugby shirt than business suit. The handshake was firm, and smiling broadly, he introduced himself.

"The M.D sends his apologies, but he's been waiting this call all day."

"No problem. I haven't had a chance to see today's paper yet. Don't let me keep you."

SAFE AS HOUSES

"You're not, I'm giving the boss a lift to Heathrow, and it's on my way. So I'm kicking my heels until you and he are all done."

"You aren't based here?"

"No. When I'm in the UK I spend most of the time at the London office. I'm with the Overseas Division. Sorry ... I should have asked. You haven't left a wife or anyone in the car park?"

Duncan considered his response in case the Brits adopted the American style of wanting to know all about a guy's appendages prior to hiring.

"Not at all. Kate had an appointment with an important client."

"That's a very English name - and you're an American? I knew a Kate once. Warm and wholesome sort of girl ...not beautiful or striking maybe..."

"But she's in the past? Duncan interrupted with a distinct lack of interest.

Heydon nodded philosophically. "In the past and no doubt married and with a brood of kids who adore her."

Duncan was irritated by such minutiae and glanced towards the staircase, then not wishing to appear indifferent towards one so obviously close to the top brass, endeavoured to continue the topic they had chanced upon. But he had misread his companion who was not to be drawn further, already surprised he could have made the error of imparting a personal detail to someone he might yet meet on a business footing, and even more to discover that an ex girlfriend was not as firmly entrenched in the past as he had imagined. There must be thousands of Kates, but the mention of the name was nonetheless evocative for him. Strange this chap was from the other side of the pond and America had been Kate's destination. Not remotely her type though.

The briefly evident impatience had not gone unnoticed and both men were relieved to see Hurst on the stairway, buttoning his jacket and adjusting pocket-handkerchief.

"I apologise for keeping you Mr. Carter. Tom, ask Jane to bring tea and see we're not disturbed."

Turning to Duncan he invited him to tell him all about himself; something Duncan was well equipped to do.

Forty-five minutes later, Hurst was visibly impressed. This man had an astute mind and knew his business.

"Well Mr. Carter, as I explained over the phone, this was an excellent opportunity to meet informally ... the Chairman doesn't appreciate having his time wasted on non-starters. Frankly I'd be delighted if you would fill in the routine application, and I can confidently say we shall be in contact."

"I look forward to that Sir and thank you for your time." They exchanged handshakes as Heydon appeared with Hurst's briefcase. Duncan smiled at him more cordially. "I hope we'll meet again."

"'Fraid not. I'm bidding the Company farewell at the end of the month."

"Tom is leaving to set up on his own," Hurst expanded. "And will lure some of our best customers in so doing I suspect."

The bonhomie between the two was obviously greater than Duncan had at first supposed and he cursed himself for failing to capitalise.

"He'll have his work cut out to survive." Hurst was continuing. "The days of the one man band are numbered. He'll be knocking at my door again within the year I'll be bound!"

"I'm willing to take bets on that," Heydon laughed, "And with respect Sir, we should get a move on or you'll miss your plane as well as a few orders!"

As he walked to the car park, Duncan watched the Ferrari enter the main road. "So that's the prize for playing my cards right," he murmured. "Not bad at all."

Hurst adjusted the passenger seat into a more relaxed position. "So what did you think of him Tom?"

"Sorry Sir. I didn't do a particularly good job of getting to know him."

"No matter. I had time to do that, He's had, in fact still has, his own company in the States and knows that survival is all about profits. Seems his wife has an invalid father over here and as she's a high flier in a company that operates on both sides of the Atlantic there's no problem about her getting a transfer to UK. Carter has left his capital in his company and put in a Manager. Good move. A less courageous bloke would have just sold up. Wasn't much he didn't know about balance sheets either . . . could think on his feet too. I told him there would be a fair amount of travelling - seems both of them have already adjusted to that kind of lifestyle."

"You're reminding me how lucky I am not to have to worry about such things."

"No plans to remarry then eh?"

"Nope."

"You'll just settle for a harem to run your office eh?"

"Sounds fine to me," Heydon grinned, "if that's what you meant by a one man band!"

"You watch that reputation of yours doesn't cause your downfall."

"It won't as long as I'm single. And that's the way I intend to stay."

Hurst detected an edge of bitterness. "Once bitten, twice shy eh?"

SAFE AS HOUSES

"You forget. I did the biting. Nobody's fault but my own."

Hurst recognised the subject was not for discussion. "Anyhow, first impression? You like the chap? Think he'd fit?"

"Very much," Heydon replied, adding to himself, 'as a competitor'.

"Good. Damn time consuming business, finding the right staff."

"You've got Personnel to do the groundwork surely?"

"Personnel send me the people who are right on paper. Instinct's the only accurate judge - instinct to tell me one, whether he'll do the job, and two, whether I can stay King of the heap while he does it."

"That's remarkably honest of you Sir."

"Why not. You're about to embark on exactly the same course. And before you get any high falutin' ideas that I can only accept your departure because I feared a challenge, let me inform you otherwise. You're too outspoken on the wrong carpet Tom ... you'd never have got the Board's backing. Licking boots is not always the sign of a yes-man. I wish you well but by God you've set yourself a target!"

"What did I tell you? We're on our way honey!" Duncan greeted his wife across the hotel lounge and the several occupants lifted their gaze from china cups and journals to observe the sudden intrusion on the teatime calm.

"They've offered you the job? Oh Duncan congratulations."

"Usual formalities have to be completed, but it's as good as in the bag."

"Will they take up references?"

"Oh Kate, don't look so worried. As it was my company. . . . . or partially so, I can arrange the references. Come on, live a little. And we'll begin with a swell meal. Go and get your finery on - I'll wait in the bar."

As she dressed, Kate thought only of the cottage. Duplicity was not in her nature, and yet how to tell him, and more significantly, with what result? Before she left the States, he had been emphatic that he neither wanted nor would see her again. True, experience had taught her that the word did not pre-empt the deed, and this time it was she who had acted rather than waited, as if motivated by a force outside herself. Picking up her bag, she recalled Mr. Charlesworth's maxim, 'When in doubt, do nowt.'

"And that's precisely what I shall do," she determined. "Fate must take its course. I shall deal with the job in hand and enjoy my dinner!"

As she saw him within a group of businessmen enjoying a pre-dinner drink, she regretted her delay. Tell tale signs alerted her to the fact that he had already consumed more than one glass.

SAFE AS HOUSES

"Kate where have you been? Hell of a nice couple I wanted to introduce you to. We could have eaten with them if you hadn't been so long."

She took his arm. "We'll meet up with them afterwards. Look there's a table for two by the window. You can tell me about the interview."

Annoyed at being deprived of company, Duncan was unforthcoming and Kate, recognising the all too familiar signs knew she must humour him.

"So this Mr. Hurst.... you liked him?"

"Fine. I'm to await a letter - I told you."

"What's the Company? I'm longing to hear everything."

"Which is why you were so long coming down?"

"I was trying to make myself look special for a celebration meal."

"The Company was Hallerton Chemicals. Quite a big outfit over here."

Her smile concealed the jolt to her memory. Surely that was the name of the company Tom had worked for - but that had been in London... maybe they had other branches... She recovered her composure before asking, "Did you get to speak with anyone else?"

"Receptionist, secretary .. oh and a guy sent to look after me while Hurst was on the phone. Can't recall his name - bit of a bore to be honest. In any case he's leaving to set up on his own. Got the impression Hurst considered the move somewhat foolhardy, but that's his problem."

She relaxed. Tom could never, by any stretch of the imagination, be described either as a bore or foolhardy. By now he would have moved on to new pastures. In any event, the likelihood of their ever meeting was remote. Even so what quirk of fate had caused both men to apply to the same organisation? As she mused on the coincidence, a middle-aged man paused at their table and nodded affably to acknowledge her. From Duncan's reaction she supposed him to have been one of the people to whom he had been anxious to introduce her.

"We're in the small lounge," the man said. "Miriam forgot her cigarettes - just popping back to the room for them. Join us for coffee after your meal?"

"Great idea. We'll do that. And Bill, I'd like you to meet my wife."

"Nice to meet you Kate. From what Duncan was saying, he's a damn lucky chap."

As so often before, she was mystified that the wife he described in glowing terms to others, was not adequate company at a candlelit table even when the meal was a celebration of something that affected them solely as a couple. He was immediately enlivened and turned to Kate as if he had been so for the past half hour. "Let's eat. And yeah, the job - I told you hon - it's in the bag. I can work with Hurst. Now come on, I could do justice to an American sized steak!"

"Then prepare to be disappointed - they are an endangered species here!"

Lucy and Alex were openly relieved by Duncan's news and Kate did not feel disposed to enlighten them concerning the normally protracted nature of such appointments. Grateful that Mam was genuinely welcoming of such a diverse personality, she would do nothing to fragment the warmth that accompanied their return.

"Duncan, is the offer of that pint still on?" Alex asked, and his uncharacteristic boldness amazed his womenfolk.

"Why sure!" Duncan replied. "You say the word Alex!"

"You won't mind Lucy, will you? It'll only be an hour."

Before Lucy could suggest that they both go, Kate said, "You and I can get to know each other in the shop then Mam!"

"That wasn't like your Dad," Lucy said. "Wonder what got into him?"

They were gone longer than an hour. Losing track of time was something else Dad never did, but he had a job to do and would be relieved to get it out of the way. He had waited too long for his peace of mind already.

"Duncan - if this job works out - and from what you say, it will.."

"Nothing more certain Alex....Dad.. Oh hell, what do I call you?" Duncan asked, inclined to do the right thing for winning the respect of her father would be instrumental in regaining Kate's affection.

"Alex when we are out. Dad in front of Lucy," his father in law stated simply. "She's a stickler for convention."

"Won't that be confusing?"

"Seems straightforward enough to me." Alex was anxious to get on to the purpose of his invitation.

"As you wish. There's something on your mind old fella. Anything I can help with?"

"You're the only one who can."

Intrigued, Duncan gave Alex his full attention.

"Duncan...this job.. You'll settle in the Warwick area if you take it?"

"You'd rather Kate lived nearer to you?"

"No. No. Warwick's no distance, I mean..... will you buy a house there?"

"Eventually, yeah. We'll have to rent for a while until I can arrange cash to put down a deposit. My capital is kinda tied up in the States just now.

SAFE AS HOUSES

You need money for something?" he asked, unable to follow Alex' line of questioning.

"No. No. Quite the reverse. I want to get rid of some."

Duncan lifted his pint of unappetisingly warm beer with a relief Alex failed to notice. "That doesn't sound like a problem to me!"

"It darn well is to me." Alex refused to be cajoled out of his dilemma. "Kate must have told you how we used to work for a man called Charlesworth. I was his chauffeur, and she worked in the office. He thought a lot of our Kate."

"She's often spoken of him."

"When he died, he left a fortune to his wives - he had two, - and Emmeline, his girl. He left a little to me and Kate. He hadn't heard she'd gone to America and he didn't specify exactly how much to each. In fact the lawyer said he had left it to me to sort out, as it says in this note. Look."

Duncan read Charlesworth's words carefully.

'Benson....this is a matter between you and me. Use what you need to make you comfortable, and if ever your Kate sets herself up in business, buy yourself into it in a small way. That will help her indirectly for she would be too proud to accept charity. Besides she'll know that it isn't the same if you don't take all the risks on your own shoulders - she'll insist on doing it for herself. You've a fine lass there: you're a lucky man. I shall always feel privileged to have employed you both.
Charlesworth.'

"How much was it?" Duncan asked. And Alex interpreted the directness as being indicative of a businessman used to dealing in large sums.

"Over two thousand pounds. I bought our first family car out of it and an electric sewing machine for Lucy. That met with his first instruction. The car's been a real pleasure for us - we've been places I'd never have dreamed of. But Kate didn't set up in business. She's married to you, and with this new job, you'll be settling down in England it seems. At first I had to be really sure you were looking after Kate. It seemed a bit odd 'er coming 'ome alone, and we did wonder whether you were going to materialise. But that's all sorted now - she looked really happy when you came back today. And the job and everything - why that's champion news."

"Alex, I'm an accountant; I have marketing experience and my own business. You don't need to fear for Kate's future."

"You don't know what it means to hear that, Duncan."

"Does Lucy know about the money?"

SAFE AS HOUSES

"I wish she did, but Mr. Charlesworth said it was a matter between him and me as you saw in the note. He mebbe thought Lucy would have her own ideas on telling Kate - with the best of intentions of course. I told her it was Mr. Charlesworth's money that bought us the car and sewing machine, and she was well pleased. But the instructions about the rest were clear enough. And simple enough too, if only Kate had been in England and set up on her own, though what gave him that idea I can't fathom. We're not that kind 'o folks. As I see it, he wouldn't mind if it was used now for a deposit, seeing as 'ow things are. Only she 'asn't to know of course - just as he said."

"Gee if you're certain Alex. I'll admit the timing couldn't have been better with my assets straddled across the Atlantic as they are. This will mean the difference between an apartment which we would want to offload in six months, and getting the type of house we'd prefer straight away - and can afford, once finances are transferred. If Kate wants to set up her own business then I can arrange for that with no problem."

"So that's settled then."

Incredulous at the unanticipated windfall, Duncan felt constrained to say, "Old fella, you're sure about this ... I mean you could invest.."

"Wouldn't know where to start. Anyway it's not mine. It's Kate's. Buy her a home - one that's worthy of her eh?"

"Sure will Alex. I know how lucky I am to have found her."

The older man drained his glass, visibly relieved. "I'm well pleased to have that sorted out," he declared, "It's been fair botherin' me for too long."

"Two thousand you say. Your boss must have thought a lot of you both."

"Less the car and the sewing machine. Well over eighteen hundred left. I'll get it out of the building society as soon as you find a place. 'Aven't liked having secret cash."

Duncan chose to ignore the last comment and said, "From what I see of the market we should get ourselves a very comfortable place for three, three and a half thousand. That cash will go a considerable way towards it. Mighty generous of you Alex - and thank you."

"Mr. Charlesworth, not me. I never had that kind of money. And it'll be better than having a mortgage round your necks." He took out his pocket watch. "Reckon as 'ow we should be off eh"

"I think we should stay put and enjoy another drink whilst you reflect for half an hour. Wouldn't want you to harbour regrets a month from now."

"I won't. I've honoured the boss' wishes to the letter now - using the money to help Kate without her knowing. If she has 'ouse better than the one she grew up in, then that's champion. And once there's a wedding band, I don't see as 'ow you can 'elp one half of a partnership without the other."

"I can - and will - look after Kate Alex, but don't forget you don't own your shop."

"Lucy reckons when we come out, the proceeds should buy us a place of our own - just big enough for us and Bob. And that money's not ours. I'd be breaking trust with Mr. Charlesworth if I did other than what I'm doing. But you're right - we will have another."

Duncan rose, and then stooped his tall frame to avoid the beams. "Something stronger this time?"

"Ale's fine. But don't let me stop you."

Was there no limit to the man's integrity, he mused as he approached the bar. Or indeed naivety? He asked for a Tom Collins to celebrate his good fortune but the barmaid raised quizzical eyebrows. No matter he would stomach another pint of this disgusting beer in the unexpected circumstances. Not only had he a solution to his cash flow problem but at her father's own insistence, Kate was to know nothing about it. No deceit called for; no manipulation of figures. A mighty productive evening. The matter having been closed to both men's satisfaction, they drank in companionable silence, each content with his own thoughts before returning to the womenfolk.

Duncan was to commence work the following month and meanwhile agreed Alex and Lucy should take their first holiday for many years.

"They are long hours - and seven days a week," Alex said, inanely Lucy thought, since how could Kate have forgotten"

"It won't give you much chance for house hunting," Alex said aside to Duncan.

"Don't worry - I've done the groundwork," Duncan assured him. "I've narrowed it down to a couple of very pleasant areas. Nothing but the best for Kate eh?"

"Champion!"

Lucy pushed her fingers wearily through her hair recalling orders still to be delivered.

"Mam, leave me a note of suppliers you need to phone, and then get your clothes together this evening," Kate suggested, observing that already the prospect of preparing for a break might be more trouble than it was worth to

SAFE AS HOUSES

her mother. And by the way there's a bag on the stairs for you. Better hang it up before it gets creased."

"Kate you didn't.....? The one I put back when I saw the price tag?"

"Some things shouldn't have price tags." She put her arm around Lucy's thin shoulders. "Enjoy every minute of it."

"I still feel guilty about not taking Bob."

"Bob had a holiday in Wales with me."

"Aye. You never did tell me why you went. Duncan didn't seem to know much about business contacts there our Kate." Lucy smiled mischievously, knowing it was a matter that would always be left to conjecture.

The apparently genuine change in attitude perplexed Kate. "You're very sure this time Duncan?" she asked, to which he insisted all he needed was her faith in him, which had not always been forthcoming. She refrained from saying his lifestyle had not readily inspired confidence.

"With me on the road to success again, we need a home commensurate with our expectations," he insisted. "Forget renting. And don't look so startled honey. I know you thought I'd mismanaged the company money but you see I wasn't as remiss as you feared." He took her in his arms. "It was a rotten time for you and I sure am sorry."

"But the Receivers.. . . ?"

"I had money put by.....arranged for us to start again. You didn't think I cared Kate, but let's put it behind us now. We'll search Warwickshire until we find exactly what you'd like. I know the perfect place to begin - pity we can't stay over, but there it is."

"I don't understand," Kate began, "And Duncan, we really must talk."

"You don't *have* to understand. Just trust me. You're not very good at that."

They settled on a house whose seclusion and large undulating garden appealed instantly to Kate, and the scope for development did not escape her husband's professional eye.

"The vendors have already emigrated," the agent explained, "so a speedy conclusion would be in their interests too."

"In that case they'll likely consider my offer," Duncan said in the manner of one who would not waste time haggling. "You'll call them tonight, Mr. Stokes?"

"I will Sir, though it's a little on the low side. However, I'll be in touch. I should point out there has been interest from other prospective buyers."

SAFE AS HOUSES

"We have nothing to sell," Duncan said in reply.

The agent recognised the nature of his client, and wasted no further time on pleasantries.

Kate's mind was taut, but how to tell her husband, and simultaneously ensure the continuity of Mr.Rees' tenancy, was seemingly impossible, for to satisfy the one she would inevitably break trust with the other. She was in fact suffering the very situation of which the Mr. Griffiths had warned her, though even he couldn't have guessed it would be the husband who had terminated their relationship only two months ago, who would now be at the centre of the dilemma. Indecision held her firm in its grasp but that evening she got as far as saying she had brought a little money back

"To set yourself up again Kate? Because you didn't believe I would come and find you? That's yours. From now on I'll be looking after you."

Once working, Duncan had asked her to send all paperwork concerning the house for him to deal with. One envelope had been ineffectively sealed, and withdrawing the contents she noted with relief the confirmation of a mortgage and acknowledgement of his cheque for ten per cent of the purchase price. The fact that the house was to be in his name, served only to relieve her conscience concerning Two Ways cottage. She forwarded the forms and told him of her willingness to help with repayments.

"It really isn't necessary honey. The mortgage is well within my means."

"I'd like to help. Besides I need something to occupy my mind," she lied.

"Rag trade again?" he teased, his words cleverly denigrating her previous involvement in the fashion industry. "Just leave some time for entertaining. It will be an important part of my job. Maybe something less ambitious than you had with Uncle Sam. Secretarial work shouldn't be difficult to find if you insist, but there's really no hurry."

"You'll come first," she assured, aware of his need for her to play a subordinate role if he were to have a chance to prove his stated intent.

She had learned that her cousin Jonathan was still involved in fabric design; a metier that still drew her. When they were installed and the house met with approval for entertaining, she would look up the younger relative of whose career she knew only through correspondence with Uncle David.

CHAPTER FIFTEEN

Knowing Uncle David would read between the lines, letters to him had become less frequent after her marriage, greetings cards being the only tenuous evidence of the bond between them. And then to her remorse he had died, so soon after retirement and less than a year before she unexpectedly returned to England.

"Sudden stroke - no warning at all," Jonathan told her. "He'd have been thrilled at the prospect of your coming home again Kate."

"As I would have been to see him." She handed him a coffee. "Let's talk. There are so many years to catch up on."

So like his father in appearance and ability, they were immediately at ease as they brought each other up to date with news and ideas for the future.

"I'm much too junior in the Company to pull any strings for you Kate," he said, on hearing her plans. "But get in touch with Philips and Larkin on the commercial side, and wait an opportunity."

She refilled his cup. "I don't want strings pulled - and I've got an interview with them on Monday. Just a clerical post. I'll let you know how I get on."

"So why am I here Kate?"

"I'm intrigued to know why, with all your talent, you've decided to go on the sales side. Why not still designing?"

"I think with your experience you already know the answer to that."

"I accept you need to be a fair way up the ladder in order to be the one to capitalise on your own ability. Am I warm?"

"Spot on. And I'm not sufficiently modest to compromise. I wanted to influence fashion rather than supply its demands and didn't appreciate my boss getting fat on any skill I might have, whilst I struggled to get off the first rung. In Europe, I have access to the latest fabric weaving techniques as well as the Company balance sheets that reflect their success in the markets. I'm involved with fashion houses that set the trends, successful outlets and the advertising campaigns that launch each new season."

"And why would you want to chase around after all that know-how if it were not your intention to fly solo one day?"

SAFE AS HOUSES

"I see we speak the same language Kate."

"It's one I understand."

He looked about him, and then back to her. "Why do I get the impression all isn't as rosy as this house suggests?"

"We obviously don't have to spend time getting to know each other!" she admitted, gaining the few vital seconds needed to regain a composure he had momentarily toppled. There was little point in fencing. "Duncan and I weren't altogether happy in the States."

"Is that why you came back to Blighty?"

"It's why I, but not we, returned. Duncan's not English. American. I'm sorry, I'm being ridiculously oblique."

She sat quietly for some moments trying to sort through the torrent of thoughts tumbling through her head.

"Words aren't important - not until you feel comfortable. But someone like you shouldn't be sad - though Dad suspected it; reckoned that's why you stopped writing."

"I might have known I couldn't fool him."

"He was very close to you; I was jealous sometimes."

"Oh but you shouldn't. He waited so long for you. No one could have meant more."

"I learned that later, but for years I felt I competed for his approval with a cousin of whom I knew practically nothing. Yet occasionally I learned a lot about you - just from a chance comment."

"Such as?"

"He said how well you'd done, yet thought you'd chosen the wrong career - that you should have gone into journalism."

"Didn't have the courage, Kate mused. "The kind necessary to a be pavement artist."

"You've lost me."

"Just something he once said to me in London - before you were born. In fact, had he chosen that path, you wouldn't have been here. We shared the same drive to escape the same circumstances."

"Which is what made you so close. What does your husband do?"

"He's with a large chemical concern now. In America he had his own company, but the receivers were called in last year."

"Can't have been any fun. Is that what put pressure on your marriage?"

"Jonathan, I'm sure it wasn't just unfortunate investment as he claimed. There was something else - money unaccounted for. He refused to discuss it

- wouldn't let me get near to him. Still won't, despite insisting I'm the one lacking in trust."

"Trust is earned. Women? Drink?"

"I don't think so. He drinks but not to excess. Instinct would have sounded warning bells on the other front."

"So likely he took risks or got involved in dodgy deals."

"I stopped thinking about it when he said our marriage, as well as the company, was at an end. He wanted the freedom to start over - without me as an encumbrance."

"Is that how you saw yourself?"

"I don't think *he* did really, but he knew how to hurt and thought he would make me feel vulnerable without him. Which might have worked if it was only my lack of confidence. But surviving Brierley taught me that vulnerability comes from allowing people to know too much about you. You can't get hurt by losing people if you don't put yourself in the position of needing them in the first place, or at least letting them know that you do."

"It's quite nice to need someone Kate."

She looked at him squarely. "I know. But it's all about feeling safe isn't it." Watching as her fingers played around her mouth he knew why his father had loved her, and why never again would he feel any resentment. He didn't interrupt the silence in which an almost palpable bond was developing, recognising the need in her to talk, perhaps more tonight than ever again, and said quietly, "So you came back to base?"

"I'm not sure it was wise. I knew he was using words as missiles and that I should have dismissed them as angry frustration. I had a job I loved...."

"But no roots and all the time your confidence was being sapped."

Finally she asked, "And you? Things have worked out well?"

"I'm lucky. You must meet Val soon - and you'll be at our wedding next month. You, or both of you - whichever seems appropriate."

"We'd like that." He accepted her reply as the official state of affairs and she found herself telling him about the cottage.

"Um. Not the most shrewd financial move maybe. But you returned to where life must at one time have felt right."

"It wasn't an investment," she insisted, shaken by the strength of his intuition. "I bought it because I wanted to. My first act as a free agent. I would have conducted a business arrangement considerably more rationally, and I realise how ludicrous it must appear, having an asset in the middle of nowhere that I can't access."

"Is that how it seems to you?"

"Only since Duncan's return."

"Because you are not after all a free agent?"

"Because it should have been a decision taken together."

"Would you ever have taken it together?" She shook her head. "Then all you need to ask yourself now is whether you now regret your course of action. Do you?"

She withdrew into the comfortable depth of the armchair and stretched her toes towards the fire. "Not at all," she replied, and smiled with the air of one relieved by confession.

"In that case, ensure Mr. Rees' discretion, and say nothing."

There were no barriers now, and he asked, "So is my cousin still holding a torch for her Welshman?" And he noted the sudden light in her eyes at the mention of him.

"Tom wasn't Welsh - Geordie in fact. And I haven't seen him since I emigrated."

"That doesn't answer my question."

"Surely all of us at some time in our lives have to come to terms with the fact of falling in love with someone who doesn't reciprocate. Unrequited love is not just the stuff of poetry - it's a common human condition."

"But that does," he thought. Given her earlier comments she must have felt on safe enough ground then, to risk being vulnerable. He had a strong suspicion that too, she was one of those people who only love once, and that would explain why she accepted the lack of magic in her subsequent marriage to Duncan.

"I think you were shocked to discover it wasn't reciprocated?"

"Which goes to show how naive I was."

"But hurt nevertheless."

It was a statement, not a question, but it shocked her to realise just how much she would have enjoyed telling him about Tom; to relive those precious weeks, the memories of which would outlast all others. And when Jonathan had left, she would have regretted her indiscretion, as he already knew would have been the case. He recognised that while she may not truthfully wish to change the subject, she did want to shift the emphasis.

"But you were willing to risk rejection again?"

"I love Duncan, but his inconsistency frightens me. There were wonderful days together - I found him very attractive. He needed me, and I think still does. But you're right, this time I held onto my head - wouldn't allow myself to be swept on a tidal wave again that I couldn't control. Just because the fairytale element isn't there doesn't mean I made less of a commitment. Which is why the cottage troubles me in that I've used money I could have put towards this house for which Duncan has taken on a considerable mortgage."

"That's no big deal; we all do. Mortgages are based, on the husband's salary, which presumably is a good one. And it isn't incumbent on you to provide a home especially after being given the heave-ho. Wait until you see how things pan out or you could certainly jeopardise Mr. Rees' future, which is really what bothers you. Right?"

She nodded. "I'm glad you came. I'm sure things are going to be fine now. The job, company car, he seems to feel secure - and happier as a result."

"What did you actually do in the States Kate?"

"I started off as a secretary, became P.A to the director of a textile company, and then the opportunity arose to become a buyer."

"Really? Off the peg? ... Haute couture?"

"Neither. Fabrics."

His face broke into the broadest smile and he shook his head in disbelief. "Well who knows what the future may hold eh? That's a partnership I could contemplate!" He flicked a piece of coal that had fallen to the hearth. "But first I'm going to marry Val, get a mortgage like Duncan and have kids. All very conventional but extremely pleasant and for which I need my current well paid job." He paused, smiling, "But um, what a prospect..."

The time was not ripe; they had separate lives to lead yet. As yet her own ambitions were fanciful and must be put on hold whilst being supportive to Duncan. Whatever his reasons or motivation, he seemed genuinely to be considering her. The house she now occupied was testimony to that.

Jonathan looked at his watch, unsurprised by the lateness of the hour.

"Don't worry about the cottage Kate. You thought you were on your own and took a decision with money belonging to you. Duncan has only put the minimum deposit on the house, and you intend helping with repayments, so he's getting a lot more financial help than most men. Involve Mr. Rees in the conspiracy, then don't give it another thought."

As he prepared to leave, the confidence that had enabled her to anticipate future success was ebbing away.

"Jonathan you will stay in touch won't you?" A serene demeanour belied a nagging fear inside, and he reacted to what he thought was a rhetorical question.

"Try and stop me! Night Kate. Take care of yourself."

But he was concerned about the cousin with whom he had only now become properly acquainted. Too trusting for her own good. Worse, she trusted because she wanted to, and with no solid basis for doing so. And he rather suspected that she knew that.

"Maybe offspring will take precedence soon Kate?"

"Duncan doesn't want children - not yet anyway. And I agree it would be best to make sure we are on a firmer footing."

'Too much competition for him,' was what came to mind, for he was already disliking the man.

"We'll have dinner together one night next week," he said. "I know you and Val will get along. Wednesday?"

"I hardly need to consult my social diary!"

She sat for a time reliving the past hours that had done much to restore an inner calm she was only now aware had been absent for too long. There had been no awkward moments or need for preamble. Indeed they had seemed to talk to each other through the occasional silences in the manner of those fortunate enough to be bound not only by mutual regard, but also by the work they shared. The fear that had surfaced as he left, receded. She suddenly felt a strong urge to get on with life; to reach out, to be creative. Unconsciously she delayed going to bed lest the resurgence of energy be lost in sleep by morning.

By the time Duncan had completed the induction programme, Kate was installed at Philips and Larkins. The job was, undemanding of someone of her experience, but presented the opportunity to glean information from departments relative to the operation as an integrated whole. Several times she came near to telling him about the cottage, but knowing it would prove impossible for him to apply anything other than a financial logic to the situation, resulting in the ousting of Mr.Rees, she drew back. By taking no action, just biding her time as Jonathan had counselled, there was nothing to prevent the asset becoming jointly owned in the future. It had already been intimated that Duncan would be spending time in Europe; maybe she would take Bobby to Wales again. As swiftly as the thought entered her head, so also did the resolve that would make the visit a certainty.

CHAPTER SIXTEEN

"Morning Mrs. Carter! What a honey of a morning to be sure. Here we are - recorded delivery for you."
Kate unkinked her back from weeding. "Hello Paddy. Yes, the sunshine gives us all a lift." Removing her gloves she pocketed the unmistakable letter from the Bank. She did not go inside immediately, but stood awhile, her eyes scanning the now established garden as if to draw strength from it. The copper beech was in tiny leaf, spreading a warm hue over the intricacy of branches. The dew was still on the grass, drops of moisture shimmered on the hawthorn hedge, and flowerbeds offered up the scent of hyacinth.
A warm day of pleasure had promised in the early morning sunshine. Somewhere high above, a lark vied with another. And then the robin had come - never far away from her as she worked. But it was all spoiled now; she could feel the tightening in her chest as she thrust the spade into the earth and went indoors. She confronted him as he read the morning paper propped against the teapot.
"We've both worked for over two years now, yet can't manage a credit balance at *this* point in the month."
It wasn't the smartest of moves she knew. She would have achieved more had she waited until he had had a second coffee, but frustration and worry combined to wear down her ability to hold fire and choose the moment.
"Kate we've set up house, run two cars, entertain. What's your problem?"
"My car is an runabout; yours a company car which costs us absolutely nothing. We rarely eat out, and apart from an occasional theatre, we live simply. It doesn't add up." Her calm response was a fair accomplishment, for rarely did she make such a lengthy statement without interruption or argument. He breathed deeply and tight lips betrayed a growing anger.
"Point to any waste on my part," he challenged. "You may have noticed that I don't patronise Saville Row, nor do I dine at the Ritz. And no, I don't want to finish my breakfast. I'll have some at the Club where the company is less abrasive. And in case you hadn't noticed, we owe nothing to anyone."

SAFE AS HOUSES

"Except the Bank! Duncan you say I don't have to go to work...."

"Nor do you," he retorted curtly, gathering his jacket and golf clubs. "It has always been a matter of choice - your choice."

"How would we live on one salary if we can get rid of two so easily?"

"Cut you coat according to your cloth. If we had to manage, we would. I suppose you're going to tell me you'd like a family now? Are you aware that children too cost money?"

Ignoring the sarcasm she said, "I made a list of our outgoings the other day. Look. Can you think of anything else?"

"I have better things to do with my Saturdays."

"Duncan why do you make so many cash withdrawals?"

"For Christ's sake, you surely don't grudge a daily paper and pack of cigarettes?"

"I'm not talking about pennies."

"Oh you think I'm keeping a fancy woman?"

"I didn't say that!"

"You inferred it."

"I inferred nothing."

"So what do you suspect me of? Drink?" His tone was seething. "But somehow I manage to sober up before I come home!" It was getting out of hand now. "It all amounts to the same thing. No trust. After giving up my business, my country, buying a house near your family, there's still no trust"

"Oh let's drop it," she pleaded. "It's not important. I'm sorry."

But he was in command now and capitalised on the advantage. "I suppose you go to your precious father with all these worries?"

"I wouldn't dream of involving anyone in our disagreements."

He slammed the door emphatically, and smiled as he drove away.

It didn't make sense to her. There had to be an explanation, even if the discovery of one proved more painful than remaining in ignorance of it.

Increasingly her fascination for fabrics lured her, but their current financial situation would make the even a modest commercial venture impossible. Guilt associated with the cottage made it incumbent on her to pay her salary into their joint account, but it had not been intended to compensate for a regular shortfall. She put some Grieg on the record player to stem the downward spiralling of negative thoughts. Well what didn't go into the Bank couldn't be taken out; she must adopt a different philosophy.

"I'll have a market stall on Saturdays," she decided. "But a stall selling quality fabrics that would be double the price in select department stores."

SAFE AS HOUSES

She bought two journals relevant to her quest. A few minutes to reflect on the technicalities, and then a call to Jonathan.

"A market stall? But Kate, you're a professional woman."

"One you won't be too proud to partner in the future I hope," she said defiantly to herself, for it would take so little to shake her resolve.

"Tell me about it." He listened to her plan and then said, "Fine. But do you feel a market stall is the right outlet for designer fabrics? Surely those who can afford them will go to quality suppliers, even the West End?"

"Those who can afford them, yes. But there are those who appreciate them and for whom they are out of reach. They will be my customers."

"Long shot. It'll take time. And Duncan's hardly going to approve."

"Which is why I shall begin with Saturdays. He spends every weekend at golf. If he doesn't have to be involved, he won't object for long. Jonathan, I need to do this."

"OK I'll send you the names of wholesalers, but they're normally only interested in supplying vast yardage," he warned.

"No doubt I shall have some persuading to do."

"Sorry, I forgot. You've done all that! OK, any leads I can help you with, I'll pass them on. Let me know how you fare."

Her initial requirements were small and she had no strong position from which to negotiate price. "But one day I will have," she promised herself. "One day they'll have to sweet-talk me!" She felt alive and capable. A momentary wave of dismay as she contemplated telling Alex and Lucy of her plans. Market stalls were what the folks in the street had been used to; a backcloth to the life she had left behind when she had gone to the 'toffs' school. And wasn't she fighting herself too? Ever since she had left Mr. Charlesworth's employ, she had struggled to base her life on the supposition that it mattered little what other people thought as long as one's own integrity was intact. But a stubborn streak of social conditioning had ever impeded her efforts, and the foundations of her jerry built elation would have been in danger of cracking were not the necessity to keep her word stronger than the fear of humiliation.

"Fifty pounds up front," said a man whose demeanour was clearly stating 'take it or leave it', "and ten a week rent if you only use it on a Sat'day."

"For the time being."

"Just playing shops are we?" The derisory tone accompanied a total lack of interest in her as a person. She was a mere entry in his book that would soon be deleted. "Take the pitch over there by the coffee bar."

SAFE AS HOUSES

"You have nowhere else?"

"We'll see 'ow regular you are," was the curt reply.

"If I'm here in six weeks I shall expect to move." She adopted a similar tone to convince him she would not be sat upon.

She had not needed to fold down the back seat to accommodate the few rolls that two hundred pounds borrowed from the bank had enabled her to purchase, and the sidelong glances and raised eyebrows did not escape her.

"You forgot your Wendy House luv," someone called.

"I'm Kate," she introduced herself defensively. "May I ask you to keep an eye on my stall while I park my car?"

"We're all in the same boat ducky." With an amazing deftness he removed a further two columns of cartons from van to stall. "Scuse me - you're in the way."

As she turned, he called out, "Go on, finish unloading - I'll watch it."

"I have," she said, not waiting to be subjected to ridicule. She joined the general exit of drivers who knew their vans to the inch, and made light of negotiating narrow passes. This was not something she had bargained for.

"Come on luv, 'urry up. We'll 'ave the punters 'ere soon." Nervously she manoeuvred between stalls and vans and rushed back to her pitch.

"It's still there!" the shirt-man grinned, "Don't think the masked bandits noticed it!" His smile was surprisingly not contemptuous, and returning his gaze, she acknowledged she was having her leg pulled.

"I'll probably have sold out before you come back," she countered, "so I'll serve your customers if you like, while you move your van."

He held out his hand. "Thanks Kate. Joseph's the name."

She had made the comment in jest to let him know she would survive any taunts he might choose to make and was caught off balance when he responded so trustingly.

Within half an hour, trade was brisk - for seemingly everyone except Kate. Despite draping the fabrics artistically to fill her stall, she failed to attract a single customer. Outward smiles at those who glanced tentatively at her merchandise concealed a gnawing anxiety. It was difficult to see where she had gone wrong, for several people with a discerning eye commented favourably, but none ventured to buy. She was aware of Joseph watching her in between his many customers. The short, stocky, dark haired stallholder had little difficulty in rapidly calculating the cost of purchases, and his easy familiarity with customers who had obviously patronised his stall for years, drew many a smile or light-hearted response.

SAFE AS HOUSES

"You won't do anything today Kate. Markets are all the same. They'll see if you turn up next week or if you're just a fly-by-night. Once they can count on you, they'll come up with the readies."

"I'm glad there's a reason. Anything I can do for you, if I'm not going to do anything for myself?"

"Ay. Go and get some tea. It's hard work taking all this money!"

"Will you look after my stall for me!" she laughed.

"You won't get nowt pinched from another stall holder Kate. But I will watch now with Joe Public around. Be hard though for somebody to walk off with a roll of fabric under her arm, and not be a mite conspicuous! Wouldn't you be better with offcuts? You might lose one or two to the Artful Dodgers but the price must be better. And you get a lot thrown in when the suppliers get to know you."

"I'll think it over Joseph. Tea coming up." She may not have made a sale, but she had learned a great deal about her new metier in this first morning.

"Do any other markets?" he asked as they sipped the strong brew.

"Just this one."

"Not the real McCoy then? Don't depend on it for a living?" Reluctant to deepen the conversation, Kate was grateful for the appearance of an elderly, classically dressed woman. "Excuse me Jo - this might just be the one!"

"Those are most attractive fabrics. Are they seconds?"

"No Madam. Quite perfect, all of them."

"Intriguing." She paused. "I meant you dear, not the fabrics." Kate awaited explanation, but none was forthcoming. "If they are perfect as you say, I'll take three yards each of the turquoise leaf and the brown daisies." Kate cut confidently across the width of the rolls, folding each length deftly, but with the care befitting a major purchase. "I look forward to seeing you in them Madam."

"I trust they will launder well - they are not the cheapest fabrics."

"Quality is rarely cheap Madame." And Madame returned her smile.

"Your first customer luv, eh?" Bill on the provisions stall was now less rushed, and consuming a substantial sandwich with obvious relish, said, "You'll never forget 'er no matter how many you have. She'll stick in your mind 'til your dyin' day."

"I think you're right. And she has paid my petrol if not my rent."

"Maybe your next one will do that. Want a coffee?" Without waiting for a reply he added, "Ow many sugars?"

"Just one please, I'll get the next one."

148

SAFE AS HOUSES

"You bet," he laughed. "Take on the market and yer fights yer corner."

"All talk that one," Joseph grumbled, having watched the conversation develop. "Don't you go thinking the' ain't no gents on the market Kate."

"How could I Joseph when it's been your encouragement that has kept me going all morning," she placated, hiding her amusement that it had been his offhand manner when the day began that had almost made her flee.

The coffee slopped over the mug Bill handed to her, and she moved towards him to prevent damage to the fabrics.

"Don't worry luv. I knows quality when I sees it. Funny choice though. You won't have many customers like that uppercrust old biddy. They get driven up to town in their Rolls and never have to ask the price of anything. People 'ere look for a bargain."

"And a bargain is what they'll get. Taste isn't the prerogative of the rich."

"Now if you're gonna use big words like that, you'll 'ave to find another mate. Good luck to ye Kate. Bit of a lark, is it?"

Lack of clientèle made her aware of the damp chill in the air, and she wouldn't be sorry to call it a day. She sold only one more length before threatening skies caused the market to close early. Jo Public had gone home, and so must they.

"Bye Kate. See you next week?" Joseph wove his van between those still being loaded, and with his departure, her spirits fell. Whilst most of the stallholders had ignored her presence, she knew they had not failed to note her miserable takings. The rolls seemed heavier than when she had left home with such expectation ten hours ago. But tiredness had never beaten her yet, and as she heaved the last one into the car, she heard someone call,

"Take these mushrooms Kate? They won't last till Monday."

She was momentarily thrown by the fear she had given the impression she needed charity, her mind racing headlong back to her childhood. How grateful the family would have been for a box of mushrooms then. But she saw no intent to humiliate.

"Why that's really kind.".

"Take 'em. I'm Sophy, and that's my man Chas."

"How did you know my name," Kate asked diffidently. More had been happening around her than she had registered.

"Asked Joseph," was the matter of fact response.

So he had been the one designated to see if she was worthy of general approval. She smiled her thanks and two or three voices called out to her as van doors were slammed. "Cheerio Kate. See you next week!"

SAFE AS HOUSES

She had sold virtually nothing, but suddenly and overwhelmingly, felt she had gained so much. In her notebook, she wrote the date, and '£8.2.6d.' She would remember that amount as well as her first customer, and wouldn't have missed coming for the world."

Duncan put in an appearance before she had completely emptied the car.

"Kate, I'm not too thrilled about all this. Heaven knows I'm no snob, but you know what business is like......if it gets abroad that my wife runs a market stall ...And it's hardly something our neighbours have to do... Look you don't need me to spell it out."

Having been up since half past five she was utterly drained, and said testily, "When we can manage on one salary, I won't need a lucrative interest, will I?"

"It has proved lucrative then?"

"That depends what value you place on £8.2.6d."

He relaxed. It had all been a flash in the pan; she would give up. Not immediately, for he knew his wife would cling to her pride, but soon.

"You're tired," he said solicitously. "I'll get something to eat at the club."

"There's no need. I left everything ready to put in the oven."

"We can have it tomorrow."

"As you like," she conceded, realising he had expected to slip in and out unnoticed. "But the speciality of the day won't keep until tomorrow."

"What?" But he didn't wait for an answer.

Leaving the casserole she had prepared in the fridge, she made herself mushrooms on toast. They were, after all, firm and succulent, and would have lasted until Monday. She would look forward eagerly to the following Saturday. When the phone rang, she knew it would be Jonathan.

"I won't exactly be reordering tonight," she admitted, "but I made a start."

"Just covering expenses is all you can expect at the beginning. Well done Kate." He had no idea of the overestimation he'd made of her takings.

"Thanks for phoning Jonathan. I will make it work."

"I know you will. Just don't kill yourself in the attempt. You already have a full time job. Put your feet up tonight."

"I have. And the armchair is Heaven. Night Jonathan."

By midnight Duncan had not come home. She used to wait up but that had irritated him, so she slept fitfully until she heard his car on the drive.

SAFE AS HOUSES

The smell of tobacco lay heavily on him, and he'd certainly had a drink but was not the worse for it.

"Nice evening?" She tried to sound neither concerned nor inquisitive.

"Got talking to Stan, and Jim Saunders - business stuff you know. What say we go off for the day tomorrow - just the two of us?"

"I'd like that. Night."

When she awoke, he was still sleeping soundly, and she decided to pack a picnic hamper before waking him. Job done, she was sliding some bacon rashers under the grill, when the phone rang.

"Kate! How are you my dear? Have a good day yesterday?" Amazed that Duncan should have told Stan about her venture, she was on the point of responding. But of course he hadn't. "How was your mother?"

"Oh well, thank you Stan. And you?"

"Fine. Actually m'dear I was wondering if Duncan would mind starting half an hour later this morning? Wife's sister is staying with us, so I'm doing the courtesy bit before leaving. I've telephoned the club."

"Starting?"

"Eleven instead of ten-thirty. Why don't you join Win later - haven't seen much of you recently."

"Maybe. You're up early Stan, after talking into the early hours."

"Come again Kate. I thought I was a good boy last night - playing mine host and all that."

Duncan had obviously been woken by the phone, and languidly sat at the kitchen table. "Bacon smells good. Sure I'm a lucky fella."

"Because I'm so gullible? Duncan, I can't say don't take me for a fool, because that's obviously what I have been. If there's someone you've become close to, have the courage to break us up cleanly." She'd always felt she would know if there were anyone else, but instinct had not suggested it. He took her hands firmly in his own. "Kate there isn't and never has been. Corny as it sounds, I love and need you."

"So much, that having arranged to play golf, you suggested we spent the day out together?"

"I really did mean to wake early and cancel with Stan. I only made the arrangement because I was piqued you went out the whole of Saturday."

"But you're out anyway on Saturdays. Evenings too. Why do you think I felt free to take on the market? Where were you Duncan?"

"I drank with Stan. Win had gone to get her sister, and he ate at the club."

"And afterwards?"

SAFE AS HOUSES

Endeavouring to assess just how much his friend had told her, he said, "Stan went home. I stayed talking to one or two others and must have fallen asleep in the members lounge. The caretaker woke me. Guess that's why I wasn't tired when I came home." His explanation sounded plausible enough and he showed none of the discomfiture of a liar. "Kate, come and have lunch at the club. Win will be there - you get on with her."

"I like Win perfectly well. It's just that after three or four G and T's she isn't Win anymore and I don't know who I'm talking to."

"And there are other more interesting things you can do alone?" He left her to make her own decision about lunch.

The aloneness dragged like a weight on her efforts to reach out for the exhilaration of yesterday, and duster in hand, she sank dispiritedly into the armchair. Why didn't she admit it; she had wanted the security of his support and approbation, not the bleak benefit of knowing that if she achieved success, it would have been all on her own.

Having pierced the bubble of her own dishonesty, she asked herself if it wasn't a child she wanted, not a fabric stall. So what if Duncan left? They'd struggle through somehow. Pushing resolutely on the arm of the chair she said, "That's me selfishly deciding what I want. What would the baby get out of it? Jam but no butter. Shoes too big so they'd last twice as long?"

And in those moments she recognised the longing would always be countered by experience; by memories of Mam's constant weary battling to stay afloat. Her fear of poverty was such an integral part of her; she had known it, felt its pangs. No, it was fortuitous that children did not feature in Duncan's plans - at least he would have none to reject.

As always, when pruned of her alertness, she drew on the resilience that had sustained her from childhood, and attended first to house and then herself. It would be churlish not to join them for lunch; there might even be vindication of Duncan's excuses. And she knew this was her strongest reason for going, for she had no wish to discover she was married to a liar.

In the event, circumstances contrived to make the day blandly pleasant. There was a distinct absence of undercurrent and all seemed aware that Duncan had fallen asleep and been locked in the club the previous evening until discovered by Duggie who came on night watch. None attempted to be secretive about it, suggesting there was nothing suspect.

CHAPTER SEVENTEEN

The site manager was pleased she was coming regularly - too many casuals destroyed the traditional image. He offered her a better position, but Sam who sold second-hand silver advised her to stay put. "It's not the best place but wait until you've enough customers to bother informing you're moving, or you'll start all over again."
Advice that coincided with her intuition, and she declined the offer.
"I wish I'd allocated you a better spot in the beginning, but I didn't give you more than a week or so."
"I'm glad I've proved appearances deceptive!" she said.
He wished her well and warned it was hard going in the winter.
"Longjohns are ready! I'll be here to wish you Happy Christmas!"
He reckoned she would too, and adroitly stepped out of the way of a young woman whose attention was caught by the fabric Kate had hung at the end of the stall. She had her back to Kate who said, "Do say if you'd like it taken down Madam. It's no problem."
At the sound of Kate's voice the customer spun round, unable to believe her ears and the two faced each other, both speechless. It was her customer who recovered first. "Kate. Kate Benson!"
"Emmeline! What a surprise. How are you?"
"Never mind me. Kate why are you here? What's happened?"
Angry that she had herself momentarily shared Duncan's contempt and disapproval of her stall, Kate said calmly, "I'm here because it's where I want to be Emmeline."
"I'm sorry... I mean.. it's just that I heard you were in the States .. a buyer or PA or something.. must have been at one of the reunions."
"I was. And this is something of a change, which is no bad thing. What are you doing now?"
"Since my divorce, I've been helping Mummy in the boutique."
"Your mother is in business?"
Emmeline grinned at Kate's reaction. "Yes, she took Daddy for everything he had after he left with 'that piece' as she refers to Miss Forbes."

"Who was actually very nice," Kate felt impelled to interject.

"She must have been for Daddy to go. Anyhow Mummy managed to get through a fair amount on cruises etc, but eventually got bored, and bought a boutique. I'm waiting for her now."

"So who's looking after the shop?"

"We have part time staff to call on - and frequently do. By the way don't let her hear you call it a shop!"

"Sorry! But what brings you to a market stall when you have haute couture at your disposal?"

"Kate, can you imagine what it's like fitting expensive clothes on sixty year old matrons. 'You don't think it emphasises my bulge dear?' 'Have you anything a wee bit more décolleté darling?'"

Kate had forgotten Emmeline's talent for mimicry and laughing appreciatively asked, "So why don't you cater for younger people?"

"They can't afford Mummy's prices."

"Adjust your range."

"Kate you're talking common sense when it's snobbery that dictates Mummy's reasoning. Anyway I prefer designing to selling. These fabrics are quite something."

"So why aren't you designing? That's what you trained for."

"Kate, you know what a lazy so and so I am. I didn't finish my course so no fashion house would be interested. And the boutique is all so easy ... I work when I want to... Daddy was the grafter; we just spent what he earned. You heard about his heart attack?"

"Yes. I really was sorry Emmeline. I liked him a lot."

"I know. And I was jealous of you - not that you didn't deserve his high opinion. He'd be sad to know you were here though."

"I don't think so. Intrigued maybe - but not sad."

"What *are* you up to Kate? And why here?"

"Boutiques don't come gift wrapped too often Emmeline. Right now I wouldn't swap my stall for Harrods itself."

"I don't believe you would. But Kate *why* not?"

"Because I didn't build Harrods."

Emmeline's expression was serious. "You're talking Daddy's language," she said softly. "It's something I don't know anything about because it isn't in me. I've never built anything - which is why my marriage went on the rocks I suppose. Like my mother, I only know how to take. Whilst Daddy provided for our every whim there was no motivation to do otherwise."

SAFE AS HOUSES

"But now there is, surely - ordering... marketing and expanding..... staying within a budget."

"Ordering and expanding - yes. Mummy's an expert. But in line with budgets! The accountant is constantly nagging her. Only last week, two elegant chaise-longues were delivered; fitting rooms equipped with floor to ceiling mirrors...fresh flowers delivered every day, clients are served coffee in none but the best china etc etc. Fur rugs for the poodles will follow."

Kate smiled, suddenly feeling free to embark on a friendship that had been barred to her at school. Maturity and experience now enabled the building of a bridge instead of the walls she had conditioned herself to erect.

"I haven't brought the best china, but there's coffee in the flask."

"Yes please. I'll help myself. Looks as if *you're* going to be busy."

Indeed a flurry of customers in the next half hour made quite an impression on the display. Rearranging the stall she said, "It's good to see you again Emm. I was embarrassed when I first realised it was you but.."

"It was OK when you discovered I wasn't quite the bitch I used to be?"

"I didn't say that."

"I did. Mind if I call again Kate?"

"I'd be over the moon."

Neither noticed the appearance of Mrs. Charlesworth, whose horror at the sight of her daughter drinking coffee on a market stall preceded her actual presence. "Emmeline, I have been kept waiting."

"Sorry Mummy. I met an old friend. You remember Kate Benson?"

Thrown by the distasteful environment, Mrs. Charlesworth's brow creased impatiently. "I don't think so." She was agitated, eager to be away, but Emmeline stood her ground quite literally. "Benson? Oh you mean the chauffeur's girl?" she finally conceded.

"Kate was Daddy's assistant, Mummy."

"Really?" She glanced at her watch. "Emmeline, we must go."

"Is it difficult to find a reliable chauffeur these days Mrs. Charlesworth?" Kate asked, recognising it was for her to release Emmeline from her stance of loyalty, and her mother from further discomfort. She was content to have had the strongest indication of Emmeline's wish to stay in touch, and had no need of her mother's patronage.

"I really don't have time..." Mrs. Charlesworth made an attempt to establish her superiority, but Emmeline winked broadly. "We don't have a chauffeur now Kate. I've driven us here in the mini and there really is no hurry, but we'll go anyway."

SAFE AS HOUSES

Mrs. Charlesworth's expression was one of ill-concealed annoyance at her daughter's public lack of respect, for it was obvious this was not a chance meeting that would be relegated to oblivion.

Trade was buoyant for the next hour or so, but slackened as the afternoon grew cold and grey. Joseph tossed a chocolate bar to her. "Told you it would get better Kate. Make the most of the run up to Christmas."

"You've been busy too Jo."

"Yep. Reckon I'll take my old lady to the flicks. You going anywhere tonight?"

"Expect so." She declined the bait. "Enjoy the film."

"Don't hang about. Just as important to have a reg'lar packing up as starting time."

"Which is why you're going early," she teased.

"I can afford too. I'm almost cleared out."

"And I shall stay because I haven't! See you next week."

"Make sure you do. You're one of us now."

"It's taken long enough!"

"Almost as long as your customers," he bantered.

Three young women ran up to her. "Oh good, you're still here. Pity the shirt man's going. Now I'll have to go to Marks," one said.

Joseph wound down the window of his van as he manoeuvred past her stall. "Mind how you go - the roads may be slippery."

Smiling her thanks she whispered, "You've just missed a sale – sure you don't want to wait?"

"No, we can't put all the Big Boys out of business can we? 'Sides," he winked, "I've sold out of her husband's size!"

For the first time she repacked her car in less than half an hour.

"That's the ticket Kate," Sam called. " Best go home light!"

"Too right. I'll just collect my veg from Sophy. Anything you want?"

"No. I eat out. No fun peeling spuds for one." His loneliness loomed up at her. So that was why he was always last to leave, despite a trade that was at best inconsistent. There must be a story behind each one of these people. Maybe now that she was established, she would become better acquainted.

Sophy was tired after heavy trading "Times like this we wish the stall was ours," Chas sighed wearily.

"I thought it was."

"Nah. Boss is in the Canaries," Sophy told her.

"Are you sure it's alright my having greengrocery at cost?"

SAFE AS HOUSES

"Course. We all do. Traders don't make a profit out of each other."

So that was why stallholders hadn't purchased from her.

Sophy read her thoughts. "We'll all come when you are on your feet ducky. 'Til then you make your cash out of Jo Public."

Kate put her arm around the old woman. "It's a privilege to know you all."

It was the kind of delicious tiredness that follows a satisfying day, and the long drive home, far from being tedious, was given over to pipe dreaming. Tonight she must double up on her orders. Her spirits bounced almost ludicrously in the knowledge that in coping with Duncan's resistance, and Emmeline's unexpected appearance -something that would have unsteadied her in the past - she had eluded the lure of comfortable conformity. She was stronger as an individual; she was on her way.

"I can see you did well," Duncan said half heartedly as she climbed out of the car with an alacrity belying the fact that her day had begun over twelve hours ago. "I'll give you a hand."

He appeared strained and she asked, "Did the rain spoil your plans?"

"Kind of." He was trying to conceal the cause of his brittleness.

"Do you want to tell me what's wrong?"

"You wouldn't be interested," he replied, unable to quell the tart and unfair response. She was always interested, and genuinely so. "And in any case it isn't important. I was merely reflecting on one of the many small occurrences of the day."

"In particular?"

"Oh I imagine you will hear it from Win anyway. It really doesn't affect us. Felt kinda sorry for a damn nice guy. Duggie the night watchman, got the push. Something went missing from the club - the board felt his carelessness was to blame."

"We all make mistakes. Hardly seems grounds for dismissal," she commented, wondering why Duncan was so concerned. Welfare of his fellow men was rarely a priority. But the name had a familiar ring. She paused for a moment and then said, "Wasn't that the man who woke you up one Saturday night some weeks ago?"

"What? Oh yes. Good Lord Kate, what trivia you choose to remember! You'd do the chap a good turn if you avoided the subject. You know how a bunch of females can turn a mere incident into a full blown scandal."

She did not appreciate being bunched with 'scandalmongers', but knew that discretion would prevent an argument in his current mood, and said only, "If it troubles you I won't mention him at all."

SAFE AS HOUSES

"I didn't say it troubled me. God you're doing it already."

The familiar, rapid escalation of emotion towards anger was the cue for immediate capitulation or change of subject. Indeed it was difficult nowadays to find anything they could discuss without animosity.

"I miss the golf to relieve the week's tension," he grumbled. "Filthy English weather."

His departure brought a measure of relief to both, and deciding to freshen up before making a cup of tea, she went upstairs to their room. He had left his jacket in a heap on the bed, and his chequebook was visible from the inside pocket. He must have been worried to go out without spending power, and unable to resist checking the stubs, she spent some moments speculating on who or what DG might be. And then the colour drained from her face. Replacing the chequebook in the jacket, she took a clean blouse from the wardrobe, but it was sometime before she actually put it on. Just why did they owe Duggie Grant the equivalent of a month's salary? And was it debt or compensation?

CHAPTER EIGHTEEN

"Thank you; that will be two pounds four and tuppence."
As the customer left, Lucy's hands met on the small of her back and she arched wearily, unknowing which bit of her body ached most. Alex was in hospital again, having his ulcers treated for the second time in six months.

It was as well Bobby had strength to lift the barrels; for him at least the days were rewarding, for Mam really needed him now. He could hoist things beyond her strength and was fulfilled and content as a result. Tomorrow, Gill would visit and then on Sunday, in the precious hours the shop was closed, Kate would drive Lucy for the longer afternoon visit, returning in the evening with Duncan, if he should come too. Lucy hoped so; they didn't seem to do much together nowadays. And now Kate was giving up her office job to buy a shop. It was beyond her; all that education and business experience just to be a shopkeeper. And after Duncan had set her up in that lovely house. But they must sort out their own lives now, for she could barely find strength to cope with her own. All that mattered was that Alex' legs healed and then they could grow old together with only Bobby left to care for.

Beth seemed to have found her niche, and Gill was doing well in the catering business. Both girls were climbing the ladder without any help from her now, which was a blessing. Only Kate was inexplicably on the way down again. She must talk some sense into her when she arrived: perhaps it would be better if she did come alone. No doubt Duncan would have made his feelings clear, and maybe a well-chosen word from Lucy would be enough to tilt the balance. He'd certainly left her in no doubt about the market stall, and understandably, for they hadn't needed the money with Duncan in his position. If Kate were not careful she'd be risking her marriage next. She had grown less timorous since leaving home; prior to going to America, Lucy could have talked her out of anything.

No matter. Alex' recovery was all that mattered; everything else was insignificant. It had been a shock enough last time when he'd given consent to have his toe removed. The poison had affected it so as to leave no option,

SAFE AS HOUSES

and now his leg had flared up. His depression was deepening too; some days it was impossible to lighten his spirits, and she would leave him desolate, trying to suppress her own fears until she was clear of the ward.

"Keep fighting Alex," she implored, but he insisted each time that it mattered little what he did. "Seems the ulcers'll not be beaten."

"Yer state of mind makes all the difference. Try luv," she begged. But he succumbed to his private dread, and ignored her plea.

Bob lifted the crates for her to refill the shelves for the evening trade. Her husband's meticulously organised cellar had made his absence easier to cope with than might otherwise have been the case, but she dreaded to think of his reaction to it now that it had been left largely to delivery men. He wouldn't be annoyed; only anxious to have it ship shape again.

She was serving draught bitter as Beth came into the shop looking pale and drawn and knowing that Mam, despite the introspection of the past weeks, would be unprepared for the news she must impart.

"What is it Beth? He's not worse?"

"Come and sit down. Bob, call me if anyone needs serving."

"Tell me." Lucy's impatience surfaced. "What's 'appened?"

"They've told Dad they must amputate."

Lucy, white and silent, was unable to react beyond, "What does Dad say?"

"Nothing. Nothing at all. He won't talk. He'd signed the form before I arrived. He realises there's no choice, but he's afraid, and doesn't trust their assurance that he'll master an artificial limb in time."

"Did he ask for me?"

"He asked if it would be your turn tomorrow."

"Damn shop." Lucy gained some relief from the release of tears. "I should've gone tonight. I'll be first on that Ward tomorrow."

"I'm afraid the poison began to spread, leaving us no alternative," the consultant explained to Kate the following day.

"Will he be in a wheelchair always?"

"Good heavens no! We'll fit an artificial limb as soon as the stump is receptive, and it's possible that very quickly he'll be walking normally - at least in so far as other people are concerned. Given a positive attitude, he may even cope with things like gardening."

"Is that the key?"

He nodded. "Your father is prone to depression."

SAFE AS HOUSES

"Only when taken from where he belongs," Kate corrected him staunchly. "Such people can't be uprooted without agony."

"He's in his local hospital," the consultant reminded her gently. He had so far found Alex only grudgingly cooperative.

"I wasn't referring to places," she added patiently. "You could move him to Timbuktu as long as he was still looking after his family. He is doubly wretched because he is not only away from them, but facing the intolerable situation of not being their strength - perhaps even becoming a burden."

"We'll get him home as soon as possible," he promised, smiling at Kate's earnestness, "and then he'll be able to test his will and ability. But I can't guarantee he won't be back if he succumbs to self pity."

"Not pity; anger at himself."

"For something he wasn't responsible for?"

She did not want to explain that which was so irrational, yet understandable if you had grown up with Dad, for wasn't she a part of him who knew exactly how he functioned. The consultant rose. "He's a lucky man. Don't deprive him of your company."

She returned to the ward to find Gillian had arrived unexpectedly and was challenging her father. "So, you want to be a burden on Mam. One limb short and your whole body is a wreck, is that it?"

"Gill! That's enough!" Lucy interceded. But instinct told her it would be like trying to stop an avalanche.

"May as well put me three feet under for all the use I'll be to her."

"Well, she could marry again and get someone else to tap the barrels."

The grey eyes, sad and defeated, suddenly blazed with a passion unexpressed for so many years. For a moment Lucy thought he would hit out at his daughter. "Over my dead body!"

"Which is exactly what it will be if you are three feet under," Gillian retaliated seeing the first positive reaction to her bravely cruel gamble, for she knew she would be forgiven by none of them if she failed. "I'm going now Dad. Work on getting home eh?" She said no more and Kate, who followed her to the door, knew it had cost her dearly.

"Thanks Gill. Not even Mam could have done that."

"Not this time at any rate. She's only half a person without him. Just as long as he forgives me. Kate, we won't lose him will we?"

"Not after what you did," Kate hugged her sister. "We've never thought what it would be like without him. You going to be alright?"

"Just as long as he is."

SAFE AS HOUSES

"I guess that goes for all of us. I'll see you before I leave."

The gauntlet had been thrown, and though in sombre mood for the rest of the day, the corner had been turned, and by midweek Alex was being treated at home. Before long he was using his crutches to get into the shop and refill the shelves. The stump remained tender and sore for a long time, and eventually when the limb was fitted, progress was painful and slow because it chafed so. Eventually it was agreed for a second to be made, which was not a great deal better than the first.

"Darned if I'll let a bit of plastic get the better of me," he asserted with a conviction he was far from feeling. "I have to get down those cellar steps Lucy. Tapping barrels ain't woman's work."

"Bob helps. There's no hurry. Maybe the stump's too sore yet," she warned, and smiling in the direction of Beth whispered, "He'll be alright. He's fighting again!"

Handing him a mug of strong tea, Lucy told him that Gill had made an appointment to see Mr. Bowers to tell him the leg wasn't right, and Beth was going with her. "And Kate has written a letter, so between them they'll get summat sorted," she added.

They did, and it was agreed a third limb should be fitted.

"By God that's easier," he announced. "I could walk for miles with this." And the relief that lightened his face made Lucy's heart sing.

"A little each day," Sister counselled. Short steps and turning corners."

It took fifteen minutes, and more than a few anxious intakes of breath - Lucy's, not his, for him to make his first foray down the winding stairwell.

"You know darned well Sister didn't mean these steps," Lucy scolded, but pride and stubbornness were his driving force.

"Don't get in the way Luce." His curtness indicated that argument would be to no avail, and sweat pouring from his brow, he picked up the wooden mallet, and swung at the barrel. The sheer effort of tapping caught him off balance, for he had not yet the co-ordination needed for such exertion, and though the bung was firmly positioned, he himself having nothing on which to break his fall, crumpled in a heap on the damp floor.

"Quick Bob!" Lucy screamed. "Down the cellar! Help me!"

Never before impatient with his slowness, she pleaded, "Oh Bobby, do hurry up." But Bob only had one pace, and a hand on each rail, he lumbered ponderously down the steps. His eyes became troubled at the sight of their predicament, and then his concern receded in the triumph of being needed, which was *his* greatest need. Here at last was a task that could not be snatched from him, for Lucy couldn't perform what he would now accomplish. He needed not help, but time; time to plant his feet where they could not stumble and then he scooped, rather than lifted his father, his strong arms encircling the older man's waist. For a moment the two were locked together as Alex struggled to regain control of a limb he could not feel, and which itself did not respond to mental intent.

"Damn thing has a will of its own," he muttered.

"It has no will at all Alex. We'll have to learn the new controls."

"All very well for you to know it all," he complained, instantly despising himself for taking out his frustration on she who had just linked herself with the learning process that now confronted him.

"If I could suffer it for you, I would." Lucy wept.

"Don't say that Luce. Thump me when I talk such tripe. Here girl - give me your hand. Hold me up Bob. I want to give yer Mam a kiss."

That he had lifted his father from the floor without mishap was of no surprise to him, but to have brought about such a rare show of affection caused him to beam with pleasure. He stood like a happy guard of honour holding Dad's heavy wooden crutch for the moment it would be needed, but concealing the shock the fall had inflicted, Alex dismissed it.

"Leave the crutch – one's enough – gi' me your shoulder son."

"Wait Dad," Bob instructed, revelling in the importance the incident had attributed to him. He undid Alex' tie and tied his own leg to his father's inanimate limb. "Three legs race," he grinned. "We climb together."

Lucy remonstrated, but Alex laid a restraining hand on hers. "Let him be. Thanks Bob. Come on then fella - up we go."

Bob supported his father to the head of the steps, and Lucy positioned a stool for her husband's momentary respite.

"Right Luce, go and rest," Alex insisted. "We'll mind the shop."

"But...."

"I said rest woman, and that's what I mean."

Drained by weeks of worrying and waiting, she withdrew to the living room, felt the comforting support of the fireside chair, and though not sleeping, closed her eyes and sighed out her weariness. Bob came to collect two glasses. "Dad and me going to have a pint," he announced, grinning broadly. "Me a man now!"

"Drinking on duty, the pair of you eh?" she smiled weakly.

She would listen in case they called, but for the moment she could doze. Her man was home again, and together they would find a way forward.

CHAPTER NINETEEN

As apprehensive as on the day she had stepped from her known world into the daunting atmosphere of public school at eleven years old, Kate, now in her mid-thirties and with four years of successful trading behind her, received a congratulatory handshake from Philip Jensen who was to be her new company's accountant.

Mrs. Charlesworth stood somewhat piqued in the background - an 'emplacement' to which she was clearly unaccustomed. Disposed no more than superficially to disguise her irritation, she was impatient to finalise courtesies, and said acidly, "I wish you well. Of course Mrs. Carter you have a head start having purchased at such a remarkable price."

"Remarkable as in something above the reserve price before you knew of my interest Mrs. Charlesworth - and one you would have been happy to realise in any event." Kate smiled in an endeavour to ensure they parted on other than acrimonious terms. "Will you be staying on in the area?"

"Good Lord no! I can't wait to escape this debilitating climate. My architect will be consulting with me later today to finalise plans for my villa; I have so many friends in the south of France you understand."

"Of course."

Jensen, recalling the boutique accounts he had inspected on Kate's behalf, raised his eyebrows aloft. "Ladies if you will excuse me – I'll see you at three tomorrow Mrs. Carter?"

Veronica Charlesworth's relief at his departure was evident. "Mrs.Carter before we go our separate ways I must make clear my opinion I've not been dealt with entirely professionally, There was no agreement, implicit or otherwise, that the expertise of the staff was included in the purchase price. I had no idea the buyer would assume my daughter's continued services thus saving on the expense of training a new assistant."

Kate flinched at such a flimsy attempt to cast doubt on her integrity; one that even Mrs. Charlesworth had not uttered in the presence of her solicitor.

"Emmeline isn't staying on Mrs. Charlesworth. Her job as Sales Assistant - that is how she is described and paid in your accounts - came to an end when you sold the business. But yes, I have made her an offer, and she, as a free agent and currently unemployed, has agreed to join me in a different capacity."

"Oh?" Curiosity aroused, Mrs. Charlesworth found it impossible to maintain her stance of apparent indifference to Kate's plans or to conceal her frustration at the woman's minimal communication.

"Quite different. And now I must ask you to excuse me for I have a pressing engagement. I hope everything goes well for you in France."

"Who does she think she is?" Veronica Charlesworth seethed between clenched teeth. She was welcome to it. The novelty would soon wear off when she realised what was involved to cream off an income to be expected from such an enterprise. As for Emmeline, what did she think she was doing associating the family with their ex chauffeur's daughter?

"Kate!" Emm saw her as she entered the Bank. "Has it all gone through? Mummy actually resisted pulling any last minute stunts?"

"I don't honestly think she had many cards left to play. When I left her, she was looking forward to the villa, and an eternal summer!"

"I do believe I'm more excited than you, and it's your business!"

"I doubt it!" Kate laughed. "I'm just better at hiding it."

"I don't for the life of me understand why you'd want to."

"Neither do I. I'm just made that way."

"So when do I start?"

"Tomorrow at eight thirty?"

"You expect inspiration to flow at such an uncivilised hour!"

"If I'm paying for it, yes!"

Emmeline regarded her new employer with affection and respect. "Aye aye boss lady!"

"I've found you a seamstress. Solid, conscientious and thorough."

"Flair?" Emmeline mimicked Kate's economy with words.

"That's your department. She'll translate your designs into perfect ensembles. I want nothing left to her imagination; that way argument will be excluded, and we shall maximise on production."

"You couldn't be a little more specific?" Kate was teased, both recognising that given tolerance of each other's traits, they would rapidly from a perfectly balanced team. "When can I see the selection you made?"

"It's in the stock room already. Come on!"

Emmeline smoothed the fabrics, appreciating both quality and colour tones.

"Superb. You must be over the moon Kate?"

Kate nodded and knew that her dream would be realised when she had persuaded Jonathan to join them.... exclusive designs in exclusive fabrics. But that was the future. "Right now my priority is to secure the exclusive agency for these fabrics."

"Think we'll get enough clients? We weren't that busy in the boutique."

"Yes we shall, but not all through the boutique, which for wider custom will merely be our base. But that's my department. You just keep the designs coming." She looked around and thought the glow within her must surely set her afire.

"Kate don't you have any apprehension?"

"Apprehension? I'm terrified!"

"It doesn't show. But then, it never was allowed to surface, was it?" Emmeline looked away and then, as if not really wanting to know the answer asked, "Kate, why did you invite me to join you?"

"Talent. Talent that was never put to the test because you already had everything you wanted. Only when you stopped living on your family was there a chance you'd realise your own potential. Needing to survive sharpens everything. I'll just have to keep you away from rich men!"

"You still haven't answered my question."

"Alright, you were the friend I always wanted at school, but your social status, and my total lack of it, kept us apart."

"And that's all?"

"Of course. What did you think?"

"That it might give you a buzz to employ a Charlesworth?"

Kate bristled. "If that was my reason, why didn't I ask your mother to stay on? That surely would have been the coup de grâce!"

"Wonder if you'll enjoy it as much as the market stall? I'll never forget finding you there!"

"Neither will I! Reckon I earned an Academy Award that day, - And I still have that stall, and a couple of others beside. They'll keep my feet on the ground until we're established at the other end of the market."

"I might have known, Oh if only Daddy could see you now!"

"He was my best teacher - I watched his every move. And yes, I confess I'd like his approval; none more in fact."

"You weren't jealous of me Kate?"

There was not the slightest hesitation. "No. I already had the only man I'd ever want as a father. But I admired yours as employer and business man."

"And when he left Mummy?"

"By that time I, like everyone else who worked for him was totally biased in his favour, and found reason to understand."

"And mother?"

"I have no sentiments about your mother."

"You mean she's hollow?"

"I've never had anything to do with her. She's had no impact on my life."

"I'm like her Kate."

"Is that a warning to me, or a reason for you to change your mind?"

"I'm not renowned for doing the decent thing, but it's definitely not the latter for I've never felt more sure about anything."

"Good. Shouldn't we be thinking about something to eat?"

"Super idea if you're free. Is Duncan not at home?"

"No, still in the States."

"Job-hunting?"

"Just visiting."

"Do you love him Kate?"

"Yes. Just afraid to follow it through. I don't feel like explaining Emm." Nodding her acceptance of the reply, Emmeline flung wide her arms at the realisation she would have a routine, a sense of worth and purpose to hold her together, without which she had for so long been empty and insecure.

"At last I have a reason to get up each day! I'm actually part of a team whose success depends just a teenie bit on me. Kate Benson, I thank you with every fibre of my being!"

"Emm it depends as *much* on you as me - which renders me vulnerable enough to convince you I could not have afforded to take you on to indulge a whim! If either one of us fails we're done for!"

Both reflected on their new situation which presented a first time for each; the one on whom no-one had ever before depended, and the other who had, all her life, clung stubbornly to her independence.

"Why don't we eat at my flat tonight - then you can look over the sketches I've been working on," Emmeline suggested.

"Perfect. You shoot off if you're doing the cooking. I'll check over a few details and be with you in an hour."

Alone to savour the day's events, Kate mentally reorganised the space available. She would set up office at home initially; paperwork could be done in the evenings leaving the days free for chasing business. Already she could hear Jonathan warning her of all work and no play, but at this moment none of it remotely resembled work, only the most exhilarating challenge.

SAFE AS HOUSES

More immediately she must reach a decision on a separate issue. Having paid a weekly rent for the stalls, she now had the option to pay a lump sum that would guarantee her right to trade for life. But the timing could hardly have been worse for she had already borrowed heavily to buy the boutique. The Bank Manager, having watched the progress of her original venture for which he had loaned her the princely sum of two hundred pounds, was more than willing to extend her credit, but would require collateral. Kate had produced the deeds of the cottage.

"This is not the house in which you live Mrs. Carter?"

"That isn't mine to risk. And I would not use the cottage to support anything less than a certainty." He had paused for her to qualify her statement, but she said only, "I have an obligation to the occupant."

"From whom you receive a rent." Assuming he had completed her statement for her, pen in hand, he awaited the figure.

"I receive no rent. Mr. Rees' right to live in the cottage was reflected in the price I paid for it."

"A remarkably trusting arrangement," he commented, "and for a long standing customer, one of which we shall forget I was made cognisant. A sitting tenant is not as financially attractive as one without complications."

Kate had never considered Mr. Rees a complication in her life; indeed he was one of the more serene elements of it. The Manager pointed out his slight concern, though it would, he said, not affect his agreement to back her should she wish to proceed.

She had inherited neither Lucy's decisiveness, nor her subsequent confidence in the wisdom of her decisions, and recognised much of her father in herself. "I've felt some of the agony you went through Dad, when Mam bought the shop," she said aloud. "But at least you had her to blame if things went wrong!"

She confirmed her acceptance of the terms, and put the note through the Bank letterbox on her way to Emm's flat. As it fell to the floor, so the weight of decision-making went with it. "Of course, there was a simpler way," she told herself as she rang the bell. "I should have asked myself what Mr. Charlesworth would have done, then it would have been easy!" Even so it was reassuring to have the confirmation that such a thought evoked.

Disguising none of her excitement, Emmeline flung open the door. "Come on in. Everything's ready!"

"So quickly?"

"TV Dinners don't take long Kate!"

SAFE AS HOUSES

The sketches were all Kate needed to complete a perfect day. There was no disguising Emm's ability, to which she must now do justice. She was taken aback therefore when Emm said, "Kate, I don't care what you have to do, keep me at it. No throwing in the towel this time. I mustn't let you down."

"What is it you fear? You couldn't let me down with all this talent. I'm just so glad we were able to build on that meeting at the market. You have to agree, it could have turned out differently!"

"I might have cocked a snoop, made you feel two inches high and walked away you mean?"

"No that's not what I meant. We might have missed an opportunity. We didn't, so what's the problem?"

"The problem is the money I have in the Bank - Daddy's money. I don't have the fight in me that you said comes from having to survive Kate. Even now he's dead, he's still protecting me. You're the one with the vision and the enterprise. I'm grateful to be part of it, but will it last when hard work takes over from the excitement?"

The frank and unexpected outburst troubled Kate, but she said only, "The commercial headaches will be mine. You concentrate on the design side until you're so caught up in the business, you won't be able to tell one from the other. I'm going to collect Mrs. Grant. That way she'll be in at the beginning and know she's an essential part of the team."

"Sure. Just seems crazy that you've an overdraft from the same bank that manages my surplus."

"Forget it. That's your personal life; my connection is with your professional one. The risk I've taken will generate the energy I need to make my target attainable."

"Tell me about Mrs. Grant. Where did you find her?"

"She does dressmaking for golf club wives, hence my opportunity to see her work at close hand - I sit by it often enough."

Kate pondered her own motive for collecting Mrs. Grant. Both had sought assurance concerning her reasons for appointing them, though in Mrs. Grant's case, there appeared a wariness of charity as opposed to the revenge her friend had suspected. How complex human beings were, and with what sensitivity they must be handled if they were to achieve their potential. The only explanation she had ever elicited from Duncan for his cheque to Duggie Grant, over three years ago now, was that it was an affordable loan until the poor man could find alternative employment. The ensuing invective had followed a familiar pattern. 'Was Kate with her high

SAFE AS HOUSES

principles telling him that he should not now be the Good Samaritan when it was within his power to be so? How illuminating, how interesting, to realise it was she who would pass by on the other side when a friend was down on his luck, or was it that Duggie was lower class that she objected?' He lashed out with his tongue with no realisation of effect or consequence, and yet when she could no longer restrain herself from retaliating, he was astonished and hurt that such wounding comments could be uttered by one who supposedly loved him.

As always, faced with the logic of his argument, the reasonableness of his proposed course of action - if with no real conviction of the validity of his motive, she had accepted his explanation of events. But when two years into his job, he had given as reason for being asked to resign, the fact that he couldn't substantiate his expenses because his briefcase had been stolen from his hotel in Kenya, suspicions she had repeatedly thrust away would no longer be denied.

Mrs. Grant was waiting, and as Kate, who was obviously not going to be asked inside where she might have had an opportunity to speak with Duggie, pulled on the handbrake, so her new seamstress dropped the catch on her front door and got into the car.

"Mrs. Carter I can't thank you enough for offering me the job. There must have been so many others you could have considered."

"I chose you on merit Mrs. Grant - a decision I don't think for one moment I'll live to regret." The pause she allowed herself was of such brevity it was barely discernible, and with apparent indifference she added, "There were no favours involved because I know of none that are outstanding. Are there?"

Mrs. Grant was unprepared for such a rapid opening, obviously made to enable her to throw light on a subject she was ill equipped to discuss, and of which she too would like to know the full facts. "No indeed Mrs. Carter. Your husband was generous to Duggie in the past; and things have turned out in such a way that you are now being kind to me, that's all."

Accepting she would make an inept detective, Kate insisted it was a business arrangement from which she hoped both would gain.

Having offloaded her earlier apprehension, Emmeline directed them towards the easel. Mrs. Grant expressed genuine admiration, and having sensed Kate had enjoyed the drive here no more than she, was now happily contributing to the enthusiasm for the venture in which they were all three committed. She surmised that her host might not be quite as comfortable to get along with as Mrs. Carter, but she'd certainly enjoy creating the designs on the drawing board.

When she was better acquainted with her new employer - poor soul, did she really think no one knew about that husband of hers - they might be able to talk about the awful night when Duggie had stupidly been persuaded to turn a blind eye to the poker game that shouldn't have been going on, on club premises in the first place. And then to get himself blamed for the missing drink - she could only assume he'd lost the brain he was born with. The cronies Mr. Carter had brought in hadn't even been members. Business guests indeed! She would have told him that rules were rules, but no, Duggie had always revered those with money.

The Directors hadn't wanted adverse publicity either, so it was in their best interests to let the dust settle quickly, and given his past loyal service they had no wish to add to his difficulties. The impact of being involved, however unintentionally, had, they felt, been a chastening warning. The bar bill had to be met of course but Mr. Carter had graciously condescended to 'lend' him the money for that, and gave them, what she had to admit, was a generous sum to tide them over until things were sorted. They had explained the improbability of repaying, but he obviously felt Duggie's compliance to protect his good name to be a fair return, and insisted they lose no sleep over it.

And now Mrs. Carter had said he was in America. No doubt he had contacts and capital all over the world - must have to be setting up his wife like this. One thing, she hoped *she'd* never set eyes on him again, except to give him a piece of her mind, though she wouldn't want to risk her own job this time. It might be Mrs. Carter running the show but doubtless it would be her husband's money behind it.

CHAPTER TWENTY

Kate studied the notes Jonathan had sent, following visits to Paris and Cologne. As yet operating on a modest scale, she was nonetheless keeping abreast of leading fashion houses, and by forming a liaison with his Company had circumvented a multitude of difficulties that may have beset her had she expanded too soon, and independently. Accounts showed an excellent return on investment and to no small degree she had benefited from his intuitive perception of the likely take-up of European markets, which was to be the next stage in her company's development.

Mrs. Grant now managed a team of seamstresses, whilst Duggie collected finished garments from those working at home. Kate had several times asked Lucy if she would like to join her but the answer had been predictably the same.

"You know me Kate, I'd need to run the ship. Don't think my pride could stand working for my own daughter. No, the shop's ours to run just as the Company is yours. It gives Bob something to do, and," she had added on the last occasion, "it provides for our needs without worrying about competition and expansion."

Kate's lips had tightened at her mother's veiled disapproval of her activities. And then, as always after seeing her comment had gone home, Lucy relented, and with a genuine wish to have made the point without hurting - though she could never have refrained from actually making it - insisted gently, "We're glad everything's going well for you. And now Beth has found someone, I'm even more content - even if Australia is half a world away. She won't bother about a career with a brood to look after. To think she was the one that wanted children most - an' the one that couldn't have 'em. God must be as contrary as all the other fellas he made."

Kate smiled at her mother's perception of the Almighty and though she longed, she could not tell Lucy how she too had yearned for a family. To do so would necessitate explaining Duncan's refusal to have one, thus opening the door for awkward questions. Better to let her continue with the assumption it had been a mutual choice.

SAFE AS HOUSE

They had all been so pleased for Beth when she had met and married a widowed doctor with three young offspring who, being assured of her love for all four of them, had accepted a consultant's post in Sydney.

"Why don't you and Duncan go for a visit? Seems Gill and Stuart won't be able to go for a year or more now they're buying the hotel," Lucy suggested.

"Strange to think of Gill in the north of Scotland. I would have put her down for London life any day," Kate sidetracked.

"Me an' all. But Scotland's where they've found the hotel. She's got plans to make it attractive to them on expense accounts." Lucy sniffed her lack of conviction. "Thought she'd have been as well off with family visitors."

But Kate disagreed "No, the season's too short. She's wise to consider the oil-business opportunities."

Lucy regarded her eldest daughter keenly, other matters on her mind. If the gossips were to be believed, Kate had been supporting Duncan this past year, though to her credit Lucy had neither time nor patience for those who deflected attention from their own affairs by concerning themselves with others. She had tried to get to the bottom of it, but Kate had insisted all was well and beyond that she couldn't get her to talk. That was the problem; she was always such a closed book if she so much as suspected intrusion. Neither had she gained any help from Alex, for wasn't he just the same?

Accompanying Jonathan to Paris, Kate had helped on several occasions over the past two years to entertain selectors from the stores that provided his company's bread and butter business. There would be times, he said, when lavish individual attention would pay dividends and was confident the experience would prove invaluable to her. How accurately he had attuned himself to their thinking; how closely he observed what caught their attention in the window displays of Marie Gabard, St. Gervain, Boulevard Hausmann. And privately Kate had thought, 'Keep 'em coming Emm and there'll be a Charlesworth-Benson House here one day.'

She had physically felt the magic of that city. Beautiful, elegant and assured as the models who made fashion its password; she knew she would return to it again and again. Its architecture excited, its atmosphere wooed her, whilst its tree lined avenues were evocative of the beauty she had sought from childhood. And thus with an aim to have a branch here, her future plans were mapped out.

SAFE AS HOUSE

Sheer adrenaline had, and would, keep her going, her chosen métier being meat and drink to her. So many developments fell into place she felt she was walking in step with destiny itself, and when an opportunity arose to buy into another innovative concern, Emm insisted on adding her capital.

"It's too exciting not to Kate," she insisted. "I sometimes feel we shall take off! I can't believe how far we've come." Pressing home her point she said, "You keep me so busy, I don't have time to spend my capital. It's insane to have it in the bank whilst you borrow even more. And don't forget it will be to my advantage too."

But Kate was not easily won over to the idea, remembering the doubts Emm had expressed six years ago when she had bought the boutique.

Eventually they had compromised on an agreement whereby Emm could withdraw her money at three month's notice. If such a need arose in the future, it would surely be at a time when Kate could afford to repay. Phil Jensen had asked why she had been reluctant for Emm to invest on a proper business footing.

"Emm has never had to worry about money and consequently has not taken an interest in how it works in business. Because we've enjoyed success - and the signs are that it will continue – she finds it impossible to contemplate a loss. If the Company, or the work ceases to appeal to her, she is capable of quitting overnight, in which case she'll need her money."

"But you've made no provision for her so doing?"

"You don't replace people until they actually leave. Added to which I've not yet met anyone to match her. And frankly I wouldn't want to run the business in its present form, without her. Having surrounded myself with people whose competency I admire and respect, I've built a company compatible with their abilities. The idea was mine; I then sought those who would perpetuate it, since when our direction has had most to do with our combined talents."

"Different. You aren't a business woman in the true sense, are you Kate?"

"I didn't think I was doing too badly!"

"Magnificently. I'd back you any day. But you aren't motivated by money; the balance sheet isn't your focal point, nor does it generate you."

"I certainly take it into account!"

"But as a tool; not as the centre of your activities."

"Life's too precious Phil."

She stretched herself free of fatigue, deciding it was time for a coffee break, just as Jonathan phoned.

SAFE AS HOUSE

"Come to Zurich with me Kate," he said. "See all the processes in one place. Massive factory - seems to employ the whole town! It's bound to provide valuable contacts for you. How's the clientèle in Europe building up?"

"Excellent. I've to visit three new customers in Germany next month."

"So we can tie in the two trips! Firm up on your dates and get back to me eh?"

"You in a hurry?"

"Only to get home. Flew in an hour ago. Stopped off at the office to leave some typing. Haven't seen the kids for ages. Night Kate."

Replacing the receiver, she knew that their shared enthusiasm was the most essential element in her success.

And success was almost self-perpetuating as they went from strength to strength. As the hurdles increased in height and number, so apparently did their ability to jump them. The factory operated at maximum capacity almost two years ahead of schedule, whilst contracts in Germany led to equally substantial ones in France, and office, factory and sewing room staff were increased commensurately. Had she had time to stop and ask 'how' she would have marvelled at the heights they were scaling; might even have queried how they could keep up the momentum, but every waking moment was geared to a dizzying rate of growth, and satisfying demand.

And the progress was intoxicating, and provided all the adrenalin she needed.

CHAPTER TWENTY ONE

Emmeline thrust a glass of sherry into her hand. "Good trip?"
"Emm there is nowhere in the world I adore as much as Paris. If we lived in a story book world we'd open a branch there by next week at the latest." Ignoring Kate's eulogising, Emmeline smiled as one who had discovered a closely guarded secret that, for the time being at least, could rival a mere city in its intrigue.
"You've had a visitor in your absence. Said he was a family friend. I told him I expected you back this afternoon - or tomorrow at the latest."
Kate kicked off her shoes and glanced cursorily through the mail. "You know all my friends. Lots of reps try that approach. Anyway he's probably got his foot in another door by now. Much more importantly, did we get the order from Ennals?"
"That too!"
The news she had hoped for dispelled any fatigue that threatened as a result of ten days negotiating on the Continent. Jubilant, she tossed a pile of circulars into the air. "Marvellous! That's the big one. Oh and Emm - we can get a government subsidy to import knitted fabric from Turkey - half the cost of producing in the U.K. Check the colours and rationale against my report and we'll arrange an order. I've made all the necessary contacts."
"Kate you're incorrigible! Aren't you the least bit curious about your visitor?"
"What's so different about this one? - Aren't we always having callers?"
Emm smiled. "I think you ought. That's his car that just pulled up."
Kate glanced indifferently out of the window. "Never seen it before. Get rid of him for me. I need to tie up ends from the trip... Did you arrange for the caterers for the summer show? The invitations are ready... Oh and tomorrow we must place the order for flowers.... Look have a meal with me tonight - there's so much to discuss."
"I was rather hoping you'd have dinner with me this evening," interjected a voice from the doorway; someone on whom Emmeline had expectantly fixed her attention.

SAFE AS HOUSES

Kate, about to empty her briefcase, stood transfixed before turning towards the person who, with a few words, melted away the past seventeen years. Tom Heydon held her gaze with his own, openly admiring what he saw.

"Tom." Neither the acknowledgement when it finally came in a mere whisper, nor the visitor's impact on her employer, escaped Emmeline, who having no intention of absenting herself until discretion absolutely demanded it, luxuriated in the revelation that Katie Benson had 'a past'.

"Business of course." Tom recognised he would not convince her.

'Why' and 'how' were the only words occupying Kate's head until the professional in her rushed to the rescue. She would insult neither Emm's intelligence nor observation, but she must be relieved of the skeleton-in-the cupboard notion she was obviously entertaining.

"Emm, may I introduce Tom Heydon - a friend I haven't seen since my pre-America days - hence the shock. Tom - Emmeline Charlesworth, my friend and partner."

"I really just work for her - which is why I'm so interested in the fascinating dilemma in which my boss now finds herself!" Emmeline told him. "But complying with the dictates of my better nature - which I might add, rarely dominates - I shall go and perc you both some coffee."

"Not for me thanks," Tom said. "I've an appointment in Warwick in an hour. I really only called to see if you had any news of Kate's return so I could fix a time to meet."

"I'll make some anyway - she runs on the stuff."

"Tom, how on earth did you find me? And why after all these years?"

"I'll explain everything tonight - here isn't the place. You will have dinner with me? If only not to disappoint Emmeline! Sorry my entrance lacked finesse. Haven't improved have I? Pick you up sometime after seven?"

"I'll be here."

He paused before leaving; his expression becoming serious. "Something I need to talk about. Had to see you Kate. I've put it off too long already. Tonight then?"

She nodded, her mind reeling. He had said enough to elicit her agreement to being taken out to dine, and kissing her casually on the cheek he called 'Cheerio' to Emmeline. Kate, knowing there would be no peace until Emm had been acquainted with 'background information', sank into the chair.

"I knew him many years ago Emm. I was living in London ... we were both young and unattached... Then I went to America and he to Africa."

SAFE AS HOUSES

"But he was special Kate? And any denial you are about to fabricate will be futile! Why the chemistry almost sparked - and if that's after so many years what must it have been like at the time! Her tone was nonetheless solicitous for she was not oblivious to the fact that Kate was shaken to learn that whatever emotion had existed in the past had, albeit unconsciously, been fermenting ever since.

"Special? For me, yes. But it wasn't reciprocal - I was just another girl."

"Then why.. . ?"

"You heard him – it's a business appointment - though I can't imagine in what connection."

"Which wasn't true of course."

"Emm. I don't know. Truly. Nor do I know how he heard of the boutique - or indeed of my whereabouts. I'm as mystified as you."

"But you have agreed to see him?"

"He's collecting me here this evening."

"Good. This time, don't let him slip away!"

"Emm I am married - or had you forgotten?"

"You'll let that make a difference? Kate I despair. Even though I don't understand - for that handsome husband of yours was some catch - I can see what your marriage does to you. While there was no one else I was prepared to let you feel you had fooled me all was well. That was obviously the way you wanted it. But this Tom has come all the way from Africa to find you!"

"Emm your romanticism is running away with you. He was in the area ... seemed to know I was also here and for reasons best known to himself, decided to look me up." Privately she conceded he seemed to have a more substantial purpose.

"Conscience is your department, not mine. If I smell an opportunity for you to be happy I shall not collaborate with you in keeping a promise for 'better or for worse'. At least give the bloke a chance."

Kate rose from her chair and peremptorily brought the conversation to a close. "I once did," she said quietly.

And Emmeline, recognising the signs, knew she must wait patiently before raising the subject again, or most surely it would be closed to her forever.

Kate dressed with meticulous care after the staff had gone home. She and Emm kept a wardrobe on the premises; expedient when the occasion demanded a hurried change of plan. Emm gave her approval to Kate's final

SAFE AS HOUSES

choice of dress but insisted on driving to her flat to fetch some ear-rings. "You don't do justice to those classic features of yours my friend and I know you need only the slightest nudge to be adventurous. Won't be long. You'll love them!"

"And if I don't?"

"You'll wear them anyway, because you trust my judgement more than your own on such matters. Only your upbringing will dismiss them as flamboyant and deliberately eye-catching," she called, as the door swung behind her.

But tonight Kate wanted to be eye-catching. No matter the reason for his coming, how he had found her, or what he had to say, she could not quell a joy so strong that it shut out both past and future as completely as only the fiercest pain can do. She would savour this hour as she prepared to meet the man who for the second time in her life had emerged from nowhere and knocked her sideways. Now, as had happened before, even if years passed before she saw him again, there would be days of recollection from mere moments of incident.

She radiated joy as Emm smoothed her hair back and upwards into an elegant chignon, and stood to admire her handiwork.

"Emm you won't speak of this .."

"I did inherit just a soupçon of Daddy's discretion - talking of whom, remember even he gave up on a marriage that was doing nothing but destroy him - and believe me that in itself was world shattering. It's alright; not another word shall escape my lips. And if Duncan returns unexpectedly I shall compromise him myself rather than your evening be ruined."

"He's coming home next month, and I'm sure I shall have no reason not to tell him of tonight's meeting."

"Katie Benson, I sincerely hope you will!"

The success of her career assured, Kate possessed a natural poise and dignity, and yet tonight she trembled as a seventeen year old on a first date. The moment she had longed for was upon her, and though she knew it could have no permanence, she did not wish to lose its transitory magic through the shyness that was her real self. Yet no words seemed available to her as she opened the door to him and he took both her hands in his own, grinned in the way she had never forgotten and lightly kissed her cheek.

"Ready?"

SAFE AS HOUSES

She nodded, amused that the characteristic impatience to get on with things once he had a plan, had not left him. But this time she had misread him. He wanted to get what he had come to tell her out of the way once and for all; only then could he start the process of getting to know her again.

They walked to the car and she smiled to herself when he climbed into the driving seat leaving her to open the passenger door. Gallantry had never been his strong point. Nevertheless it gave her pleasure that he treated her in familiar fashion; polite formality would somehow have indicated he had forgotten the comfortable way they had been with each other. As he released the handbrake he turned briefly to wink at her before pulling away from the kerb. "You look fabulous."

She returned his smile, as unable as she had been on the night she had met him at the theatre all those years ago, to find words that would tell him that she was so glad he was here, without also letting him know that her heart was about to take flight.

To learn Tom had discovered her through a meeting with Duncan, stunned her, and she listened engrossed as he explained how he had met her husband prior to his joining the company that he, Tom, was preparing to leave.

"He did actually mention you, but the description he included in a conversation in which neither was remotely interested, was so unlike you, that never for a moment did I imagine his wife could be my Kate."

She made no attempt to suppress the glow that the possessive reference had ignited. "So you didn't forget me immediately then?"

"Idiot!"

"When was it you realised?"

"Later. Much later when our paths crossed again."

He refilled their glasses, and suddenly changed the course of the conversation, asking her to tell him about Paris. If she hadn't known him better she would have sworn he was prevaricating, but Tom was the last person to feel uncomfortable, or dither about finding the most tactful way of saying something.

"Where do you stay?" he asked, and was surprised to hear about the small hotel in Reuil Malmaison whose owners now numbered amongst her closest friends. "Don't you prefer something more central?"

She supposed that now it could be afforded, it would make more sense, but in the early days when financial constraints had dictated outlay, the Cardules had made her so welcome that now it was impossible to think of staying anywhere else.

SAFE AS HOUSES

Throughout the meal he wanted to hear all about the intervening years. To discover that she had so much to tell; that her life had not been without event and interest to others, excited her. For his part he realised that the shyness and diffidence he had previously associated with her concealed a latent vivacity which tonight, through his own sudden reluctance to discuss the purpose of his visit, he had somehow released, and found enchanting. She was unaffectedly sophisticated now, and there was about her an elegance that had not been evident before. The hairstyle perhaps - it complimented her bone structure in a way the conventional cut she had had at twenty two had failed to do. But the eyes were the same, deep and trusting just as he remembered, but now with the sobering effect of years and experience, he felt less worthy of their gaze; flattered to be her escort; even more so to see clearly that she was far from indifferent to his presence.

He ordered liqueurs knowing he could no longer delay imparting news that would cut abruptly across this most tangible of atmospheres, in which they had resumed conversation as if it had continued from only yesterday, and in which their allusions had caught, and held, and needed no explanation. They had fallen into an easy silence now, and watching her sip her coffee, her warm dark eyes reflecting the candlelight, he wanted only to take her in his arms and tell her what an arrogant youthful fool he had been to let her slip away to America. And yet, if he were honest with himself, prior to finding her he had been prepared to discuss the situation without sentiment, had the circumstances been more in line with his expectation that she would be immersed in domesticity. Abruptly he said at last, "Kate this isn't going to be easy for either of us so I'm not going to dress it up. And if I'd any sense I'd probably let the matter rest and hope you'd never discover."

"Discover what?"

"That I had a hand in your husband's dismissal. I can't even pretend that had I known he was married to you it would have made any difference; in fact I might have enjoyed twisting the knife even more."

She raised her eyes slowly to meet his own; the glow that had characterised her demeanour since he had driven her from the boutique was snuffed out in an instant, and he could not have surmised, nor did she intimate, that her first reaction was one of bitterness that even in his absence, Duncan had managed to taint this most fairytale of evenings.

Assuming the brief flash of anger and dismay to be directed at him on her husband's behalf, he yet assumed she had known of events, even if unaware of the cast involved. He grasped at the tenuous link of their being at the same table, which was all of the bond that seemed to remain.

"I knew I would hurt you. I'd like you to know my side."

"Please tell me exactly what happened." Her voice was barely audible as she struggled to hold herself together.

"I don't mind a fair fight Kate. We were both out to win customers and I figured that even with a sizeable concern behind him, I could, knowing contacts he would have been allocated, still handle the competition."

She was perplexed. "But you have a Company behind you - that's why you went to Africa?"

"At first, yes. Then I decided to set up on my own, and for a while things went well. I made it my business to socialise; many of my customers had become friends who switched their allegiance when they learned of my plans. I undercut the big boys for a time but was soon operating on an equal footing. There's a healthy profit margin in pharmaceuticals."

"And Duncan came along and undercut *your* prices?" she asked numbly.

"Hell no. Nobody minds that Kate. We all do it to get established. It was par for the course and something I foresaw before I quit - and why I decided to have my base at the source of need, rather than supply. I was surprised they didn't offer to base Duncan out there for the same reason."

She pondered the irony of a situation in which she might have gone out to Africa as Duncan's wife, only to meet Tom who had left her behind. She resisted questions that would betray her ignorance, knowing she was only on the periphery of discovering what she should have been the first to know.

"I'm sorry Kate. I don't come out of this very well either, but when generally accepted sweeteners were replaced by cash bribes....... Africa is a young country in terms of business.... It wasn't difficult."

"How did you find out?"

"I didn't need to. My own fellow was African. He told me of the vast sums Duncan was paying to those who could pull strings."

There were other, more straightforward questions she wanted to ask in order to contract this ordeal, but only by letting him assume she knew the background, would he provide the full picture.

"Was it personal?"

"Only to the extent he wanted to convince the Company he could win as much business for them as I did. He was ambitious for board level status."

"He's not the most secure person; I expect he needed to prove himself."

But Heydon was not prepared for her to delude him. "Sufficiently secure to gamble his shirt, and the Company's money at the tables every night, and then to use his winnings to put me out of business?"

So now she had it. The blood drained from her face, and she gripped the sides of her chair so he should not see how fundamentally he had shaken her. "Did he always win?"

Heydon drained his glass angrily. "Of course not. But then he'd cash cheques .... borrow .. even on one occasion sold his airline ticket and arranged for his wallet and briefcase to be stolen from his room... Of course my rep knew other locals working at the hotel who didn't appreciate police investigation. That's when I phoned the Company Kate. And not until afterwards did I discover you were his wife; I swear."

"I don't understand how one led to the other."

"He reported the loss and offered a reward for the briefcase containing company documents - even tried to involve me. When that didn't wash he asked me to revoke my call to the U.K. ... say it was all a mistake. Pleaded with me to play the white man and consider what it might do to his wife and family. Sorry Kate, but the only decent thing about him was that he loved you and the kids - absolutely distraught at the effect his stupidity would have on you all. He took out a photograph and there you were looking up at me. You can imagine the impact. Guess that was the first time in my life I had proof that fact could be stranger than fiction."

"Did you tell Duncan about us?"

"No. Would you rather I had?"

She shook her head. Time in the past with Tom was something Duncan could not be allowed to ruin. If only there could somehow have been a memento, a photograph of this evening; something to which she could refer in the future and know that it had actually been real. But that which has faded and disappeared cannot be recorded. Desolation encased her like lead and kept her from him. "Tom .. I think I'd like to go home."

"I didn't mean for it to be like this Kate. I don't understand – you're more shaken than I thought."

"You knew what you were coming to tell me."

"But you look so devastated."

"It surprises you?"

He supposed it did. Having assumed she not only knew the facts behind her husband's dismissal but had had time to come to terms with circumstances, he had thought she would the more easily handle the explanation of his own reason for taking action. He had even hoped she might agree to see him again. It seemed fate played its cruellest tricks at times of deepest happiness for that which he now hoped for was surely what she had long dreamed of.

"You thought we would have separated over it?" she asked directly, but the appearance of the waiter spared him a reply, and he covered the bill with bank notes and dismissed the change. "I may as well come clean Tom, We didn't, because I've never been honest enough to face the possibility that Duncan was the compulsive gambler you've confirmed. I always looked for other explanations."

"You mean you didn't know? Oh my God."

She shook her head, and though now tightly in control, her eyes glistened in the candlelight. "You said the only decent thing about him was that his love for me was genuine."

He did not respond, regretting the sensitivity he had attributed to his adversary who would have appropriated it without a qualm had he been party to the conversation. He was aware of Kate continuing. "Which means that he needs me, and that being so, I know that I won't find the strength to rebuff him. I'm sorry you were badly affected Tom."

"You'll stay with him! Kate I don't understand you." He did not look at her; her rejection now openly offending him.

"I don't think I understand myself."

The beautiful, fragile bubble that had gathered again with such speed around her dreams, had burst with no warning at all, leaving her bereft, alone and vulnerable.

"Please take me home Tom."

He drove her back to the boutique. "Kate we can't ... I won't part from you like this. Look. I'd no idea – we must talk."

Not through any will, but rather because she had been rendered numb, she was unresponsive. His voice became taut. "I'll check up on you now and then." The kiss he had given so casually when he had collected her, but which had aroused such intensity in her, and for which she now hungered again, was withheld.

"Oh yes," she wept as she drove home from the boutique. "I'd like so much, so very much for someone to check on me, to be cherished for my own sake. How could I have been so dumb; so moronic as not to realise?"

In three weeks Duncan would be back, trying to convince her that he had been selected for a lucrative job with a high profile company. She could already hear the persuasive tones. 'We'll, just have to go through a period of adjustment Kate. Stick with me honey - we'll soon be flying, you'll see.'

SAFE AS HOUSES

And how despicable, how dishonest that in being dutifully solicitous of he who needed her strength but had never given a damn for her own well being, she had turned away from the one man for whom she had yearned. Today he had held out his hand, fired her again, but stunned and overwhelmed by what he had told her, she had held back from him.

She derived some measure of comfort from the solitary stretches of the long night if only by allowing herself to be convinced that it was all a ghastly nightmare. But if Duncan's gambling were unreal, then the evening with Tom must also have been so. And to have experienced the sheer joy, the untroubled peace of the latter, necessitated the profound pain of the other. If only the numbness that followed enlightenment had not prevented her from talking, and taking comfort from his reappearance, she might not now feel so disembodied, so remote and abstract, so keenly blank where Tom wasn't. And though he may not have provided her with dispassionate answers, in talking together she might have been helped towards a clearer conclusion. She yearned for him and having no tangible evidence of their togetherness, she clung to the sense of loss, the desolate feeling of emptiness, because that was all she now had of him.

Next morning she put a call through to International Enquiries. If Charles had moved house, it would surely be to a larger one to accommodate a family that must have materialised by now. The agony since she had known, the anxiety and resentment, all combined to feed the panic that had begun at the dinner table last night and today threatened to make rational and pertinent questions impossible.

"Why Kate! Hi there! Ella-Mae - it's Kate .. no .... Kate from Blighty!"
She hadn't bargained for a social call and said quickly, "Charles I'm just off to a business meeting but needed to contact Duncan urgently."

"Business meeting." She could feel he was groping for time. "Why Kate that sounds pretty high powered. Congratulations - I'd no idea you were back in harness." He was trying to assess why, in view of the way circumstances had evolved, she should imagine Duncan was here.

"Duncan's been in the States for some weeks now Charles. I understood he was calling on you to finalise matters."

The ensuing silence provided the answer she should not have needed. Duncan had, he told her awkwardly, wound things up years ago - as soon as Kate had returned to England in fact. As he had understood the situation, her husband had decided to invest elsewhere.

"At your request Charles?"

There was an indistinct murmuring that she assumed to be an indication to his wife that this was not after all the occasion for social exchanges.

"Water under the bridge now Kate. Let's just say our views on company policy didn't exactly coincide."

"Or business ethics?"

"Kate, just let it go honey. Hell .. - why are you asking me now?"

"Because I didn't know to ask you then. Charles why didn't you tell me? Does Duncan have any outstanding debts to you?"

"The answer to your first question is, I suppose, cowardice. Then I figured you upped and left because he *had* told you. To the second, none that haven't been dealt with. But neither were there any assets Kate."

"That comes as no surprise. I just need to know where we stand."

"Sure."

So evidently it was still 'we', but notwithstanding, he told her that if ever she was on their side of the pond she'd be mighty welcome. She hadn't after all seen their brood - there were four of them now.

"My love to them all Charles. I envy you."

"Yeah? You should be here at bedtime! Bye Kate. Take care of yourself honey eh?"

She nodded because no words would come. She put down the receiver and tried to hug the loneliness from herself, but the longing for Tom left her hollow and desolate.

CHAPTER TWENTY TWO

Duncan twice delayed his return, and Kate who had resumed a punishing schedule in the north, returned one day to be handed a cable from him.

"I opened it in case it was an e.t.a. and he needed collecting," Emmeline explained.

'Postponing homecoming for further month,' she read. 'Am onto something really promising. Can't wait to tell you. Duncan.'

"You seem to specialise in men who love you from a distance Kate." And Kate recognised the request for an update on both Tom and Duncan.

"The evening I spent with Tom was truly memorable, and thanks to your encouragement Emm, I really enjoyed it. We didn't embark on a relationship, and I doubt I shall see him again for a long time."

"Um, acquired a wife and family in the intervening years, eh? Don't they all?"

"Including Duncan," Kate mused. "Wonder how many we were supposed to have had."

When he did appear, it was flamboyantly, by taxi, and bearing expensive gifts. "Got a last minute cancellation - didn't want to drag you out at such an ungodly hour honey, so I stayed in London and took the afternoon train." She put the roses in water. "They're beautiful. How was Charles?"

"Fine. Sends his love. Good to get everything wound up satisfactorily."

"It must have been a relief to you both."

"That's in the past Kate. It's the future that matters." Nonchalantly he poured two brandies, and wandered into the lounge.

"I agree. It's time we discussed the future."

He drew a small package from his inside pocket. There was no mistaking the Tiffany wrapping. Swallowing hard, she realised that despite her affluence and success, she still didn't buy expensive jewellery. Her suits were beautifully cut, the accessories tastefully appropriate, but habits of a lifetime containing neither waste nor excess, clung tight. But this was not the time for reflection. If she were not careful, the moment for confronting him would elude her.

SAFE AS HOUSES

"Open it," he urged with impatience at her lack of overt gratitude.

She turned the package over in her hands several times before handing it back to him. "A good night at the tables was it Duncan?"

"What!"

Having recouped the initiative, she said calmly, "Shall we stop pretending? I know what happened six years ago. Stupidly I've buried my head in the sand ever since because I wanted to believe you were in contract work."

He tossed back the brandy and hands sought refuge deep inside his pockets as he faced the French window. "How did you find out?"

"It's not important. Not even what you did is important now."

He turned abruptly and gripped her shoulders. "The gift is to show how much I love you. I swear it Kate. I don't want a life without you."

"Give it to someone who'll ignore its cost. For me the price is too high."

Releasing his hold, he asked abjectly, "Kate, if I were ill would you leave me? The compulsion to gamble is something I can no more help than having a brain tumour. I need you. I can't make it without you."

He had touched the conscience that for her was destructive of self. She knew that whatever argument she would enact, she would ultimately make the renunciation it demanded of her. She would pay the price of the gift from Tiffanys, and all that it signified, but perhaps when she had paid there would come a sort of peace. She was surprised by her lack of emotion.

"When did it start?"

"In a casual way, before you came to the States. It gave me a buzz -that's all it was in the beginning. Then I did well and got a bit of a name in certain circles - it's how I got the capital to set up. Then you happened along and I genuinely intended to work for every cent that came my way. I watched when you came to help - coming down at weekends after holding down a demanding job all week. I marvelled at your energy - you got such a kick out of doing so much. But Kate - it was unadulterated hard work! With clients for whom I could hide a little of the truth from the tax authorities, and have my palm greased in return, I guess the temptation was too great."

"You mean lie."

"Oh honey .. don't be naive. You surely don't imagine it doesn't go on?"

She ignored the jibe and he continued. "Later I met up with Charles again at a ball game ... he asked if I was interested in setting up a partnership."

"Because of your ability to defraud ... surely not."

"Because of my ability, period - proven when we were students together. Sadly I didn't have his background to capitalise on that ability. Not much use being brain of the year if you haven't got a pater to go with it. Charles was always gonna take over from his old man. Anyway, I needed more capital than we had."

"Which is when you started playing around with our investments. Why on earth didn't you just say. We could have sold them to raise the money you needed - and taken a loan out for the rest."

"Not quite that simple. And if I'd told you I was playing a high risk strategy to avoid having debts around our necks?"

"I wouldn't have agreed to the type of high risk I now know about."

In the past it had not been difficult to convince her - because he had convinced himself - that their problems could be laid at her door, but now he was forced to recognise that she was completely unmoved by his argument. Her anger, so justified, gave her strength, but even in that strength she could not allow herself to break free; a healing, forbidden freedom. She wished she could define her emotions for it would make them more tolerable. He forced a smile, advancing a little towards her, but she was in control; had no need to draw away to indicate he was cutting no ice.

"Can you believe it Kate - my biggest reason was to be able to give you the best? I was always afraid of losing you."

"No. And if we are to discuss the subject - and I must be insane to do so - you'd better dispense with the make-believe Duncan."

Tacitly he yielded to her demand, asking meekly, "What did Charles say?"

"Nothing at the time. He assumed my departure was a result of developments. I gather you took similar risks with money belonging to the partnership?"

"So how...?"

"I telephoned Charles some weeks ago."

She provided no clue as to how he stood with her and he decided to press home the advantage he had been aware of when appealing to her conscience. "I've been jealous of you Kate. If you hadn't been so involved in your business we'd have been OK. If only you'd needed me, leaned on me...I wouldn't have taken risks with the job. I'd have been strong for you."

She thought what it would have been like to lean against someone; really lean with all the weight of trust in another's capacity to care for her, and wondered which came first - the demonstration of a greater strength by the one, or absolute trust from the other. Recalling Mrs. Charlesworth she decided it was neither. People incapable, or too selfish, to carry themselves, generally found those who could find the resources for two.

SAFE AS HOUSES

"Duncan don't seek my sympathy by trying to delude either of us. You didn't want children, so God help me I sought fulfilment in a market stall." He pleaded with her to credit him with at least the refusal to bring up children on a game of chance. "I wanted them just as much as you did Kate - truly I did!"

"Enough to invent them? To use them to gain sympathy?" He threw a questioning glance at her, but she ignored it and said, "You don't have the capacity to love Duncan. You need, but you don't love."

"I'm sorry, I forgot to leave money. Did you pay the mortgage?"

"I imagine we would have been repossessed if I hadn't."

"Hell Kate, the cash for that necklace would pay for my default, and I've brought money home to clear any overdraft." His eyes, devoid now of arrogance and deception, were pleading with her. "You can't abandon me. You'll see a year from now, I'll buy you something with money I've really earned." He threw his arms around her, his head heavy on her shoulder. "I will try. You gotta help me. Kate you're the only one who can."

She pulled away but he saw the sudden sharp intake of breath and eyes close in surrender to the inevitable, and knew he had stumbled on the right phrase in the nick of time. She wouldn't leave him now.

"I met with Tom Heydon," she said. "He was in England on a visit." And in that split second, by harbouring no deceit, she knew she had committed herself to standing by him. But he appeared peculiarly disinterested in where they had met, or under what circumstances; did not even register surprise that they had known each other, and said finally, "Heydon? Tom Heydon eh. Now there's a chap who would have given you cause to worry about other women and no mistake!"

Certain he was unaware of the pain he inflicted, she pulled from him.

"Guess we are both drained," he said warily. "It's been quite a day."

She knew of Tom's ability to reach right down through all the accumulated layers of defence to the woman she really was, but if life offered her a choice between gambler and womaniser, she would trust herself to neither. Strangely the resolve enabled her to rise above the raw hurt burning inside.

"I'll go back to what I was before Tom came back," she vowed silently. "I'll cope on my own. I don't need him. How could I have been so wrong?" In a mist of confusion she wondered whether the one's inclination to stray would have troubled her less than the other's obsession with the tables. But only for a moment. Deep down she knew she would have been powerless to stop loving Tom whatever he had done had fate decreed her life differently.

SAFE AS HOUSES

So perhaps she was fortunate in that Duncan, who would no longer possess the power to break her heart, was the husband to whom she was committed.

To avoid having time and temptation on his hands, he suggested that until Duggie Grant was out of hospital, he should take over the local deliveries until his own schedules were developed.

"I shall be away often in the next few months," she said, grateful that in Emm he would have a tougher taskmaster than she, if he stepped out of line.

When and wherever possible, she and Jonathan planned their schedules to allow for a meeting somewhere in Europe, to exchange ideas and contacts. Soon his plane would be landing at Orly. She repaired her make-up, donned an emerald green jacket over the navy skirt and added some sheets of rough estimates to her briefcase. She could work on those if he were delayed; a routine she had perfected long since in order to get her 'sixty seconds worth of distance run'. She ordered coffee, then seeing him framed in the doorway, raised her hand to catch his eye.

"You've had a good trip, I can tell!" Kate said.
"One of the best. What about you?"
"I'm going to need wings on my suitcase soon!"
"You'll have to get another assistant Kate - here at the marketing end I mean. I know you've increased the factory staff and given Emm a 2 I.C."
She interrupted. "I've got an experienced PA in the office now."
"Even so, you can't keep this rate up."
Regaling her with developments he said suddenly, "You want outlets here in Paris Kate! That's why you've not expanded further in UK."
"I've got an idea I intend to put to the Cardules tonight."
"Don't make yourself vulnerable."
"I'm not about to lease premises in central Paris. And I promise you I've thought through every angle."
"Of course you will have done."
They laughed in the relaxed, unfettered way of those totally comfortable both with each other and the surroundings in which they find themselves.
"Keep me posted. Meanwhile I'll wine and dine the Simpson buyers and fly home tomorrow. Then a whole two weeks leave with Val and the boys. And I wish my cousin would do the same."
"I don't think Duncan would welcome two whole weeks of me, and you well know I'd swap the whole of this to have had a family to spend time

SAFE AS HOUSES

with. But as I haven't, the Company makes a good substitute. And the Cardules may provide all the break I need," she assured him.

In fact they responded positively to her request to rent office space. "Une excellente idée, ma chérie!" Madame enthused, and Armand absorbed the financial advantage of sharing a secretary, and providing accommodation for Kate's clients. She had expected to do at least some persuading and was thrilled her suggestion had met with such unequivocal acceptance.

Armand turned to his wife. "We shall go to Kate's favourite restaurant and celebrate our collaboration. Wizout any paperwork at all, we make ze contract! Ze best kind I think."

Indeed the contracts that had proved most tenacious over the years, had been those entered into without formality. Despite years of practice, decision-making still took its toll, but tonight she relaxed at her favourite restaurant. Close proximity of tables with red checked tablecloths and candle-grease laden bottles precluded the separateness of groups, whilst crescendos of conversation and laughter contained the very essence of Paris. As she manoeuvred herself into a seat, an elderly man with effervescent eyes and white shoulder length hair, sat down at an adjacent table and acknowledged her in the courteous manner of his countrymen. "Madame," he said simply, with a slow nod of the head that rose again to reveal a disarming smile. He assumed her to be French also, "but not Parisian, Madame," he observed after some minutes. And as evenings are prone to do when congenial company share good food and wine, this one no less, passed rapidly and with immense pleasure for all concerned.

"One day I think Paris will adopt you," he said. "Maybe not yet, but certainly one day, for you have already fallen under her spell."

"And that of her people," she said, aided by the wine and general conviviality into feeling serenely content in a way she had not known for so long; a way that allowed her to enjoy the moment for its own sake, conditioned by neither past nor future. Not since buying the cottage from Mr. Rees had she felt so at ease. Even if subsequent events made it difficult to sustain the correctness of her decision, she knew she would not regret the making of it. It may yet exact its price, but she would be willing to pay.

He stood as she prepared to leave, gently moving her chair in the restricted space. "Madame, it 'as been a great pleasure, even if as an old man I 'ave indulged in a little self delusion. But what is ze harm in that?" His English was impeccable.

"None at all Monsieur. Of that I'm certain."

SAFE AS HOUSES

As they left, the air was warm, fresh, and gently in unison with their mood. Armand stepped between Marie-Jeanne and Kate, linking arms with both.

"How you say in England? We make a good pretty team, yes?"

"A good pretty team," she agreed as they climbed into a taxi. And then, "Tomorrow I must advertise. "I need a bright young woman with the right attitude. She'll have time to learn as the business expands."

"Then I shall introduce you to le directeur of a business school I know. I am sure he will have ze student to recommend," Armand promised.

Memorising those who had been commended, she singled out a quiet young woman who was doing an equally efficient job of summing up Kate. 'Makes her own clothes,' Kate observed, 'and doesn't make a bad job of it either. Sticks to simple lines and depends on accessories to ring the changes. Aware of other people too; her popularity was evident from their spontaneous reactions. Looks as if she could stand alone when necessary.'

And so Danielle Létrange was the first appointee in Kate's European base.

"The appointment will be on a temporary basis for six months during which time I look forward to being impressed." Smiling at her newest recruit, Kate was reminded that she herself was no longer young. "Enjoy the vacation. I shall meet with you in four week's to help you establish a routine that will mirror the one in England. One third of your time will be for the Cardules, though of course you will need to exercise flexibility. Keep a schedule, and as long as you are working a ratio of two to one, all will be as we anticipate. If not, I shall review the situation. I would not wish them to be at a disadvantage." They walked out into the college gardens to discuss the appointment in more detail. "You are sure you don't mind working alone for so many hours? You're very young and might miss your friends. That will be the nature of the job for some time. Phone immediately if there are situations you can't handle. My secretary will always find me."

"I will try not to escalate your telephone, Madame."

"The phone will be a small price to pay for getting things right. And now I suggest you enjoy the end of term. Where are you going for a holiday?"

"I shall remain in Paris Madame. I 'ad to pay for my room until August end, so if you wish me to go to ze hotel to receive office equipment, I can easily do. I do not wish payment; I am yet a student."

Suspecting from the conversation there were no strong family ties, Kate said, "If you can be released from college for a few days, why don't you

SAFE AS HOUSES

come to England with me tomorrow and see the organisation at first hand? Be at the hotel by 8.30 and we'll visit a client and go direct to Orly."

"It is all so incroyable. I did not go to England since I was sixteen."

"Such a long time ago!"

"It seem a long time because so much 'appen. My mother she die in my first year at college, and my Papa he is already marry wiz someone else."

'She wanted me to know that, and having got it off her chest, she'll probably never mention it again,' Kate thought. 'She's still hurting, and the someone is resented.' The younger woman was looking at her quizzically. "Was there something you wanted to ask me?"

"Madame, only...I ask do you always make up your mind so rapide?"

Kate was relieved that no substantial skeleton was to be released from a cupboard. "Only when my instinct is very strong! Most often I spend tortuous weeks weighing the pros and cons."

A warm summer evening enabled Danielle to see England at its best. Stopping just once at an old coaching inn for refreshment, they made light of the rest of the journey before drawing up at the boutique with its expansive bow windows on either side of a Georgian doorway. Kate was aware of someone above in the sewing room but before she could investigate, Mrs. Grant appeared on the staircase.

"Why Mrs. Carter, you're back early. I was just finishing off the last of the 'Country Lass' collection."

"You shouldn't be working so late! Mrs. Grant, this is Danielle."

The seamstress greeted the newcomer genially and they followed her to the dressmaker's model where cool blue and white daisies in finest lawn were thrown into dramatic effect by the much deeper blue of the satin trim. Just a hint of cotton lace petticoat peeped from beneath. Danielle knelt to admire the hem stitching more closely. "Never have I seen such work! So Engleesh .... but Swiss too. And I can also see it by ze Seine. Please what is 'lass'?"

"Someone like you!" Mrs. Grant was delighted by such appreciation. Turning to Kate, she asked, "How did the orders go Mrs. Carter?"

"Enough to keep you all busy from dawn to dusk," Kate assured her, the travel weariness ebbing away. "And that, by the way, is the title of the next collection - Dawn to Dusk. Where's Emmeline? Did she leave a message?"

Mrs. Grant appeared uncomfortable. "No... no she didn't."

"Never mind. I'll call her."

"I think maybe she isn't there tonight. Tomorrow will be better."

"But I can see her here tomorrow. I'll leave a note on my way home."

SAFE AS HOUSES

"I can do that for you - I expect I shall go before you."

Mrs. Grant delved in her bag for a pen. Though she could not fathom why, Kate knew by complying, she would relieve her of a very obvious stress.

"Does Mrs. Grant make all the dresses?" Danielle asked.

"When we first had the boutique, but not any longer. She always makes the first copy of Emm's designs, and each is beautifully cut in top quality fabrics as you see. It is with those I create interest in both home and European markets. From each of our individual designs, less exacting and cheaper versions are made for department stores - hence the factory."

"Just one designer and one chief executive?" And Kate admired the young woman's astuteness in picking up where they were vulnerable.

"Not quite. We both now have assistants. But I have not yet found another designer of the same calibre."

"Or your own commitment?"

"That we shall have to wait and see," Kate smiled. "Yes, we are a little thin at the top. It has been a question of economics and survival."

"And if you were ill Madame? The Cardules tell how hard you work."

"I won't be. I thrive with the business; we are mutually perpetuating." She looked at her watch. "I'll install you in the flat and make tracks for home." Mrs. Grant shot her an anguished glance, and Danielle, observing the questioning raise of Kate's eyebrows, said she would go and unpack.

"I'll show you where everything is, and then yes I would like a few minutes with Mrs. Grant. Thank you Danielle."

"C'est vraiment joli!" Danielle's delight was spontaneous as she moved towards the window overlooking the woods.

"A version of a room I once occupied as a little girl" Kate said and the nostalgia was unmistakable. She retraced her steps to Mrs. Grant.

"What is it Mrs. G? Duncan?"

"I don't think he's at home this evening." Their acquaintance was too long established for signals not to have been transmitted.

"Is he gambling again?"

"Maybe. I could be wrong. A store rang up because deliveries were late."

"Our deliveries are never late," Kate flashed angrily, and Mrs Grant laid a hand on her arm, wanting somehow to take away the invidious hurt.

"Mr. Carter was detained in Cambridge. He still had deliveries on the van and promised to take them next day. But that meant he couldn't collect the silk order, so there had to be some rearranging. Duggie offered, and Miss Charlesworth agreed so all would be on schedule by the time you got back."

SAFE AS HOUSES

The tiredness was there again as her embarrassment turned to humiliation.

"And Mr. Jonathan phoned to say why not drive over at the weekend?"

"But I only saw him on Tuesday."

That Mrs. Grant had engaged Jonathan in conversation was evident; for what reason she had yet to discover. There was something she had not felt it in her place to divulge - not a problem from which Emm would suffer. Knowing Kate was due back this evening, she would likely have coffee percing, eager for a Paris report. She would get an update on developments that for some reason Mrs Grant didn't want her to become aware of tonight. To Kate's knowledge, the Grants were the only one connected with the business who knew of his past activities.

But when she rang Emm's bell, there was no reply, and a brief glance through the window confirmed her absence. Disappointed, for it was with Emm more than anyone that she could unwind, she got back behind the wheel. She would telephone later, for Emm must be the first to know of Danielle's official appointment. She knew precisely what her rejoinder would be - 'So, you've got a foothold in your precious Paris at last! Knew it was only a matter of time!'

CHAPTER TWENTY THREE

Strangely Emm was disconcerted on meeting Danielle. "Morning," she greeted them both quietly, and the effusive hug, and 'Hi - had a good trip?' were notably absent. To Kate she said flatly, "Glad you're back. How were the new designs received?"
"As always my talented friend - rapturously!" Then aside, "You alright?"
"Fine. I didn't realise you'd bring a visitor."
"Not a visitor. One of the team! I did what you've always challenged me to do - acted totally on instinct without consulting anyone! I've opened up our French office."
Emmeline leaned forward, her fingers seeking support from the desk.
"Emm, it's alright. I haven't bought a whole avenue!" And even as she uttered the assurance, she knew that normally, trusting implicitly in her judgement on the business front, Emm wouldn't have given a tinker's cuss if she had. As it was, her reaction punctured Kate's confidence both in the new acquisition, and her own perspicacity.
"You've committed us?"
"I've given my word."
"Which for you is the same thing."
Emmeline apologised to Danielle. "Forgive me. I don't feel too well. You'll love working for Kate. She's the best, as I expect you've already discovered."
So much for the claim that verbal communication was barely necessary between them, and for surmising Emm's opening gambit would have been 'Welcome aboard! Kate's a menace but we manage to survive despite her!'
The atmosphere manifestly tense, Danielle turned her attention elsewhere.
"Emm what is it?" Her whispered question was urgent and pleading.
"Not now Kate. I hadn't expected you to bring someone back." She forced a grin. "You see how we all depend on the predictability we tease you about. Hell what a mess...what timing. And here's another one right on cue." Angry bitterness spilled over as she signalled the arrival of Mrs. Grant, who offered the merest nod in Emmeline's direction making it plain

that were it not for the visitor, she would have ignored her completely. Kate could hardly conceive of such a situation. A harmony born of a regard for each other's skill, and affectionate tolerance of characteristics, had been the keynote of their relationship. Any differences were immediately thrown into the open and afforded the degree of vehemence they merited. True there had been strain when working against the clock or competing with fatigue, but nothing like this. On any occasion in the past, she could have guaranteed a visitor the warmest reception with exactly the right balance of light hearted banter from Emm, and deferential politeness from Mrs. Grant. So why today the inordinate tension?

She would insult neither Danielle's perception nor Emm's genuine dilemma, by pretence or excuse and said, "Mrs. Grant please show Danielle around the workroom and introduce her as a new member of staff."

"She's joining the company? Oh I'm sorry Mrs. Carter, I had no idea."

"Fortunately last evening provided for a more favourable first impression. I had intended to make the position clear to you as soon as I had introduced her to Emmeline, but sadly the atmosphere has hardly been conducive.."

"Forgive me, I don't speak any French m'dear." Her manner distinctly subdued, Mrs. Grant indicated the direction of the sewing room.

"Danielle's English is excellent," Kate intervened tersely. It was an unmistakable warning not to allow anyone to discuss the matter that was causing such abrasion here in the boutique, and of which she herself was as yet in ignorance. She supposed Duncan to be at the bottom of it and that perhaps Emm had handled the situation in such a manner as to incur the strongest antipathy from Mrs. Grant. That being so, the older employee was at fault since in her own absence, Emm's word was law.

The two left the salon, and Kate, conscious of the most extraordinary negativity, apologised for Duncan's failure to deliver on time. "It can only have added to the frustration. I know you were all working full tilt on the collection, and he must have been the last straw. I can't tackle him about it because he didn't come home last night. Emm, as soon as Danielle returns to Paris, I will discuss it with you, I promise."

"Kate stop! Stop being so self-effacing as if you are responsible. How the hell have we got into a situation where *you* are apologising to *me*? I'm sorry; that must be the first time anyone has pleaded with you to shut up when the hardest thing in the world is to get you to talk."

Intuition warning her that what she was about to hear was going to strain every nerve, Kate sat down, her mind racing ahead to the possibilities... a

SAFE AS HOUSES

lost client ...money borrowed from staff.... newspapers... court action... "Just tell me."

Whatever in the next moments she imagined, she only knew that nothing could have prepared her for what she actually heard.

"Kate." There was a devastating pause whilst Emm came to terms with the fact that the truth could not be made less virulent by the choice of one phrase over another to give it expression. "Duncan didn't come home last night because he was with me."

No words came. Kate stared, dumbly incredulous, and Emm waited, as she had prepared herself, for her words to become a reality for the last person in the world she would have chosen to destroy. She met Kate's disbelieving eyes and saw a girl made vulnerable by poverty and gentle nature, fighting to survive the mordant acerbity of those whose school she had been told it was a privilege to share.

"I'm the same bitch I was then Kate."

"No!"

Gazing into a space somewhere between them, Kate was sickened by the implication of the changed circumstances. The surface of her mind was frozen by the brutal realisation that in losing the marital partner, she would also lose the professional, and she could find no more than a superficial response. Questions reverberated in her head with the dizzy repetition of a roller coaster, whilst she herself sat motionless. Panic began to envelop her as if at any moment she would break in pieces, as she made a desperate mental clutch at that which was slipping away, and her body shook with the thoughts that tumbled through it.

"Kate please say something! Anything... Oh God."

Her desperate plea drew a response. "Emm, that I'm not enough for Duncan is something I've long accepted and can't pretend to be shocked by. But for my replacement to be you is something I can no more describe than define my own lifeblood. I don't have any words. There are things you must know. I should have told you before. We must talk. Not now, I'm too stunned. Later."

Both were grateful for the tentative reappearance of Danielle who was deferring to Mrs. Grant's cognisance of the situation to decide whether the moment was opportune. Almost audibly, Kate ordered herself to be composed, whilst Emmeline, holding her partner in the greatest affection for so doing, made no such attempt, since in her own case it would have been futile.

SAFE AS HOUSES

"They are exquisite," Danielle addressed Emmeline with genuine admiration. "Madame told me so much about your work on ze flight to England, but I did not dream to see so many such beautiful clothings."

"They are for beautiful occasions Danielle. But it's Kate who has found the fabrics, and created the markets for them." Emm was obviously near to tears, whilst Kate could only think that nothing in the world was worth this. "Kate is the Company, Danielle. I'm glad she has found you."

"I think it is as Madame explained - ze partnership of minds and expertise; it is ze combination which has ze puissance."

Emmeline's eyes dropped to avoid Mrs. Grant's challenging gaze at the innocent expression of such a poignant observation, and said merely, "I hope Kate has found a like mind in you Danielle."

"I hope also Madame. I am so happy to be ze Paris secretary."

"I'll take Danielle over to the factory then perhaps you will have your lunch with her in the flat Mrs. Grant. Emmeline and I have business to discuss." Kate's tone, though curt, made Mrs. Grant aware there was no need for hints and innuendoes. The problem was in the open, and waited to be addressed by the only people it concerned.

In the car, Danielle glanced at Kate. That something was seriously amiss beneath that ultimate professionalism there could be no doubt, as indeed was Madame's intent that she collude with the deception. Madame Emmeline had said none of the things her employer had predicted on the flight; instead she had been abrasive, as if she, Danielle were an unforeseen encumbrance. There was no option other than to use her lack of the English understatement to pierce the barrier Kate was determined to maintain, and then to hope her intrusion would not result in it being restructured, for she had no money to follow through the offer she was about to make.

"Madame I see there are problems to correct. I zink it good idée for me to go to London; I will comply your schedule whenever you wish it."

Kate placed her hand on the younger woman's arm. "Danielle, London is very expensive unless you have friends there, which I suspect is not the case. You are correct in sensing a problem I didn't anticipate, and which does need my attention. I very much regret that your introduction to the Company has been marred in this way. Thank you for being sensitive. If you are agreeable, I shall telephone my cousin with whom I work closely. He will arrange for you to see his larger manufacturing unit."

"I am happy wiz anything you arrange Madame. And I give you my condolences."

SAFE AS HOUSES

Kate smiled at the choice of word, yet perhaps after all it was the most appropriate since a loss was most definitely going to be involved.

Of course he would be happy to have Danielle, Jonathan assured her, and yes his P. A. would arrange a full itinerary. She could stay the night - Val wouldn't mind - and accompany him to London next day.

"Jonathan if only I'd known before I left Paris."

"That's sorted Danielle out. What about you?"

She caught her breath, but uncertain how much he knew, left space for him to continue. "Emm phoned - asked me when you were due, and hinted at trouble. I gather Duncan is involved. Kate isn't it time you kicked him out?"

So Emmeline had allowed discretion to rule.

When at last they had the time and privacy to talk, Emm said, "If Jonathan hadn't told me you were following on his heels I would have flown out to tell you rather than deceive you any longer."

"Emm, are you trying to say it wasn't just a fling....an affair that's over?"

"Years ago I warned you I was like my mother, capable only of taking."

"Not true. You've given more than I could have dreamed of."

"I've designed because I love doing exactly that, and am damn lucky you gave me the chance. No one else would have taken me on."

"That was their loss. This company has thrived on your talent."

"Talent that needed you to give it credence. I've had none of the angst whilst you've worn yourself to a shred finding markets, only to burn midnight oil on the admin."

"Do you think I have one single regret! It's been my reason to be. And Emm I wouldn't have had any other partner."

"I'm an employee."

"You'll always be my partner."

"Not when you learn I'm about to steal your husband."

Suddenly that which they had met to discuss, and for a while contrived to put aside, was again sharply in focus. Each accepted without awkwardness the silence that followed. It was necessary to draw strength from it; to ensure that whatever needed to be faced could be tackled without emotion. Assuming an onus to acquaint Emm with facts she had long concealed. Kate said, "I don't blame Duncan for looking elsewhere. I haven't been as open minded as I might have been, but there things you ought to know."

"Kate, I know Duncan gambles if that's what you are about to tell me."

The revelation, with all its implications was so stunning that Kate was stupefied. At last she said weakly, "Why doesn't it matter?"

SAFE AS HOUSES

It was if she had just discovered some dreadful failing within herself. What needless distance had she allowed his gambling to put between them, and what harm had really been done? What destruction of another had she caused in allowing it to assume such proportions.

Recognising the strange mixture of maturity and childlike gullibility in the friend with whom she had worked for so long, Emm asked, "Shall I leave you alone?"

Kate nodded helplessly. "But first tell me why it doesn't matter Emm"

"Isn't everything we do a gamble? Another man could plan his career to give his family security, and then on an ordinary day be told he's redundant; he can't handle it, takes to drink, and goes down hill at speed. Everyone who sets up a business is a gambler to some extent Kate."

The words went home. The enormity of her own gamble was, in these moments, being forcibly brought home to her as a cavernous crack rent the foundations of the friendship and trust on which she had built her company.

"We don't know that this might be the day we walk under a bus, or be told we have cancer. Why shouldn't someone make a profession out of dealing with chance, if that's what he does best? You have made an analogy with 'a bob on the dogs' and reduced his gambling to a matter of shame to be hidden at all costs. Kate, I *like* pretty things from Tiffany's. You won't find me handing them back!"

Kate cringed as she pictured them discussing her. "Have you thought of the consequences of losing?"

"I imagine the risks are commensurate with the Stock Exchange. But the financial markets are upper crust and respectable aren't they Kate?" She was deliberately cruel in an effort to give Kate the release of hating her, and added with a calculated casualness, "And you know damn well I wouldn't stay with a loser."

"Does everyone know?"

"About his being a gambler? Yes. And it's a measure of their love that they respected your obvious wish for it to remain undiscovered. And Mrs Grant knows about last night damn her. Don't worry, she adores you too much to have told anyone else." It was unbearable seeing Kate so broken but she could bring no comfort to such anguish since she herself was its cause. She couldn't feel pain as Kate did; didn't allow it to get inside her. Kindness, she decided, was an awful thing to be saddled with. The words had all been said, and were getting in the way. She closed the door quietly behind her, and left to warn Duncan that their secret was no longer.

SAFE AS HOUSES

Kate sat motionless, making no effort to dispel the numbness that for the moment was protective. Mrs. Grant tapped on the door. "Your favourite paté m'dear. Got it when I took Danielle to the shops this morning. She's taken a fair shine to you. I told her how lucky she was you chose her."

Kate brightened theatrically. "We must have a celebration to mark the opening of our Paris office, before Danielle goes back. Would you help me?" She reached the end of the sentence before her voice gave any hint of emotion.

"Course I will," and seeing the trembling that played around Kate's lips, said, "You don't deserve this. If I had liberty to speak my mind..."

"It's perhaps as well we don't voice our thoughts just now Mrs. Grant. There's been enough of that for one day."

"If you say so, but in my book there's a darned site more needs a saying."

Kate clasped her hand appreciatively. "May I leave you to arrange a small buffet - just for the staff?" She delved into her bag. "I suggest lunchtime on Friday." Fragile emotionally, she felt the need to keep a certain private space around her.

A professional gambler. She repeated the words over and over, and remembered Mr. Charlesworth's advice. "Find out what you're good at and go for it. No looking back." Bitterly she conceded to herself that the addition of one qualifying word - 'professional' separated her husband's gambling from her own mental association with the men in Big Grandma's pub who had raucously placed their bets, and then either losing their stakes or drinking their winnings, forced long suffering wives to find ways of making ends meet. Never had she divorced it from the fear of shame and squalor.

An army of questions charged through her consciousness. Was her perception of gambling, and not the act itself, the cause of the rift between them? She may have built a successful company but had she really changed from the timid child who had sat on the cellar steps listening to Dad maintain that the toffs and the poor were very similar - for didn't they both play with money they hadn't got? It was the folk in between with their aspirations and scruples who got hurt. Alex with intuitive wisdom had discerned some basic truths.

CHAPTER TWENTY FOUR

Duncan had a large brandy in his hand when she got home, but at least he was there.
"Don't be brittle Kate. I want to explain."
"Emmeline has already."
"Kate you know I can't bear to hurt you. We must talk."
"It's only my pride you've succeeded in wounding," she lied, wanting only to rush to his arms now that the stigma had been removed from his gambling. She had made it a problem and now, as Emm had left her in no doubt, she had only herself to blame.
"I understand why you've sought other company. Just a shock that it's Emm."
Aware of Kate's affinity with old-fashioned values, he had expected a mental battle lasting weeks, if not months. Now amazed by the unexpected reaction, he appropriated the long-suffering characteristics she attributed to him. It was expedient to appear bereft of protest, and meekly he said, "It means more than I can say that you don't hate me."
"I love you!" was all she wanted to cry out, but instead went to the kitchen to make coffee she didn't want, and with which she was already awash. She would return to Paris with Danielle, and stay, if only for one night. In her absence, they, as she, could decide on the next move.
Duncan followed her into the kitchen and with a need for activity she mechanically poured two cups. She would move out of the house that in any case she had always considered his. Finance would need to be arranged. The new office had swallowed up all current available equity, but as the Bank Manager seemed to fall over himself to increase her borrowing power she supposed there was no problem.
"How soon do you plan to make it official?" She posed a question to which he had given no serious consideration.
"It's not important."
"I think it is," she whispered. "I'll vacate as soon as is practicable."
"This is your home too."

SAFE AS HOUSES

It was as if they were two strangers, their responses taking each other by surprise, causing the situation to grow by the moment more brittle, and the artificially reasonable verbal interchange in danger of collapse.

"You'll want the equity. As at this point I can't buy you out, I see no alternative."

"And there we have the root of the problem Kate. No faith in me to provide for you."

Drained by guilt, she nodded meekly, "You found the house and raised the deposit, which I confess surprised me. Even then I doubted you. Emm's right. I'm sorry."

Composed, and confidently reassuring, he put an arm around her shoulder.

"Honey you've insisted on paying half the mortgage - it is *our* house. And as for the deeds - I've had that piece of youthful arrogance rectified. Look." He produced an envelope from his pocket. "I've turned it over to you. That's one decent thing I've done - maybe make up just a little?"

"But.."

"No. I won't listen to any protest. It is now solely in your name. You just need to sign here and I'll get the forms back to the Building Society. Then the house is yours. I guess you won't have a problem paying the mortgage alone from now on?"

"Of course not, but Duncan, I can't let you do this."

He pressed his finger lightly to her lips and smiled. "Allow me to do this for you, so your memories of me will not all be bad." He indicated again where she should sign. I should have taken it out in joint names from the start - selfish bastard that I am. Correction. Was a selfish bastard. Now my name can be deleted in favour of yours. At least I won't have that on my conscience for the rest of my life." He replaced the forms in the envelope. "Guess there's nothing more to say Kate. I'll go now and......"

"Duncan, before you go, there's something I have to tell you. Something I've wanted to tell you so often. It's pointless going into reasons now."

He listened intently as she told him about the cottage.... how she had bought it on impulse assuming the separation was destined to be permanent.

"Thanks for telling me. I wish you'd done it sooner but I guess you feared I would have gambled it away uh? Gambler I may be, but a fool, no. Gambling is a business - there are risks - but calculated ones. And the overall pattern is positive." He laughed. "This is a fine time to be telling each other so much - like husband and wife!"

"It's been my fault."

SAFE AS HOUSES

"I think maybe so honey. I guess that's why... well Emm doesn't make me feel guilty for playing the tables or not wanting a family. She enjoys my personality and the fun it can generate. You on the other hand take everything so seriously. Look, I don't wanna hurt you, but if you get involved in another relationship.."

"That isn't likely. I've no wish to mess up anyone else's life." Remorse was rapidly destroying her self-esteem and conscience exacted its price. "I shall raise a loan, and give you a cheque for half the current value of the cottage, which simply means it's been an asset you didn't know you had."

"OK. If it makes you feel better. And I shall arrange for what must be the most amicable of separations, with each looking after the other's interests in the manner I would have expected of you, and the manner you have at last realised, is also mine." He paused, "Not that it matters, but have you been receiving rent over the years?"

"No."

"None at all! You mean it's been empty . . . . just a refuge?"

"An elderly gentleman lives there."

"For nothing!"

"Yes."

"I don't want to criticise, but that doesn't seem very businesslike."

She made no response, and he left the room.

So she still had no inkling it had been her old fella, or rather the guy they had both worked for, who had enabled the purchase of the house. Amazing Alex had said nothing all these years, though given the nature of the man, not so incredible. He had stated the terms, had assumed trust on both sides. Duncan smiled wryly. His father-in-law wouldn't be too pleased at how little there was to show for the bulk that hadn't been included on the down payment, but as Kate had lacked for nothing, neither had he been given cause for concern. And in any case his precious daughter was more than capable of financing her own nest.

Kate slept badly that night, and woke gripped by anxiety that borrowing to set up the French office and privately paying Duncan his share of the cottage might prove a greater strain than she had considered when insisting on her course of action. But for her there had been no alternative and her resolve that the situation could and would be managed, afforded a strange sense of release. Thank God Emm had stopped her from destroying him.

She flew to Paris to discover its magic had faded; the emptiness inside her seeming to invade the very aspects of the city that had previously made her heart sing. And if Danielle in youthful deference felt unable to indicate she was not fooled by Kate's attempt at geniality, the Cardules demonstrated no such inhibition. Madame went straight to the point. "So did you lose your heart to another, or discover your 'usband as been ze unfaithful?"

Shocked by her accuracy, Kate smiled at the clean sweep administered to her English reserve. "It is possible to get upset about other things!"

"If there had been a death in the family or your business had collapsed, you would hardly have run away." Armand said softly.

"Your marriage was not always so 'appy Kate?" Madame said. "So ze pain will be bitter, because guilt must also play ze part and because our English friend must do ze right thing, no matter if it is not right for 'er."

"Your observation is acute Armand," Kate said.

"I live fully and observe human nature wiz great interest. Unlike in your country, we do not avoid experience; we get our fingers burned as you say, and waste no time in regret or hypocrisy."

He responded to a call from Reception, and Kate said, "Madame, you asked if I had lost my heart, but whether my husband had merely had an affair."

"For men it is enough."

"Surely many women too?"

"But not you." Madame paused. "You are hurt, but I am glad it is over. I hope you will not deny yourself when ze chance for happiness comes."

Kate shook her head. "There won't be a second time."

"Which means you blame yourself. Quite wrongly I suspect."

"But you've never met Duncan."

"You have never inspired me wiz the wish to do so, Kate. And Armand and I, do you think we too have not had ze problems?"

"You mean Armand? And you don't mind!"

"E is still handsome and a man. If I 'ad divorced I would also lose him. I am not so stupide."

"But he loves you."

"Exactement."

They made no attempt to affect a change of subject as Armand returned, or to curtail the silence that followed.

"Female talk, je suppose," he said. "And you are fatigué Kate!"

And as so often happened as the evening grew late, they spoke in a mélange of language. It had always pleased her that they should presume upon intimacy not to go on searching for the right word when tiredness made it a chore to do so.

SAFE AS HOUSES

The familiar bedroom offered a place to lick her wounds. Both Madame and Emmeline had ignored the accepted code of ethics in dealing with their menfolk; had forgiven the part so as to remain in possession of the whole. She on the other hand, had worked herself into a silent lather about another's shortcomings; had tried to conceal them from public disapproval. And was not all that had happened really the result of her decision to marry a man whom she had loved, but not loved enough, so that he in turn lacked the confidence to build on their combined strength?

Settling into the soft, enveloping warmth of the duvet, she wondered if she would have tried to alter any part of Tom or cared what anyone thought, and knew there was nothing she would have changed, for his wholeness was indivisible. To set about changing any individual is to begin a process of destruction. That at least had been halted. Oblivious of her host passing the room she wept quietly without fight or remonstrance, allowing the tears to begin their therapy.

"Bon," Marie Jeanne nodded on hearing the gentle sound. "She will recover, but maybe not so quickly."

Whether due the cognac or the safety of being with friends, Kate knew only that she had slept, creating a fragile bridge between despair and hope. As arranged, Danielle joined her for breakfast.

"I make ze registration to begin my Engleesh commerçiale lessons," she told her, and then sensing this was probably the most propitious moment to pose a question she would never repeat, asked, "Madame remains 'appy about opening ze French office?"

And knowing she referred to the situation England, Kate looked up first to catch the eye of Armand who was replenishing the servery, and then smiling with a courageous defiance she did not feel, replied, "Pas de regret Danielle," and added, "burnt fingers où non!"

"Madame?"

But it had been Armand to whom the comment was addressed, as she immediately realised from the murmured "Bravo!"

The peace Kate had grasped in their company deserted her on her return to England, and the emptiness inside threatened at moments, to turn into a frightening enveloping depression. Only with friends available can one comfortably discover the joy of being alone; without them life has to be coped with in a tenuous, insecure vacuum.

"They're functioning, but not creating, and certainly not getting any joy out of it," Mrs. Grant observed to Helen one morning. Those who had spontaneously kept it alive were now stifling the effervescence that had been an intrinsic part of their working relationship. A trust Kate had assumed inviolable had been destroyed, and she too, broken in the process. The job that had been as natural to her as breathing suddenly demanded mental and physical reserves of which she was virtually deplete. Though both longed for those times when they bantered, raged or eulogised on the day's events, to each came the realisation that a way of life was at an end.

A brittle discussion followed an agreement Kate had made with a client and uncharacteristically Emm assumed a concern for the wider concept of the Company that had always been Kate's domain.

"We'll find a way," Kate insisted almost desperately, and Emmeline, perturbed by the change in Kate's demeanour, found it impossible to conceive of a Kate without the strength of purpose that had characterised her every decision. There was about her now, a porcelain fragility.

"Duncan I can't bear to see her like this," she told him next morning.

"Garbage. Kate's tougher than any of us. Just be the friend you've always been and see her through a bad patch. She's punishing herself. OK, so she's temporarily off balance, but nothing will cause her to risk her precious company. Hell knows I've been desolate and she's barely noticed, but one ripple from the office and she switches on like radar. No, the kindest action is to let her think everything is normal."

"But it isn't!"

He stifled his irritation, smiled indulgently and said, "And that my honey is because it never has been. You two have mixed business and friendship to the point you now feel guilty for having a life of your own. Continue to run your side of things and Kate will be mortified when she realises she's the one letting the side down. She'd rather die than be a passenger."

"That's unfair. There are times when we all need to be carried along."

He threw his hands up almost triumphantly. "I know that, you know that. But not Kate. Kate must never presume on anyone. She doesn't even need friends. She despises failure and weakness - but never more than in herself."

"That isn't true. In herself maybe, but never in others. You're just bitter."

"And with good reason. Having suffered from Kate's insistence on perfection, I'm darned well not going to stand by and watch the same happen to you. Now promise you'll take a tougher line; I guarantee it will have an immediate effect."

SAFE AS HOUSES

"You seem very sure."

"After seventeen years of marriage what do you expect? Maybe this much maligned husband will at last be seen as having good reason for failing."

"I never heard Kate say one word against you!"

"Only because in the world she created, I didn't exist. Now come on, where's my good time girl who knows how to handle life?"

Emmeline poured herself another coffee. "Kate's the dearest, perhaps the only real friend, I ever had. She freed me from a phoney lifestyle and made me feel I was worth more than the money I inherited. I've repaid her by sleeping with her husband for God's sake. How can she be unaffected!"

He took both her hands in his. "Our first spat - and who has caused it? I tell you Kate would rather be married to a counter clerk bringing home an honest penny than someone who could shower her with money... take her round the world... free her from the necessity to work. That would mean admitting that gambling could involve a high degree of professionalism."

She laughed lightly. "That's where we do disagree - and I told her so. I suffer from no such middle class principles." She became reflective. "Must admit I was perplexed by her reaction. It was as if I'd suddenly released her from an attitude in which she'd been imprisoned all her life."

"That's probably what you did. She has never really questioned the maxims on which she was raised. And I'm sorry if I seemed impatient but Kate has had my past and rejected it. Now I want to share my future with someone who is vital enough to enjoy it."

"You are going to let her have the house aren't you?"

"Honey I've already agreed it." He walked away from her. "I'm disappointed you doubt me."

"It would be so easy to have second thoughts, that's all. And I suppose I can't really think why anyone would give up Kate for me."

He embraced her saying, "I can give you a hundred reasons - not least that you are infinitely more beautiful." He reached into his pocket. "Look I wasn't going to give you these until dinner tonight, but you need cheering up and I really can't bear to see you so."

The gems reflected the morning sunlight, and Kate was gone from her mind.

CHAPTER TWENTY FIVE

The interview with the Bank Manager had been less than comfortable; not because he had warned her of an over-commitment as she had anticipated, but because he seemed more familiar with her situation than she supposed.

"It's a reorganisation of our accounts," she explained awkwardly. "We're separating."

Evidently aware that Duncan had not had an income for some time other than the recent modest wage from her company, he insisted it was not incumbent on her to make such a gesture.

"But I need to do it for me," she reminded herself. And in any case, she had agreed it. And when it was done she would be freed of a responsibility she had never truly known how to handle.

To her relief, it now seemed as if after all, Emm would stay. Only their sustained friendship would allow for the continuity of their professional relationship, despite the disruption of their personal lives. And things would become easier as time passed. She must cultivate a strictly business attitude, for a whole workforce was depending on her carrying on as usual. Methods and management may change, but a company should not cease to function because of personal crises. Nor would it.

Emm was finalising a waistline when she returned, and had the look of determination that would preface a statement she had rehearsed, but about which she remained unconvinced.

"Kate, Newmans called. Evidently you promised a quote last Friday. I know it's been hell but we can't risk our reputation at this stage."

As Duncan had predicted, just a hint of blame had an immediate effect.

"Thanks for reminding me. The figures will be in tonight's post."

"Oh God Kate, you don't have to excuse yourself to me!"

The frankly unexpected vindication of Duncan's advice jolted Emm into the realisation that she personally would find a businesslike approach impossibly daunting.

"I'll get the quote finished, and later perhaps we could spend an hour checking the draft costing I've prepared for next season's collection."

SAFE AS HOUSES

"Kate, you must have been up all night on that lot!"

And Kate could not say that she had been grateful to have it to do in the long hours through which sleep had eluded her. Indeed there were so many simple, natural things she could no longer say. But she had set her course and would not be deflected, because to do so would be to surrender all her defences against a terrible, surging emotional tiredness.

"She's either a machine or near a breakdown," Emm decided, and fearing the latter, must comply with the rôle-play she had been instructed to initiate.

"You must assume more regular hours," Kate said. "Remind me if I forget; it won't be intentional, only enthusiasm for whatever we're involved in. You know what I'm like."

It was as if Kate had overheard the breakfast time conversation. And Emm knew she wanted her to believe she was in control again, and with Kate the will was the deed, for which, whatever Duncan might say, she was mightily relieved. From that moment of expressed decision, Kate would throw herself into her work with the vehemence of her early twenties, but this time not to build or scale heights; just to keep afloat. The wretched situation that was suddenly added to a sustained period of overwork and travelling, had taken her close to the edge. She closed, then opened again, the door of her own office. But in trying to conceal her vulnerability, she had put an unfamiliar gulf between them, for the door was only closed as a courtesy to visitors. She paused, aware of Emm staring at her.

"It'll be alright, you'll see. We'll make it so eh?"

And the words simultaneously healed, and openly confessed, that though it was to be a private and lonely battle, the friendship was stronger than the trust that had been fractured.

Mrs.Grant tapped at the door and asked if she'd like some tea.

"Yes please, that would be nice," and well knowing she could be overheard, added, "I imagine Emmeline could do with one too. And if those threads are for my approval, you know they are her department. It's business as usual Mrs. Grant, whatever else has changed."

"If you say so Mrs. Carter."

"I do."

Kate's weary eyes smiled her thanks but left no doubt as to the modus vivendi. "It won't help for the current tensions to continue. I suggest we all accept our rôles within a larger business than the cosy unit we began with. Sometimes it takes a jolt like this to bring about necessary changes."

"Some things won't ever change Mrs. Carter."

SAFE AS HOUSES

"Like the excellence for which we've all three striven, and together achieved?" Kate deliberately misunderstood. "Please try - for me?"

"It's the hardest thing you've ever asked me to do."

"You wait until the season's orders start coming in!"

The seamstress shook her head, closing the door as she went. And this time Kate did not feel disposed to open it. With indifferent attitude, tea was placed on Emmeline's table. Not so indifferently, Emmeline chose to leave it to get cold.

It was after five when Emm reported as requested. The awkwardness she felt on the other side of the door, communicated itself before a determined knock preceded her entry. Laughter was the only solution.

"For Heaven's sake, we don't need to go that far you idiot!"

"You don't usually close your door."

"Mrs.Grant did. By the way I hope you drank your tea."

"No." And when Kate affected a disapproving countenance, she conceded, "OK. Childish petulance on my part. But she's been a bitch - and it's none of her business. And yes, before you say anything, I understand why. If it had been anyone else, she would have dismissed it as my colourful life style. Anyway, before we get down to paperwork, there's something I've wanted to say. The other stuff got in the way."

"Go on."

"On top of everything else, I'm damn sorry about my attitude to Danielle. You don't usually go in for surprises - and knowing I'd got everything else to offload, I couldn't absorb her as well."

"I'd have given a lot for her to have seen us as we were. I'd told her so much about you. She was terribly impressed as you gathered."

"Your account of the fun we have must have seemed hollow in the circumstances."

"The atmosphere didn't exactly bear testimony to it!"

"I'm sorry. Kate, why don't you hit back? You don't have to put up with everything - you aren't some kind of punch bag."

"We're getting personal again, and we agreed."

"Sure. Come on, let's get down to it, and then...." She was about to say, 'and then go and have a bite to eat,' as they usually did, until she remembered she was dining with Duncan. So instead she said with an anger turned inwards, "and then I'll go off to your husband, while you'll no doubt stay on working. Hell Kate why don't you scratch my eyes out - or something."

SAFE AS HOUSES

"You got that off your chest for both of us. At least *I* feel better! The laughter and tears at the situation in which they were immersed became an absurd mixture. Finally Kate said, "Emm, I'm going to say something I won't be able to say again. When I first learned what had happened, my first thought was not what I'd lost, but fear that you'd taken on Duncan not knowing he was a gambler; that you too would get hurt. The shock was in realising that not only did you know, but didn't care. You could make light of what I'd utterly failed to handle - even enjoy it. So yes, my pride is hurt. Yes, I wish it had been anyone but you, but you're *not* guilty of destroying me, and as soon as we can remove the melodrama surrounding us, so will everyone else. There, now we can make a start."

"Do you really feel like tackling it?"

"No, But a certain person only this morning reminded me we shouldn't let the competition get ahead!"

"Touché." Emmeline filled their cups. "As if you ever would!"

For two hours an onlooker would have failed to notice any change, not because they were endeavouring to play a part, but because it was effortless, and frankly preferable, to believe in the past than the rawness of the present. They were occupying furniture and space that had been the backdrop of every such routine after office-hours session, and the bond that had grown over the years would not be denied - until the phone rang, jerking them back to reality, and Duncan. Each knew he was calling to remind Emm that despite Kate, she had a private life.

"The time's flown."

"It always did."

Emm cut an elegant figure and unable to say her usual 'Don't stay too long', because she recognised that working late was probably going to bring its own solace, she cast a solicitous smile in Kate's direction. If she hung on to herself hard, it was going to be all right.

She visited the family at the end of the following week, and it took all of two minutes for Lucy to ask, "You got something on your mind our Kate?"

Alex looked beyond the smiles, to dark rings under her eyes, and said quietly to Bob, "Go and make your sister a cup o' rosie-lee, there's a good chap."

Delighted to be of need, Bob shuffled purposefully in the direction of the kitchen, laboriously filled the kettle and settled himself to watch it boil.

Kate said immediately, "I came to tell you Duncan and I are going our separate ways."

SAFE AS HOUSES

"Never! You don't mean it?" Duster in hand, Lucy sat down to digest the news. Alex knew she would never have intimated such a thing were there any remaining doubt. Besides, he'd suspected as much. Lucy might have swallowed the excuses because she liked having a son in law who travelled the world on business, but he hadn't. And just as he would have resented intrusion into his innermost thoughts, so too would his Kate. If decisions or actions were to be taken, she'd do so at the right time for her, and until then he neither sought to invade her privacy nor offer advice. Not that he saw there was any to be offered, for marriage was for life and you had to find your own way with it. People could only look from outside; they couldn't feel, or live for you. And anyway, no words were needed to tell her he was always there. It was something they'd known together since she was small and he had taken her by the hand to Little Gran's.

"Is there anything you need Kate?" he asked simply, and when she shook her head, because she couldn't speak to him without emotion, something with which she knew he was unable to deal, he nodded and went on cleaning the shoes he had lined up on two sheets of newspaper in the way he'd done every week since she was a little girl.

"How you going to manage? Is someone else involved?" Kate stemmed the flow of Lucy's agitated questions. "I shall stay on in the house: Duncan has offered to find alternative accommodation."

"That was decent of 'im at any rate," Lucy commented.

"No more'n he should," Alex muttered, polishing the heel of his boot the more fiercely, for the first time questioning the wisdom of handing over Mr.Charlesworth's money to Duncan and worse, insisting Kate wasn't told.

"It is 'im who needs a change?" Lucy asked. Kate nodded, knowing that had she been the one, her mother would have had a great deal more to say. Alex was less perturbed on hearing Duncan was about to give his half of the property to Kate. At least the man had remembered where the purchase money had come from. "Needs his 'ead looking at," was his final pronouncement on the subject.

"A marriage that's held together by a bit o' paper ain't worth much," Lucy said, feeling very modern now that they had rented a television and she had seen some of the new dramas. "Best end it."

Amused by her blatant hypocrisy, Alex raised his eyebrows and grinned. "Well in that case I'd best start looking round for what's on offer."

"Don't talk daft Al." And to dismiss his stupidity she turned to Kate and said, "You know where we are when you need us."

SAFE AS HOUSES

"Just as we know who's been paying for Mrs. Osborne to give yer Mam a hand's turn in the house all this while," Alex said. "Fancy thinking we'd swallow the story about her being hard up for company!"

"We haven't any financial problems. In fact I've just opened an office in Paris," Kate assured them.

"Paris! Oh where's Bob got to with the tea. Tell us all about it!" And then completely wrong footing her daughter she asked, "What does Emmeline think of all this? She still not married?" The juxtaposing of the two questions left Kate wondering whether her mother was referring to the new office or the separation. Intoning her reply with as little significance as possible to give Lucy no clue she had so effectively thrown her off guard, she said casually, "We're all adjusting to a number of changes." Then adroitly steering the conversation back into a more comfortable area, she told them of the agreement with the Cardules and Danielle's appointment. And though Lucy, who had never surrendered the maternal need to know best, cautioned her about expansion, she glowed with anticipation at the prospect of one day going abroad.

"We might see the Eiffel Tower yet Dad, eh?"

"Of course you will," Kate said, relieved to have diverted them. "We'll ask the Brewery if they can arrange cover for a couple of days."

Lucy glowed. "Oh Kate, that's given me a proper lift. I shall look in the winders of all them big fashion stores - do you remember that dress I made you to go to the ball? And Dad taking you in Mr. Charlesworth's Bentley? Wonder if he ever found out?"

Though she was back on dangerous ground, Kate recollected the times she and Emmeline had laughed about it.

"All them purple sequins I stuck on. My eyes wouldn't cope now!"

And thus it was in high spirits she left them, and knew that had they felt more than a superficial, dutiful affection for Duncan, that would not have been the case. They had played a part for her sake because she had chosen him. Today it had been just the three of them again, with Bob too of course. Dear Bob, who absorbed atmosphere rather than conversation to which he was able to contribute so little. "It's like having a bottle of love-concentrate in the house," Lucy had said, having no eloquence at her disposal, yet nevertheless most aptly describing her son.

The effect of the passing years was more evident now, and perhaps because of her own new solitary state, for the first time she contemplated the one without the other; they who had been an inseparable unit seemingly for all of time. Never had she seen the one resting while the other had work still to do. They had been content with each other, and their children had been their world, and as each member grew up and left so that world shrank back by degrees to encompass only the two of them - and Bob. Always there would be Bob.

She turned her attention to the itinerary she had planned for the coming weeks; a deliberately gruelling schedule to enable her to do some of the forgetting that must be accomplished if she and Emm were to continue. Work, she decided, was as good a place as any to begin the uphill process of fighting back.

Duncan had thought better of his resolve to stay in the house to affect respectability. A note lay on the coffee table alongside the bank's letter thanking her for the agent's valuation of the cottage. 'Sorry hon,' she read, 'haven't got used to checking they are not for the both of us. Lucky there are no secrets between us any more! I think we'll both feel more comfortable with me out of here. Say if you need anything.' The last sentence was scrubbed out at the realisation of his lack of tact, but not well enough to prevent her seeing, 'You know where I am.'

It was evident he had done a thorough job of removing his own, and many of their joint possessions. 'Things, only things,' she whispered philosophically, 'but I must replace the pictures.' Without them the place had the feeling of nowhere in particular, a large cell almost, and she its prisoner. An icy fear gripped her, a fear that having all her life harboured no distaste for solitude, she might now discover she could not be alone. She picked up the phone to call Emm, replacing it as she was forced abruptly to come to terms with the fact that Emm was no longer available.

For two hours, she moved about in a vacuum, the familiarities confronting her in anticipated progression as she walked from one silent room to another, feeling the tearing of threads of a life interwoven with another. Everything from bed to teapot seemed a ludicrous size for one. Nothing seemed to matter except the enormous sadness that it had all been so unnecessary. If only she had been able to make allowances for his failings, had enjoyed him for all the positive aspects of his character instead of living by a set of rules to which she had offered no challenge, resulting now in this empty, frightening vista opening in front of her.

Work had been the solution when she had learned of the gambling, and must be so again in combating the effects of Duncan's adultery. But aim and motivation had evaporated, and the recovery she'd believed had already begun whilst enthusing to Alex and Lucy about the Paris office, now seemed insubstantial, and a deal less tenuous than the void that stretched ahead without him. She looked yearningly at all that was safe and familiar, questions taunting her weariness. Had the gambling been a necessary part of their marriage to test her affection, and would surviving it have been proof of the strength of the bond - a strength she had often felt, despite herself?

She was confused and hurting again, just when she thought she had it under control. She could not see his guilt behind the apparent enormity of her own. And the house, which she would always think of as his, suddenly felt as feasible a place to live as a wigwam in the Arctic. Delaying not even long enough to make herself a coffee, she packed and called a taxi to connect with the night train to York.

"Stop here first please," she requested the driver, indicating the boutique. The windows were always left lit through the night, and as they drew up in front of them, the artistry that enticed passers-by, still pleased her. She too paused before going inside, determined to rekindle that which had driven her, lured her on to achieve success beyond her wildest hopes. When Lucy finally condescended to look in these windows, she would take her to those in Paris she longed to see. 'Not that she won't have had Dad drive her past often enough,' Kate thought. 'She just won't let me know that she's delighted it wasn't a corner shop after all.'

She left a note for her secretary saying she had decided to make an early start. When she returned she would move into the flat for a while. She stopped. Always in the past she had left a note on Emm's desk. Whatever she now wrote would appear trite or melodramatic. Better just to go.

CHAPTER TWENTY SIX

"Penny for 'em, Luce."

"Reckon they'd be worth a lot more if only I could sort 'em out." She leaned her head back against the chair. "My daughter told me last week her marriage is over, yet I've been able to think of nowt but a trip to Paris. To think I was always the one to lecture about getting priorities right."

"Mebbe yer didn't like him as much as yer made out?"

"I just wanted to see her make something of 'erself after that posh schooling an' all. He seemed to fit the lifestyle... different from us."

"Didn't love her enough. Never did."

"You're not sorry then..... that he's gone?"

"Don't care about 'im. But I don't like to see her hurting."

"She was, wasn't she?"

"Aye." He poured himself a second cup of tea not wanting her to see his concern. "Still can't get used to this stuff without sugar. Do you think Doc's right about the diabetes?"

"I don't care what he tests you for as long as he gets to the bottom 'o them faints. Frightened the life out o' me, yer did."

"Aye and meantime you get off to Paris. Do you both good."

"She meant you as well."

"What would I want with Paris fashions Luce. I ask yer."

"It's not only shops.... the sights as well. Jonathan's always over there."

"Well he would be wouldn't he? He's in the same trade."

"And been a real good friend to her by all accounts."

Alex concealed the pang of jealousy that sparked. "She was always drawn to your David when he was alive. Remember 'ow he went on at us to let her live with them when she was little? Thought he'd give her a better chance."

"She made it on her own though didn't she?"

"She did that. And you know Luce I reckon it's about time you told her so. Our Kate's got so high in her job I don't rightly know where she's at, but having a shop and a factory and office, and traders from across the Channel can't be bad, and I don't think I've ever 'eard you tell her."

SAFE AS HOUSES

Though not conceding, she determined to rectify matters. She'd tell her in Paris that her frocks were every bit as stylish as them in the windows there. Alex stirred the contents of his cup, and then stopped, realising it would make no difference to the bitter taste. He looked at Lucy who was pale, and kept creasing her brow. "Do you want an aspirin?"

"Later if it doesn't ease up."

"It's all that excitement about Paris!"

"Must be. It's been on and off since our Kate came. She 'as done well, but she's got 'er 'ead screwed on - she'll know it without me tellin' 'er "

"You tell her. 'Specially now."

He took his father's watch from his waistcoat. "Nearly time to open up. I'll just see Bob's finished stacking."

"He loves that. You know I thought the end of the world had come when the Doctor said he wasn't right, yet he's turned out a real treasure."

As they locked up after the last customer, Lucy put the takings in a bag. She would total them when her headache had gone. "It's a scorcher. Can you and Bob get your cocoa - I must lie down."

"Why couldn't you give in afore now?" he remonstrated. "Take some more aspirin, and I'll bring your drink up. You would keep on. Get to bed."

So rarely ill, she had, all her life suffered from headaches for which she maintained the only cure was to lie down with a rag soaked in vinegar and cloves across her forehead. Best stick with Nature's own remedies. When he went upstairs she was already asleep. Bobby sorted the coins, and after tapping a new barrel, Alex totted them up, noting the amount for her to put in her book next day. "Thinks nobody can do it like she can," he laughed at Bob. "Good job she didn't see how long it took! Off you go now fella."

"Mam better soon Dad?"

"She'll be right as rain come morning, don't you worry."

But for the first time in their married life Lucy didn't sit up before the alarm had stopped ringing, and as Alex stirred, an incoherent plea made him turn.

"Lucy what's wrong. Not still got your head?"

She drew his gaze to her face. Horror-stricken he looked at her contorted mouth, "Lucy no! Can you move...sit up?"

Her left arm lay lifeless beside her, and feebly she shook her head. Unable to assist her effectively, he reached out for his limb, fumbling in his panic. "Blasted thing," he muttered. "Just hold in there Lucy. I'll get the doc."

Instead he phoned directly for an ambulance explaining in hushed tones that his wife appeared to have had a stroke, and would they please hurry. As the

SAFE AS HOUSES

stretcher was lifted into the ambulance, Lucy indicated that Bob mustn't be left, attempting encouragement to her distraught partner.

"You'll see her when they've settled her in," the driver assured him. "You'd only be in the way now, Sir."

Bob appeared at the shop doorway, dishevelled and disorientated at not finding Mam in the kitchen and the kettle boiling for breakfast tea. Neither age nor sex a barrier to his emotions, he put his hand into his father's, his eyes clouded and confused.

"Mam's gone to the hospital Bob. She'll come home soon." Then as if to assure himself, "It can't be a bad 'un - she's still giving us our orders."

With the mystery of Mam's whereabouts solved, though much distressed, his sentiments were totally selfless. He couldn't help Mam, but he could comfort the one equally precious, and filling the kettle, put bread in the toaster as Mam did each day. Eggs were better, but marmalade was simpler.

Alex looked at his watch; barely half past seven. He must phone Kate's place. Duncan would tell him where to get hold of her. But there was no reply. "Come on will you. Get out of bed man," he muttered agitatedly, until realisation dawned that given what Kate had told them, her husband probably wasn't there either.

"By gum, that was champion Bob." He had no appetite, but Bobby was watching every mouthful. "Good as Mam makes. Thanks pal."

Praise was music to him and Bob set about adjusting the routine that had been disrupted. Meanwhile Alex pondered his problem. Maybe Miss Charlesworth could help him: she would know Kate's whereabouts. His daughter would never forgive him if he kept it from her, 'specially if anything happened. But it wasn't going to happen; Lucy was indestructible. Even so Kate would want to be in touch every day. She'd once pointed out the flat to him, somewhere in Cressington Gardens he seemed to remember. He'd recognise it when he got there and if he hurried, he could be back to open up as usual. And if he were not, folks would have to get their groceries elsewhere if they'd run out of stuff for breakfast. Teach 'em to think further than their own noses.

His limb, hurriedly attached, was now chafing. Bending, he tried to adjust it but the confines of the car were restricting. It was more important to catch Miss Charlesworth before she left for work. Pressing the bell above her name, he apologised for calling at an unsocial hour. There was a pause that he found not the least disturbing since he too would have been disinclined to visitors at such an hour. And then he heard her voice again. "Mr. Benson,

221

SAFE AS HOUSES

yes of course, please come up. There's a lift to the right of where you're standing."

Alex admired the beautifully proportioned staircase, and in a less tense state would have trailed his hand along the polished handrail. Now, anxious and breathless he could do without the climb and did as she suggested.

"What the hell's going on," Duncan demanded as he heard the name. "Why didn't you tell him to come back later?"

"He said it was important. And if Daddy's description of him was correct, he didn't waste words or time. He can hardly be visiting on a whim."

"Obviously Kate has talked and he's come to persuade me otherwise."

"Duncan, Kate's in her forties, not a seventeen year old."

"You don't know the vehemence of his affection for her."

"Lucky Kate! You could always do a piece of theatre and hide in the dining room whilst I deny your existence!"

"Emm don't be facetious. Of course I'll meet the chap. But I'd rather have been appropriately dressed and on neutral ground."

"It's not a situation I envisaged, but it will add a degree of zest to the day. Do you think he's going to knock you down darling!"

Alex tapped deferentially at the door, and not hearing her tread over the thick carpet, was about to knock again when it was opened.

"Miss Charlesworth, I really am sorry to come like this..." His demeanour indicated that whatever he'd come to say, he was not in aggressive mood, and though struggling to maintain his dignity, was obviously distraught.

"Mr. Benson come and sit down. I'll get you a cup of tea."

"Thank you all the same Miss, but I've to get back quickly. It's the Missus you see. I just need to talk to Kate, and I thought you might..." But the words froze as Duncan, now in jacket and tie, entered the lounge. Alex stared first at one, then the other, unable to cope with this added crisis. "Duncan... Miss Charlesworth. . . I .....why."

"Mr.Benson, drink this. Kate told me how sweet you like tea."

"I'm not allowed sugar anymore, and anyway no thank you Miss. If I'm seeing what I think I'm seeing, I'll take no favours."

The shock, and the pain from his upper limb, made getting up from the chair a struggle, and Duncan put out a hand to steady him.

"Dad, Alex, you mustn't let it affect you like this. It's all been arranged amicably and with no bitterness on either side."

Alex pushed him aside. "Aye, I can see how amicable it is. Apologies for disturbing you Miss Charlesworth. I'll be off."

SAFE AS HOUSES

"But you needed to talk....."

He moved towards the door and Duncan, completely mystified, said, "But that's why you came...and Alex, you do know that I've arranged for Kate to have the house?"

"That's the only reason I'm not blacking your eye! I'll take my leave." Leaving them both bewildered, he pulled the door behind him, and in his misery forgot the lift, and painfully negotiated each tread of the staircase.

"I don't understand.... he'd obviously come to give me the benefit of his opinion, yet was totally thrown by the two of us together."

"The man's in trouble. Before you came in, he mentioned Kate's mother." Emmeline went to the window overlooking the car park. "Look he's fallen over! Come on Duncan: he needs help."

Her heels sank into the gravel and by the time she reached him, Alex had heaved himself into the driving seat.

"Mr. Benson, we thought Kate had told you. Please let me help."

His lips were tight as his shaking hands took hold of the steering wheel. "Thank you but I can manage without your kind of help." Releasing the brake that seemed also to release his hold on himself, his voice quavered. "I just want Kate." He pulled away and the wheels spun on the gravel.

"Mr. Benson, you really shouldn't be driving!" But her words echoed around her ears, and he was gone.

"Same damn pride," Duncan muttered. "You just can't help them."

The pain was excruciating by the time Alex drew up in front of the shop and saw Bob looking out for him.

"Hospital lady phoned Dad. You phone back."

It was confirmed Lucy had suffered a stroke, but her condition was stable.

"Put the kettle on Bob, while I get this gammy leg fixed. Mam's fine and maybe Kate'll phone us tonight. No need to worry her now. By gum I'm as tired as if I'd done a day's collar. Put a bit 'o sugar in that tea son - it'll not do any harm to replace the energy I've just used."

Meanwhile the woman he had rebuffed threw a change of clothes into an overnight bag and grabbed her keys. "I'll call you tonight darling. Bye."

"Where are you going?" But the sports car zoomed out of view. The old man's arrival had unsettled him and he poured a drink. The sooner all ties were cut with the Bensons, the better.

Emmeline left the engine running and ran upstairs to the office to check Kate's current hotel. "Helen, I'm going to join Kate. If her father phones tell him we'll get her to call him as soon as she makes contact."

SAFE AS HOUSES

"That'll be at 1.30. She rang last night to dictate some letters, said she was seeing suppliers all this morning, and would call me from the hotel before she entertained one of them for lunch."

"By which time I shall be with her. Sorry Helen, there isn't time to explain... Tell Mrs. Grant where I am but don't give her any details."

"I don't have any!"

"Be in touch as soon as I can. Bye. Ask Mrs. Grant to look after the buyer coming from Heseltines this afternoon. She knows what to show her."

"And where's Madam going?" Mrs. Grant enquired as Emmeline slammed her car door shut before pulling out into the traffic.

"To find Mrs. Carter, and I don't have any details. She asked that you please look after the buyer from Heseltine's at 2.30."

"Not more trouble!" The senior seamstress threw up her hands in a gesture of desperation. "And she knows I don't like dealing with visitors."

"It did seem urgent."

"Usually is with that lady. And if I'm in charge I'll have a cup of tea."

The Receptionist mistook Emmeline for one of Kate's luncheon guests. "Mrs.Carter will be down shortly if you would care to wait in the lounge. May I get you a drink?"

"Please call her room, and tell her that her partner must see her urgently." The receptionist spoke in subdued tones to Kate, and then said, "Room 42, Madam. Second floor."

"Emm, what on earth are you doing here?"

Emmeline sat unceremoniously on the bed. "I'm not sure Kate - except that I know you have to go home. Your father came to the flat this morning."

"What!"

"Exactly. So it must be important. And I think perhaps your mother is ill."

"But why didn't he tell you?"

"Because he found Duncan there. Hence he wouldn't explain or allow us to help. Told us what we could do with our help. But he was shaken Kate."

"I hadn't told him... It must be serious.... the suppliers will be here."

"No problem. Give me a quick briefing and I'll entertain and explain your absence. Here." She threw her car keys into Kate's hand. "Leave the ones for the hire car. Who else needs a visit?"

"Hollingtons tomorrow morning. Bradburys at 3. Here's my diary. Details and contracts are in my briefcase...the train ticket home, too. I'll meet you."

SAFE AS HOUSES

"No need. I'll take a taxi. Just get yourself back." Emmeline retrieved the silk blouse Kate threw into her suitcase. "I only stopped to pack the minimum - this will provide a quick change. May I?"

"Take what you want – and thanks Emm."

Glancing from the window she saw the first of her guests. "That's Mr.Wilkinson. Not much time for pleasantries - prefers a large whisky and soda, and straight into figures. Appreciates a spade being called a shovel!"

"I'll escort him into the bar before he sets eyes on you. Don't worry about a thing. I hope you mother's alright."

"So do I." Kate snapped her suitcase shut and was soon heading south.

"Dad!" Her father was about to draw away from the kerb, as she pulled in ahead of the old Vauxhall to impede his departure.

"Damn the woman," he cursed, believing the driver to be Emmeline, until Kate ran to his offside window.

"Oh thank God. Mam's had a stroke - I'm just off to the hospital again."

"Come in this one," she said opening his door, but he pulled it from her.

"We'll go in mine."

She tried to release his tension. "You didn't mind her father's!"

"Her father never did the dirty on us!" He was outraged and she slid into his passenger seat. Exhaustion was evident and she put her hand on his. "Stop at the entrance. I'll park it. Mam would rather see you first

She watched as he bent awkwardly over Lucy's semi prostrate figure in a rare, public gesture of affection. "Our Kate's come, Luce."

Lucy's face had undergone a change that seemed to rob her of her own personality and unable to believe the deteriorating effect of last night's event, Kate embraced the inert form on the pillow. Gradually, a tight nervous smile trembled from one to the other as if seeking recognition, and both moved quickly to own it by grasping the hand that was nearest. The fingers that Alex now held, closed around his own, and Lucy strained to say indistinctly, "Hold Kate." And Kate could not say that she was indeed holding, but the hand seemed not to belong. White and limp, it yielded no reaction to the gentle caressing. And then the thread of talk slipped away from her again as her eyes closed and the three remained silent whilst the bond that had held them over the years, drew even tighter.

A young nurse entered brusquely, scattering the silence. "The physio will tell you what exercises to do to get the fingers moving." A glance shot from Kate to Alex, a hopefulness taking shape. "You mean...?" But the nurse had in her youthful nonchalance, moved to the next unplumped pillow that caught her attention.

"Rub harder Kate!" Alex urged and Kate smiled her compliance as if the years were washed away and she was sitting on the cellar steps again. She drew his broad hand to the lifeless fingers. "Just going to see if I can hurry things up a bit," she promised.

"Your mother is a very determined lady, and I've known worse cases make almost complete recoveries," the consultant said. "Age is against her of course and some change to her lifestyle will be inevitable." He introduced the physiotherapist. "Miss Thomas - Mrs.Carter would like to know how best to help."

"Nothing today but rest and massage. Then no matter how tedious, she must exercise. You know there are no guarantees?"

"Only one," Kate thought to herself, "Lucy's own will power."

"We'll start as soon as equipment is available," Miss Thomas promised. "We hope tomorrow, but even the best laid plans are subject to cutbacks."

"Not in this case," Kate decided, and headed for the physio department.

"These were some of the things being used by stroke patients Dad. Shouldn't be any problem for you, should they?" she asked, producing scribbled sketches.

"I'll knock 'em together after closing tonight. But Kate, what if we don't know about the rest of her yet. I've just been so pleased she's alive but..."

"We can find out when she wakes. I'll massage while she sleeps."

"She'll be alright won't she?"

"Is her name Lucy Benson?"

Lucy's eyes opened for a moment and the shyly communicated affection, and pleading eagerness of his face were still behind her lids when they dropped again of their own weight. "Legs alright Kate. Just face and arm."

"Thank God," Alex put his large white handkerchief to momentary but effective use.

"No good worrying about more'n we 'ave to," Lucy urged, and in seconds was deeply asleep again.

"She really does need to rest," a voice from behind assured them, and Kate turned to see the Consultant with whom she had spoken earlier. "Her body has started to make its own recovery, which may or may not be sustained long term. She's out of immediate danger, and the degree of receptivity to your help will become obvious." He turned his attention to

SAFE AS HOUSES

Alex who appeared a little unsteady. "You can't look after her without looking after yourself old chap."

Kate drew her father from the bed. "Let's go home Dad," she persuaded, and the inference that they belonged in one place was comfort to him.

"He meant for us to sell the shop didn't he? She's not going to like that."

"You may have to make the decision for her."

"By God, that'll be worse than war!"

She smiled. "But it's not today's problem. You rest. I'll open up."

"I did already," beamed Bob, handing his father a mug of steaming tea. "People banged on the door."

"You did what! Kate nobody'll have had the right change."

"Didn't give change." Bob said categorically. "Give the people paper bags and they put the money inside and wrote what they had. They said get change when you come home."

Kate encircled her brother's ample form. "Bob you're a treasure!"

"Like pebbles by the sea," he stated simply. "We go again one day Kate?"

"You bet! When Mam's better. I love you Bobby Boyo."

"Long time Kate. Lots of years."

"Much too long Bobby. I'm sorry."

"See Mr.Rees. He say Bobby Boyo."

Kate took his plump hands in her own. "Mr.Rees is dead now. Don't you remember?" she whispered. "But our cottage is still there. We'll go back."

Slowly her brother traced his hand around the edge of the table and then lumbered into the kitchen. He put his head into his hands and gave silent expression to his desolation at the news he had refused to believe previously, it being beyond his comprehension. He had had no visual evidence of illness; had been able to put it from his mind as if it had never been said. And because his world was a confusing muddle of fact and fantasy, he believed events could be eradicated if you ignored them. But Kate had told him again now and he must accept.

Perplexed and excluded, Alex asked, "Who was Mr.Rees. Kate?"

"Someone a lot like you Dad. I introduced Bobby to him when I took him to Wales soon after I came back from the States - do you remember?"

"Aye, I do. That was a journey your Mam couldn't get to the bottom of."

"I'm sorry. I wasn't deliberately being secretive. It was a difficult time."

"Nothing wrong in being secretive if it's nobody else's business."

Kate looked at him earnestly. "There's nothing I'd ever want to keep secret from you unless it would give you pain."

SAFE AS HOUSES

"And going to Wales would?"

This of all days was not the time to be dragging skeletons from the cupboard but the moment had presented itself. Their love of each other was profound, yet the similarity of their personalities strangely prevented them from simply talking when to talk would have been the best therapy.

"I hadn't intended to, but I went to Wales because I was hurting and didn't want to involve you. At the time, the fact of Bobby needing a holiday gave me the opportunity to go without admitting it."

"To us or yourself?"

"Mam would have tried to organise me and you would have been so upset because you couldn't solve my problem - and I didn't want either."

Alex nodded but for a reason that mystified him, and yet seemed to have something to do with Lucy's absence, he too seemed suddenly felt able to talk over that which affected him deeply. However inarticulately expressed, the thoughts would be his, and not influenced by the Lucy's strongly held convictions. "So what *was* the problem Kate?"

"Duncan and I hadn't been getting on too well..... that's why I came back to U.K. I thought it was all over... I went to Wales - saw Mr.Rees whom I'd met before I went to the States, and for no logical or rational reason, I bought his cottage. You could hardly describe it as a sensible move but it was one of those gut feelings - I never once regretted it, and in the event Duncan and I made a go of things."

"Kate if only I'd known. And Duncan - what did he have to say?"

"I didn't tell him until recently. That doesn't say much for me does it?"

"I don't know all the circumstances. The way I see it now, the less he knows the better." How could he have been so daft as to hand over Mr. Charlesworth's money. "But you were alright - for some time I mean?"

"Yes - for a long time after."

"And Kate ... he has done right by you ... the house I mean?"

"Duncan has been very generous. Although I shall assume full responsibility for the mortgage, he insists the house is mine."

Alex sighed with relief. So it had all worked out. With Mr.Charlesworth's money being enough to pay for half of it, the outstanding mortgage wouldn't be a lot on her own. He was about to ask her when Bob, in some distress, came into the room.

"I don't want Mam die like Mr.Rees," he sobbed.

Both knew they should take the fear from him but he had sparked the thoughts lodged in them too. "No Bob, neither do I," Alex heard himself pleading. Then, taking a hold of himself, said reassuringly, "And we are all going to see that she don't."

Propped up by pillows, Lucy's functioning hand was manipulating the fingers of the other when Kate returned, and her face was less contorted.

"I can't feel a darned thing," she said, "but the doctor reckons there's every chance I will, if I keep at it."

"I've brought these," Kate said, pulling a box of coins from her basket. "As the feeling returns you can try gripping different sizes. And Dad made this to exercise your arm - Bob helped him with the sandpapering."

"What a team," Lucy enthused. "Push it under my arm now Kate and press down."

She was soon tired but before succumbing to a snooze, made Kate promise to continue to move the arm whilst she slept. "The older you get, the less time there is to waste."

"And fewer opportunities," Kate thought, Bob's reaction still in her mind.

In the event, Lucy was home again within the week, and with Mrs. Osborne agreeing to come in every day until matters improved, the show was ostensibly on the road again. But there were orders to be made for the reps; wholesalers to be visited, books to be kept up to date and the family to be cared for in addition to Lucy's therapy, and Kate's organising ability over the ensuing weeks was tested to the limit.

"Don't want you cracking up as well girl," Lucy commented one evening when Kate called late. "Best let that partner of yours do a bit more."

"Emm isn't my partner Mam, though because of her support you could mistake her for one. She's technically an employee and puts in a hundred per cent."

"Which is what she's tecken out." Lucy's tongue had lost none of its acerbity. "You're too soft Kate - always were."

But her mother was coping with the affliction she had suffered - like a Trojan, and it would not do for heightened emotions to be the cause of a setback. Already, feeling had returned to the index finger. Alex suddenly steered the conversation with an immediacy that took both of his womenfolk by surprise. "I've asked Mr. Clayton to call this afternoon. Best he should know the situation."

Lucy bridled. "With me like this! What you go and do that for Al?"

"Because I'm not prepared to fool myself any longer Luce."

"And I'll tell him that when you 'ave the toothache, ye just chew on the other side for a bit. We'll manage."

SAFE AS HOUSES

"You can if ye like Luce, but I'm tired of walking on t'other leg. I'm ready to stop." He had taken the decision and would also be the reason for it. "We're well past retiring age," he insisted quietly.

"I won't stop. We can't. We ain't got there yet."

"Got where for Heaven's sake. Just where is it we're going?"

"We said we'd come out of here with enough to buy our own place."

"And so we shall."

"Not one like our David 'ad."

"Then we'll have one a bit smaller."

"Over my dead body ." She stopped short, and gently he took her hands in his.

"Aye Luce. That's just about what it will be. We're stopping."

Tears of frustration came first, and then unexpectedly the smile. He sighed his relief. "I'm glad you've seen sense love."

"I 'aven't," she grinned. "I just got another finger back!"

CHAPTER TWENTY SEVEN

"We'll be sorry to let you go: you've been good tenants. But I can see it's out of the question." Mr. Clayton from the Brewery accepted a glass of beer. "Got somewhere to go?"
That it was merely a rhetorical question was not appreciated by his less sophisticated hosts who could reasonably assume some interest in their misfortune given the significant increase in turnover during their tenancy.

"We're looking." Lucy judged his thinking. "Trade won't suffer."

"With your hands on the tiller, my dear, I'm sure it won't." He drained his glass and smiled disarmingly. "Decision making is tiring. Get some rest."

"Then it shouldn't be me that's tired, for it was no decision of mine." She looked at the hand that was now fully recovered and knew if Alex hadn't lost his nerve, they could have stayed on, though watching him limp back behind the counter, she knew he was right. But folks were not going to say she'd let a stroke dictate what she did.

Clayton drove away. Pity. Tenants like the Bensons were not easily found. It would come as a shock when they found the Brewery, not they, had been the beneficiary of all their effort. But with a Board Meeting scheduled for ten, they were dismissed them from his mind.

"All them years ago Al...I was so excited about 'avin a shop of our own."

"Do you think you could get excited about having a *life* of our own?" He continued to turn the pages of the local paper, but she knew he was vitally interested in her reply, and yearned for him to let her see his eyes. But he'd never demonstrated the love he had for her and wouldn't start now.

"As long as its always with you, I reckon as 'ow I could," she said.
Unable to find the words he desperately sought, he said gruffly, "That's alright then."

"Kate'll be back from Wales on Friday. We can show her that bungalow."

"I was damn relieved when the Doc insisted she 'ad a break. Like a shadow she was."

"It's the hours she puts in on that business that's to blame," Lucy asserted. "There are family crises in everybody's life. You don't think I 'ad a stroke

SAFE AS HOUSES

on purpose do you? And I'll tell you something for nothing. It won't be just a long weekend Emmeline'll take. Nor alone. She'll be tecken by the one as should be lookin' after our Kate. He can count 'imself lucky you wouldn't take me to give him a piece of my mind."

"I'll not argue with that pal."

She wanted Kate to come back; to see the strain had been a temporary thing. Funny this fascination she had for Wales

"Why did he die Kate?" Brother and sister sat on either side of the range.

"Because he was very old Bob. But he had a good life here."

"All by himself." Bob's brow creased. "I don't want be on my own."

"You're not going to be."

"Mam nearly die. Gill and Beth gone away."

Kate recognised fear born of anxiety. "Mam's much better now and Dad's legs won't get so tired when they leave the shop. Don't worry." She hugged him in the bear-like fashion he loved and slid a snapshot from an album.

"Who is it Kate?"

"That was Mrs. Rees."

Bob placed a stubby finger on the print. "And that man?"

"He was a friend of mine." She faltered slightly over the words that were intended to be casual. Where was Tom now? Had she chilled him away too? If only she could have given him some indication of her longing that he should have taken her in his arms and told her what they were *going* to do; not give her the chance to decide what she *ought* to do.

She had escaped the poverty of her childhood with a scholarship to an elite school and only now did she question the price she had paid. She had clung like a limpet to its principles, as if by abandoning them she would slip back into poverty's grip. They were the safety net that kept her from being imprisoned for life in the dingy back street into which she was born. One digression, one lapse - even wearing the wrong shoes - and she risked losing everything. With a jolt, she realised she clung to them yet; they were the barrier between her, and an existence that could ensnare her still if she lost her guard. Tom and Duncan on the other hand had set their own agendas. Sent to 'good schools' by professional parents, their education had performed the function of boosting a confidence that was already a part of their makeup, had equipped them to be assertive in the manner of those to whom stewardship is a right, and success an expectation.

SAFE AS HOUSES

They could never have understood how she'd had to manoeuvre her way through the maze of respectability on the one hand, and chameleon like, remain hidden in a another world where stocks and shares and financial security were aliens. And in drawing no attention to herself, she had suppressed her personality too, to such an extent that often she believed she had created her Company by default. Only in Mr. Charlesworth's employ had she breathed more freely, knowing he too had survived in a world ready to ridicule his aspirations. Like Tom, Emm had also been 'second generation wealth'; had none of Kate's inhibitions. However outwardly poised, she was still, inside, the scholarship kid from the back streets.

Bob was gazing at her intently. His sister's contemplative mood troubled him, and suddenly aware of it, Kate returned to the task in hand. They walked again by the shore in the evening, Bobby absorbing the luxury of seeing his sister at ease, rushing neither to meeting nor airport. The dreadful tiredness that had frightened him recently, had disappeared from around her eyes, and just a little, her face glowed again. There was about her tonight a tranquillity that made him feel more secure.

"I like you here Kate."

She pinched the barely defined cheek affectionately. "Not anywhere else?"

"All the time." He could not articulate that which he knew she understood.

It would be no easy task to keep the cottage aired from such a distance. Stout walls may have kept the gales out but in long periods of unabated rain, they also kept the damp in. Future visits would offer less relaxation than maintenance on a significant scale. There was the sound of footsteps, then a tap at the kitchen door. An instruction to 'Lie there. Stay,' and Jim Cole stepped inside.

"Ullo there Bobby Boyo!" he called out, nodding at Kate. Bob beamed his response to the greeting Mr. Rees had made synonymous with an unpatronising acceptance. "Good to feel welcome still in this kitchen."

"You've come at the right time Jim - we've been sorting Mr.Rees' things. Is there anything you'd like?" And as Bobby looked concerned. "Except the biscuit tin that is!"

"Aye aye. But first I must give you this - and I'll ask you to look in the drawer for the one I wrote to my daughter should I be the one to go first."

It pleased her to think of Mr. Rees discussing her with Jim as if she were family.

'Dear Kate,' she read, 'I still remember young Thomas warning you of longevity - that you might not do well out of our agreement. But I never sensed any resentment and have spent my old age free from financial anxiety in the place I love most. I've been able to travel too sometimes, but I enjoyed coming home more, for I never found anywhere in the world more beautiful.

When you talk to me about your work, I know you have found satisfaction. But happiness is another matter. It was there for you on the day you and Tom chanced upon us. Don't let whatever is hurting, stop you from recognising it again Kate.

Jim will be with you, as you read this for his curiosity will get the better of his manners. Tell him to take my fishing rod, and the picture on the wall in my bedroom. It is the creek where we used to fish as boys, and his mother had to call him so often for we never kept an eye on the time.

My love and gratitude to you Kate, for I owe my peace of mind these nineteen years, to you.
Haydn Rees.'

She told Jim of Mr. Rees' wishes but he said merely, "Aye aye, but something else I've got on my mind."

"I'm listening."

"It's about your field Kate. What would you be a wanting for grazing rights now?"

"I thought your sheep grazed on Morgan's land?"

"They do indeed. But it won't be convenient after Ladyday. I find myself on a sticky wicket for I don't know what I'd do with idle hands now Haydn's gone." He levered himself from his chair. "If 'tis time you need, I'll call again tomorrow."

The night was turning chill and she added more coal to the range. "Sit down Jim." She paused and then said, "I pay for the materials for fencing: you organise the labour."

"And the rent Kate?"

"Open my windows every fine day when you bring the sheep. Keep an eye and let me know of any problems." She refilled their glasses. "Do we have a deal?"

He delved into his pocket for matches, lit his pipe and laughed robustly. "Oh we do indeed!"

He left her and she re-read the letter. The sandpipers and kittiwakes had long ceased their calling, but they would waken her in the morning. Tonight she too was content. She slept soundly, and surprisingly it was Bob who woke first. He brought her a cup of tea and sat heavily on the edge of her

SAFE AS HOUSES

bed. "I like little houses better than shops Kate," he confided suddenly, and she knew he had gone to bed with a troubled mind."
"I thought you enjoyed filling the shelves and carrying crates for Dad."
"Mam's tired now. This is better."
"You know they have found a little house for the three of you to live in?"
"By the sea?"
"No, but it has a garden where you can have tea just as we do here. Look, it's a beautiful morning – we'll have breakfast outside." A suggestion that met with instant approval, for here was something tangible. She considered the intuition that had warned Bob of the need for change, realising the past weeks had affected him deeply. She watched as he plodded from kitchen to garden laying the table one item at a time, and unconsciously absorbing the stillness, as the ringdoves called monotonously and bluetits darted in and out. "Would you like to bring Mam and Dad here Bob?"
"Mr. Rees say so?"
"The cottage is ours now – yours and mine to look after. But I won't have much time so you could be in charge for me eh? I'd be really grateful if I knew the cottage was in your hands."
"Me! Love you Kate."
"And I love you too." She hesitated before adding, "So you won't mind going home to tell Mam and Dad the news?" He grimaced in the most genial manner because he trusted her implicitly. "Of course you will," she smiled. "And so will I Bobby Boyo."

"It's a semi bungalow." Lucy said. "We got it at a good price."
"You wouldn't have bought it if you hadn't!"
"Survival. The Brewery didn't know all I sold in the shop, so I didn't put it through the books. We weren't just there to line *their* pockets. Your Dad fretted about it, so I didn't tell him half. I wasn't doing anything wrong - just looking after our old age. Left to the Brewery, we'd be out on our ear by now crying for a council house. We'd to open all hours so why let the till be idle for most of 'em. Folks need more than ale - and it took no longer to sell something for ten pounds than ten pence." She was silent for a moment or two, her eyes misting over. "Fancy, me - a lady of leisure at last."
Kate shook her head. There were other ways to describe looking after a house with a disabled partner, and caring for the needs of a handicapped son, oneself having suffered a major stroke!

CHAPTER TWENTY EIGHT

It had been a marathon to accomplish the equivalent of two month's travelling in one. Major clients were visited and arrangements finely tuned to ensure their continued confidence as Kate trod the precipice between ongoing success and the one fatal error that could topple her company into the waiting arms of competitors. Attention to detail had not failed her yet, but it exacted its price. Catching sight of herself in the taxi mirror, she decided the time had come for a discreet colour rinse.

In Paris, Danielle was doing a first rate job and Kate was enormously impressed by the increased poise of her young assistant, who possessing a natural talent for putting clients at ease, then patiently earned their trust.

"You were right to suggest renting further space Danielle. And full marks for the arrangement. I'm delighted. Send me a detailed progress report of the plans we've agreed but don't write for the sake of it. Where there's no comment I shall assume no change. Now I must catch the night flight."

Despite the late hour, she stopped the taxi at the boutique, wanting to confirm her decision to move into the flat.

"Somebody working late," the driver said, indicating Emm's workroom.

"Would you wait please?"

He switched of the engine, his head falling back in anticipation of a brief shuteye.

Tentatively opening the door she was startled to discover Emm sticking down an envelope, her desk littered with discarded sheets of paper. Wearily she held the waste paper bin to the desk and swept them into it wholesale.

"Go and get rid of your taxi Kate."

"Emm it's after one. And you look terrible - what's wrong?"

"Only the effect of unaccustomed paperwork and an unrepaired makeup."

"Am I meant to notice or ignore the letter addressed to me?"

"Neither. You're going to read it before we talk."

"Can't we just discuss it?"

"Not this time. Let's get it over with." Emm's lips were tight.

"I think I'd prefer the usual spontaneity than a polished delivery."

SAFE AS HOUSES

"We'd deflect each other - argue to change the course. And as the end result will be the same, we'll spare ourselves the misery."

"Which means you've made up your mind, and are going to win."

"On this one. Though it won't make me feel like a victor. And that doesn't mean to say I haven't looked at the alternatives."

A fear began to tighten around Kate as she withdrew the letter. That it would contain uncomfortable reading was evident, but as possibilities sped in succession through her mind, she locked on the one most awful to contemplate. "Em, you're not...."

"I'm going to tart myself up."

That to which they had given life was about to be snuffed out. She knew it before she read 'My very dear Kate,' four words that could have prefaced any sort of note, but on this occasion contained all that was to follow. Unable to continue, she placed the pages on the desk, until a sudden irrational hope that her dread was without foundation, forced her to resume.

'As always, you, not I, have produced the necessary strength. And I cannot stay to watch you struggling to hide your misery. Duncan wants to tie up some business and can't wait to return to the States. I won't pretend the prospect isn't exciting for me too, and I honestly think this way will be the least painful for all three of us.

In the past I've watched you respond to problems as if they were a direct challenge to your ability to cope, and once over that initial lack of confidence from which you suffer so intensely, you've pushed us on to greater heights. And you'll do so again Kate, whilst I've never subscribed to the philosophy that you get out of life what you are prepared to put in. You get out what you opportunist enough to take. We can't put the clock back, and however we try, things can never be the same again. Remember, you were the one to insist change was inevitable, and necessary, to stop us growing stale. I shall seek contacts in the Big Apple for you, and maybe your next step will be New York now that Paris is throbbing.

I've at least left you free from your own conscience to seek out the chap who had once so obviously won your heart. Whatever he did that made you ditch him when he came to find you, he could make you want him again I know it.

Bye Kate, Love you, Emm.'

Her fingers gripped the desk. "No Emm," she whispered. "Not you."

Staring around the boutique, she felt no more than a resident ghost in the place that had been their joint creation. No Mrs. Grant this time to steady her nerve; no Danielle to require attention. An empty room in which for the second time she was taking a battering that was both vehement, yet remote.

When Emm returned, she could feel rational reasoning slipping away from her whilst no words were spoken in what strangely was not an uncomfortable silence. Neither tried to affect stoicism; the one unresenting and subdued, the other accepting the responsibility for the necessity to wound if honesty were not to be compromised. The long silence was embarrassing to neither for each recognised its exigency. Eventually Kate said, "Thanks for taking a straight course."

"I'll phone for taxis. It's not exactly the night to share one is it?"

"I'd prefer to stay at the flat. You go ahead."

In the solitude of the night she embarked on the mental futility of tracing the collapse of her marriage back to its beginning. Her thoughts raced headlong to decipher a pattern in the events that had brought her to this point. Terrifyingly aware that she lacked vision of the way forward, she was stifled by the fear of becoming solitary and isolated, her life a barren treadmill stripped of zest and creativity. At last, exhausted, and not remembering when, she finally slept. But it was a troubled sleep, which did little to lift her above the problems that now confronted her. In the light of events, Paris was a major error; a drain on her resources. Arresting the spiralling down from error to disaster must now be her priority, though she had no stomach for such a momentous task.

She took her coffee into the tiny walled garden, shaded by the trees that were now tall enough to hide the factory, recalling how they had collected them in pots and joked about being mature matrons by the time the trees had fulfilled such a purpose. "Either they grew extraordinarily well or we've done a good job of staving off our dotage," she mused.

She smiled despite the tears that since none was there to see, she allowed to fall unchecked, and longed for the soothing therapeutic effect of Pembrokeshire that had first cast its magic so many years ago with Tom.

She had married, but not built with Duncan, so he could only hurt her pride by leaving. But Emm had tugged and broken that which was at the very centre of her life, the work to which she had linked herself in the absence of someone to trust and be a part. She had expected to wake this morning to discover her world had fragmented; had become a heap of rubble. And in a strange way that would have been a relief from pain. But the factory and the boutique remained obstinately whole, relentlessly awaiting her ability to manage them again. It was she who was broken.

SAFE AS HOUSES

She supposed the catastrophe that faced her was a small matter compared to the vast tragedies that tore the world apart, yet this particular small matter had wrenched at her world to the point where she no longer knew how to put the pieces together again. She sat awhile and mentally took herself to the place of her childhood. Her mother would remonstrate and tell her what a fool she had been. Hadn't she put her on the right lines when she had exhorted her to be a secretary? If only she'd been satisfied and not wanted the moon ... had had a family like any sensible woman instead of a career that had tested her to breaking point. And when she had finished her censure, she would remind her that she had a home, food in her belly and money to buy a few comforts; something that she, at the same age would have given her right arm for. It was more than a strong enough base from which to start over again.

"Only this time Mam," she wept, "I'm not at all sure I want to."

Lucy was still not recovered. She would acquaint them with developments when she had come nearer to finding a solution.

"Why couldn't they have gone when they first faced you with it! And what business needed him to stay around after he'd destroyed you," Mrs. Grant protested.

"A small matter of half a cottage would have been one such item," Kate thought bitterly. "Though of course he neither wanted nor needed it."

Mechanically she adjusted her timetable to accommodate the enforced changes, not because she had any heart for it, but in an attempt to convince the workforce she was still at the helm, and able to separate business from private life. She smiled wryly; there was precious little of her privacy left.

She made a frank statement to the staff, but even as she addressed them, knew that without the right replacement, any amount of reorganising would be for nought; a fact that escaped no-one. All recognised the Company's vulnerability. Even Mrs. Grant conceded the greatest respect for Emm's work, and in all honesty did not know how she would manage to produce the goods without the often infuriating, spontaneous flashes of inspiration that dictated a change minutes after the initial design had been made up.

"Used to make me so angry after I'd spent the day copying what she gave me in the morning only to throw it overboard in favour of an idea that came to her just as it was time to go home. But drat her, the changes were downright winners." She looked at Kate imploring. "Mrs. Carter, I'm sorry

SAFE AS HOUSES

but I don't see how I can carry the responsibility. I was going to tell you when you came back from your Paris trip that it was time to call it a day - though Heaven knows I didn't expect all this. And I know in the circumstances I shouldn't, but it's all too much. Maybe it's as well if you have a complete change whilst you're about it."

Kate made a desperate attempt to stem the panic that flared, but knew that even if she wrought a change of heart, there would be less commitment, less zeal, in the gentle surrender to old age. "And Mr. Grant too?"

The older woman nodded. "Soon as it's convenient Mrs. Carter."

Kate faced them all squarely. "Are there any others whilst we're about it?"

"Of course not!" Helen intended to silence anyone about to speak.

"Thank you Helen. But it's best if things are out in the open."

She looked from one to the other, knowing that for each of the factory hands wondering what job would be left without designer or assistant, another more blithely optimistic would glimpse the prospect of promotion.

"In that case, I suggest an early coffee break."

As a buzz of speculation was released, Kate looked at her secretary. "A scandal loses its spice once it's been talked about. If they'd had to wait for another hour, the story would have merited the national press. I think you and I should go and prepare an ad."

"Only one?"

"The one that's going to give me problems."

But before she had pen to paper, Mrs. Grant tapped at the door. "Mrs. Carter - I'm sorry. I didn't mean to say it in front of everyone like that."

"You've every right to retire, and you shall go out in style. How else, when you've been a part of our success – and a friend. I'll miss you." The words were out even if the emotions remained imprisoned.

"Oh Mrs. Carter, so many times I've wanted to help you...but you were so loyal to that husband of yours I never dared speak out. You make it hard for anyone to get near ...."

Kate swallowed hard. "I didn't mean to be distant. You've been very close - my Company mother as it were. And there are some things you can't discuss with your mother you know!"

Mrs. Grant's statement had troubled her more than a little for she seemed to be having so many indications that, wittingly or not, she had put a ring fence around herself. And yet she needed people - not necessarily en masse, but most assuredly the close circle she had assumed would find her anything but difficult to approach.

"If we want help we make a beeline for you. Oh I don't have the words."

"Do try," Kate urged.

"I mean inside you. We can see and reach - love you, and not know what's hurting or driving you to despair even if you allowed it to show, which you don't. You don't let anything show - almost as if you don't have a right to be - as if everybody else can be and say what they like and that's alright, but not you. I can't bear to think of you shouldering so much and yet here I am like everyone else, adding to your problems. And I wish I could have been a help with all that business with your husband - first at the golf club and then Miss Charlesworth...."

"For whose work you have enormous regard."

"She was the best. Being partners from the very beginning, and friends too, you somehow made her see the people you dealt with when you went off to get business - brought back a feel about them so she knew what they wanted as sure as if she'd been there herself." She wiped her glasses hard. "Are you going to be alright?"

"When have I not been Mrs. Grant? This show will stay on the road for a long time yet, don't you worry. In fact you've just given me the impetus I need. If I can paint word pictures as you say for Emmeline, then I can do it for someone else too. Now what about staying on - say three months? Someone familiar and trustworthy to give me moral support - not if and when I need it, but because I *know* I'm going to need it."

"Of course m'dear. But you can't hurdle alone forever you know. Nobody can. One obstacle after another - sometimes there are just too damn many of 'em!"

CHAPTER TWENTY NINE

In the days that followed Kate knew what it was to have a mind diseased; fearing that at any moment hers would break in pieces. Only by absorbing herself for long hours in routine duties could she find not peace, but simply a means of continuing to exist. So often she stared at the familiarity of the fabrics hanging in the order Emm had left them, and she would fight with her subconscious to deny the prevailing circumstances. Depression came in waves and gusts, sweeping her along haphazardly so that on some days she appeared as much in control as ever, whilst on others, having difficulty in maintaining perspective. On such days she could do no more than affect an interest in the activity that still miraculously surrounded her and which was a tribute to the efficient routine she had established for her work force.

"Say when I should phone your next accommodation," Helen attempted encouragement. Yorkshire soon gets booked up at this time of year,"

"You think I'm slipping Helen? I think our priority is to find a new designer. Perhaps you'd let me have the interview list if it's complete." She was being brittle and hated herself for it.

"A call to Mr. Brightman wouldn't be a bad idea." Mrs. Grant whispered.

"Surely he'd have been the first one she talked to?"

"I get the feeling she hasn't told a soul. She's fighting but frightened. I've told her I'll stay on 'til she finds someone but then I'm not the problem."

"But you were the final straw maybe?" Helen did not disguise her anger.

"That's not fair young Madam. I'm already past retiring age."

"Your timing could have been better."

"I've discussed it with Mrs. Carter and it's no concern of yours."

The two parted, and the vexatious atmosphere they created permeated through to Kate, despite her disinterest in their exchange.

"Don't go Emm," she murmured. "We were coping, and neither Duncan nor America will be what you think." She replaced the list she had barely scanned. She would go to a film - anything, just to lose herself in it.

Perplexed and holding hands, Jonathan and Val were outside the flat when she finally returned.

SAFE AS HOUSES

"Kate! There you are. We saw your car...... where have you been?"
Throbbing with the deprivation of all that holding hands signified, she said brightly, "I went to a film... you know how difficult it is to park, and I needed a walk." Her words trailed as she failed to fool them.

"Enjoy the film?" Val asked, to break the silence.

"What?"

"The film - was it good?"

"Oh yes...... It's such a long time since I went to the cinema."

Jonathan took her shoulders and it felt as if her whole body would collapse under his grasp. "Kate, you've seen it round twice and have no idea what you saw."

She slumped into a chair, her hand covering her mouth as he continued. "It's one hell of a situation Kate."

"The vulnerability you always warned me about."

"So that's why you didn't call."

"I'd rather make a blunder in front of anyone but you."

Val grimaced. "Mistakes are for the rest of us eh? Not you and Jonny!"

Fond as she was of Val, Kate wished Jonathan were here alone. He, because he was the same ilk, understood that which drove her. He looked hard at the shadow of the vibrant, elegant cousin with whom he had attended the Trade Fair only two months ago. "Kate stop beating yourself. I have a personnel department, finance and a whole Board behind me. To get this off the ground, you and Emm had to be everything."

"I still didn't expand when I should have done."

"You were hardly to know Emm would push off like that."

She couldn't find the energy to explain that Emm hadn't just worked for the Company - the two of them together were the Company, and more than a mere job had disintegrated.

Jonathan got up. "I'll use your phone Kate, and then we'll be off." When he returned it was to say she was booked the early morning plane to Paris. "I've a meeting at ten. Should be free for lunch; if not you can help me entertain."

"Jonathan no. It's impossible ... there's so much to organise here."

"Which is why you went to a film?"

She looked at him with undisguised fear in her eyes. "The fight's gone out of me Jonathan. What if it doesn't come back?"

"Then I shall lose someone to enthuse with when the new fabrics come out; not a prospect I relish. See you in the morning."

SAFE AS HOUSES

She responded in the confused manner of someone grateful for another to channel operations.

"I've never seen her so desperate," Val said. "She looks terrible."

"Her ambition is crushed and she's been rejected twice in the process - at least that's how she sees it. And the inevitable crack is appearing. Nobody can drive as hard as she does and have reserves when disaster strikes."

"Jonny she's ill. Why Paris for Heaven's sake? A visit to the doctor...a week in bed would make more sense."

Raising his eyebrows in mock remonstration he smiled at his wife. "Like you said Val -such things are for other mortals! Don't worry. If anything can do it, Paris will."

"You're taking a gamble. I hope you're right. What if she doesn't cope?"

"Having opened the French office, she's got to. Otherwise the company will bleed to death. And I'm not sure Kate has recognised the fact."

"That doesn't sound like her."

"You can only adjust to so many shocks at once. She's lost her motivation just when she needs to pull out all the stops. God, I couldn't bear to see her go under, not now."

"Is there a danger?"

"As for any company. But with most, there's young blood waiting in the wings."

Kate had no desire to wake up let alone continue running a company, and with eyes stinging with the need to weep, she looked aghast at the state of her face and hair. "I've got to get a grip. There's too much at stake," and then hopelessly, "For whom?" And in that moment she had identified at least part of the deeper problem. She, like Fred Charlesworth, had needed to subjugate humble background and lack of privilege, and prove an ability to compete with the best, but equally for the resulting success to be acknowledged by their assumed superiors. And like him she was scathed by the fear of failure that menaced always in the background. She washed her hair and towelled away the tears along with the spray that had performed a more useful function.

Jonathan was finding conversation difficult; a situation that had never been part of their experience. "Remember you're replacing a talent, not a person. Kate you've got to divorce commerce from personal relationships." And for the first time she smiled the way she always did when bemused by the human race. "You mean as you are doing by taking me to Paris."

He grinned. "Touché! But you know what I mean."

SAFE AS HOUSES

She tightened her lips. "Yes. I must settle for a business that is no longer also a way of life - which makes it less valuable. I did recognise what I had Jonathan. Every day I knew, and was thankful."

"How did your ad read?" She pulled a copy from her briefcase, and handed it to him.

"Fine. You may have to offer a greater incentive though."

"Then she'd be earning more than the M.D."

"Good Lord, Kate. When did you last update your salary?"

"Can't remember. You see it's only two minutes since I embarked on a policy of divorcing the commercial from the personal!"

He was relieved at the first sign of a lessening tension and saw his opportunity. "Give yourself a nice fat pay rise to boost a wilting ego - as soon as you get back."

"Currently it's hardly warranted."

"It's overdue. And you haven't an option if you're to attract the right designer."

"Supposing Emm wants her money out?"

He registered alarm. "Kate you did have a legal contract drawn up?"

"One that suited us both."

"Has she said...?"

"No. At this moment she doesn't think she'll ever need it. You know Emm - live for today. She believes Duncan will take over where her father left off."

"But you know otherwise."

"I don't know anything anymore. Maybe her faith in him will be justified."

He recognised she had brought the line of enquiry to a close; not because she resented it, but rather because she herself feared to pursue it. "Kate you're stunned, but you *have* to keep up the momentum. Now more than ever. It's crucial."

Abruptly she turned her face to him, anxiety prevalent in every pore. "Help me Jonathan," she pleaded desperately. "Only you know how we tick."

"I also know where! Come on, belt up - we're almost there."

"Kate chérie! Quelle bonne surprise!" Marie Jeanne enveloped her visitor, and as she did so, Kate noticed an elegant silver tray supporting a bottle and three glasses. So Jonathan had telephoned ahead of her arrival.

SAFE AS HOUSES

"Oh I would not make ze good criminal Kate! Yes your cousin, en avance he speak wiz me to say you come. Eh puis alors, we 'ave ze coffee before Armand arrive. And zen we drink to ze future eh?"

So Jonathan had told them no more than was sufficient to explain her drawn appearance and need to see old friends - had perhaps let them think she had not got over Duncan.

"Wonderful. But first I must tell Danielle I am here."

"Zat is not possible because Danielle is not 'ere. She go seek a new client for you - a client wiz much promise, she say."

"I'm intrigued. When do you expect her back?"

"Not before tomorrow. She will be sad to miss you, but I sink maybe better she does not see her ideal Kate looking so defeated."

"Am I such a wreck?"

"Yes. But we remedy after lunch."

Kate smiled weakly. There was something reassuring about being organised by friends. "Danielle *is* doing the work agreed for the hotel?"

"Of course. And when she 'as no time, Brigitte, she come to 'elp. At ziz moment, she types ze menus."

"Why hasn't Danielle mentioned her? I must go and meet her."

"Because she is like boss-lady. When somesing is successful, the world may be informed. Until zen - silence."

Kate tapped at the office door that stood ajar.

"Please come in. You must not knock at ze door of your own company!"

An attractive woman whom Kate assessed to be in her late thirties held out her hand in greeting, but strangely did not get up. But as she leaned forward, the sweater casually thrown over the back of her chair dropped to the floor, revealing a wheelchair.

"Madame Cardules she tell me you are coming. I hope you forgive I do ze work for Danielle from time to time. Danielle she pay me from her own salaire whenever she need my help."

Kate sat down. "Why don't you tell me something about yourself?"

"Certainement. I am Danielle's cousin. My husband, we are separé after my accident and Danielle and I rent un appartement to save ze expense."

She misunderstood the fleeting expression of bitterness that clouded Kate's face. "Madame please do not be angry wiz Danielle. Now zat I live in Paris I am available to help her when she need."

"I'm not angry Brigitte - except of course for not charging the Company for your work, which we shall remedy immediately. Perhaps just a little cross with the world in general. I'm asuming the accident was not so long ago?"

"Less than two years Madame."

"And your husband caused the accident?" As Brigitte appeared disconcerted, Kate added quickly. "Forgive me. It's none of my business."

"Why do you ask zat Madame?"

"Because if he hadn't, he would be sufficiently angry with whom, or what was to blame, to care for you."

The younger woman nodded. "He had drunk a lot perhaps - but only because he was anxious you understand, about his business. Ze car swerved on the road... It is difficult to stay and be reminded each morning of one's guilt. I understand why he need to go."

"And you loved him enough to insist he took his freedom." Kate stood now. "Brigitte, it's been a privilege to meet you. Tell Danielle to put you on the books and to backdate your pay."

"You are not staying Madame?"

"Not this time. I've a few local difficulties to iron out in England. But when I come again, I look forward to seeing you." Observant of tight fingers relaxing, Kate added, "Oh and tell Danielle I approve of the curtains."

"Madame?"

"Les rideaux... sont beaux. Impeccables."

"I am pleased you like them."

"So it was you who made them. And that was why I was only billed for the fabric!"

"I trained in interior design Madame. I enjoyed ze making."

"And I shall enjoy hearing about your career."

"After my legs, I do not try so much... pity for self no good, but so difficult. It is good I 'elp Danielle."

"You're right. Pity for self is no good. But broken dreams need repairing Brigitte." 'And you'd better do just that Kate Benson,' she told herself.

As she retraced her steps to Madame's kitchen, she decided that unhurt people were not much use in the world. Somehow, and soon, she must find the energy and motivation to do what must be done. But where and how, at this moment she had no idea.

Armand was installed in his favourite chair when she returned, and with characteristic disregard of preliminaries, said, "Et puis alors chérie – so you are free at last."

SAFE AS HOUSES

Wanting to know the background to her visit he must first hazard a guess for her to correct. "So Kate, as one becomes older and ze cards have been dealt, we can only exchange them one by one in ze hope of gaining ultimately a better hand n'est-ce pas? But make no mistake, whilst the exchanging of the first card may not prove so 'elpful, it is in itself ze beginning of changing ze whole hand – ze point at which fate makes an intervention." He caressed her hand and Madame, ignoring the gesture, poured coffee.

"Armand, I didn't decide to change anything, and if you're telling me that this is only the beginning of a whole series of changes, I don't think I can bear to listen. But you're right. It's not possible for anything to happen in isolation. And yes I would like to know what other cards I've been dealt, to plan for the survival of my Company." The desperation was evident. "I can't crumble and wait for Providence to take over."

"But it will in any event Kate. We can steer around potential obstacles but it is not given to us to see ze places where we must trust Destiny's own charts. And thank God, for such certainty of direction would destroy the beautiful mystery of life."

Succinctly, if not painlessly, she told what had happened. Madame placed a cocktail beside her. "I zink better than coffee at ziz moment Kate –and also some shouting or a long cry to 'elp you – and also to stop Armand from more armchair philosophy."

"When Duncan left there was relief muddled with the hurt," she went on, "relief that the rows and accusations would come to an end. Had he left me for anyone else, I would have been glad he'd found happiness, and that consequently I'd be relieved of a marriage that had become a millstone. But when Emmeline left the Company, I couldn't affect any such pretence, for the company mattered more than my marriage. I felt destroyed as a person. And you see this isn't the first time I've driven someone away..........Tom came back to find me once but I.... Do you think I'm afraid of loving? Is there something wrong with me ... Might I become an embittered old woman, incapable of loving or being loved?"

Flinging her arms around Kate, uncaring that her most precious crystal was knocked to the ground, Madame shook her head in disbelief. "Kate non! Absolument pas! You are warm creature, and one day you will love again, and wiz spontaneous love – not a dutiful one."

Armand surprising them both, said, "Kate you are a most feminine woman, and Marie Jeanne will on this occasion forgive me my pronouncement. By being ze faithful wife in a futile marriage, you have denied yourself fulfilment in all but your work. Ze friendship wiz Emmeline was an essential part of ze Company into which you 'ave so wrongly thrown your whole life. And it is the Company you love with such puissance. But at this moment, it is your friend who has ze healthy attitude to life. She had her work in perspective, whilst you feel greater confidence to work than to abandon yourself to love, because always you must do what is expected of you – as if ze Company gives you the right to exist. You cannot believe you are valued for what you are. And I do not know why Kate."

His eyes betrayed emotion, and in that moment she knew he had desired her. The moment was electric and Madame moved to collect the glasses. "Loneliness and anxiety create fear, Kate; the mind is greatly harmed by them. Now we dispense with ze notion you will be a dried up matron, what will you do before your cousin come?"

"In the absence of the knight in shining armour you prescribe, I will go to the coiffeuse. That way I shall be ready for him when he arrives!"

"La meilleure idée! And I shall come too so I have less chance of losing the knight I already have!" The direct gaze towards Armand, though intended to be challenging, revealed instead the hurt he had inflicted.

"Jamais chérie," he whispered as she passed him. "Despite his many wanderings."

The whisper had not been inaudible; merely a stage-like indication that the exchange was a private intimacy with the assumption that Kate would treat it so, being inherent in the situation. What was the point of making secret something they knew she already understood.

"To love; to laugh; to 'ave friends Kate. Without these nothing is worth ze battle. Come back. You are good for us also," Madame whispered.

They had clarified her resolution and she could not imagine a future that did not include them.

Jonathan was waiting for her at Orly and grinned broadly at the cousin unrecognisable as the crumpled Kate he had deposited with the Cardules. His gamble had paid off.

"So tell me," he said, taking her bag. "Do I get the impression your French venture is still on the agenda? You didn't decide to offload.... incorporate Danielle into Innovation U.K.?"

"On the contrary," she assured him with a confidence she was reaching for but did not quite yet have in her grasp. "There's another name on the books!"

"Hey! That so? Am I allowed to ask why?"

"Because it was the right thing to do. And now I have to go home and justify it." She saw him smile to himself. "Are you not going to challenge me?"

"Nope." he said. "It's quite enough for me that you're trusting your own intuition again! Tells me everything I need to know!"

The plane soared into the sky heading homewards, and as the lights of the Champs Elysée twinkled below, he leaned back and closed his eyes in relief. Yes, as Kate had reminded him, he knew how they ticked.

Lucy shook her head in disbelief. "Kate! What are you going to do? Mrs.Grant going too!"

"You just watch yourself girl." Alex was concerned. "You can't tackle three jobs."

"Nor will she," Lucy asserted. "Another month you say? Right, keep her 'til then and no longer. Go on calling the shots Kate. By then I'll be recovered."

Alex spun round, his jaw falling open. "Lucy what are you saying!" But he neither expected nor received a response and instantly resigned himself to the fact that the thought would be the deed if she so determined. "We've not yet had a year out o' the shop, you're getting over a stroke, and you want to start work again. Woman if we live to be a hundred I won't never understand ye."

Lucy barely reacted, but continued her thinking aloud. "Exactly. I'm getting over it. And we're family ain't we?"

"Mam, there's no question...." But Alex didn't rate Kate's chances against her mother.

"There's no question cos I didn't ask one. You say Emmeline's left her designs with you? So if you don't find a replacement, ye can count on ye Dad an' me." At which statement, father and daughter's eyebrows shot up simultaneously. "You'll be losing Duggie too surely?"

Acquiring a driver was the least of her worries but Alex said quietly, "I'd really enjoy giving you a hand with the deliveries Kate, 'til yer find somebody."

She left them with the belief they had saved her from imminent collapse, but the necessity to prevent Lucy attempting work again was now imperative.

SAFE AS HOUSES

Applications had occupied her desk for some days. She could prevaricate no longer. "A scoop of inexperienced college graduates," she complained as she dictated further advertisements.

"Didn't you say your mother has offered Mrs. Carter?" Helen asked.

"I did. But I didn't say it was a good idea; certainly something I'd prefer to avoid. Regrettably there won't be a chance of keeping her out if she discovers I haven't found a replacement for Mrs. Grant. Arrange visits for me to Lamberts, and Belle Hélène - better make it lunch for the latter."

"Lamberts sent a reminder whilst you were away – payment is overdue."

"Oh Helen Why didn't you say?"

"I did leave you a note. Actually rather a lot of things have been mounting up. I'm happy to work late if it would help."

"I'm sorry. It's entirely my fault. And yes if you possibly could, I'd be very grateful. Is there pressure from any other supplier?"

"No but two orders are still waiting completion on your approval."

"I'll deal with them immediately."

"Mr. Jensen is due at 11.30."

"Phil! What does he want? Helen put him off... Tell him .. oh anything."

"Mrs. Carter, you asked him to come, remember? - To discuss the loan for the new machinery. I rather think he's already on his way."

"Then I must see him. I'll work late by myself tonight and leave you a batch of typing for tomorrow. Meanwhile get the visits arranged, adverts placed and these quotations in today's post." She withdrew paperwork from her briefcase. "Fabric samples are to be included wherever indicated."

Her secretary looked aghast. "Did you get any sleep last night Mrs. Carter?"

"I shall tonight, knowing they're done! Aren't I seeing a buyer this afternoon?"

"3.30. She rang to confirm yesterday."

"Good. As soon as Mr. Jensen leaves, stave off any further interruptions."

She was, in the event, pleased to see him.

"Real body blow Kate. Especially as Paris isn't up and running at a profit yet - not that it's to be expected." His pencil shadowed a column of figures, and she perused the paperwork he presented.

"Timing and cash flow are the problem?"

"Don't be too ambitious about repayments on the new plant. Your borrowing is about right. Join me for a lunch time drink?"

"Another time Phil. Just now it's full sail into the wind."

"And in uncharted waters?"

SAFE AS HOUSES

She nodded and he sensed the fear in her; a fear that manifested itself in a bruised confidence that concerned him much more than the balance sheet.

Lucy carried out her threat when Mrs. Grant left, and Kate was forced to admit the skill that had lain latent for years was even sharper for the long respite. Fingers that had been so cruelly restricted, now flew dextrously over the creations that took shape under her supervision. Alex, unobtrusive as always, not only regained the dignity of performing a job despite disability but was of practical help to a daughter he still idolised. They slipped back into each other's lives, finding recovery in the powerful strength of familiarity that cocooned them.

And so with a temporary stability at base, Kate began to rebuild a shattered ego. She forged new contacts, concealing apprehension behind a practised mask of assurance. She was stunned to discover that two long-standing clients had been tempted away, and intent on preventing further slippage, redoubled her efforts, being forced to realise how near the precipice she had walked. It was a lonely acceptance of a salutary lesson, and she determined to focus solely on marketing and was thus disquieted when Helen told her that one of the seniors in the workroom had left in high dudgeon.

"What prompted that?"

"There was an altercation." Helen was embarrassed. "I think Mrs. Benson was involved."

"My mother! Helen, tell me the whole story." Kate slumped into a chair, listening without interruption to an account of how Lucy had 'perhaps a little tactlessly' criticised the positioning of a pocket trim, and had 'somehow' incurred the wrath of the recipient of her remarks.

"And not for the first time Helen - is that what you don't want to tell me?" Her secretary paused, relieved to have offloaded an awkward duty. "I think perhaps Doris found it difficult to adjust to Mrs. Benson. I'm sure it would have been the same whoever had taken over."

"And just how many does Doris represent, Helen?" Kate ignored the platitude. The hesitation that followed made the reply superfluous.

"Designer interviews are fixed for the 26th. It would be politic to let it be known that the ad for Mrs. Grant's position will be in this week's press, offering immediate appointment. I thought it was understood my mother was only here temporarily."

SAFE AS HOUSES

"I think they did at first. Then when things were going well and you decided to wait for the new designer to take a hand in choosing her own number two..."

Kate smiled. "They thought there was a possibility she would choose my mother? Well that's an admission of her ability and no mistake!"

"So there's no need to upset Mrs. Benson?"

Kate smiled. "Helen you are as twitchy as I am to think of the consequences if I did! But I shall speak with her. She can't be allowed to empty the sewing room before the new designer arrives."

"She was probably right Mrs. Carter ... about the pocket I mean."

"Oh undoubtedly Helen." And to herself added, "When was she not! But it's Dad I must see first, for he'll be the one most affected."

"I hope you're not going to sack us both Kate!" Alex asked as she joined him in the greenhouse that evening. "You know how outspoken she can be when she's ruffled."

"I should by now! I've been more than grateful to you both for coming to the rescue. Mam realises the job must come to an end soon. But Dad, if you want to carry on..."

He covered her hand with his own. "I couldn't leave her all day on her own, but I'd appreciate the chance to fill in when you're busy so ye don't have to pay overtime rates. I've really enjoyed working together. Just like the Charlesworth days eh?"

"Me too."

"Kate."

"Yes?"

"You will be happy again soon won't you?"

Squeezing his hand she feigned conviction, and in the language of her childhood said, "Course I will Dad."

"Let's go and put her out of her misery for she's ready to bite off her own tongue."

Lucy had the kettle boiling. "Another difficult day for you Kate," she said casually. "Here, drink this up. I've made some of your favourite scones as well."

An outsider would think she had no part in it, Kate reflected wryly. "And for you too Mam I hear."

"Not the pleasantest when all a body is trying to do is 'elp her own." Pausing to ascertain no rejoinder, she continued, "Seems to me our Kate, you've been too soft on those girls by half."

SAFE AS HOUSES

"Possibly." Kate's tone was deliberately conciliatory. "So it will be helpful all round when we appoint Mrs. Grant's successor."

Only briefly wrong footed, Lucy asked, "That going to be soon then?"

"Immediately after the designer. It's best she chooses her own assistant."

Lucy quickly regained the upper hand. "Probably as well. Ye Dad's legs were playing up again last night."

"Lucy they were not!" Alex was visibly annoyed. "I've thoroughly enjoyed being mobile again. It's been a change for both of us."

Lucy looked crestfallen in a bid for benevolence. "So it was a good decision then - to help our Kate?"

"One of your best pal," Alex conceded with a sigh.

A satisfactory outcome achieved in that both husband and daughter were now grateful to her, she would make the most of the time left before she must hand over. After all these years she was doing the job that was sheer unmitigated joy to her. And she had proved herself a match for Mrs. Grant. But tired, uncannily tired. It was the tiredness that had made her snap at Doris. Surely the woman could see that. It annoyed her that fatigue could suddenly envelop her for no reason. One minute she was as alert as a cock robin and the next could fall asleep in the middle of a task if she didn't keep the tightest grip on herself. If only she could stay in Kate's workroom to the end of her days, she would have at last realised her wildest dream.

Tears of frustration filled her eyes. She'd never lost her temper in the shop no matter what provocation. Why today? Well, there was no going back; the damage was done now. She must make every moment count until Kate appointed someone. The fabrics, the creations, the excitement - they all added up to Paradise. To think she had turned down Kate's offer all those years ago because she had to be 'top dog' in her own shop.

CHAPTER THIRTY

For her office Kate preferred bunches of flowers picked from the garden, to the exotic arrangements from the florist that adorned the main entrance and stairways. She had for years picked snowdrops and daffodils from the copse behind the factory on her way from flat to boutique; rediscovering the thrill she had felt as a little townie, gathering buttercups with Aunt Polly who had called them treasure. Treasure. A tree laden with plums, the delicious smell of apple pies from the range, hearing the drone of the engines that told the pilots were safely home, and then falling into a deep and blissful sleep between cool crisp sheets. Most of all, walking the lanes in a togetherness that turned the ordinary into something special; sharing thoughts and feelings that were to fill the diary for Oliver.

She would wander from room to room, examining work in progress, samples, trimmings and haberdashery. Kate loved this time of the morning before the machines whirred and phones began to ring. And then, as they who were part of her world could be heard arriving, she would gravitate to the sketches on Emm's drawing board; sketches that held promise of new creations, and that in the months ahead would give reason to their future. People, ideas and skills; the fusing of them into an integrated whole. Treasure.

But today marked the beginning of the most fundamental change to which her enterprise had been subjected, and one that still threatened to tear her apart, for Emm was so central a lack.

"Was it difficult when you appointed Miss Charlesworth, Mrs Carter?" Helen asked as she handed Kate the shortlist.

"Not at all. Just intuitive one hundred per cent certainty!"

She recalled the backdrop against which she had put her suggestion to Emmeline. Today's setting, like the ad in the quality press, was infinitely more up-market. She would hardly be interrupted by traders shouting 'Mind yer backs now!'

Apologising that the day would be peppered with interruptions as candidates were shown the organisation, she knew she was eliciting unspoken assurances from foremen and senior staff, of courteous cooperation and the traditional welcome to visitors, ironically with which only Lucy was as yet unfamiliar.

A tall, assured young woman, nudging thirty Kate guessed, gave shape and form to the application bearing her name. Cruelly she was not unlike Emm, but forty minutes later, the differences were pronounced and the first 'No' was pencilled.

"Ready for Mrs. O'Mahn Mrs. Carter?" Helen asked.

"As ready as I'll ever be, Helen."

She hid her amusement behind a welcoming smile as the second applicant beamed herself into the room. Plump, hair as dishevelled as if she had ridden a point to point, shiny nose and face aglow with sheer good health, she took Kate's hand in the manner of greeting a much loved Granny. Without ado, she unclasped the huge folder, spilling numerous small sketches from between the full sized ones intended for presentation.

"Blessed if I don't get myself organised one day," she breezed, immediately winning the heart of one who adored characters unfettered by convention.

"I can at least give her some interview experience," Kate decided.

But when the sketches were retrieved and order restored, it was obvious that interview experience was all that was needed.

"What d'ye think Mrs. Carter? D'ye like them?"

"Very impressive. Mrs. O'Mahn, you have real talent."

"So just me that needs smartening up! And 'tis Molly I am."

Her personality would have defied any attempt to pull rank and Kate looked again at the stylish, upbeat outfits. "This is Chelsea territory Molly."

"So will I do?"

"My initial reaction is that I may not do for you."

"Because they are not for the cocktail set?"

"Maybe their daughters though." Kate was suddenly feeling invigorated. "Problem is even those daughters like to be independent nowadays and have no compunction about buying off the peg. Department stores would have to be the main outlet."

"You do supply both markets Mrs. Carter?"

"You did your homework. I wonder why you didn't bring styles relevant to our mainstream clientèle?"

"I figured you had that side covered and were looking to expand."

"I see." She liked Molly O'Mahn, admired her work though it would not satisfy current orders. "I'd like to help you Molly. I have a number of people to see - but if you felt able to leave your work with me, there's someone....."

"No problem Mrs. Carter. I don't plan on going back until...." But she was interrupted by an agitated Helen opening the door.

"I'm so sorry." Turning to Molly she stammered, "Please excuse me. Mrs. Carter is needed urgently. Would you mind waiting outside please?" Fear and apprehension were palpable.

"Helen what's happened?"

"Mrs. Carter, your mother. She's very ill. Please come quickly. Jenny found her collapsed after showing Miss Cheverton off the premises. It was all so sudden."

Someone had covered Lucy with a blanket. "It's happening again," she forced a whisper. "The tingling in my arm. Feel it Kate. Don't leave me." She shuddered as her voice assumed a strange slur, and the arm slumped beside her.

"Call an ambulance. Tell them to hurry - second stroke patient," Kate instructed hoarsely. She eased a pillow someone handed her, beneath Lucy's head, and felt the sweating and tumultuous pulse in the back of her neck. "Lie quietly Mam. Don't talk. The ambulance is coming." Holding both hands and oblivious of those who stood solicitously but helplessly around, Kate whispered over and over, "I love you."

"Kate." Lucy's voice strained now, barely audible. "Look after Bob. Stay with him - don't leave him."

"I will. Ssh now." She spoke gently with a calm she did not feel.

"The ambulance is here!" the junior watching from the window, called.

Lucy died before they reached the hospital. For a long time Alex could not speak, but stared into a space somewhere beyond the room. Numb and detached, wrapped in an icy unreality, the tears would not come. They clung tautly to each other, he and Kate, feeling somehow abstract and superficial, disbelieving of this enormous irreversible happening, yet unable to flee its hollow grasp. Calls to Scotland and Australia; funeral arrangements that somehow, once set in motion, seemed to be happening despite them. And Bob to be comforted. Bob whose acceptance of each day's fate demanded no explanation, only Kate to fill the cavernous void of Mam not being there.

On the eve of the funeral, Kate took him to the office whilst Alex, heavily sedated, at last slept.

SAFE AS HOUSES

"Mrs. Carter, I didn't expect to see you," Helen said.
"I wanted to thank you for holding the fort."
"I've hardly done that. You're the one who makes things happen. I cancelled the interviews of course, and postponed any visits."
"Yes ... Frankfurt... were they willing?"
"I didn't need to contact Frankfurt. When I explained to Mr. Brightman what had happened, he did some rescheduling to include your new clients - personal visits on your behalf to keep them interested. Said to tell you he's desperately sorry and that his wife will be at the funeral for both of them - that your mother would understand that you're just as important."
Kate grimaced. "I'm not sure she would. She was a stickler for protocol. He'd be on the carpet if she were here!"
Helen smiled at the incongruity of the statement, and Kate said, "I'm not sure how things will fit together yet Helen. My father is still in shock and..." With Bob present she did not continue, but there was no doubting from Helen's sympathetic nod that her promise to Lucy had been the subject of office speculation.

They followed the cortège out into the churchyard, Alex and Kate, with Gill and Bob close behind. Her father's grip on her fingers made her knuckles whiten as he stared blankly into the hole that received his wife's body, whilst someone put soil into his hand to shower down on her. Devoid of the comfort, stability and protection that being married meant for him, he whispered, "I don't want to be without you Luce. Nothing means anything now. We should've gone together."
Jimmy and George Corfield were among the mourners. "Saw it in the paper." George explained. "No mistakin' who it was when we read you girls' names. Ye Ma were good to us as kids. Couldn't not come."
"You'll come back to Dad's home?" Kate invited.
"Thanks Kate but I've left the 'ot dog stall down the road. Didn't want to park it wi' all the other cars. But Jim could stay, couldn't yer brov?"
Jim smoothed the ill fitting, borrowed suit, and sought words to convey that though he had not come with that expectation, he would very much like to.
No-one stayed long. Dr.Bostin's anxious glances at Alex left them in no doubt that the sooner he could rest, the better. One by one they offered condolences and left.
"Alright to phone for a cab Mr. Benson?" Jim asked.

"Kate'd create if I let ye," Alex replied. "And I don't need two lasses to guard me."

As her car pulled away, he sat wearily and said, "He's been wanting to talk to our Kate ever since he came. Thick as thieves when they were kids."

"I didn't notice Dad. And I didn't think you'd been aware of much."

"It's ye Mam I've lost Gill, not my wits." The abruptness was something she knew Kate would have understood. To her he was curt in a way that prevented her getting as close as each yearned.

"If ye drop me in the town centre, Kate, that'll be fine."

"Where's home Jim?"

"Nowhere you need see. I've got lodgings - I'm alright."

"No family." She made an assessment rather than posed a question.

"Not since I did a stretch inside. You married?"

"Separated."

"Thought you were the 'death-us-do-part' sort o girl."

"I won't argue with that. Why did you go inside?"

"Cos I got caught."

"Sorry."

"Where do you work – or maybe yer don't 'ave to?"

"In a boutique."

"That's a posh name for a shop ain't it? Funny, that don't seem to fit you either - shop assistant I mean." His hands thrust deeper in his pockets. "Always envied you as a kid. But you know what I envied you most?" He grinned for the first time. "Even more'n yer Mam's cooking? That trip you made to the country. Fields to kick a ball.... all that green. I was so mad at you when you didn't want to go."

As they approached a junction she waited for him to indicate which way.

"Drop me here. Sorry about yer Ma. Missed yer when yer left the street."

She pulled off the road, and scribbling the address of the cottage on an envelope, pushed it into his hand. "If ever you need space again, just get on a train. Call me. I'll arrange the rest. And thanks for coming Jim. Mam would have been really pleased."

She picked up the road again, suddenly registering Val hadn't been at the funeral. Strange. She would check when she got back. Then tomorrow they must all begin a life without Lucy.

Gill was on the phone when she let herself in. "I'll tell her as soon as she comes. Try not to worry. Oh she's here now." Gill covered the mouthpiece.

"It's Val. Jonathan's been involved in an accident."

SAFE AS HOUSES

A chill struck through Kate as she took the receiver. "What happened?"

"Kate thank goodness. I got a call this afternoon just as I was leaving for the funeral. Seems he was in a collision...I'll fly out in the morning. Kate you will come? I don't speak any German... and oh Kate, what if..."

"Val, give me the hospital number. It might be something minor; an overnight check. Does his company know?"

"It was his secretary who phoned. Kate this is awful - you've just had Aunt Lucy's funeral. I'm sorry - was everything alright, and Uncle Alex - is he bearing up? Bob - poor thing, he'll be so bewildered and oh Kate I'm out of my mind with worry."

"Dad and Bob are both resting. Val give me the number. I'll get back to you as soon as I've made contact."

She recognised the Frankfurt prefix. He had been rushing to do her job as well as his own, adding her clients to his already full schedule... exceeding speed limits ... too fast round a corner and now lying in the casualty ward of a Frankfurt hospital. 'Jonathan, be alright,' she pleaded as she dialled.

An eternity passed before she was linked to the ward. She rang as his wife, and aghast at what she heard, said she would be out on the first available flight. Her face ashen, and mind reeling, she signalled to Gill to come to the kitchen. "Jonathan's in Intensive Care. Can you stay with Dad and Bob for another day whilst I go to Frankfurt with Val." Gill hesitated. "Gill I must go. Surely you've got staff to put in overtime. Bill it to me. Anything. If there's a plane, we'll go tonight."

"You can't Kate. You're all in." And then, "It's that serious?"

Minutes later she lied, "Val the morning flight's booked. There's one in four hours if.."

"We'll go. But Kate what about your father....."

Believing she was responsible, she recoiled at the thanks. "Gill's staying on. Get a taxi to the boutique. I'll leave a message and drive us to the airport."

"Kate, you're mad." Gill's whisper was insistent. "You're exhausted."

"Not anymore," she said. Truthfully, for adrenalin had taken over.

"You've got some problems Kate. I can see in your eyes," Alex said.

She explained, and pressed him to go to bed. "For Mam. She's at rest now."

"I'd rather she was here."

"I know."

"You do what you have to do love. Bob and me'll be all right. Wish Jonathan well for me. He's a fine man Kate."

"The best," she whispered. "And please God let him live."

SAFE AS HOUSES

Dawn was breaking as Val, stunned and shaking, stared at the stranger in front of her.

"I am sorry Frau Brightman. Your husband did not regain consciousness. I can only comfort you with the assurance he suffered no pain."

It was for Kate to be strong, and she struggled violently with her emotions. But her love of the cousin now dead was as fierce in its own way as that of the wife who mourned him. "We are staying at the Mannheim," she heard herself saying. "Perhaps you'd prescribe a sedative for my sister in law..."

Then they walked silently away, arms linked, feeling a strange and fearful amputation.

CHAPTER THIRTY-ONE

Urgency written across his face, Phil Jensen strode towards Helen. "Is Kate in her office?"

"She mostly is these days. And she must have spoken with clients because I'm not having to make excuses. All routine orders are going out but there are no new orders... "

"Helen she's got to pull out all the stops. The Company is heading for trouble - and fast. It doesn't take long. I'll have to play the heavy with her. Meanwhile you get on to all the candidates and re-arrange interviews."

"I'll talk with Kate and tell her what you suggest," Helen replied testily.

"It's urgent."

"It's also Kate's company."

"One that she's in danger of losing! She hasn't been out in the field. There are no new orders or contracts. Business is not just about an efficiently run base. And she still has no designer. A fashion house without a designer Helen! It's as crucial as that."

"It's exactly four weeks since she buried her mother and Jonathan was killed, and before that the minor detail of her partner stealing her husband. It would have driven most people into an institution, let alone put them on hold for awhile."

Jenson relaxed his tone. "Helen, I've the greatest regard for Kate. Her energy and achievements have left me nothing short of breathless, which is why I'm so anxious not to let her go down the pan now. But this is the price she pays for going solo. She can't afford time to recover, for the simple reason the Company won't be here when she does."

Helen was grateful to be interrupted by a buzz from Kate's extension, and placing a warning finger on her lips, picked up the receiver.

"You seem to have a nettled visitor, Helen. Can you handle it, or would you like me to see him?"

"It's Mr. Jensen Mrs.Carter."

"Ask him to come in. And bring him a cup of tea to calm him down."

"Kate! Good to see you."

SAFE AS HOUSES

"Phil. Are you well?" She was pale, had lost weight, but was composed.

"Sorry you heard me getting hot under the collar with Helen," he said.

"Sorry you did, or sorry I heard you?" she teased gently. "I'd prefer the former. It's not for employees to deal with the heat in my kitchen."

"Kate – it's the heat I'm here to warn you about."

"I don't need warnings about the prevailing winds and currents, Phil. I've been around a long time too you know - or had you forgotten?"

She was wrong footing him, and he sought inspiration as Helen came in with tea. "But if you realise the extent of the difficulties......."

"Why am I not rushing across Europe to rescue the situation?"

"Well, yes. I just thought you had been too punch drunk to have realised. If you've already faced the problem, then thankfully we're further ahead than I supposed. Just pick up the phone and tell Helen to reorganise the interviews for designer. We'll raise a temporary loan to cover the outstanding invoices and use available cash to buy in more fabrics etc. If you start now you can pull it back. Kate with you ready to go again, the problem isn't major. This is wonderful news! Do it Kate. Do it now!"

Her tone quiet, almost tranquil, was unquestionably intransigent. "No."

Frustrated and perplexed, he brought his hand down on the desk. "Hell why not? Are you going to sit and let a tide of bankruptcy lap around your feet whilst you consider the options, because I warn you Kate, there are none!"

Patience was not his strong suit. "Kate stop playing cat and mouse with me. Unless you act swiftly, the Company you've lived for will bleed to death."

"You could hardly have put it more succinctly."

Again she was in control. He leaned both elbows on her desk and supporting his head, exhaled his exasperation. "You've lost me. You realise the Company's on its uppers, but you're refusing to do a damn thing about it!"

"The Company's already dead, Phil." Her voice was shaking now.

"No Kate. No! You can pull it round!" he insisted vehemently."

"It died with Emm and Jonathan," she continued. "I've no wish to resurrect it. Indeed I'm grateful not to have appointed a designer."

Putting his hand over hers, he said, "Helen was right. It's all been too much. Kate you are the Company. It is not dead, nor ever will be! Just think for a moment. If you gave up on this, what would you do?"

"I shall be with Bob, and my father for whatever time he has left."

"If you sell now," he persisted, "without a designer.... without yourself at the helm, and clients falling away, it will be at a serious financial loss. Play

SAFE AS HOUSES

your cards right and you can remain a very rich woman. What you are proposing is little short of financial suicide!"

"I've already informed our major clients that we shall not continue, so that they can make alternative arrangements with other fashion houses."

"What!"

"You have to have a reason to do things Phil - or not to do them. The boutique can be advertised as a separate unit. That's what it was when we began. The machinery can be sold to pay off the workforce; I'd like them to be given at least a month's notice. Many have families depending on them."

"A week is all that's required," her accountant interrupted sullenly.

"You've had no cause to criticize my style of management in the past."

"Management has not been my job."

"Exactly."

Polite restraint beyond him, he refused to allow her to have the last word. "You've no shareholders; you've resisted offers to be taken over. Spend a year bringing the company back to peak, then pull out – put in an MD."

"I don't claim that wisdom has much to do with it, but I've made my decision. It wasn't difficult."

Plainly incensed, he thrust her file into his briefcase and stood to go, but he could not be so churlish as to stalk out, refusing the hand she proffered. "Kate, let me come back tomorrow. Maybe I haven't been as tactful today as you had a right to expect."

"On the contrary, you've been as businesslike as ever. I chose you years ago as our financial watchdog, and never once regretted my choice."

"Then why won't you listen to my advice for God's sake!"

"Its very good advice. And if I still had a company, I wouldn't hesitate to take it. But I haven't. The Company is over. The creation of it was exhilarating; and competing with the best in the business and working with the two people I most esteemed, was the ultimate satisfaction."

He made one last attempt to score where it hurt. "What about senior staff who've been loyal to you... have seen themselves as part of the business. - Helen... Mrs Gr.." He had to accept she was in fact standing almost alone.

"There's a right time for everything Phil, and this is it. I have in fact, a plan to put to Helen and Danielle and if they find it attractive, I shan't hesitate to ask you to stay with us. But I'd appreciate it now if you'd leave me or I shall become very unbusinesslike and bawl my head off as Emm would have said."

"Kate." He drew her to him as her defence crumbled.

SAFE AS HOUSES

"Please Phil. Just leave me."

Helen was covering her typewriter as he closed the door of Kate's office behind him. "Goodnight Mr. Jensen. I'll just collect the tea tray."

He put a restraining hand on her arm, and suggested it could wait 'til morning. "Is she alright? ... Kate's not going under is she?"

"Possibly Helen. But I suspect not for long - though I'm damned if I know how. She'll talk with you tomorrow. Best if we go now."

Their dropping of the Yale latch echoed in the stillness. Kate opened the door to the workroom and sat in the window seat from where she had admired so many final fittings, and didn't move for some time, at first unaware of a fear - almost hysteria - that was growing within her, setting her whole body trembling. It was as if all the striving, the tenacity and discipline of the past twenty odd years were being replaced with bewilderment and panic. She couldn't put it all together yet, but knew intuitively the futility of clinging to that that had passed. There was a time to let go - even of one's own creation - and that time was now.

Relationships, meaningful work. She had been fortunate to have both, but the price they exacted was grief. The tremendous energy she had once possessed had, since Jonathan's accident, consumed itself in perpetuating doubt. Nothing seemed of consequence any more, except the enormous sadness of his death; that a simple matter of making a call for her could result in a changed world. She had reached her decision. Maybe there could now be interludes of calm on this voyage into the unknown. Yearning for that which could not be, she made her way up to the flat. The application forms lay scattered on the kitchen worktop. She picked up Molly O'Mahn's and dialled the number provided.

"Why Mrs. Carter of course I remember. What a dreadful day that was for you."

Kate told her that circumstances were now radically changed, but that she could offer interim help should it be of interest.

"Oh yes please, Mrs. Carter. However interim, I'm interested. I don't know what's wrong with my interview technique. Maybe you'll tell me."

"I'll help you all I can. Tomorrow at 4.30?"

The shriek of delight was not quite withheld until the receiver had been replaced.

She made one further call to Paris. Danielle would fly to UK next day. Of course she could; there was so little business being generated that she must be wondering how to justify her position. Tomorrow, one way or another, tension would be eased. The choking feeling at last began to subside, and if she felt just a little peace, it was not because the burden had been lifted, but rather she had found a way to accept it. She could even feel the beginnings of a creative urge to get on with whatever had to be changed; only a frightening nausea drained her yet of the energy to do it. It was not the end of the darkness, but the first bit of comfort in it.

Next morning she informed Helen of her decision. Handing her a sheaf of typing, Kate said, "With these out of the way, I propose we run down everything in this order."

Helen looked at the list, and then back again imploringly. "But you've put your whole life into this business."

"Three lives actually Helen. And yes, you know I'm sure because I'm talking about it. I've asked Danielle over. A train from Euston links with her flight and arrives at 11. We'll have a working lunch in the flat and if she's receptive to my proposal, I shall ask you to consider staying on in a similar capacity. I'll speak to the workforce this morning so they can leave as and when opportunities arise over the next weeks. There'll be items we shall need legal advice on." Her lips tightened. "I'm not so experienced in winding things down!"

There were few recriminations once it became clear that no-one would be pushed out in a hurry, and time off would be allowed for interviews, for there was plenty of work in the town.

"Ask prospective employers to telephone your supervisors and we shall be happy to speak for each of you," she assured them. "In the meanwhile, the boundaries of your positions are likely to be less rigidly defined. I would appreciate it if we could all work together to do what has to be done."

She suggested to the duty foreman he allow an extended coffee break for the topic to be given a thorough airing. Having worked for her long enough to appreciate the pain the decision would have caused her, he knew better than to fear it had been hurriedly made. Recognised too that without her characteristic vigour, she could not perform, as she had always done, work that was more than enough for two. She must have felt that not only had she lost Miss Charlesworth and Mr. Brightman, but half of her very self.

"I'll stay 'til it's all wound up M'm," he said.

"Not if you get a good offer Ted. Don't miss an opportunity."

"If I'm not good enough to wait for, they can find somebody else."

"I'm grateful. And so very sorry to do this."

"Anyone with half a brain'll know that. Tea help - if I'm not presuming?"

SAFE AS HOUSES

In the event it was the perching on two stools surrounded by worksheets, duty rosters and deadlines, that comforted. Ted moved to cover the girlie calendar his young assistant had insisted every works office should have, but she waved his gesture aside as the notice he pinned over the provocative bosom, fell to the floor. "I have seen such almanacs before Ted"

"I expect so M'm."

"Are they going to be alright?" she asked.

"The women will have no problem; they're all good workers. Danny will find it a bit harder, being only used to the steam press as yet."

"Give him all the help he needs. And thanks for the tea."

"You alright now M'm?"

"When weren't we Ted?"

"That's the ticket. You take care now." He watched as the woman whose resilience he had long admired, walked back to her office.

"Try Mr.Jensen's number for me Helen please," she said. "Then go and meet Danielle. Take her for a coffee."

So it was carte blanche to spill the beans, and grave though it was for her, Kate was playing down the significance of the business ceasing to trade as far as they were concerned. But whatever idea she was entertaining, it was an academic exercise; she was not on fire as she had been when she had discussed a new design with Miss Charlesworth, or planned an itinerary with Mr.Brightman. Dark rings still circled the eyes that lacked the fervour and enthusiasm that had previously made them sparkle so expressively. Sometimes, Helen thought, she looked as if she were planning for tomorrow without the conviction of getting through today.

Phil Jensen listened attentively as she put forward her plan. "Can be done of course. As I said yesterday, winding a business down is not going to yield either income or capital commensurate with selling one that's flourishing internationally. But you know that without my shouting the odds, and for reasons I have trouble accepting, you want to do it this way. It's your business."

"You're still sore."

"I've watched you make a roaring success on the strength of investing a few quid years ago on a market stall. What reaction do you expect? Sure you've some problems now, but it's the first time you've been in troubled waters - business-wise, that is," he added hurriedly. "Watching the incredible growth over the years, I just know you could steer the thing through. I thought you knew better than to bring sentiment into business."

SAFE AS HOUSES

"On the contrary, it's probably what mine was founded on, as I told you yesterday. Today I'm asking if what I propose is feasible financially."

"On the face of it, yes," he agreed reluctantly. "But you'll lose money in the process."

"I've already lost the only things that matter. Shall we talk again when I've had a reaction from the girls?"

She put a call through to the bungalow to check all was well on the domestic front. Now that he had become familiar with the fact of her calling around the same time each day, Bobby was invariably the one to pick up the receiver. "Hello Kate. Love you. When you come?"

"Not so late tonight Bob. Soon I'll have more time to spend with you."

"Like that Kate. Go to Wales again? Long time now."

She had made him his own telephone book with the few numbers he was ever likely to need, written in bold black pen with a photograph beside each to remind him whose numbers they were. Learning to dial had been a major achievement, and it was a while before the novelty wore off.

She heard Helen's car and went out to greet her visitor. They looked at each other for a moment before Kate dispensed with formal greeting and opened her arms to Danielle.

"Oh Madame. It is very 'appy to be wiz you...... I remember I stay 'ere when we first come to England. In ze early morning I walk in ze wood and know for me I find exactly ze right organisation." Helen shot her a warning glance. "I am so sorry. Now I make your speech to me ze more difficile for I understand you wish a termination."

"On the contrary, hearing that you find us so much to your liking gives me hope to think you might want to stay." She looked from one to the other and her French protégé thought how much she had aged. "Helen will have told you that I'm unable to continue, in fact I'm bringing everything to a close."

"You will close ze Paris office too Madame?"

"I've no option. My agreement with the Cardules will be honoured to the letter, but the fashion business will cease there, as here." She paused. "When you've had time to freshen up, we'll have lunch and I'll put an idea to you. If it has any initial appeal, we can thrash out a possible strategy."

She set out her plans to dispose of the business as it stood, but only the nature of it. She would retain the land and factory, converting them into a Conference Centre. "This is where you come in Danielle. You've demonstrated an aptitude that has impressed me enormously. But it would mean moving to England."

SAFE AS HOUSES

Turning to her secretary she said, "It goes without saying Helen that I very much hope you'd be willing to double as secretary and receptionist until we generate enough business to engage further personnel. From the projections I've done, the three of us, plus janitor and domestic staff, could cover most aspects until we are up and running ... very much as Emmeline, Mrs. Grant and I functioned in the early stages of Innovation. What I'm warning you about is that it certainly won't be a nine to five affair, and a job description impossible to write. We'd turn our hands to whatever required attention."

She had engaged their interest. "The flat would provide accommodation for you Danielle - with a room for each of us, to use as and when required."

"But Madame, this is your apartement.... it 'as your charactère."

"I have a large house which at last will be useful to me when, as I expect will be the case my brother comes to live with me."

A comfortable silence claimed the room as each thought her own thoughts. .

"Won't such a conversion be very expensive," Helen asked.

"New beginnings are always expensive Helen. And yes, from a coldly financial point of view it might be more sensible to dispense with the whole thing lock stock and barrel. You said earlier that I had put my whole life into it. And you were right. But even if I can no longer live with the business as it is, I do have to go on living. And I have an innate desire to create rather than merely function. But whatever I now create must be tailored to a new life style. I think it perfectly feasible that Bob will be capable of simple caretaking duties, under supervision - but that is for later. Today we are here to consider working as a team. Or not - as you decide. You may feel this is the time to move to other organisations. I've merely put forward an idea. That's all it can be at this stage until I have your reactions. Mr. Jensen agrees it's possible - though with distinct lack of enthusiasm. Overall, given a positive reaction from you, I'm hopeful."

Helen, physically closer to the business on a day-to-day basis was finding it difficult to disassociate herself from the numerous questions that had occupied Kate's mind over the past weeks, whilst Danielle, having been stunned over coffee as Helen had regaled her with developments, now weighed the possibilities and found the prospect agreeable.

"Absolutely no hard feelings if you reject the idea," Kate assured them. "Whatever you decide, I shall always be grateful to have worked with you. I must go to the boutique now; I'm meeting someone at three."

Walking back through the copse, she knew if the project had any hope of success, the two younger women had to feel as right about each other as she

SAFE AS HOUSES

and Emm had done all those years ago, and neither preparation nor planning could make that happen. She was already fatigued. Doing what must be done to save her sanity was draining her, for her mind persisted in the notion that the past months had been a nightmare and at any moment, Jonathan's car would swerve into the drive. Which all made it incredibly difficult to hold tenaciously to her resolve.

"Mrs. Carter! Hello again. How are you? I can't wait to hear what you want to discuss! Are you really closing the whole operation down? I can't believe it! I couldn't see your secretary, so I just came in."

"Whoa!" Kate laughed. "Sit down - or do I have to lasso you?"

In the course of the next hour her visitor listened in quiet amazement as she was offered use of all Kate's business facilities for the duration of the closing down exercise. "I don't know how quickly the machinery will take to offload, but as long as it, and the personnel to operate it, are here, they are yours to capitalise on," Kate informed her, "though obviously any outstanding orders on my books must take precedence."

Kate would continue to display models in the boutique window to the left of the main entrance, whilst Miss O'Mahn could utilise the one to the right. There was only one stipulation: her designs must be labelled 'Innovation – Jeunesse.' As far as the boutique was concerned, it would be sold as a healthy going-concern.

"Think it over," Kate said, her energy deserting her now.

"That won't be necessary Mrs. Carter. I'll go and buy a toothbrush and a pair of knics. I'll be here to start in the morning."

Suddenly, the thought of someone else using Emm's desk caused a pain so sharp, it was discernible to the one who had unwittingly inflicted it.

"Mrs. Carter are you OK? Can I get you a drink...aspirin?"

"Thank you Molly. I'm fine now."

She was committing to the past that on which she had dreamed of building her future. If there was pain, it was all part of the process of letting go, and had to be endured.

A call came through from Helen. "Mrs.Carter, we were wondering if you'd mind if we made a meal in the flat before I go home?"

"Nothing would please me more. Do I take it you're near a decision?"

"Could have given you mine yesterday when you hinted there was a possibility of continuing to work with you!"

SAFE AS HOUSES

"I can't tell you what it means to hear that. But you do realise that once we are up and running I won't be putting in a hundred per cent as I did with Innovation - unless of course Danielle doesn't come up to scratch. What I mean is....."

"You reserve the right to grow old like anyone else." Helen finished her sentence for her, though somewhat more brutally than she herself might have given it expression. It was the first indication she had had that the years were beginning to tell - in which case she'd have to show these youngsters a thing or two! Much more likely than she wilting of old age was the possibility of two such attractive mademoiselles being whisked up the aisle. She was replacing the receiver as Danielle came in. "Oh Madame - Helen 'as asked you?"

"Have you got everything you need?"

"The kitchen is so well full. I always enjoy so much to visit England."

"But not to stay?"

"Mais oui! I like so much. I hesitate only because I take small apartement in Paris wiz my cousin as you know. Already you dismiss one anxiété wiz offer of ze flat."

"Your salary will enable you to retain your base in Paris. In the morning we'll discuss the possibility of Brigitte designing the Centre interior." Intuitively she knew they had now dispensed with the only obstacle. Danielle seized Kate's hands. "I sink tomorrow we celebrate yes?" And then her eyes clouded. "Oh but Madame forgets. Brigitte, she in ze wheelchair."

"Good Lord Danielle. If we are going to see this venture through, we'll be moving mountains, not just wheelchairs!"

"Now at last I see ze Madame Monsieur Armand describe me - ze lady who builds Innovation before I join her. Oh, quelle bonne journée!"

"An older, battle scarred version maybe!"

Kate glanced at her watch. If she hurried to the factory she would catch Ted. With plans in her head already seeking fulfilment, he could go home a less worried man with the offer of Site Manager's job at the new Conference Centre.

PART THREE
CHAPTER THIRTY TWO

Phil Jensen scanned the room for her. "Kate! Congratulations! What a take-off!" He was impressed, not only by the attention to every conceivable detail - which he would have anticipated, but by the sheer flamboyance of the event, with which he did not so readily associate her. Intrigued, he said, "You usually nibble away quietly at something and then surface having achieved your objective. Is this the new Kate?"

"Horses for courses Phil. A different strategy was needed - immediate impact to recoup some of the investment. Wearing down the competition was yesterday's policy for which there isn't time if we're not to be destroyed by interest charges. All my eggs in one basket – definitely not my usual style - nor a comfortable one!"

He felt a surge of admiration for the friend who, with an innate drive that refused as naturally as she breathed, to be denied, had picked herself up, and was flying again. But she corrected his persuasion. "Too often I'm a coward Phil. But I grant I'm more generously endowed with persistence, and in the absence of courage, that has had to suffice." All that had been necessitated was a change to her life style, which was the way of all families, and not something to get steamed up about.

There were others waiting to speak with her, and he moved away through cascades of spring flowers whose scent filled the hall. Strolling through the sunlit corridors, he looked approvingly at the succession of Georgian style display areas built into the wall, providing advertising space selling quality merchandise. 'Nice one Kate. Saves buying pictures and generates revenue you badly need - an idea that will definitely catch on.'

The cost of factory conversion, salaries and costs, had far exceeded funds available and the lack of cash flow meant digging deep into collateral. But there could be no half measures this time, nor a dependence on minimal staffing and he had been forced to warn her that there would be such a delay on breaking even as to make the investment risky.

"So the very situation that you claimed made me vulnerable last time, is now a pre-requisite!" she laughed

SAFE AS HOUSES

Undeterred, since the solution lay in the only way of life she knew, and one that could also accommodate Bob's needs, she had gone ahead; relieved almost that such would be the demands on her concentration as to liberate her from the nightmare of recrimination when guilt and anguish hit her like blows to the stomach. From some deep recess of the mind she had tapped the source of strength she needed.

She had decided against selling the boutique following Molly's unexpected request to take out a lease. Jensen been surprised that though she had insisted the fashion business was dead, she had retained the most tangible aspect of it, but doubtless she had her reason. Assuming success in the initial development, the next stage would be to make the Centre residential. At such time the boutique would prove an invaluable asset and thus she could not afford to be distracted by sentiment. Though Molly had not been forthcoming on the subject of her guarantor who paid through a London agent, the cheques were regular. A substantial deposit had dispelled any doubts and she presumed Molly's husband was the interested party.

Shaking hands of those last to depart, she glanced through the window to where her father was proudly pointing out to Bob the sign 'Benson Centre' high above the main entrance. Now debilitated by ulceration, Alex had worked with Ted to train Bob as 'assistant caretaker', and aware of his own limitations, was content there was no better man to keep an eye on his son. Pride lit his face as she joined them. She was his kith and kin, and no matter the dignitaries littering the lawns, she had come to be with him and Bob. He wanted to give her a hug and tell her what it all meant to him, but words wouldn't come and anyway that wasn't what you were supposed to do in public. So instead he said, "You'll tell Ted I'll collect Bob when you go to Paris, Kate?"

"I'll only be away one night to check that everything's been finalised to the Cardules' satisfaction. They've been good friends over the years."

Kate had explained to Ted that though initiative and responsibility were never to be assumed, Bob would do anything to please, and earn praise - as long as rapport and trust existed. Ted would have the patience not to snatch a job from her brother's hands when he needed time rather than help. His limitations would be far outweighed by the number of times he would surprise them. When Ted required further staff, it would be hired. Bob was there simply because he was Bob and needed fulfilment as any other.

She suggested the three of them went into the kitchen for the decent cuppa she knew Alex was craving, whilst she went to collect her briefcase. Words

SAFE AS HOUSES

she had read at some time rushed in on her. 'Upon the wreckage of thy yesterday, design the structure of tomorrow.' and she wished she could recall whose they were. The loneliness came back for a moment. This was a day that should have left her on a cloud, but she was still painfully empty inside; yearning for the two people without whom she felt raw and solitary. But her turbulence was a state she now knew the nature of, and until a genuine sense of purpose could be renewed, she must play the expected part

Helen popped her head round the door. "Wasn't that wonderful Mrs. Carter! I can't wait to see the press coverage......Oh Danielle said there was a call for you - I've put the number on your pad. No message - asked for you to phone back when it was convenient."

"Let's hope it's a reservation. I'll do it now. And yes - everything went superbly! Wonderful day. I'm deeply indebted to you both."

"Reckon we'll make a team?"

"No question!"

She had begun to dial the number before its familiarity jolted her. The area code had altered but the number following was the one Tom Heydon had left with her the last time they met. Such an eternity ago – before Emm and Duncan had had their affair, or Mam had died, or Jonathan killed.

Though irksome that her brain had retained that particular sequence of digits, her pulse quickened at the recollection of the evening he had taken her out to dine. Best to ignore the call, return to the lounge and avoid further pain. But her legs refused, and there remained the possibility he'd call again and then his persistence would intrigue Helen.

"Tom - Kate here. I understand you called earlier. How are you?"

"Kate! Good to hear you. Yeh I did. Hell of a noise going on in the background - got a sale on or something?" Of course he thought he had called the boutique, and this was hardly the moment to update him.

"There have been a lot of people here today."

"Look old thing, I've got a couple of weeks leave in U.K. Wondered if you'd like to get together for a meal or something ... Tuesday any good?"

It might well have been only a month, not years, since their last meeting, and one so routine that the emotional upheaval it had caused a mere figment of her imagination. Incredulous, yet instantly charmed by the familiar tones, she told him that on Tuesday, she would in fact be going to Paris.

"Why that's perfect. I'll come with you! I need to visit the pharmaceutical concern I've tied up with - would have gone the following week anyway. What's your flight number - I'll book on the same plane."

"Tom....wait." She was trembling, desperately seeking words that would neither deter nor encourage him. "You can't just invite yourself along. How do you know it's convenient, that I won't be accompanied....."

"Because you'd tell me if you were. Are you?"

She paused, irritated by her own feeble response. "No."

He laughed, and she could feel her resistance crumbling against his will to overcome any obstacle she might invent. Noting the details, he grunted affably, "So you still insist on getting up at the crack of dawn! Ah well, daresay the prospect of meeting you again will entice me out of my pit. Take care now. See you at the terminal. And don't look for the handsome model of yesteryear - I'm practically bald!"

"That's a relief. I've more than a few grey hairs too now. Bye Tom."

She clung to the receiver. So he still remembered Wales when they had got up early to go to the coast on a day when they believed they would never grow old. Well she was a free agent again now, and if Fate were providing a second chance, then this time, neither conscience nor loyalty must get in the way. He would not have phoned after so many years if there were no special memories for him too. Suddenly she felt as if she were stepping out of a weight that had enveloped and held her in it grip for so long, and it was necessary to make a conscious, determined effort not to float down the central staircase, where Danielle caught sight of her.

"C'était magnfique aujourd'hui Madame. You must be so 'appy."

Kate smiled. "Do you know Danielle. I think that's just what I am! Very happy!"

There was a new serenity about her. She felt it; radiated it; marvelled that it could so instantaneously renewed. And a bemused Danielle wondered what could have taken place – surely more than the success of the day itself - for the tension that had cloaked her employer for the past months, to be so rapidly dispelled.

"I didn't realise it had been such a worry for you love," Alex said as she drove them out of the grounds. "Why you look ten years younger now it's all over. I expect it's that executive stress everybody talks about nowadays. You'll be alright; you always did do things proper - that extra bit o' thinking and planning. Nice speech you made too. Do you know what I was reminded of? The night I took you to the school ball in the boss' Bentley. I was driving a princess. For all his brass, his girl couldn't hold a candle to mine."

"That's because you were biased."

SAFE AS HOUSES

"Don't know what that means. And it wasn't because I was anything. You knocked spots off 'em. And you did again today." He took a sidelong glance at her. "Look luv, why don't you stay a bit longer than one night in Paris. Bob an' me are fine. And I'm sure Helen and Danielle can cope now that today's over."

"Perhaps an extra day *could* be arranged - but the diary is full on Friday."

"Do you know how long it is since you took a day off? Over two years."

"Put like that, perhaps I could be persuaded!"

Alex switched on the gas fire before taking off his coat. "Kate, I ain't got no 'ead for business, but there was a hell of a lot of money involved today. Is that what's been causing you so much strain? You know I'm proud as a peacock - but your business ventures - they're bigger than I can begin to think about. And some days I wish you'd ended up on that Post Office Counter. You'd 'ave gone 'ome to a brood of kids and let someone else have the worryin'. Then there's that cottage o' yours. Ages since you enjoyed it. It can't improve the place to stand empty."

"I was lucky to have it cared for as long as I did. Yes, I do love it. And so does Bob."

"And when Lucy an' me went, we could see why. But people don't last for ever - me no more'n Mr. Rees. And this house won't yield much between four of you."

She put down the cutlery she had begun to arrange and her eyes met his. "Dad, I wouldn't care if you owned Buckingham Palace, I would rather have you here. My finances are all in hand; there's absolutely no need for you to worry."

He nodded. "Fair enough. We never liked to be in debt - Lucy and me. Saved up for everything we had."

She almost replied, "I didn't say I wasn't in debt," but it was better he remained untouched by the world of high finance. "I know how you feel without Mam here. You've got to check up on us all, the way she did."

"But I don't get the results she did!" Nor had he learned that of which he needed assurance. "But it must've helped not having to spend years paying for your 'ome."

She regarded him quizzically. "I don't quite follow you Dad."

"Well Duncan paying for fifty per cent of it outright. Made it easier to put money into the business I should think."

"Dad, Duncan didn't buy half a house! In fact I was amazed when he raised the ten per cent deposit."

SAFE AS HOUSES

Alex turned abruptly towards her, and then back again, passionate anger surging within. With vehement desire to lash out at the man who had made a fool of him, came the realisation of his own guilt in misplacing his trust. Wracked and confused, his breathing was more pronounced; his colour heightened.

"Dad what's wrong?"

Quelling his silent rage, he said only, "I'll get some water. Mebbe too near the fire." He needed time to collect his thoughts. Kate must suspect nothing - not until he had sorted it out in his head - or she wouldn't go to Paris. For some reason the prospect of seeing her friends again was having a transforming effect on her. He pushed his chair back from the heat he found so comforting. There was a pause, a tension she didn't understand. "Well so long as he paid for it before he left you so you haven't got that to bother about as well as the business."

"Dad there isn't a problem. Duncan very generously abandoned his claim. I've been happy to go on paying for it. Please don't worry."

"I just wish you had a man beside you to share some of the responsibility. Why you take on so much is beyond me."

"Would you rather Duncan had stayed?"

"By God no." The urge to thump the object of his bitter thoughts enervated him. He had handed him a fortune in trust for his girl and she'd seen nothing more than the miserable amount he'd put down as deposit. A reason for living now raged and vibrated in every nerve. Given the opportunity just once to cross his path, he vowed he would swing for the man.

CHAPTER THIRTY THREE

He took her hand in a most familiar, ordinary way as if Wales had been only yesterday and they had belonged together all the intervening years. The joy that welled inside her made the sky incredibly bright, and the murky water of the Seine assumed the clarity and brilliance of the Mediterranean. The setting was perfection; the bustle that surrounded them not the least invasive, but an artistic backdrop to their togetherness. Paris charmed her with its magic and she surrendered herself willingly.

She knew then, as she had always known, that she didn't want memories to be all she had left of her love for him; that she had never recovered from his not being part of her life, even though somehow the years had been got through. She had only been half a person without him but now suddenly there was purpose and focus again. Surely, surely he was here with her now because he too had found that life was meaningless and empty alone; that loving so deeply, they would never truly grow old. Only he could take away the fear of failing; only with him could she feel a complete person. Without him, she had forgotten what real happiness was.

Strolling in the warm morning sunshine, he stopped to remove his jacket and she stared lovingly at him for signs of what the years had been for him. Her eyes travelled over his features as if reconciling the memories she already held. He was a little stiffer now, his gait less fluent, though he still walked tall. Even after half a lifetime apart she felt she knew him with a pleasing comfortable thoroughness, still attracted most by his lack of inhibition, the audacious twinkle in his eyes, and a love of life that had no need of self-consciousness or pretence. Most exhilarating of all was the sweet discovery that they were still not too old to be romantic; that love was as potent in age as in youth.

An old woman approached them with a basket of dried lavender, and he pinned a sprig on her dress. He lightly touched her cheek and tenderly held her gaze with his. "Don't say I never gave you flowers! Not your birthday by some lucky chance is it?" Just a twinge of pain here, for she had remembered his without need of diary to remind her over the years. But then he had never professed to be good at dates; in fact, distinctly forgetful. She remembered how he had hummed 'I won't send roses' from the Mac and Mabel production they had seen together in their twenties. Flowers would come spontaneously, but on the right day, never, he warned.

His arm was around her shoulder now and they were speaking to each other in the silence, for their companionship was so tested a thing that it could be rested on without the need for words. Oh how she had yearned for a man's arms about her again; to have safe boundaries against which to lean and support her weakness; once more for flowers to come unexpectedly and for no reason other than to assure her she was thought of and valued. But today at last, her existence was rescued from a lifetime of missing all that. It could still happen; surely *would* happen now that he was here again, for he was all she ever wanted in a man.

"I don't want to lie in my bed and be gnawed by fear and loneliness ever again," she admitted to herself. "I want to be with Tom; to love his mortal being, not his memory, and for him to hold me tight against him, for no matter what I've pretended in the past, my happiness depends on him." She wanted so much to tell him that, but being herself, did not.

He glanced at his watch. "Time for a quick coffee and then we'll get on with the business we came for. What time are you seeing the Cardules? I have to take Dupont for lunch before the meeting, but we'll meet up again this evening - can you come to the hotel?" She was jerked back to reality; had deluded herself into thinking that this *was* what she had come for; had quite forgotten there was another reason.

"Let's celebrate! We'll go to Maxims."

Celebrate he had said. A celebration, not for some extraneous business reason, but surely because he had found her again. The long loneliness was ebbing away at last. She looked about her at the busy sidewalks, the pavement artists, people discussing ardently or just relaxing and enjoying coffee under the parasols, and thought how dreadfully she was going to miss being part of it all. The enormity of the void now that Innovation was no longer, and which had been raw and open since Jonathan's death, would be unbearable had not Tom re-entered the scene. Her life, so insignificant by comparison, would be lost inside such a vacuum.

He seemed suddenly fired by the prospect of tying up a contract. Draining his coffee he stood, kissed her lightly and arranged a time to meet. It was a strange, confused feeling. Often casual, yet he also talked and behaved sometimes in the familiar way of their being married, simultaneously

SAFE AS HOUSES

evoking in her the excitement of a new love. They were easy in each other's company; were of the same age; had experienced the same years and culture, and now shared a love of this most exhilarating of cities. And above all else, they were here together. He turned and waved and she watched him weave his way through the crowd; this man whom she loved and needed, and without whom she was not properly herself. Happiness reverberating through her, she ordered another coffee, loathe to leave the table he had shared, and when the waiter removed his cup, put her hand out, almost restraining him.

"Je m'excuse Madame. Le Monsieur reviendra?"

"No, no he's not coming back," she said. "I'm sorry. Do take the cup. But perhaps I could have a little more milk?"

He laughed. "Café au lait engleesh style! Ugh!"

She smiled, her mind elsewhere. "I yearn for you Tom," she thought. "I want to be in your arms and for you to be content for me to be there." He had swept her off her feet again despite a determination to stay rooted to the ground, and her heart had soared. She sat for some time, recalling his looks, his teasing, intimate smile, his voice, and the feel of his hand holding hers. Anyone would think I was seventeen," she smiled. But as her thoughts turned to the evening ahead, she *was* seventeen, recklessly wishing the hours away to the moment she could rush to his arms. But she could no longer delay her return to Reuill, signalled her thanks to the waiter and fought to turn her thoughts to the task in hand.

The three walked together in the park, appreciative that Kate hadn't to maintain a punishing schedule of visits to clients. It was ironic, Armand thought, that they were enjoying such a rare chance to relax together because there was no other call on her time, and yet only with the continuation of such pressure had she been able to visit so often. They would miss her enormously, for whilst it had amused him for her to believe that all the colour and charm was on the side of the Parisians, they had no illusion about the appeal of their so-English friend. He would not contemplate months, perhaps years without seeing her, knowing she was in the hotel and feeling safe in their company, her expressions of gratitude so heartfelt and genuine. She had trusted them with her innermost thoughts when at her lowest ebb; had provided strength whenever they in turn had demonstrated a need. She had simply the gift of love. Not a disturbing turbulent passion, but something almost old-fashioned; peaceful and still and very, very deep in her. Yet she seemed unable to tap those reserves to quell her own turmoil. Her solace at such times had been in their Latin, extrovert personalities. Bereft of her presence and without the prospect of regular visits, life would be less interesting; mundane almost. And he could not tell her. For the moment it did not matter for they had never expressed their trust in words; each was so aware of it, they acted on it with the certainty that it would never cause them to fear for its strength.

Alors, the course of her life had been changed, as was the manner of living. He had noticed a difference this time; still signs of strain, but something definitely light-hearted about her; a joy, that most real joy that seemed to come from within.

"Do you remember Kate when you were troubled you were destined to be a solitary Madame wiz whom no-one could feel comfortable?"

"I do. What miserable company I must have been for you!"

"For us, never. But I hope since you start your new company you have not the same sentiments; that you can see things in ze better proportion now."

She gave him a sideways glance before replying. He had been the astute observer for so long now that she suspected it would not have been an idle comment, and he in turn acknowledged her recognition of his thought with a barely discernible smile before resuming interest in the world about him.

"As you know Kate," Marie-Jeanne smiled, "Armand is 'indiscrèt' and asks if you have anozer amour, which is not his business of course. But zat will not prevent him asking."

"On the contrary ma chérie." Armand paused to address them both. "Kate was unable to accept my suggestion we should all dine together tonight, and yet she does not fly home before ze morrow. She 'as no business contacts now - it can only be zat she is in love! Maybe wiz a Frenchman which means we see her often, and shall be ze most pleased."

The demise of a friendship that had so often sustained her was not a pleasing prospect and she looked at them both fondly. "I'm sorry about dinner. And yes, I do have an engagement. And no, it's not business."

"So Armand is correct! You are in love. Oh Kate I am so 'appy for you!" Madame had contained her curiosity for too long; had, despite her remonstrance, been glad that Armand had raised the subject. She was incapable any longer of appearing indifferent.

The dilemma was Kate's. How could she deny she was in love when she could feel the emotion throbbing from every pore? But to admit it when it had been less than forty-eight hours since Tom had phoned; that up until then she had planned on coming to Paris alone, and would have thought of dining with none but them, would sound ridiculous.

"Stop! Both of you! Yes, I am to dine with an old friend who contacted me unexpectedly just hours before I came, and coincidentally has business in Paris."

"And ziz friend is?" Armand asked.

"Tu est impertinent," Marie-Jeanne declared, eagerly awaiting the name.

"I think I've spoken of Tom before." Kate made a controlled effort to attribute no more significance to the name than Dick or Harry.

"Yes, chérie, you have mentioned him in the past." And to herself Marie Jeanne added, "Perhaps a little more souvent than you have realised."

Armand said nothing at all, and at that moment he didn't know why. And then, "I sink perhaps we return. We can 'ave some English tea and you can tell us all your news."

"We 'ave ze tea Kate, but j'imagine you need time to prepare for ze rendezvous tonight." Marie Jeanne intervened.

"He will come to collect you Kate?" Armand persisted. "We can become acquainted over cocktails before you go?"

Kate was aware of a slight tension growing. "Thank you Armand. But I'll take the metro. Tom is reserving a table at Maxims. He had business this afternoon and it saves time if we meet in the City."

"How gallant of the fellow, Armand grunted inaudibly. "Mon Dieu, did he not know how to escort a lady, despite being able to afford Maxims?"

They dined, and danced into the early hours, and afterwards, for no reason other than their steps took them there, walked through the cobbled streets of Montmartre towards Sacre Coeur, and stood in the light it shed. Drawing her gently to him, he closed his arms around her, and as he kissed her tenderly, Kate knew that if Fate decreed this were to be the only day left to her, she would have experienced happiness sufficient for a lifetime.

They had recounted all that had happened over the years; those with whom their lives had been entwined, and the events that had forced changes of direction. She was surprised - for he had not mentioned it on their previous meeting – to hear Tom had a son, though why it should have surprised her she wasn't sure. It was after all the usual outcome of a marriage, of which he had had two.

SAFE AS HOUSES

He traced a finger over her cheek. "You know Kate, there's a part of you that hasn't changed. Growing old was what happened to other people we said - not us. Do you remember in Wales when..."

And of course she remembered every detail, for the time with Tom had been indelibly etched on her heart and the years had not erased them. Those months she had subsequently longed for and relived a thousand times.

"We go back a long way you and I, Katie Benson. More years than most married couples come to think of it." He grinned. "I remember how you'd call out when you saw me first, and run to me through the crowd."

"Wasn't very sophisticated was I? Should have kept my emotions under wraps."

"I don't think it's much to do with sophistication. You're a most sophisticated woman now - and you're still not hiding them," he teased.

"Do you want me to hide them?"

"Could you?"

She shook her head, and then shivered involuntarily at the thought of being required to quell this wonderful effervescence whirling inside her.

He misread her. "You're cold. Come on let's get a taxi."

Her body pliant in his arms, all the long years of loneliness and longing gave way to the whirling momentous sensation, as she gave herself to his embrace. The fierceness of her love was finally allowed to surface and she did not, could not, summon one iota of physical resistance to the only man to whom she could have yielded in joyous, ecstatic surrender. And when her senses had calmed at last, she knew the supreme comfort of falling asleep in his arms. Somehow Tom, with whom she was completely at peace, had, she knew now, loved for a lifetime, was at last miraculously beside her.

An unfamiliar noise woke her some hours later, and reaching out to her bedside light, she sensed Tom was not fully asleep, was aware of his unease, a suffering almost.

"Tom what is it?"

"Ssh. Go back to sleep."

"Tom. I love you."

He stroked her eyelids closed. "I know. I love you too."

Whilst he had been in and out of another marriage, her love had lain latent, grown in strength so that despite the gentleness and reticence that characterised her every reaction, he had evoked a passion in her that had

SAFE AS HOUSES

frankly taken him by surprise, yet seemed for her the most natural progression to a sureness and serenity in the life they would have together. But as sleep claimed her again he recognised a barrier that would prevent him from the total commitment she would expect, because that was the only kind she understood. He couldn't analyse his feelings at this moment; failed to isolate them from the tenderness he felt for her. But by the time they shared a table for breakfast, he knew.

She sensed immediately his awkwardness though for some time he insisted she was imagining it. "You regret last night?" she asked with a directness he did not anticipate.

"Not unless you do. Kate, I've loved every moment of the time we've had together. I was never so much at ease, or so content in anyone's company."

She was bewildered for was he not voicing her own feelings, yet the tense he used implied those times were already over. A chill sensation seeped through her, as her head began to take control. Of course she knew what was happening. Nothing more or less than what a million lovesick women before her had had to come to terms with. She would not allow the agony to be prolonged; would extract herself with as much dignity as could be salvaged in the circumstances, which was precious little at her age.

"Tom, I shouldn't have assumed... I think I expected you to have harboured the same feelings for me - and how could you. You telephoned for old times sake - nothing more - and I've made an idiot of myself, and you don't want to hurt me by explaining... If I were still a young woman, I might be forgiven, but to have made such an erroneous assumption at my age is humiliating to say the least."

"Kate, stop. No one has been an idiot. Least of all you. And Good Lord, do you think middle age has a prerogative of wisdom?"

"Of course I'm not the only woman you've brought to Paris - nor will I be the last. That's what you're saying isn't it?" Her head gave a little toss of defiance. " Well you aren't the first man...I've met so many people in business...." She was unable to continue the lie and wanted only to rush into his arms, to feel again the overwhelming rapture of loving, and being loved in return.

Kate don't do this to yourself. You know very well I've had affairs. But not you." He was looking at her earnestly now. "And knowing that, I shouldn't have allowed you to embark on this..."

"You thought I'd come out of an older woman's loneliness and physical, human longing."

SAFE AS HOUSES

"Don't be ridiculous. We're such old friends – comfortable with each other." He paused. "It could never have been trivial - not with you"

She searched in his eyes for a meaning to his words and utterly confused, said, "Yes I do love you. I've always loved you Tom. But you weren't to know."

This was not the time for deep discussion and he sought a response that wouldn't wound her. "You know me Kate. I act on impulse and let things take their course."

"Spare me the humiliation of telling me I was just a casual affair."

His face darkened. "Now you're being stupid. For God's sake I've kept in touch over the years. It was you who turned me down when I begged you to leave Duncan."

"I hadn't forgotten. That's why I thought you'd come back to ask me again. I'm sorry, I shouldn't have leapt to such a conclusion."

"I phoned you because I don't ever want to lose touch with you. When you said you were coming to Paris I was over the moon at the prospect of some time with you - yes even hoped that something might evolve that we could build on."

"But it has!" Her eyes were pleading now. "But you mean not for you." Her heart felt like a stone in her breast. Before she had come to Paris there had been nothing else to lose, nothing to throb with the pain that pierced her now, nothing to make her feel as bereft as the loss of Tom would do. It shocked her to realise that not even Innovation would leave her so scarred.

"Everything has been perfect. It's simply that I couldn't live the kind of life you'd need me to live, given all that we told each other last night," he said eventually.

She had been unaware of making any demands, and confusion clouding her brain, she was reluctant to say the words that would speed the end of this most precious relationship that last night had seemed as strong as steel in its ardour, but which the morning light had rendered so fragile. Bewildered, she remained silent. It was no time for argument or persuasion; had he woken with the same surfeit of emotion, this conversation would not now be taking place. Words would have been superfluous, yet here they were struggling awkwardly to employ them like unfamiliar tools that must be mastered to be of effective use.

And then she said in something approaching a whisper, "I didn't realise I'd made any demands. I'm sorry if that's how it felt. I want nothing other than to be with you."

SAFE AS HOUSES

"Not consciously Kate. But your lifestyle makes demands - of you most of all, and ultimately of the person who marries you."

"If you mean the time I give to the business - I've had to survive Tom. I haven't had someone else to support me. What did you expect me to do?" But even as she sought to rationalise, she realised that if such an exercise were necessary, then it was over.

"Kate it's not what you think. I want to explain and don't want to hurt you."

A waiter coughed with elaborate discretion. "Monsieur.. Madame -Your taxi - it is 'ere. You would like me to say you come?"

Tom glanced at his watch. "Thank you. A moment please." And then turning again to her, he said, "I can miss the flight. It makes no difference if I get a later one, but.."

"I can't," she said abruptly. "I've appointments I must keep."

Tom handed the waiter a note. "Please have our bags brought down and tell the driver we'll be with him in ten minutes." He placed his hands on her shoulders, looking earnestly into her eyes. "We can talk about it - about us - on the way home Kate. We must."

But the fences were about her again. The long practised impression of 'I can cope on my own' had fallen over her like a mantle. She wouldn't need anyone else. How could she have let this affair be so crucial; how could she have been so wrong. But as she rose from the table and he put out a hand to her, she was forced to lower her gaze to prevent him seeing the emotion. She didn't want to cope on her own. She needed him with all her being, wanted to cling to him, to tell him she would give up everything to be with him. In a future that did not contain him, whether she recalled his kindnesses or his hurts, the pain would be the same; she would ache for the comfort of his presence.

She tried to imagine life without him but her imagination refused to rise to the demand. She could not believe that the intimacy had meant nothing to him. What had she done or said to destroy that which had made him take her hand and say 'I love you.' She would hold in her memory the way he walked, gestured, teased and held her, the way he brushed his teeth, looked at a menu or loosened his tie. Every vivid physical detail of him would stay with her; the steep shiny forehead where his hair receded, the cleft of his chin that deepened when he smiled, the curve of his middle, the suggestion of a stiffness in one knee. And most, his vitality and anticipation of what each day might bring. There was so much ahead of them; an exciting road to map out together, years to catch up on. Years that spent alone, would be empty and meaningless; a meagre, barren existence.

She walked towards Reception with all the outward appearance of calm whilst inside she was pleading, 'I don't want to live without you. Please don't go away, don't leave me. Tell me again that you love me.' For Tom to think of her as Duncan had done was intolerably painful. But intolerable or not, if both men gave her the same message, then the fault was hers.

"Kate you haven't understood, we've got to talk. Don't clamp up on me." But as they were intercepted first by one then another, he resigned himself to waiting at least until they were on their way to Orly. Perhaps he could make her understand the impossibility of the situation as it stood, maybe even work out a solution.

She did not resist when he sought her hand again, but savoured every second of the feel of his fingers around hers, knowing with awful certainty that the fairytale was near its end. She would move in crowds again, with people grey and ordinary by comparison, and the only person who mattered would be absent. That was the agony of loving someone more than you are loved. Even his absence would be a positive factor; would affect her all the time he wasn't there. And the grief would be a pain that couldn't be analysed in the suspension between past and future - only endured.

CHAPTER THIRTY FOUR

"Don't want you to die Kate."
She put her arm around Bob's ample shoulders and they crunched through autumn leaves in the hospital car park. "People go to hospital for all sorts of reasons - they need to be mended like cars. All those people you saw in the clinic will be going home again as we are. Everything's fine Bob."
But she had misread his apprehension. "Mam and Dad die." He trembled.
"But not us. Not for years yet. Tell you what - we'll both die on the same day when we're a hundred and ten!"
The comforting illogicality brought a tremulous smile to his lips, and his grip was less tight as he said, "Both at supper time when we say goodnight."
"Supper time it shall be! What about lunch before you go back on duty?"
"Ted get beer and sandwiches in the bar - he say."
"Oh so you've already had a better offer!"
He grinned, amiably disposed to man's talk in the bar. Grateful to Ted for his support in helping Bob to adjust after Alex' heart attack, Kate's own desolation had become blurred in the enormity of his.
"Give me two ticks to get out of my overalls, and I'll be with you Bob old fella," Ted greeted them. "Just pop these last few boxes in the store." But Bob had seen them and needed no prompting. Then to Kate, "You're back earlier than I expected. How was he?"
"They've diagnosed a thyroid problem, but medication should keep it controlled. Went to pieces when a coronary was rushed in though."
"Damn bad luck he was with Alex when he collapsed."
"I'll never forget it Ted. He was beside himself... traumatized and curled up in a tight ball. Insisted Dad was shouting - but my father never shouted. Never did I hear him raise his voice."
"The phone was off the hook you said. I expect Alex was calling for help. You'll never know Mrs. Carter and it's best you put it out of your mind."
She shook her head. "Bob knows the difference between calling out and shouting in anger. May not be able to articulate it, but knows intuitively what mood people are in. No - something happened that day."

SAFE AS HOUSES

"Your father went whilst he was enjoying life. Three years longer than you expected."

"And each a bonus. But what it was that so upset Bob? And what made Dad so furious?"

"Easy to mistake panic for anger." Indicating Bob's return he said, "I'll take him for lunch now. Get a bite yourself before that accountant of yours finds you. I heard him ask Helen if he could see you ahead of schedule." And watching her go, he knew that so concerned for Bob had she been, she had not yet done her own grieving.

Kate ordered lunch on a tray for two.

"Thanks for seeing me early Kate." Jensen bit into a ham sandwich. "I've no more laudable reason than the urge to play a few holes in this glorious autumn sunshine." Extracting a file from his briefcase, he said, "Half year figures don't look bad at all – better than expected."

"Not exciting enough to justify expansion without heftier borrowing than makes for peaceful sleep, but too risky a plateau ahead if I don't."

"Kate if all my clients were as succinct as you, I could enjoy a round of golf everyday, and still do the same amount of business!"

"Then I shall expect my account to be halved!" she countered. "Meanwhile I've an interview arranged with the Bank tomorrow, and shall reach a decision by Friday." She refilled his coffee cup. "You finish the sandwiches. I'm going to catch Molly. The rent hasn't been paid this month - I'll ask her to check it out."

"No problem before?"

"Not since she began trading over three years ago. Probably an oversight." Molly saw her from the window, and flung open the door. "Come in!" Kate explained the purpose of her visit, to the consternation of her lessee.

"That's unusual - and I can't imagine why."

"So unusual I'm not concerned. But better to check sooner than later." Kate returned to prepare paperwork for the bank. Devoid of the intense driving force that had marked her career in the fashion industry, she would nonetheless need all the adroitness she could muster to steer the enterprise through its next stage, for the risk would be great whichever path she took.

As it happened her Bank Manager's faith in her ability to prosper, was unwavering. And so with signatures on the appropriate dotted lines, conversion would begin on the storage areas previously utilised by the factory.

"I can't wait to telephone Brigitte!" Danielle enthused, and Kate knew that

SAFE AS HOUSES

for her French protégé, the enterprise now in hand was what Innovation had been for her. In a word, creativity. For a business should, no less than a painting or a symphony, be a vehicle for its originator's ingenuity. But when Danielle suggested she accompany her on visits, she shook her head.

"That's your department now! Sweet talk has greater effect when the recipient faces youthful expertise! Age and experience serve a better purpose operating back stage." She left them to absorb impending change and development.

"C'èst dommage. I think she misses being out in the field as she call it."

"The fashion field Danielle," Helen replied. "Don't worry; she's worked everything out. Here she's available for Bob, and can still perform a vital function - and one she enjoys. And by the way, she insists we have the wedding here!"

"I know. I sink you will 'ave ze beautiful wedding Helen."

It was in the early evening when Danielle noticed a slim, expensively dressed woman in the entrance hall. "I apologise no-one heard ze bell."

"I expect that's because I didn't ring."

"Please how may I help you? You wish to hire a room perhaps?"

"Yes....possibly."

"You would like to see ze facilities we can offer your company perhaps? It is my pleasure. May I know your name?"

"Johnson. Evelyn Johnson."

Danielle escorted the visitor with the pride of one who, involved in the enterprise since its inception, was unable to resist indicating their plans for further development. Evelyn Johnson paused frequently as if absorbing every detail, and her appreciation was genuine. "I'm most impressed..... and very happy." Her last words were almost a whisper.

"Happy Madame?"

"To have found it. You are the Manager?"

"I am Personal Assistant to our Director, Madame."

"Who is?"

"Mrs. Carter."

"Is she here now?"

"I'm sorry - no."

The visitor nodded as if having an idea confirmed. Danielle was disinclined to interrupt her thoughts, for quite plainly she was in no hurry to depart, and then suddenly, realisation dawned. Their meeting had been brief all those years ago, and indeed time had not dealt kindly with the woman who would have her believe she was Evelyn Johnson. But why? Indeed if she had not wished to see Kate, why was she here at all?

"Thank you. Perfect though everything is, I feel that perhaps the Centre may not be suitable for my purpose. I'm sorry to have wasted your time." Emmeline Charlesworth had made her sentiments clear, and having affected to go towards her car, doubled back and hurried across the copse towards the boutique where Molly O'Mahn was still at work.

"May I suggest it's time to call it a night, Madam?" The barman's practised, conciliatory tone caught a raw edge.

"I think I'm the best judge of that," the guest retorted, but nevertheless eased herself down from the high stool, and walked with determined care towards the stairs.

"If you say so, Madam," he sighed mechanically, and picked up the phone to alert Floor Service to check she had reached her room without mishap.

Kicking off her shoes, Emmeline lit a cigarette, and cursed the error of judgement that had brought her back to the Midlands. The mental picture of Kate having hit rock bottom and benevolently offering her the use of the flat in return for designs that would reverse their fortunes, was the stuff novels were made of. "So my friend, all you have touched has turned to gold. Did I sicken you so much you got out of the rag trade altogether - sold to the highest bidder while you were still at the top? Good move Kate. Nice pad you have there too. Nothing so demeaning as a factory for which you'd certainly have gained mother's approval. She's dead now you know - spent the whole bloody lot and then snuffed it. And I hear from your mademoiselle of ambitious plans. Oh well at least you won't miss my modest nest egg when I pull it out. From the set up I saw today, it'll hardly create a ripple in the petty cash account."

There was a gentle tap at the door. "Everything alright Madam?"

"Fine. Book an early call and ask the desk to check flight availability."

"Flight Madam?"

"To the States - they have the details - I spoke with someone earlier."

She lay on the bed surrendering to desolation, but the figure in the doorway remained motionless. "Well go on then. Unless you've come armed with black coffee."

"That could be arranged Madam. It's Miss Charlesworth isn't it?"

Emmeline jerked herself upright. "My God - Duggie Grant!"

SAFE AS HOUSES

"That's right. Saw your name in the register. Anything I can do?"

"It's a comfort to see you Duggie. Thanks. Coffee would be good."

"But we'd best take it in the lounge for my age would be no defence against gossip."

"I expect my face needs repairing. Join you in a jiff?"

They settled themselves away from businessmen relaxing over drinks.

"So what brings you here M'm? I'd heard you'd gone to live in America."

"So I had - with Kate's husband, as I expect you also heard." Her statement was rhetorical and he waited for her to continue. "Things worked out for awhile - longer than the cynics would have forecast - which was as long as he was winning at the tables. We might have weathered a few turbulent stretches if..." She became reflective, and quietly he prompted her. "If?"

"Losing made him vindictive - violent sometimes. The black moods were something I hadn't bargained for, much less imagined. Kate never mentioned them."

"She wouldn't would she," he said and his comment put Emmeline on the defensive. "You weren't the first to be taken in by his charm. I'd have trusted him anywhere - and did. Cost me my job at the golf club."

"Kate never mentioned that either. Is that how you came to work for her."

He nodded. "Like you say, he was two different people. A lion in a cage when he felt threatened. But only after using that sharp brain to convince others of his innocence. But when he'd lost money to the extent it affected his credentials ....." He drained back his coffee. "I take it you've left him?"

"Nothing so neat. We never married, so technically there should be no trauma. And I think he's already left me. He came to England some weeks ago - doubtless chasing rainbows - without of course telling me that he had terminated the tenancy on our swish apartment that moronically I assumed we owned."

"So you've come back to your roots?"

"No Duggie. Much as I despise myself, I crawled back to Kate. At least that was my scurrilous motive. I expected to find her working late in the office just like the old days. I intended to eat humble pie and discuss working together again. Contemptible wasn't it?"

"She isn't in the fashion business any more - least that's what I heard."

"And you heard right. From what I saw today she's gotten so darned big that lackeys do it all for her. Oh if only she'd been there, we'd have talked."

"Are you sure she wasn't?"

SAFE AS HOUSES

"Somewhere in her inner sanctum. Darned if I'd make an appointment."

"You mean you lost your nerve?"

Her face hardened. "For God's sake Duggie, Kate's father was once chauffeur to mine."

"And a very good one too, I should imagine." Duggie deliberately missed her point.

She pulled impatiently at a box of tissues. "Didn't need to ask if she was still there. Her stamp was all over the place." She poured another coffee. "No I'll find Duncan at one of his old haunts, - that shouldn't be difficult - make my position clear, and go back to the States. I certainly won't stay around to pay the price as Kate did. Knowing what I know now, I marvel at the length of time she stuck it out. He's a sod. Charming, plausible - and a con artist of the first order."

"Why don't you phone Mrs. Carter? What have you got to lose?"

"Duggie, I desperately want to phone her. And I could just about bear her to see me like this if she'd gone under as well. I still can't believe she didn't, given all that happened after I left - yes I had my informers. It does me no credit to wish she had, because then she would have forgiven everything, and I would have talked her into starting over and had as much fun as before. She forgave a hell of a lot, but even she must have a limit. And she's moved on. Bully for her."

She leant back in her chair, dark rings appearing around her eyes, and tightening her lips, she seemed to say to no one in particular, "And I'm as jealous of her as I was when we were kids at the school ball, and she wore that fabulous dress. She never did say how her family afforded it. I remember rushing home to sketch one as beautiful. Maybe that's how I came to choose designing. Never thought about it again afterwards, but I guess I owed as much to that dress designer, as to Kate for hiring me."

"Go and see her Miss," Duggie urged. "She'd want to see you."

She shook her head. "No. Water under the bridge now. And if I'm honest, Lady Luck won't have had as much to do with what I saw today, as sheer bloody determination. She'd scrub floors rather than give in. And I don't really mind going back to the Big Apple. It suits me better than England. I'll buy an apartment .....get myself a job. That's why I need to pull my money out. Thank God for dear old Daddy - and Kate too for keeping it safely invested. Left in my account it would long since have evaporated. A little nest egg Duncan knew nothing about. And I'll enjoy telling him Kate made it again without him. Go on, say it. Made it again without either of us."

SAFE AS HOUSES

Unable to formulate a response, he knew now why she wouldn't phone.

Kate had spoken again on the subject of Molly's arrears; had been assured that though her sponsor had suffered certain difficulties, all would soon be on an even keel.

"Molly I must insist you acquaint me of your circumstances. Does your husband have other business interests that are causing problems?"

Bereft of her natural ebullience, Molly drew breath and moistened her lips.

"Mrs. Carter, my sponsor is not my husband." Seeking to defer the information she must impart, she said, "You know all payments are made through Haddenhams."

Intuition warning her of trouble, Kate's reply was terse. "Presumably they have acquainted their client of the penalties for non-payment?"

"I'm sure that will be the case."

"Molly, I can only read such reticence as a private fear that the credentials of your sponsor are in some way suspect. If you persist, and payment isn't in the bank by the 29th, I shall instruct my solicitor to embark on legal proceedings. You realise the damage this will do to you personally and now that I know it's not your husband, I have no compunction about involving the law."

"Mrs. Carter, I know I should have told you, but you might never have agreed." She swallowed. "My sponsor is Emmeline Charlesworth."

There was a seemingly interminable silence as Kate struggled to believe her ears. Mind limp, the exchange was resumed as she whispered hoarsely, "Go on."

"It happened one evening after you offered me the use of the boutique. Miss Charlesworth phoned to ask for an address book she left behind to be forwarded."

"It didn't occur to you that she would have expected to speak with me?"

"She insisted I didn't trouble you – that you had too much to cope with. I enclosed a note saying why I was here - that I'd hoped to be working with you but your plans had been disrupted but that I could sell my designs from the boutique whilst you closed down."

"And her reaction?"

"She said you must have thought I was damn good to let me anywhere near the place. That's when the idea struck me. An opportunity I couldn't let slip. I put my idea to her - for her to back me. Some time later a letter came suggesting the agreement was drawn up through a third party, to avoid any hurt for you since you felt it was too painful to continue the business. I was to go to Finchley and sign the documents at Haddenhams. I was surprised – the signature I mean - with Miss Charlesworth as a witness. She looked uncertainly at Kate, and then continued. "At first I thought it was a coincidence being the same name as yours, but I dismissed it from my mind. Quite honestly I didn't care just as long as it all went through. Only later when I'd been here awhile and..... well you know how gossip slips out, and I realised who D. Carter was. I felt uncomfortable as you can imagine, but the longer it went on, the more difficult it became to raise it with you. And as there were never any problems, it seemed pointless to make one where none existed. I also needed to survive. There has to be some innocent explanation. I'm sure the money will come in a day or so."

"Are you Molly?" Kate paused. "I'm not. You may have put the idea to Emmeline, but it will have been Duncan's money backing you. He'll have been delighted at the prospect of having a finger in my affairs and gone to any lengths to raise the collateral." Assessing the sequence of events, she said, "It's my guess he's 'temporarily without means' as he described his cash flow crises, and hoping Emmeline is continuing at least to pay your rent 'for the time being.'

"And will she?" Molly asked nervously.

"No. She'll have a great deal more sense." She withheld 'than I had.' "I'm sorry but you'll quickly discover you're out on a limb."

"She wouldn't do that to me..."

"There's no sentiment in business. You didn't actually ask her face-to-face, so when your letter arrived, she would have showed it to Duncan and the enthusiasm will have been his. He'll have dealt with the financial details.

"So that's it, I'm afraid."
Incredulous at what they heard, the two young women looked anxiously at the effects of this latest onslaught on their employer. At last Helen asked, "Would you like one of us to come with you to the solicitor tomorrow, Mrs Carter? The cash flow can't be subjected to any further pressure."

"Duncan may be gambling on my finding the publicity too embarrassing to take him to court, might just want to make life uncomfortable for me." She shook her head. "Though why at this point in time I can't imagine."

"But you would sue him Mrs. Carter?" Danielle interrupted.

SAFE AS HOUSES

"There wouldn't be much point in suing a bankrupt Danielle." The statement chilled the air. "Why would he want to make things uncomfortable?" she was asked.

"I don't know .... jealousy possibly." She dismissed the idea. "No, he wouldn't know about it. Not unless...Helen, I wonder if Molly told him?" There was an uncomfortable pause as the two younger women exchanged glances. Quick as a flash, Kate intercepted them. "Something's happened?" Danielle nodded. "It was some weeks ago Mrs. Carter. Someone calling herself Evelyn Johnson arrived at Reception. I assumed her to be a potential client - she in fact accepted my offer to show her around, and then quite suddenly insisted we didn't suit her requirements. Something in the way she tossed her head made me remember her."

"Emmeline?"

"She was clear, without actually saying so, that she didn't want me to mention her visit."

"Which was no reason for not doing so Danielle," but waving aside the gesture of apology, continued. "I don't understand. She might just as easily have bumped into me on arrival; may even have intended to. What changed her mind?"

"Danielle discussed it with me," Helen said. "In view of the hurt you'd already been caused, it seemed best all round to comply with the visitor's expressed wish."

"I know you'll have acted considerately, and could hardly have handcuffed her against her will. The likelihood of her reporting back to Duncan, however innocently, gives credence to one line of thinking at least. Tell the solicitors to terminate the agreement Helen - a letter will follow. If Molly has managed her affairs well she should have the wherewithal to finance the last few months on her own - though Duncan will have commanded a healthy slice of the profits in exchange for setting her up."

"With you the only loser Mrs. Carter."

So good old fashioned jealousy was at the root of all this and Molly O'Mahn a mere pawn that could be dispensed with. What continued to concern her was the connection, if indeed there was one, between Duncan's insidious behaviour and Emm's appearance. Time was the enemy that lurked; three months without Molly's income was pushing her dangerously close to the edge of her borrowing power, and legal action an expense she could ill afford at this juncture. Disturbing that with considerable sums involved in the project overall, it should be a relatively minor amount that could prove injurious, and from which she might bleed for a long time. She glanced at her watch. It was time to visit Bob on the pretext of admiring the interior painting of the new pantry.

A large brush and huge tin of white emulsion provided obvious satisfaction, whilst Ted meticulously dealt with the gloss areas. Several times recently her brother had been subject to transitory blackouts, so fleeting it was difficult to believe they had actually happened. Only the nature of Bob's reaction had prompted them to observe him more diligently. "Why did you put the light out Ted?" he had asked on the first occasion, and nowhere near the light switch, Ted had reported the incident. Bob lived at his own pace, stress not being a word that featured and to move him from where he felt valued and enjoyed companionship might accelerate deterioration.

"I've noticed he succumbs to a catnap after lunch," Kate had said.

"Catch me at the wrong moment M'm and you might find me doing the same! That's why we're such good mates, Bob and me," Ted said gently, longing to protect her from any further hurt and loss. "Everything must take its course."

The airmail was on her desk and there was no mistaking the familiar handwriting. "Looks as if the mystery is about to be solved," Kate said. But the note offered little in the way of explanation.

"You all right?" her secretary asked, noting the change of pallor. Kate nodded and read a second time the passage that seemed finally to rob her of a friend. So uncharacteristic; so curt and direct.

'Kate - you will recall our arrangement whereby I can withdraw the amount loaned, in whatever year. I now wish to do exactly that. Please do the necessary at your earliest, sending a draft to the Chase Manhattan Bank at the address indicated.
Yours Emm.'

"Impeccable timing!" Phil Jensen exploded. "No warning?"

"Evidently Emm put in an appearance here some weeks ago."

"And didn't see you?"

"Asked specifically not to. However, she must have her money - when I've ascertained it is actually she who requires it."

"It will put an enormous strain on operations. Current expenses are at their highest and until the building is operational, it's not economically viable .."

"Part of the capital was always Emm's. As I'd no idea where she was, investing it in the Centre offered a reasonable safe return for her."

SAFE AS HOUSES

"But such an amount could have a crucial effect on the whole operation."

"It is against such an emergency I mentally reserved the cottage for collateral. I must raise a personal loan. Emm does seem to have overlooked the three months notice that was agreed - another reason to check she was not 'persuaded' to write the letter."

"You have your copy of the agreement handy?"

"I have them both – they're in the safe. Our banks have copies."

"But both originals are with you! Well I'm relieved it's that way round."

"It was a measure of the trust that existed between us."

"But past tense - the trust I mean?"

She hesitated, "Whatever else, I suspect the trust at least is intact." In a tone too flippant to fool him, she said, "I must get a valuation on the cottage, and see what I can do in tracking down Emm."

"I guess there's nowhere you'd rather lose."

"I may not have to sell. The cottage is paid for; I can offer the deeds as collateral."

"I don't know what it's worth, but you won't get a loan equal to its value."

"Then the sooner I get it valued, the better."

As he left her, he picked up a fleeting expression of fear. She signed correspondence, and then hand wrote a letter of her own marked 'strictly private and confidential', and which though finally reduced to a couple of sentences, took the best part of an hour to complete.

'Dear Emm - re your money. Will do as you ask, but the number of the account is unclear. Please phone to clarify. As always, Kate.'

"I've asked her to phone, Helen. No messages. I must speak with her." She stopped as Danielle and Brigitte joined them, inviting Kate to inspect the coffee lounge.

"You must have worked like Trojans! I'm thrilled! Thank you both."

"Bon. I have promised it for tomorrow." Danielle informed her. "Ze secretary of a sorority group called whilst we are working, to book the small hall for next month, and say if she could 'ave ze coffee lounge tomorrow, she will transfer also a celebration.

"How's that for a chip off the old block?" Helen whispered as she passed.

CHAPTER THIRTY FIVE

"Good to meet you." The estate agent looked about him. "Indeed to goodness, you've made a difference. 'Twas a most depressing sight when I was last here."

She had shared his impression; had been horrified at walls moist with mildew and dank wallpaper, grates covered in a layer of soot and cobwebs festooning the curtains. She and Bob had swung into immediate action, and happily exhausted by the impact they'd made, later commenced an effective assault on the overgrown garden. Gavin Hughes could scarcely believe he was in the same place.

Kate invited him to sit down. "So now perhaps we can discuss a revised valuation?"

He held out his hands to the blazing fire. "It would certainly pay to have someone maintain the cleaning and gardening as long as it's on the market. The way it looks now, we could add another thousand."

"The valuation is for a bank loan. I don't wish to sell," she said earnestly.

"In that case, I'm sorry, I can't help you. Within a month, the damp will have created havoc again. My figure was a fair one. At auction a builder would likely acquire it for much less. I'm aware of the price rises in England, but the ripples don't extend to us. We aren't the centre of industry or population explosion."

"But do you think they will? The ripples I mean."

"Not discernibly. No, I'm afraid if a healthy return on capital was your objective, you'd have been better off in stocks and shares."

"That was the last thing I had in mind. Who'd need a return on Paradise?"

"Not exactly Paradise when you arrived though?"

"Heavily disguised" she agreed. "Mr. Hughes, I'm going to have to rethink my strategy. May I get back to you? Bob's boiling the kettle – do have a cup of coffee."

He accepted, though uncomfortably aware he had compounded her problem. Last week she was a matter of indifference; now, accepting the coffee offered by Bob wearing the apron he shared indiscriminately with his

SAFE AS HOUSES

sister, he found himself wanting to help. He absorbed the peace they seemed to generate. "You don't come to Wales often, Mrs. Carter?"

"Not nearly enough. I have a business which is time consuming."

"But often enough for local people to speak well of you."

So that was why he had not been surprised by Bob. And if the locals had exchanged more than pleasantries with him, they trusted him, and thus she could ask her question.

"If it were your house?"

"I'd pull it down, rebuild, and move in at the first opportunity. It's a beautiful spot."

"But I can't move in. And if I had it renovated, it would still suffer from damp in my absence now that Mr. Rees and Jim aren't here."

A native himself, he had long been acquainted with those she named.

"Damp, distant and debilitating for you. And expensive to modernise. Without spending a fortune on the cottage, it can only deteriorate further - and fast."

He looked up at the ceiling where brown stains were already defying her most recent coat of paint. "You'll need a sealer to cover them, and frankly it would be a waste of time. But I can see how fond you are of the place."

He saw Bob reach for his sister's hand. As the bearer of bad news it was better he took his leave.

Watching his car out of sight, they returned to the sitting room where Bob added logs to the blaze. "Like it here Kate," he said gruffly, and she felt as if her heart would break.

"So do I Bob. Let's take lunch down to the shore and listen to those noisy kittiwakes."

She sat propped against a boulder for a long time while Bob meandered barefoot, stooping now and then to pick up a shell whose colour attracted him. His deep voice carried on the wind as he talked to himself. "One for Gill. Beth likes that one. Special one for Mam. Mam dead - can't give her shells. Dad dead. Kate here: love Kate."

She had forced back tears of exhaustion all the time they had walked across the fields to the estuary, but now they fell. "And I've got to take this away from him too," she mused.

The walk back tired him, and he sat heavily beside her. "You sell the cottage Kate?"

"We'll talk about it over supper at Manorbier. We can watch everything grow dark over the sea from there, and listen to the waves. You like that."

SAFE AS HOUSES

He nodded. He would like whatever she suggested; she was Kate. "Cottage die when we didn't come Kate. All cold."

"But we cleaned it up and got it to rights didn't we Boyo?"

"Man said it dies again. Ceiling falls down like Dad."

She gripped his hand. "Are you saying you won't mind if we have to sell the cottage Bob?"

His eyes found a boat to follow over the water. "Have nice home with you now Kate. Cottage die."

Since they'd arrived they had been too busy to be aware of the call of the gulls and guillemots; had failed to smell the thyme and sea lavender. Bobby was right. The cottage had become only a responsibility and Paradise had slipped away. It was time to let go. Next morning she told Gareth Hughes of her decision and he offered to come and take measurements; he could be with her shortly having nothing pressing until an auction at one thirty.

They had arranged chairs in the garden and from the open door of the kitchen he picked up the welcoming aroma of coffee. The convivial atmosphere was a potent tranquilliser and neither seemed in a hurry to embark on the business in hand. Eventually he said, "I suspect you no longer need a refuge - that perhaps you've already enough responsibility?"

She nodded. "Perhaps that's why there's less pain attached to my decision than I imagined. A relief even. Bob made it easier when we were by the shore yesterday."

She explained how her brother had juxtaposed death and the sorry state of the cottage. "You clarified his thoughts when you voiced the possibility of the ceilings collapsing. My father fell just before he died and Bob has never been able to rid his mind of the experience."

He took her number, promising to communicate developments as they occurred. It was doubtful the sale would come anywhere near solving her financial problems, but she felt a weight being lifted. At least she had one less thing to cope with. Now at last she could drink in the atmosphere that until this particular visit had constituted peace.

There was now the urgent matter of raising Emm's repayment. It had been lent without conditions and would be repaid with a corresponding lack of fuss.

"The initial sum was not huge by today's standards," Phil Jensen remarked as he perused the agreement Kate produced.

"But made an enormous difference at the time."

There had been no response from Emm, and payment was made via her elected solicitor who confirmed the details Kate had sought, leaving no doubt that she had initiated the request, but the solicitor was other than the one with whom the connection with Duncan had now been established.

And always there was the question of Bob. Instinctively she felt a time was imminent when he would require much more care, and though Danielle would ultimately assume full management responsibility for the Centre, she herself must have an income to cater for their joint needs. Never having been able to separate herself from her enterprise, she was now in the dilemma of having considerable capital locked into development. Indeed for a rich woman she could be said to be on the ropes. She was therefore worried to hear two substantial reservations had been cancelled.

"Danielle is out visiting one of the companies now," a perturbed Helen told her. I've made an urgent appointment with a senior director of the other. You'll want to go?"

"Absolutely. Is this the first time this has happened?"

"One whilst you were in Wales. Danielle followed it up, and though the reasons weren't convincing, she had to accept their decision. Just one cancellation can mean anything or nothing, but now of course."

"I see why she's been so hot off the mark. And rightly. It's extremely disturbing."

It was a disquieted Danielle who returned to report a complete lack of progress. Her visit had met with indifference from the Director with whom she had spoken and who had neither time nor inclination to discuss his reasons. Nor was he amused at misleading description of facilities available at the Centre, when she must have known of lax security.

"It was defamation!" she protested. "A herd of lies!"

"So who's our worried competitor?" Kate mused aloud.

"Mrs. Carter, you don't think it could be Miss Charlesworth!"

"No I don't. Emm is neither vindictive, nor in the U.K."

"But Mr. Carter is," Ted whispered to Kate as he brought urgently needed stationery into the office. Kate followed him outside in a flash.

"When and where did you see him Ted?"

"Getting in his car some way down the road. I thought he might be coming to see you, so I hung around a bit, and next thing he'd driven off."

She took no more than a few seconds to assess the implications of Ted's information, and steeling herself against any hint of emotion, returned to the

SAFE AS HOUSES

meeting. She had barely resumed her seat when the telephone rang, the atmosphere tense as she and Danielle listened to her secretary's response.

"That was Taylor's. They've cancelled their whole schedule with us."

"But they are our most big clients.... Mrs. Carter ..."

"So he's going for the jugular," Kate flashed. "I'll stop to wonder why, later. O.K. leave the sleuthing to me. You two concentrate on finding replacement bookings."

"At such short notice, it's not going to be easy."

"Well nigh impossible. But the loss of income will be catastrophic this month. Just try eh?"

Engaging Mrs. Osborne to be on hand for Bob, that evening she embarked on a round of calls to hotels in and around the city, purposefully avoiding prior phone calls that might alert her ex husband.

"I've called to see Mr. Duncan Carter," she said confidently on each occasion. "He's expecting me - would you mind calling his room?"

But it was after 10.30 when a less than perfunctory receptionist provided the answer she had sought all evening. "He's not in his room - thought I saw him come in awhile back though." Disinclined to go to any trouble, she acceded when Kate said that she would go to the lounge to look for herself.

He was alone at the bar as she approached from behind, ordered a mineral water for herself, and a substantial whisky that may prove effective in gaining her objective. He turned languidly in her direction, eyes affected by cigarette smoke, and disinterestedly resumed his drink. But glass half way to his lips, he turned again. "Kate!"

"Duncan." She paid the barman and said quietly, "Shall we sit down?" Had he consumed less, he might have proved more of a match, but as it was he responded appropriately to what in effect had been neither question nor invitation. Easing himself into the chair he sought an opportunity to collect his thoughts, but his unexpected visitor had no such intention.

"Why, Duncan?"

He looked at her for several seconds before replying. "That's a strange question after so long Kate. I guess I preferred Emm as a partner."

"You know what I mean. Why foul up bookings for the Centre?"

"Quite the Madame Poirot aren't we? Why me?"

"I don't have many enemies. Even fewer jealous ones. And none with your style. And when you've answered my question, we'll address the question of Molly's lease." The soft, firm tone was unquestionably authoritative.

SAFE AS HOUSES

"OK. I'll give it to you in the kind of nutshell you prefer as I recall. I guessed Emm was coming to ask you for money - what else are friends for?" His words were slurred. "I wanted to ruin your reputation so you'd have none to give her." He drained his glass and impassively proceeded to the whisky she had purchased.

"I've not set eyes on Emm since you both went to the States. Until your despicable attempts at a smear campaign, I'd assumed you were still there."

"So where the hell is she now?"

Kate remained silent. That Emm had left him was obvious, hence her request for repayment. His tongue well and truly loosened, he needed no lubrication. Nor was any detective work required to realise he was broke and that a few sweeteners from her competitors, wouldn't come amiss.

"I want her back Kate. At any price."

"But not at the expense of my business. It's too much to expect you to set the record straight with the Companies with whom you've already destroyed my reputation, but I warn you, if you don't halt your contemptible activities as of this moment, I won't hesitate to involve the police - you - and those who have paid you."

Her anger gave her the strength she needed, whilst he, even in his inebriated state, sensed that he could puncture that strength by affecting to be reasonable and compliant. He held up his hands in capitulation, and it shocked her to see how they shook. "OK. Sorry. Gross error of judgement. Wrong move. You have my word."

She recoiled as he tried to put an arm around her. "I'm long since through with your word Duncan. Just one more company cancels and I'll have the police onto you before you can stub out your cigarette. And I daresay they'll find more of interest than my Centre."

"Oh but.."

"So there are more in the pipeline? Well you'll just have to get to them first won't you? Or have I not made myself clear?"

"As crystal Kate. OK. I'll do what you say. Look, don't go like this after so long. I haven't even asked you about the family... Gill and Beth. Your Mom and Pop."

"My parents are dead ....."

He was nodding, only half concentrating. "Yeh, I remember now. Alex said about Lucy...."

She fired her question with a vehemence that instantly destroyed the last tenuous dregs of resistance. "When did you last see my father?"

SAFE AS HOUSES

"Hey hold it Kate. Gee I can't remember exactly. Some two.... three years ago I guess. No, no I didn't see him - I called, wanting to speak with you about something or other I guess. He got himself well uptight - completely out of character. Started shouting down the phone accusing me of every sin in the book. All over a few lousy quid. Real fired up he was, then told me to get the hell off the line." With a sudden jerk of the head he faced her again. "You say he's dead now?"

Her reply was barely more than a whisper. "Thanks to you Duncan, yes, my father is dead. And at last I know what killed him."

She was hardly aware of walking out of the hotel, and certainly not of the sweet relief that swept over Duncan as he relaxed into the armchair and ordered another whisky. He smiled contentedly. He had just one more card to play. And this one was an ace.

Sitting in her car, it was some time before she felt capable of turning the ignition. That he would now desist from his attempt to ruin her company she was confident. It would not be in his interests to draw police attention to himself. And then she realised, and cursed, that she had not forced the issue of Molly O' Mahn. She put the car into gear and pulled away - far, far away from him. Set against the accelerated demise of her father, the problems relating to the lease were void of meaning, and she could attach to them neither import nor significance.

CHAPTER THIRTY SIX

The last of the wedding guests having left, Helen's parents sought an opportunity to speak with Kate. "Mrs. Carter what a wonderful day. It's been a fairytale setting - so beautiful."

"Helen is one of us! She should benefit from what she helped to create. And Danielle and I had the world's fun with the arrangements."

"And she sure hasn't had much of that these past years," Phil whispered to Danielle. The financial strain is knocking hell out of her."

"There was a time after Miss Charlesworth visit she worry very much, but afterwards I sink all must be resolved because she not speak of it."

"It was resolved, because Kate sold her cottage and raised a personal loan towards Emmeline's repayment. Money the Centre now owes to Kate - which is why I've hung about - to tell her that at the first opportunity she must separate herself from her work - at least financially."

"Not easy!"

"Chances are better than when she was in the rag trade. Then there *was* no dividing line! Send coffee to her office. I must speak privately with her."

"More problems?"

"Let's say a post-mortem of them, assuming his antics are over."

"They certainly wrecked all our projections. Quel catastrophe!"

"Perfect description of the bastard!" Phil retorted bitterly.

Tell tale lines of fatigue were apparent as Kate approached them.

"You did her proud Kate," Jensen assured her. "Great day. But you must be tired. I promise to be gone in half an hour."

"Oh? I'm disappointed. I'd rather hoped we could have dinner together."

"Of course - but no Bob tonight?"

"He's going to supper with Ted and his wife. It's her birthday, and they suggested he stayed over. And I think we've a fair amount to discuss?"

"Dinner it is. But why don't I take you out for a break - look on it as an attempt to regulate the balance for all the times I've eaten here."

"I'd enjoy that. I must be growing old, initiating dinner with a man some years my junior!"

SAFE AS HOUSES

"Aren't we at an age when it's not supposed to matter? Pick you up at seven."

"I enjoy your company where and whenever, you know that. And I suspect you've been delaying confirmation of my own assessment."

He gave her a wry smile. "I should know by now there's no danger of shocking you! You're invariably too close on my heels."

Over dinner, her anxiety was more obvious.

"That ex of yours came close to ruining you Kate. And what he didn't accomplish, your partner did, with her withdrawal."

"But they were not in collaboration. I expect she needed the money to extricate herself from dependence on Duncan."

"Since when could anyone depend on him?"

"You're very bitter Phil."

"And I'm not the one he tried to destroy!"

She drew her fingers across her mouth, and for an instant closed her eyes. Jensen laid his hand on hers. "Sorry. You want to consign him to the past?" She took a letter from her bag. "There may be one bit of good news."

"This is not your bank."

"Exactly. I'm rather hoping I've been invited to call because the Manager is prepared to offer more favourable terms than we currently have."

"It says almost nothing, which could be a good sign if a little poaching is on the agenda. Other than that Kate, you'll have to look for backers - or another partner."

"That's why I hoped Emm would have shown."

"You're not serious!"

"We both made the same mistake - trusted Duncan. No room for condemnation on my part. She's probably designing in the States with money to invest again."

He looked hard at her. "We've worked together for some thirty years, and still I feel I won't ever really know you."

"I'll survive Phil. As my accountant that's surely all you need to know about me." Only a suspicion of a quiver in her voice before she added, "Our friendship is a bonus."

He urged her to make the appointment with the Bank.

"Do I sense you'd like to come with me?"

"We could discuss terms and conditions on the spot. The situation's dire."

"Not for the first time in my life. Yes it would be comforting to have someone hold my hand. Thank you. I'd like you to be there."

SAFE AS HOUSES

It was over their respective bowls of cornflakes that each questioned whether the wine had been responsible for assuming the Bank's benevolent purpose in inviting Kate to call. But no other reason came to mind, and Jensen called for her soon after lunch.

"May I speak wiz you when you return Madame?" Danielle asked.

"Of course." As Kate climbed into Jensen's car, she said nervously, "You don't think she's going to leave?"

"The chances of Danielle leaving you are about as high as your declaring a healthy profit next week. Come on. Let's see what your friendly new bank manager has to say."

"Your accountant, Mrs. Carter?" the Manager repeated Kate's introduction. He hesitated, and then to Jensen said, "So, I presume you are aware of the nature of our discussion?"

"We hope to have made an educated guess, but that's all Mr. Nicholson."

"And what was that guess Mrs. Carter?"

"From your discomfort, obviously an incorrect one. Please enlighten us."

Kate was aware now of a heightening tension.

Twisting his pen, Nicholson cleared his throat, and asked Kate to confirm her home address, and though bewildered, Kate obliged. "I've practically paid for it now," she said, for no other reason than to give him the time he seemed to need.

"You feel the house to be yours, Mrs. Carter?"

"My husband turned it over to me when he left. I'd assumed the greater responsibility for repayments up to that time, and have had full liability ever since. Forgive me, I can't see why it's of interest to you, Mr. Nicholson."

Nicholson looked first at Jensen, who was now ahead of the mental gymnastics, and fearing for Kate's very survival, and then continued, "Mrs. Carter, the situation is worse than I thought. I very much regret to tell you that you have, over the years, continued to pay for a house that in law is not yours."

Controlled, only because her head refused to absorb the awful truth, she said, "There must be some mistake. My husband obtained forms for me to sign renouncing his ownership. He put everything in my name when we separated."

Jensen gently gripped her arm. "*He* obtained the forms, you say Kate. Did you take them to the Building Society? Did you read the small print?"

SAFE AS HOUSES

There was a long pause in which she surrendered to the undeniable crisis. Forcing her mind back to that day when, distraught and confused at having learned Duncan and Emm were lovers, she had been stunned by his insistence that he wanted to make amends by signing the house over to her, pleaded with her to accept............ She had signed where he had indicated. And then had gone on to give him half a cottage. If she had questioned anything, it was not his honesty, but his decision to be so generous.

"I'm afraid what you signed was a joint ownership of a house previously in your husband's name only. The building society would be disinterested in which of you paid the mortgage."

The blood drained from her face as she swayed and reached for the arms of the chair. Incredulous and stunned, finally she said in a whisper that was barely audible, "You're telling me that I've made all the repayments on a house we still own jointly – only half is mine?"

Nicholson, breathed deeply, and then said sombrely, "I wish that were the case for then there might be paths open to you. As you say, half would be yours, which would be some comfort." He glanced at Jensen who moved towards her protectively. "Mrs. Carter, I very much regret to tell you that the house is now the property of the Bank. There is a charge against it. Mr. Carter offered it as collateral against a very substantial loan."

"And now the bastard's done a bunk," expostulated Jensen. "By God if I could lay my hands on him."

"The paperwork was all in order," Nicholson attempted justification.

"Oh I don't doubt that for one minute." Phil's face was set; hatred engraved in his tortuous expression.

Astonishing both men by her composure, Kate asked quietly, "When was this particular loan taken out - do you have the date?"

Nicholson thumbed through the file and turning it round to face her, indicated both date and signature. It was the day after she had tracked Duncan down at his hotel, after he had tried to ruin her business a little less than a year ago; the day after she had learned of the telephone call that had caused her father such anguish and precipitated his death. She nodded, as though accepting the logical significance of it, swayed a little, and then said "I don't think I can absorb any more. There will obviously be a procedure to follow, but I assume it need not begin today. If you will excuse me Mr. Nicholson I......"

"Come on Kate. I'm taking you home." Jensen picked up her briefcase and placed a supporting hand firmly beneath her arm.

SAFE AS HOUSES

White and devastated, she looked up at him with the porcelain fragility of an old lady. "Home Phil? It seems I no longer have one."

Neither spoke as each relived the past hour with Nicholson. The loss with which he had acquainted her made her feel as if she was emerging from anaesthesia. She was puzzled that it was strangely not the loss of the house, but the cottage that was most painful. If she were honest, she had never stopped thinking of the house as Duncan's; he had chosen it, arranged its purchase - or so she had naively believed. She knew that soon the cataclysmic, financial implication would hold her in its grip, but at this moment there was only relief like the lancing of a boil, in having finally got rid of him; the total absence of any solicitous act on his part liberating her from the self reproach that had punctuated so many nights sleep. There was nothing more he could do to her; nothing more he could take.

For Bob, she struggled to maintain the status quo that evening. If he noticed a certain quietness, he associated it with the pressure he knew instinctively that running a business caused his sister. Quiet periods did not mean that insoluble problems lurked to upset the routine of their lives, but rather that Kate, - because she was Kate - needed to have things in order. Watching him engrossed in his favourite TV soap, the panic that had so far been restrained, began to surface, as the anaesthesia of shock wore off. Where would they live?......store their belongings....Desperation hit home as the awful truth thumped relentlessly. A sudden rush of heat to her head made her throw open a window, and Bob shivered at the impact of cold air.

"You not die Kate!" A reminder that he too was yet tortured by his own private fears suctioned away the concentration on her own. Lovingly encircling his solid ample form, she pressed her lips to his head. "Bob, I am a little bit sad tonight. Sometimes by crying we can let the sadness out. Be patient with me - I will get it sorted. Promise."

He took one of her hands in both of his; a visual statement that he needed all his resources to cope with just one problem at a time, and murmured gruffly, "I get tea, nice tray, china cup for Kate. Love Kate." He beamed a suggestion that had always brought a smile to her face. "Go to Wales?"

"That's what I'd love to do, but do you remember we sold our cottage." To herself she added, "Thanks to the other half of the partnership."

He drew a picture of a bay they had visited frequently. The things he loved most - the birds, shells and rock pools were enlarged out of all proportion to the background, which nevertheless was a fair representation of his favourite haunt. It gave him pleasure that she gazed at it for several minutes, though he could not know that she was drawing strength from so doing. There was, she decided, sometimes more to be learned from the statement of a childlike mind, than the discourse of experts. Bob's instinctive philosophy would be the only way through this present mess.

When he had gone to sleep, she crept out into the garden and sat for a long time by the pond, the gentle sounds of the still night, rhythmic and comforting. But as the air grew colder, and a single aircraft broke the stillness, sheer terror of the future with its swarm of uncertainties began to exercise a vice like grip on her, and she drew her shoulders together to harness the tightening pain in her chest. When it became totally unbearable, she surrendered in a crumpled heap onto the grass, finally allowing herself the alleviating release of tears. Forlorn, hopeless tears, that she knew were not for the loss of bricks and mortar, but for Jonathan and for Emm, and all that together they had created, and she had lived for. Somehow she would make the Centre survive because it was now her chosen work. But Innovation had been of herself. She could feel it, abandoned and denied, crying out to her still.

CHAPTER THIRTY SEVEN

"No Kate. You can't possibly live here. It'll destroy you." Flamboyantly Val pushed her finger through the rotting wood of the kitchen window frame. "I'll lend you the deposit on something that at least resembles what you've been used to."
Kate swallowed. "I seem to have developed an allergy to paying mortgages Val..... I'd prefer the dust to settle...get rid of this punch drunk state..."
"But not here!"
"Sit down a moment." Gradually she persuaded Val to ignore the superficial. The spacious Edwardian rooms with their high ceilings would be receptive to her pictures, the tall windows enhanced with elegant drapes. Only the draughts that penetrated them, not their maintenance, would be her concern. Overlooking a park, the loss of her garden would not be so acute, and she could return within minutes if Bob were unwell.

Both were silent until Val nudged Kate away from dwelling on near disaster. "Pass me your sunglasses – I'll inspect the bedrooms," she joked. And Kate thought how attractive she was looking; there was a new jauntiness about her.

"My God it's enough to give you heat rash! But - you've convinced me. Lovely views from both large rooms. There was a pause, and then, "You've already signed haven't you?"
Kate nodded. "Come back to the Centre for tea?"
Val looked at her watch. "Just ten minutes. Andy's bringing a girl friend to dinner."
"And it must be two years since Greg went to the States?"
"Coming to visit in a few days. Strange with neither at home any more."
"But you're not as lonely as you have been? When Val didn't answer, she said simply, "It does show!"
"He's a good man Kate."
"That's all I need to know. If Jonathan hadn't made a call for me...."
"He would have fitted another into his own schedule. Yes, life has been empty since he died but he made sure it wouldn't be difficult for us."

SAFE AS HOUSES

"But you did feel I was responsible - for a time?"

"Not you personally. But the world you shared, yes. There was a part of him he enjoyed with you that I couldn't get close to." She turned to face Kate. "Things are fine for me now, but you're still alone. It can't be easy."

"I have Bob."

"You know that's not what I meant. What about the guy you once went to Paris with?"

"I didn't realise you knew."

"As you just said – it shows! Well, what came of it?"

Disconcerted at the effect of the question, despite the years, Kate kept her eyes directly ahead. "Nothing," she said finally. "Sadly nothing at all."

She was grateful for Vale's blunt, unexpurgated description of the apartment to Helen and Danielle before rushing away.

"Kate's ultimate challenge!" she joked. "Believe me girls, building a conference centre was a doddle in comparison!"

As she waved her off, so a taxi drew up and Kate stood open mouthed. "Marie Jeanne! Quel plaisir! But no Armand?"

"Non. Je suis toute seule. Kate may I stay wiz you one evening?"

Surmising Armand had reached the end of his rope; that his wife could forgive no more indiscretions, she poured her visitor an aperitif.

"Perhaps I may snooze for some minutes? The journey has tired me."

"You can rest in my room where none but the birds will disturb you."

"I would like that. And ziz evening we talk Kate, yes?"

The last word was an undeniable plea, and having settled her guest, Kate hurried back to discuss arrangements with Danielle. They were all working under pressure and she hated to go early when it presupposed her assistant would work late. And whatever it was that Danielle had wanted to talk about, had still not been aired.

"I don't know if the sadness of your new circumstances makes my idea impossible or ze more relevant, Madame. In case ze latter, I say it now, and please do not trouble about being wiz Madame Cardules - I see in her eyes she much need a companion,"

"Danielle. I do want desperately to increase the workforce so that at times like this we don't exert unreasonable pressure on each other, but..."

"Zat is why I speak. You know how Brigitte she adore to work 'ere. If she do so all ze time, we can sell ze appartement in Paris to invest in ze Centre."

SAFE AS HOUSES

Kate returned her paperwork to the desk. She could not allow them to take such a risk.

"You are not confident of ze Centre, Madame?"

"Yes I am. Though I couldn't blame those who would challenge such a statement. But the recovery will take some time. You know I've been affected by significant setbacks - setbacks of such a personal nature that it would be grossly unfair for anyone else's finance to be put at risk. Just one further catastrophe will be the one I can't survive." She would not allow them to risk their only capital asset - an asset that in itself was insufficient to remove the tightrope fear of collapse. "To face ruin myself would take as much courage as I possess Danielle. To be the cause of yours would render me suicidal. I have lost my home. I will not lose yours too."

The need to be with Marie Jeanne was pressing. She agreed to consider the request but insisted her stance would not change.

"So you thought I had finally run away from an errant husband, Kate!"

"That would have been preferable - at least there would have been the possibility of reconciliation. Marie Jeanne, it is really quite certain?"

"I saw ze X Rays myself." She paused. "I confess Kate I am a little afraid to die ... but Armand. I cannot tell him."

"He would prefer to know," Kate said quietly. "He'll want to do so many special things for you."

"Exactement. And each will remind me of my sentence Kate. And I do not want him to be different. All my life I am afraid of losing 'im. Every time he look at someone more beautiful; each occasion he slip away for an assignation, I die a little. But always 'e come back, and for those days I live and would change places wiz no one. Now for an invader in my body to make 'im ze faithful 'usband, I do not wish."

'But she wants me to tell him,' Kate realised, 'or at least hint at it. That way she can die believing he has chosen to be with her to the exclusion of all others.'

Her guest allowed her head to fall back, and closed her eyes whilst Kate poured two cognacs and observed the undeniable evidence of the malaise within. In the silence she suddenly felt the aloneness of being pushed herself further towards the pinnacle of old age. What did her losses amount to when set against her health? Did not death ultimately unload us of all our possessions and achievements? Life, however much was left, must be held precious. And at that moment she was able to shuffle her priorities into some sort of order.

SAFE AS HOUSES

Marie Jeanne opened her eyes, smiled and raised the glass Kate had placed beside her. "To ziz next year - for we all."

"May it be the happiest you have known."

"It will - so long as I have my friends .... and if Armand.... I suddenly have ze great longing to be back wiz him Kate."

Far from the assault they made on his sister's sensibility, the vibrant, discordant colours were a source of amusement to Bob. "We get big tub Kate. I paint orange walls first," he giggled, "Then blue ones."

"So we'll have fun living here eh Boyo?"

"Fun with Kate," he confirmed. "Feed ducks in the park." Trust Bob to find the one redeeming feature!

And so they tackled the conversion of a flat the agent was frankly amazed to have let, into a Kate-home. Stopping for a break one evening, they heard a rap on the door below. Kate gingerly pushed open the casement window and saw her nephews clad in jeans and golfing caps, grinning up at her.

"Two volunteers Aunt Kate! Let us in. You look as if you'd seen a ghost!"

"I thought I had!" Kate said to herself. How like Jonathan was his eldest son. "I can't un-jam the front door - come up the fire escape," she called.

"It's as bad as Mum described!" Andy shrieked.

"You should have seen it before we tackled the sitting room," Kate retorted with a bravado that instantly threatened to desert her. Greg circled his arms about her waist. "You've got more guts than a battalion. Where do you want us to start boss-lady?"

"The front door. I can paint but not fix. At least not the heavy things, and I don't fancy scaling the fire escape on an icy winter's night."

"Good as done. Come on Bob - we need a massive heave-ho."

Chuckling, Bob trundled down the fire escape after them. He had a natural uninhibited strength they hadn't bargained for, and both door and rusted lock were soon released.

Jumping behind the wheel, Andy called to Bob to accompany him. "You as good at navigating as you are at knocking doors down old fella?"

Greg rejoined his aunt, shocked that the youthful vitality that had accompanied her well into middle-age, had in his absence in the States, taken such a knock.

"Tell me how things are - apart from bloody awful. You going to be OK?"

SAFE AS HOUSES

She didn't reply immediately; he so incredibly resembled Jonathan as she remembered him when she had first returned from America. "Bit of a blinder Greg, but everything's on course to realise potential, given no more unforeseen dilemmas."

"What it was like to start over again.... Do you feel like telling me all about it? Sorry – not the most tactful opener."

"Don't apologise. I've missed this so much. Out of kindness I know, I'm urged to talk about what's happened, when all I want is to talk positively as I did with your father on how to build, how to beat the competition *despite* the problems. We never let hurdles block the way - we *jumped* them! And do you know I was never tired - and I certainly never felt old."

"And you do now?"

She nodded. Feeling an uncannily familiar rapport, she went on, "Only to you can I confess how I miss the team mate who shared the pace; cajoled me, as I encouraged him, into holding firm to convictions... backing gut instincts and going all out for the rewards. Oh they were good days Greg. Working in tandem with Jonathan was like climbing mountains we built for ourselves – exhausting but exhilarating. I tried to recapture it all with a new venture, but the essential ingredient was missing. Danielle is my right arm; perfect for the job. But I haven't got the fire in my belly I once had."

"From what I hear, you've built a pretty spectacular second show - and fought off crises that would have brought most people to their knees."

"I've been so near to collapse Greg."

She found herself telling him of how Danielle would like to buy into the company and how she couldn't take the risk of allowing her to skate on thin ice. "Backing a business with one's own home is one thing Greg - with someone else's is another matter. Determined I may be: ruthless I trust not."

"Maybe with her home up front, she'll provide the spark you can't find right now."

She bristled at his impudence, and he grinned at the correlative flash in her eyes that warned him off. But he stood his ground. "Better use every offer to strengthen your position Aunt Kate. I warn you, leave yourself vulnerable and I might well put in a bid myself in a year or two!" And he could not know his jocose threat was music to her ears.

'I can wait,' she thought. "And incidentally Mr. Young Entrepreneur - a word of advice from a mere burned out pro - the credibility of a guy who talks of bidding for something he hasn't inspected at first hand, is somewhat suspect!"

SAFE AS HOUSES

"Tomorrow?"

"Ten o'clock. Don't be late!"

So engrossed had they been they'd not heard Andy and Bob return. "Don't know if *I* can be organised by ten though!" her younger nephew laughed. "Voila! One lock, two keys. Come on Bob. 'Tis alas the lot of we lesser mortals, to graft!"

Kate flicked the paintbrush she had just washed in his direction, and then immersed it once more into the can.

"I thought you'd had enough." Greg laughed.

"Must be second wind." she retorted. "I feel like tackling another wall!

Danielle was receiving the report from the night porter when she arrived early next day. "You have considered Madame?"

"Danielle, I am professionally, physically, emotionally - and up-to-my-neck-in-debt - involved in the Centre. Hence why I'm not the person to give you advice." They looked at each other, recognising that detachment was incompatible with either of their temperaments. "Check the validity of your idea. If you remain convinced, my suggestion would be to raise a loan equal to your own equity in the house. That way your lender adds conviction to your own. If all goes wrong, Brigitte has the option of buying you out or finding a new co-owner. If not, you still have a base on familiar ground. Given her disabilities, she needs security."

"And after I have taken ozer advice? I know Madame zat when you listen wiz all ze points, your own instinct 'as ze last word."

"My situation should be a salutary lesson. Talk with your bank manager."

"He does not know about ze power of dreams. I ask Monsieur Jensen."

Kate knew that she must remain, if only just, on the periphery of this particular dream.

They were interrupted by Andy. "Only six minutes late! We came in my banger, and like her owner she's not disposed to dawn excursions. But she yielded to gentle persuasion, and here we are!"

"I expect she just needs a new spark plug," His aunt strangely appeared to address her remark to his brother. They could not know that for her, they represented Jonathan, and she nervously awaited their reaction.

Andy was looking around, absorbing the ambience. "You know, I reckon dukes or dustmen could feel equally at home here. Always assuming dustbin-men have conferences!"

"About as often as dukes." Kate responded dryly.

Greg said simply, "It just says you did it Aunt Kate."

Kate nudged him. "So I've still got a bit of mileage left eh?"

"Do you know, I feel as if it wouldn't disturb anyone if I put up an easel right here and began to paint! Aunt Kate, this place would make the perfect art college."

Andy's remark triggered a train of thought in Greg's mind. "An Arts Centre, where people could take time off from the rat race to enjoy creative workshops....writing, drama, painting..."

Kate listened to minds in motion, breathing life into a project as they would live it. If it took two sons to bring one Jonathan back for a while, so be it.

They visited Bob in his 'professional metier', as Andy teased. And the dark blue overalls might just as well have been a General's uniform, as he escorted them proudly on a tour of the grounds before returning to the office-cum-stockroom he shared with Ted, who, knowing how much it would delight his charge to offer hospitality, had the kettle boiling. With an irresistible attempt to pull rank befitting his staff status, Bob methodically lined up four mugs, poured hot strong tea into each, and offered the sugar packet and communal spoon first to Ted, and then to his guests.

"Now that's what I call a drink," Andy declared. "None o' these china cups you can't get your nose into! Oops, don't tell Aunt Kate I said that will you now Bob!"

Before they had finished, he had nodded off. The silver grey hairs of premature ageing caught the sunlight as his head fell forward onto his chest. Ted winked knowingly. "It looks as if we're on the home straight now. He's had a good life. Loves his job. And he's certainly enjoyed his V.I.P's today! Put a comment in his Visitors Book. Mrs. Carter has one on the reception desk - so Bob has one on the bench!"

In a flourishing style, Andy wrote "Hospitality better than the Ritz."

"Your visitors have been good for you Madame." Danielle smiled as they checked details for an after dinner lecture.

Kate nodded. Twice today she had been given the glimpse of an opportunity to let go a little; to loosen the reins on which she had kept such tight control for so long.

CHAPTER THIRTY EIGHT

Bob's funeral was held on a crisp autumn day, and Kate, unable to absorb individuals, was aware only of the silent, bewilderingly large gathering around the graveside remaining a discreet distance away as the coffin was lowered into the waiting depth. Taking one of the blooms from the flowers she had gathered in the copse, she turned to place it on the adjacent grave. Swaying slightly as she did so, as if the sudden change of direction dictated by her head had taken her body by surprise, she used the merest touch of her fingers to steady herself against the headstone on which was inscribed, 'Lucy and Alex Benson. Beloved parents of Kate, Gillian, Beth and Bob.'

Jensen moved to take her hand, as the poignancy of the scene impacted on the assembly who stepped back to allow family to move towards the car at the head of the cortège, before walking sombrely to their own vehicles.

"Bye Bob. Love you," Kate whispered, and turning to Danielle, said, "Please look after everyone. I just need to be with Bob for awhile."

"It would be better if you came, Kate," Jensen urged gently. "We can't have the hostess arriving after the guests." But his persuasion was awkward and unconvincing.

"Forgive me just once if I don't conform, Phil. I won't be long. There are so many people ... and I need to be alone with him."

From somewhere behind them Ted offered quietly, "I'll stay with Mrs. Carter, Mr. Jensen, and drive her back when she's ready." His voice was thick. "I'd appreciate a few moments myself. I won't intrude M'm."

"Not long then. We don't want our boss-lady going down with a chill."

Gill looked anxious and said, " She hardly seems to know where she is."

"She'll be alright with Ted."

"You're fond of our Kate."

"I've known her for many years - seen her ride more than a few storms." He made no attempt to dispute her observation. "She handles them, but they get right inside her. And every time I watch her being destroyed a little."

Ted had already moved to the church porch as she approached the grave, the freshly dug earth attributing a brutal newness to death. They had known each other, and shared a responsibility for Bob for too long, for his presence to be intrusive. She was calm; the inordinate grief offset minimally by the relief of his predeceasing her; knowing he'd never have to cope with bureaucracy alone.

"I'll miss you Bob. You were so special. I wish we could have convinced others who saw you as a burden, that you were such a privilege. Guess they were afraid to get close enough to understand your unconditional loving. Never a grouch or temper, no threat to anyone, and finding only the best in people. Ted saw all these things - that's why he's here somewhere now Bob. Only my eyes won't seem to look anywhere except at this mound that hides you from me. The responsibility when Mam died frightened me, but I got much more than I gave. You embodied loving and giving - couldn't help yourself. And I'm glad you liked being a caretaker with Ted. I expect one day soon he'll tell me he's ready to hang up his hat now that his best mate has gone. Mine too Bob. I feel so empty without you... I don't want to go home and find you not there. Anyway it's not a home; just that awful flat we rented when Duncan stole the other house you and I made home."

She felt a gentle touch on her shoulder. "Time to go M'm. Farewells are best not drawn out."

She took the arm he offered. "Thank you for waiting Ted. Are you cold?"

"No. Only saddened. There'll be a great deal missing from our lives from now on. But it was time if he was not to suffer the indignity, and you the misery, of his premature senility. Nature usually takes care of the things we have no solution for." He settled her in the car. "Now what about you? Life has to go on."

"I'll visit Beth. Bob has reminded me how short life is. Now that Danielle is in full charge of the day-to-day running, and Greg coming in on the finance side, the Centre's in good hands. I'll soon be a sleeping partner!"

"And that's not something you've had enough of over the years," he commented philosophically. "Sleep, nor time for yourself."

"Building a business and time for myself were one and the same thing, Ted. Don't attribute any halos to me - they wouldn't fit."

"No matter, I'd like to see you cared for at last."

"And just between two old uns, Ted, I wouldn't be averse to being cherished for awhile." She paused. "And that's an old fashioned word I haven't heard for years."

"It's said there was someone once M'm, before Mr. Carter did the dirty on you."

SAFE AS HOUSES

"Not any more. And what are your plans Ted?" A perceptible rigidity; the barriers had gone up, and he was not fool enough to ignore them. She was surprised to hear he'd like to stay on a year or so if that would suit. "Managing without you would have been more of a problem!" she declared.

It was in fact Phil who took her by surprise when, deflecting her from the day's event, he pre-empted what would more naturally have taken place at a routine meeting. "Kate, if you've decided not to be around quite so much in future, I'm thinking golf would be preferable to business."

"Why? I'm not your only client!"

"But you *are* my favourite. I never thought you'd contemplate retiring."

"Nor have I - just withdrawing from the Centre awhile. The one doesn't imply the other. But I'm not so arrogant as to think I'm essential to the enterprise. Danielle has been champing at the bit for some time, and with Greg on finance and marketing, I'm becoming superfluous."

A lecturer who had used the Centre on a number of occasions, hovered awhile, then seeing his opportunity sought to tell her that she and Bob had somehow symbolised the philosophy that no one need apologise for being who they were, nor yet indulge in pride or disdain. "You were rarely seen in each other's company, yet the bond was patently indestructible."

"You spoke with my brother?" she asked in surprise.

"Often - as indeed did others." A mischievous smile played around his lips. "How else was one to learn anything about his very private sister?"

"And what did you learn Professor?"

"Only that you were the 'bestest' sister; the person he loved most, and that you painted orange walls together." He laughed at her relief that secrets were safe, and then regarded her with a directness that was disconcerting. "Go and sit down somewhere and allow that practised composure to desert you. There are enough people to attend to the guests; I fear even today our pleasure in being here is dulling our sense of propriety. Now who will I ask to bring a cup of tea - Danielle, or one of your nephews?"

It was, as she requested, Andy who came, not quietly with any awkwardness, but with the obvious conviction that what he was about to say would be infinitely more effective in dispelling her distress than a cup of tea. "Drink up. Then come with me - I've got something for you."

"For me?"

"Specially for you, and specially today. You've been surrounded by so many people I couldn't get near you. Then the Prof told me you were actually asking for me."

SAFE AS HOUSES

She drained back the amount of tea that hadn't been slopped in the saucer.
"Bob would have made a better job of that," she teased.
"Bob wouldn't have put it into such a ridiculous container!"
"Agreed! Now where are we going?"
"Bob's stockroom." His face scrunched in apology as she winced. "It was the one place I knew you wouldn't go today. Please don't let it upset you."
His natural instinct was to bound, so animated was he by the anticipated effect of his gift. Opening the door, he said, "It's for you Aunt Kate. I wanted to do something really personal instead of flowers and things."
Delight made her cry out, and then smiling her gratitude through the tears, she gripped his hand. Hanging above the bench where Bob made his mugs of tea, was a portrait of her brother; the round, bland face enlivened by the benign smile that always followed the realisation he had given pleasure. He wore his blue overalls, and on them was pinned his identity badge, 'Bob Benson, Assistant Site Manager.'
"Do you like it? Are you pleased? Will you take it home with you?"
"Yes, yes and no Andy. It is the perfect gift. But the flat is not a fitting place. It shall hang here in the Centre that is infinitely more precious to me than any apartment. Here, where his gentleness pervaded, and he achieved far more than we imagined. Let's go and hang it before everyone goes home."
She indicted Bob's hammer in the place outlined for it by Ted so that his assistant could always match his tool to the shapes painted on the wall, thus to Ted's satisfaction, and Bob's pleasure, keeping everything ship-shape.
"You won't mind the noise?" her nephew asked tentatively.
Insisting it was Bob's funeral and he certainly would have made no objection, she said, "If only he could have seen it Andy. He would have been so proud."
"But he did!" Andrew threw an arm around her shoulder. "How do you think I caught the smile? He was going to give it to you for your birthday. There's a card he wrote, but in the circumstances I put it away."
"May I have it?"
Opening the firmly sealed envelope, she read the uneven, laboured handwriting. 'To my special sister. Always love you Kate. From Bob.' Three large crosses followed, then a childish picture of herself.
"That wasn't a good idea?" Andy grimaced.
"It was the only idea, but you'll have to go on ahead of me. I'll catch you up in a moment."

SAFE AS HOUSES

Phil met her at the door of the conference room where everyone had gathered around Andy, masonry nail between his teeth and hammer ludicrously protruding from his grey lounge suit pocket, as he held the portrait aloft. Ted had produced a stepladder and she nodded in response to the lifted eyebrows and unspoken 'Did you authorise this?'

The hanging of the portrait, and spontaneous applause that followed, turned the funeral reception into the type of occasion for which the Benson Centre was renowned; a combination of warmth and dignity, and all about people. The professor's voice was heard above the amiable buzz of approbation. "Ladies and Gentlemen - This occasion has already, without the slightest loss of respect, dispensed with convention. May I, as a client of the Benson Centre, initiate a Bobby Benson Memorial Fund, whose first purchase I suggest should be a portrait by the same talented artist, of the lady who created this Centre; the fund thereafter to be used at her discretion in whatever way she feels appropriate, in memory of her brother."

The atmosphere became electric as Greg and Phil swiftly formed a team to receive a flurry of donations.

When the Centre was finally emptied of all but residents, she sat with Jensen in her office. Danielle had brought them coffee, cognac and the boursin cheese of which Kate was so fond. She was in no hurry to return to the flat, which despite her endeavours, she had never quite made her own. Because of its proximity to the park, Bob had been happy in it, and she had been reluctant to move him again. Tired, but glad that the day had evolved in such an unexpectedly agreeable manner, they sipped their drinks in the comfortable silence of a friendship spanning over thirty years.

"So what now Kate?" Jensen asked in a tone suggesting it mattered little if she were not ready to tell him. He supposed that Greg, having raised the capital sum agreed between them, she could at last withdraw a substantial amount to allow her to move into a more compatible, even gracious home.

"Houses and I don't seem to get the best from each other Phil."

She would, she told him, leave her assets where they were for the time being, taking out an income to meet her needs. That way Greg - and Danielle too as a minor shareholder - could expand and diversify, and the Centre would not again be faced with the volatility and cash flow crises that had peppered its early stages.

"You're surely not going to stay in the flat?"

"No. But that's all I am certain of! I'll wait for the numbness to wear off and make decisions when I come back from Australia."

SAFE AS HOUSES

After a lifetime of working against schedules, meeting deadlines and delivery dates, there now seemed less need for either of them to hurry. There was in fact, more of an urge to savour every precious day. She told him that when the time came, Greg and Andy would inherit. Whilst nothing could recompense for having deprived them of their father, a business of which he would have heartily approved, and one that constituted a great deal of her own life, would at least convince them of her desire to repay. But that information was in confidence; it was essential that they should do their own building, if what resulted was to have real value.

He had remonstrated with her about these exaggerated guilt feelings so often, but he was no match for her overdeveloped conscience. But he would not get angry today, even though a recklessly driven truck, and Jonathan's preponderance for speed had far more to do with the accident than she. He would never understand why she took the world on her shoulders; maybe that irritating professor guy, who'd hovered around her today, could explain. Only figures that responded to logic made any sense to him. And why was she even thinking like this; she'd live to be a hundred. It was the funeral of course. Bob's death would have caused her to contemplate her own. He tapped his pipe into the ashtray. "You going to stay here tonight?" She nodded. "I want to feel some of those things that were put to me today. Clients never knew the rocky road we travelled; how near I came to going under."

"Were they ever intended to?"

"Of course not."

"Which is why you'll never be able to see what you've created through their eyes. It's an intrinsic part of your being: you and it are indivisible."

"But Innovation was my lifeblood Phil."

"I know. Do you ever regret closing.."

"I lost Jonathan and gained Bob. Each motivated me to build in a different way."

"And now?"

She did not reply; could not. Alone, she now occupied a void that held more fear for her than any of the crises she had faced over the years.

He levered himself out of the chair, picked up his coffee cup from the carpet, and grinning, placed it on the low table between them. "There! You said it would be a miracle if I ever remembered to do that!"

"So I did. Then I shall have to go on believing in them won't I?"

He kissed her lightly. "Night Kate. Take care."

She remained for some moments, and then, a distinctive figure still, moved with the grace of earlier years, through to the Conference Room where Bob's portrait hung over the huge fireplace. There was about it a humour, a sadness and beauty of innocence. Andy had given her the ultimate gift; one that no money could ever have bought.

Soon residents would filter in from the dining room for their after dinner coffee, but for the moment, she sat alone in a winged high back chair. A virginia creeper changing into its fiery autumn gown peeped through a nearby lattice window that overlooked the copse, and to the left, the tastefully converted annexe that had once been the boutique where she and Emm had begun all those years ago. From the pocket of her impeccably cut jacket, she withdrew a letter that had arrived only this morning, and pondered its contents. Eventually she walked over to the writing desk, and using the quality linen notepaper available to guests, penned a reply to Armand. On her return from Australia, she would accept his invitation to visit and find within the beauty of Paris, the mental resources to decide on her next course. A commitment made, she had turned to face the future.

Danielle entered with newly arrived guests, and having complied with their request for coffee and liqueurs, excused herself to speak with 'a colleague'.

The gesture did not escape Kate. "Thank you for preserving my privacy."

"Would you like me to put your letter in with the mail?"

They walked across to the reception area, and then, for no reason she understood, Kate stopped and said, "Danielle, it troubles me that by coming to England at such a young age, you've not married. We don't get an inordinate flow of French visitors. Maybe if you had stayed in Paris ."

"And Frenchmen have a monopoly of my affections Madame?"

She was being side-stepped, and so came directly to the point. "Have you never really met anyone with whom you could consider sharing your life?"

"I've seen no evidence that le marriage and happiness always go hand in hand, Madame."

"Of course, your father... and my husband," Kate conceded. "But you know with the right person...." As she reflected on her protégée's reasons for remaining solitary, Danielle stole the initiative.

"And your 'right person' Madame?"

Kate raised her eyes slowly, paused, and said only, "I wasn't right for him Danielle."

CHAPTER THIRTY NINE

"So you are finally here! You 'ave not forgotten your favourite city and ami Parisian!"
"Jamais. Not as long as I live Armand!"
"Of course I know it. Come. We drive through ze centre so Paris may welcome you." They filled in the gaps of years. Though not uneventful, his life had lacked the turbulence of hers. "You must stay more than ze few days. Time to laugh, cry perhaps, wiz friends. Or rather one old friend now Marie Jeanne is no more. Stay long enough for me to convince you that Kate, along with the rest of humanity is allowed to make mistakes." Holding up a hand to silence her, he laughed. "I know. For another zat would be a life's work. For me - two weeks! I am a master. I teach you by example!" He looked ahead, and she saw how superficial had been his whimsical eccentricity.

"It takes a long time Kate, yes? When Marie Jeanne die I feel if I was so miserable I must also inflict misery on ze world. And I know some of my grief was not for her, but selfishly for me because she leave me. Mon Dieu, worse than sleeping alone, is waking alone."

So he was still aching. He too had discovered that dawn did not necessarily bring the strength needed to face another day. And in the long silent hours of night, there was no longer a warm human recourse; just an appalling empty panic

They took the funicular that night to the Sacre Coeur where he lit a candle; something he had previously dismissed as tourist theatrical, and then walked in the balmy evening air; felt the ambience of Paris.

"We go 'ere," he said, as she knew he would, having made a charade of considering other bistros. It was where they had eaten often with Marie Jeanne and Jonathan. Memories were not dismissed by refusing to address physical reminders, nor did she want them to be. But they were easier to confront with a companion who had been part of the same ruptured past.

It was impossible not to feel attuned to those whose faces were in turn shadowed or warmly illumined by the flickering candles. 'Part of, but also privé in a way only Paris can arrange,' as Armand said. Waiters squeezed dextrously and with vocal geniality between groups, whilst the strains of a violin floated on smoke rings that seemed not to affect the delectable aromas. The room was hung around with pictures, plates and herbs, providing a tranquil backdrop to the hum of cosmopolitan conversation. It was as though she were wrapped in a soft snug duvet, yet the glow was within her too and about it she wrapped herself. She began to be free of that which had claimed her, without her having known its true identity. Suddenly time lost its power to dictate; became only the tool.

"You would like to walk before we drive home Kate?"

She shook her head. The wine, the metiér, his company, had relaxed her. "I find I am so utterly happy to be here, but now I'm tired."

Tonight no turmoil possessed her and she was unaware at which point she drifted into sleep. She woke early, hearing muffled sounds of activity but finding no evidence of coffee ready to perc or fresh croissants that would have featured had Marie Jeanne been alive, she tentatively opened a kitchen cupboard, and then more boldly, inspected the rest. Nothing. It was Armand's kitchen; male and functional - coffee, cognac, alkaseltzer. She was pondering what move would be most tactful when his nephew tapped at the door and told her that Armand ate in the dining room these days. "There is only one problem Madame," he smiled. "Mon oncle dort!"

"Then allow him to continue," she said. "He has told me of an important meeting this afternoon for which he is no doubt conserving his energy."

She was enjoying her third cup of coffee when he joined her. "I do not make ze apology Kate, because we already agree you stay en famille. And I expect Philippe has done it for me! So, what will my guest do today?"

"I shall go to the Opera House."

"Better I take you one evening."

"I shall go to look at the building only."

So she was chasing rainbows. A dangerous occupation, for memories were gilded by retrospect. Obviously the man she had once brought here - whose name he had quite forgotten - was still important to her. Well he could have today, and no more.

Armand had forced her to make a plan for which she was grateful. The morning was bright and crisp; this most beautiful of cities as breathtaking as on her first visit as a young woman. Then she had been passionate about her Company, striving for its success. And such sweet intoxicating success she had tasted, relinquished, and subsequently with the same determination but less fire and exuberance - built again. The striving for heights had gone from her now, and in its place a wish to live fully, to absorb and enjoy, if only she could discover where or what to link herself. Always in the past, Paris had provided solutions, acted as an opiate to free her thought and clarify her resolution.

Walking towards Quai d'Orsay, she stopped to admire the work of a young artist. "You should be on the bridge where more people can see you," she urged.

"Too many interruptions," he told her. "But thank you. This is actually part of my portfolio. I'm only out here because my room is so dark."

"That's a pity. I would like to have bought your sketch. Will you take a hundred francs for it?"

He lifted his arms, and placing his hands behind his head, regarded her seriously. Eventually he nodded, "Only if you let me finish it for you Madame. Where are you staying?"

"Outside the city in Rueil Malmaison."

"Of course I could post it to you but."

"...then I'd have to trust you," she finished for him. "It would not be the francs I would weep over, but I would be sad not to receive what will be a daily reminder of Paris, to hang in my apartment. And I too must find a more cheerful place to live when I return to England." She pushed some notes in his hand and he promised her purchase would be in the morning's post. Watching her disappear, he wished he had detained in conversation someone so sure of what she liked. Irritatingly he had neither age nor confidence to have enabled him to do so, but he had talent, and that would speak for him from the wall of her English apartment.

"So did you visit the Opera?" Armand asked, as she dropped into an armchair.

"I did. And I fancied I was driven in Prince Edward's carriage and wore a gown of ivory brocade!" she teased.

"Such imagination. Perhaps you should write a novel in your retirement. But meanwhile you will join me in a cocktail?"

"Your meeting went well today?"

"Better even! My condition is stabilised. Ze diet need no longer be so drastic."

"Armand. I thought it was business. I had no idea you were ill!"

"I am not. Seulement le diabetes, which is now under control."

"Wonderful. So you will be my guest tonight in Beaubourg?"

SAFE AS HOUSES

"Oh I see we are to break some plates! Merci mon amie. Avec plaisir." In celebratory mood he asked, "You would like to visit les bouquinistes beforehand? But you have already walked far today. Philippe he remind me I must take more care of my guest."

They browsed for some time that evening amongst the rare books in the Quai de Montebello. Armand made a purchase for her – "To commemorate your visit and to celebrate my good news," he said.

"You were troubled Armand?"

He nodded. "But no longer. And to be honest, the reason for my concern was I had not been as careful as I was advised, and I feared the diagnosis."

She wore momentarily, a reprimanding countenance, but his relief was infectious, and with light hearts they continued on their way. Restaurateurs cajoled from every doorway, but here were two seasoned clients who knew exactly where they wished to dine.

They were between courses when Kate recalled her encounter with the young artist.

"You bought a picture? But I didn't see it - it is a miniature?"

She explained it was still to be finished, that the student would send it.

"So nonchalant! How can someone be so organisé in business be yet so gullible," he asked incredulously. "Did you pay beaucoup d'argent?"

"No. And I'm confident he will send me the picture."

"You 'ave his name?"

"I have his promise."

Armand, opening his mouth to protest, promptly closed it again. "And if he does not?"

"Then the money will go towards rent for a better studio."

He was pensive and then asked, "You regret having no children Kate?"

Devastating as Duncan's gambling had been personally, she believed it would have been even more destructive of family life, and thus could feel only relief at the absence of one. But Armand was unconvinced and she admitted, "I would have liked that kind of loving. Being a family must be special - understanding each other's situations as no one else can... A reason to exist when worlds fall apart."

He had not intended to touch a nerve, and recognising that neither trivial comment nor profound discourse would stem the musing he had set in motion, he remained silent in the easy manner that tested companionship allows. Because he knew how much she adored it, he took a circuitous route through the capital before striking out via Bois de Boulogne towards Rueil,

SAFE AS HOUSES

and they enjoyed the pleasant tiredness that directed them homewards, when in youth, for him, the meal would have pre-empted a night-club.

"A meal, good company in pleasant surroundings, have always been for me a perfect evening," she said. But even as she spoke, she was reminded of the hypocrisy of her words, for had she not danced with Tom into the early hours. Or was it the fact of their being together, no matter where, that she would remember all her life. She recalled how he had telephoned her on the day the Conference Centre had opened, unacquainted with the prior expansion of Innovation, the subsequent departure of Emmeline, or her own painful decision to change course. And out of the blue, he had invited her to dine, totally unaware that he had filled her with such expectation and then, as if it were a routine alternative, accompanied her to Paris instead.

They had held hands as they had done in London when they were young and the world was waiting; had walked together in this most romantic of cities, had danced, dined and loved. And all the time she had eyes for no one but the man whose return she had long yearned for. Just they two. How much she had mistakenly read into their reunion: what hopes she had deluded herself into entertaining. Indeed she had presumed a future together, and embarked on a commitment she had been naive enough to believe was reciprocated. And for him, she was Kate, steady as a rock, the girl always in his background with whom he never wanted to lose contact; someone who made him feel good about himself.

The humiliation of discovering that she had assumed too much of another human being.... his awkwardness in telling her there might indeed have been a commitment in less demanding circumstances. A future - maybe not so exciting as the past - but safe after knowing each other for so long, would have been more than he could have hoped for. But just the two of them, he had insisted. Not three. Not a retarded male adult who would always be her shadow, always need her love. And, more than she realised he said, one who would always come first.

And so just when she had recaptured the magic that at twenty two had lifted her cloud high, so he, finding he could not bear to deceive her any more now than then, had explained his limitations. As a young man the world had beckoned, and he was not ready to stay with her. In Paris, after two failed marriages, he could not put a third at risk by sharing her with another man. He had phoned knowing nothing of her mother's death or the responsibility that had become hers as a result - just felt the urge to see her again. Indeed how could he have known, when the only regular contact over the years existed solely in her imagination - a trusted and silent repository for all that might have been.

She had never perceived Bob as demanding, because her love for him prevented seeing his needs as other than endearing characteristics. He was simply a brother she loved most dearly. And just as her father had not questioned the cards Fate dealt, so it had never occurred to Kate to want to change her hand; merely to assess and play it to achieve the best possible result for all concerned. And so they had returned from Paris, and when the world, and Tom, had left her alone, she had wept into her pillow for a second time, over the only man she had loved so intensely.

Armand paused at the traffic lights, and she returned the glance he threw, grateful that though he had discerned the nature of her reverie, he had allowed it to go uninterrupted.

"Armand, I'm truly enjoying my stay."

"So why return?" he asked abruptly.

She sought an answer other than the obvious. Why did one return home other than for the reason one lived there?

"You don't have to. You don't *have* to do anything anymore. Kate there is nothing, and no one, to hold you in England."

She gulped at the brutal truth of his statement. "I don't think I need to be reminded with quite such ferocity," she said testily.

"I think perhaps you do. Otherwise you will return and seek threads that are long broken; find no family to need or sustain you. Younger people who have learned much whilst you have been in Australia, are now running the Conference Centre perfectly well without you. And when realisation comes, it will only be after you have died a little."

He had caught her on the raw as he had intended. Relaxed and wrong footed, she found him difficult to counter, but he had underestimated her if he had thought she had been lulled into a false belief that future evenings could all be as this one. Facing up to reality was the reason for not staying more than a few days. Paris had recharged her to make an assault on the problems ahead, and that was precisely what she intended to do.

"I ask you again - why? I do not infer my suggestion would be only for your benefit. It would be my privilege to have your company, avoiding loneliness for both. You would have your own room as now if you insist; indeed my diabetes has rendered me impotent, so you see I could not be a bother to you Kate. And I could bring an honesty to our companionship that I was incapable of in marriage. You know of course I would not be averse

SAFE AS HOUSES

to seeking the company of any jolie jeune femme in ze café who will flatter my ego, but I am not so fool as to believe I can any longer captivate her!"

For them both, he insisted, there would be conversation and excursions.... solitude too, if and when they wished. Neither had the luxury of time any more, to make sense of the world in small safe doses. Without a companion, it was so easy to become anxious, without zest for life. He was not interested in a barren, emotionally impoverished existence stripped of conversation and joy so that he was only half alive. "Together we could go to les galleries, les concerts... all those things you love," he urged. "And before you tell me it is possible to go alone, I tell you zat wizout someone to share the experience, one simply does not. Kate will you please at least consider?"

But she was still smarting, though it would have been inaccurate to say that he, and not the subject, was the cause. "So you want me to move in as a kept woman? Armand, *you* can allow old age to intimidate you if you wish. I will not be persuaded that I am inadequate to meet it alone."

"Kate don't be so ridiculously English. And if that is your only riposte I know that you recognise mon idée as a practical means of achieving happiness - one I trust you will not allow a conventional reaction to ruin."

He rummaged for a sheet of paper from the bureau, and scribbling a few lines, handed it to her. "There, you can take this advertisement to England and put it in a magazine, or you can answer it yourself to save the bother!" Kate looked at what he had written, - 'Required: Housekeeper/carer for elderly, slightly incapacitated gentleman living in Paris suburb, in return for own room and modest remuneration' - and then at Armand, unable to sustain her aggrieved tone. "But you don't need a housekeeper!"

"No. But it makes everything respectable, which we already know it is!"

"And you are not incapa...."

"Only in ze manner I 'ave confessed - but enough to add truth to my words." Feigning perturbation, he said, " I hope you do not trivialise such a state of affairs mon ami!" And then, amused, and highly gratified to have elicited such a spirited response, he placed his hands on her shoulders.

"Kate friendship at our age is perhaps ze most value in our lives; even more zan love, which is ze more pervious to injury." Taking both her hands he whispered, "Please think about it."

Not wishing any further topic of conversation to deflect her, he suggested she delayed a decision until morning, knowing, because she was Kate, that she would turn the proposition inside out, and examine it from every angle.

"It would, after all, be too much to expect you to act on impulse." His smile was so disguised that his serious tone almost persuaded her she had imagined it.

"I have had such a wonderful day, I expect I shall just go to sleep," she said with equal pertinacity. "Bon nuit, Armand, et grand merci comme toujours."

She sat for some time before undressing. If only he had known how dangerously near she had been to acting on impulse - falling victim to the enticement of living in Paris instead of the flat to which she did not want to return. It was a lamentable lack of motivation that prevented her from setting about the simple matter of finding an alternative, which of course was exactly Armand's argument. She slid into bed and reminded herself this was neither problem nor disaster that faced her, merely the first of many choices of her retirement. As such it would not deprive her of sleep, and would be resolved when the time was right.

But by morning, surprisingly she had the answer, and creeping downstairs, slipped out of the hotel with the purpose of walking in the park to ascertain that the idea felt right, away from the warm security of her bed. Early risers were returning to their houses with long French sticks from the patisserie, one of them the hotel trainee chef.

"I should have asked you for some stale bread for the ducks, Serge."

"Madame?"

"Just something I'd like to do. Old ladies have time for such things you know!"

She walked towards the lake and found a seat in the early morning sunshine, the trees casting dappled shadows across the path. "Sorry ducks," she whispered. "Bob wouldn't have forgotten. But he's not here any more. And I need to convince myself of that."

When she had clarified and sequenced her thoughts, and was satisfied they made sense rationally, as well as intuitively, she returned to join Armand for breakfast. Serge had told him about the request for bread, and like those of his colleagues who had been interested observers of le Monsieur's obvious fondness for the visiting Madame, was intrigued by his apparent reluctance to join her, using, if indeed he needed one, the bread as an excuse. But their camaraderie was too precious for Armand to risk the certain catastrophic result of invading her space before she reached a conclusion, and thus he greeted her return as naturally as if the morning walk had been routine.

SAFE AS HOUSES

"Since you are obviously not going to ask me, I shall acquaint you with my thoughts so that we can get on with the day," she informed him good naturedly, and with the air of one who knows intimately the tactics likely to be employed by the other.

"Bon. Es-tu decidée, mon amie?"

"No. But if you are prepared to consider my proposition, it wouldn't take long!"

The croissant en route to his mouth, was abruptly returned to the plate.

Pouring coffee for both, she asked why the rooms she had once leased for her business had not been reconverted to bedrooms. He explained that a young man in the process of setting up a business had rented them soon alter Danielle had left for England, then Marie Jeanne had died, and for one reason or another, he had not troubled about them.

"Would you consider renting them to me?"

"Mon Dieu. You want to start another business!"

"Not at all!"

"Then .. .to move in and make me efficient . . .. takeover bids for other hotels?" Grinning broadly, he shuddered at the prospect of such an assault to his smooth, undemanding lifestyle.

"Tempting. But actually, I prefer you the way you are!" There was an edge of female complicity in her smile as she glanced in the direction of Armand's nephew, who despite his natural affability had been unable to disguise the fact of being a mite disturbed by her presence. "I'm sure if Paul knew exactly where he stood, he would be an excellent Manager for you. You need to take him into your confidence."

"Kate what 'as this to do with our conversation last evening?"

"Everything. And do continue to eat, or we shall attract an audience," she advised, and was amused by his involuntary obedience. She confessed that to live here in Paris would be the life she had often imagined, but though her independence had in turn been a curse and a blessing, notwithstanding, she could not, indeed would not, relinquish it.

"Meaning?"

"Meaning that I would very much like to rent a small apartment within the hotel on a permanent basis. With more than one room at my disposal, I could move myself, and my belongings. They are not numerous. Then we could indeed enjoy the companionship you described."

The point was not lost on him. She too would be unfettered by obligation, could have visitors even. He should not wince if by choosing to pay the piper, she might also wish to call the tune. He had sought a commitment from her whilst arrogantly expressing his own wish to avoid one. He should not be offended if she made the same demand of a relationship. Yet commitment was intrinsic to her nature, and his wounded pride insisted he ask her what it was about him, from which she must be free.

Never interested in playing games with emotions, she proffered an immediate, uncomplicated explanation that afforded him instant relief. She had, it seemed, no wish to be free from, but a great desire to be free for.

"But what is it that you want to do?"

She laughed. "I've no wish to sit in cafés with young men. But whilst you find your own relaxation, I shall have time to indulge a long-standing wish to write. You, in fact, gave me the idea."

"I did? What are you going to write that requires an apartment in Paris?"

"Exactly what you suggested! A novel. At least I'll try. And the experiment will afford me immense satisfaction."

"Which means you will do it," he asserted. "And I would tire after one chapter."

"It is not Paris, but *you* who will enable such an occupation," she said, and he could feel already that she had discovered that to which she would bind herself. She knew that her childhood conditioning 'scribbling is for spare time my girl and there's precious little of that', had proved stronger than efforts she had made to make her own rules. But Armand would dispel such misguided notions. "So you see, I shall also be taking from the arrangement. If in return I may offer you company, that is a fine contract."

Bemused, he shook his head, "I cannot accept ze logic of what you say, yet I am forced to accept the truth of it, simplement because you are who you are. You have all the time in the world, and more than ever before, it is for you."

"Go on telling me Armand please," she said quietly, appearing at once so vulnerable, so desirable, that he would have done anything just as long as she came.

That had all been five years ago now, since when Armand had convinced her that nothing was of any significance than the moment itself; that it was a duty to find pleasure in being alive. It had all been so damnably proper as she had indulged in the opiate of nest making in the apartment she eagerly converted to a home. Complementing each other perfectly, they had enjoyed life just as he had promised. They made no demands, needing never to beseech the other to be amenable or compliant. There had been none of the feminine emotional silence when he had chosen to spend the day in Parisian company, though she didn't know it was more often the company of men as advanced in years as he. Better for his pride he did not say, which presupposed that despite their ideal arrangement, he had nevertheless hoped to evoke some jealousy.

He hadn't told her that on two occasions he had denied her presence here when Tom Heydon - in Paris for his own reasons - had telephoned for news of her whereabouts. Old and grey he may well be by now, but Armand was convinced if the wretched man once crossed his threshold, he would lose his most precious companion. Almost forty years alliance, however distant, surely made it inevitable. But today, he had been unable to continue the deception. Whilst failing to find it within himself to be specific, he had said he 'believed Kate had an apartment here in Paris.' As a result, he was morose as they took coffee on the terrace together.

"You are not well Armand?" But her concern only succeeded in annoying him.

"Perfectly."

"Then perhaps eating out this evening would cheer you up?"

"I shall go nowhere. I must attend to the accounts Paul has prepared."

It was futile to suggest to the master of prevarication himself that he looked at them tomorrow. For a reason known only to him, Armand was not in rational mood.

"Then I shall go to the Opera by myself," she announced.

"Which is just where he'll think of looking for you," Armand muttered under his breath. Mon Dieu, why hadn't he suggested they drive out to the country. He poured himself a cocktail, knowing that if not today, the man would come again to find her. Better get it over with.

Closing her diary, she left him to prepare, and removing her linen jacket from the hanger, suddenly felt an irresistible urge to be elegant. Hurriedly she substituted her navy wrap, throwing it around her shoulder and over the dress that hung in soft silken folds from the still tiny waist so reminiscent of her grandmother. White gloves, and finally a parasol of blue daisies completed the ensemble. Releasing the upper clip that held the frill tight against the spine, she smiled approvingly at its coquettish shape. Even now that youth was long gone, it was still fun to be feminine. The deep hues of her outfit complemented her silver hair, and the parasol proved the perfect accessory, adding an air of genteel sophistication. Perhaps when he saw how much she'd enjoyed getting ready, he would change his mind and come with her.

But her appearance served only to irritate him further. Perplexed, and somewhat deflected from her purpose, she hesitated, until an observant Paul called from the reception desk, "Amusez-vous bien Madame. Would you like me to call a taxi?"

She would, she said, walk across the park and find one outside the metro, a diversion that would provide Armand with time to recover from whatever was causing such obdurate pique, and catch up with her. But it was a lone, slight figure who eventually hailed a taxi. "L'Opéra s'il vous plâit," she said without enthusiasm.

"Madame." She was his last fare for the evening and he drove gently and enjoyed helping her out and watching her smooth her dress whilst looking diffidently around. Bidding him 'bon nuit', and with a defiant tilt of the head, she approached the imposing steps. They tired her a little in the heat, but were not a major challenge.

"There's a seat over there Madame, if you'd care to wait," the man at the box office said. "It will be cooler than outside."

Thanking him, she observed the comings and goings around her; the leisurely arrival of those whose wealth had ensured the most prestigious of seats; disappointed couples who were told there were now only singles available, and last minute requests from students. So fascinated was she that an attendant beckoned to her that the performance was about to begin, and vacating the brocaded sofa, she proceeded with concentrated care in the direction of the stalls.

The young man at the box office was responding to a late request, switching languages with ease. "Just one in the rear stalls Sir."

"I'll take it. Thank you."

And time itself was halted, thrown into reverse, and the years slipped serenely away. She was in her twenties, and the place was London. Stunned, she stood still, and then was disconcerted as the throng obscured her view of him. Deliberately slow in reaching her seat, wishing to have the advantage of standing until the last possible moment, she followed his direction. Pocketing his change in the dimmed light, his brow creased as he appeared to catch sight of her, then dismissed the possibility as too remote.

And had not *her* mind been equally duped? When the house light rose for the interval, she would surely see there was no resemblance. In any case, she had already registered that the look-alike was much thinner; gaunt almost. But for the time being, disbelief need be of no consequence. Alone, since Armand had declined her company, she could indulge in dreams. This time she would remember he was here on business - how well he had done to continue until now - that there were no strings attached, and overt affection would be indiscreet. Besides, though he could still delightfully raise her blood pressure, she had grown beyond youthful yearning. There was a certain comfortable complacency in having at last accepted the inevitable, knowing that all life's major decisions had been taken.

But perhaps in the September of her years, she could be forgiven for inviting a gentleman - if by chance she were not mistaken - to join her in the interval. Indeed, as Armand would have declared, 'Mon Dieu, from whom do you need permission at your age!

CHAPTER FORTY

Danielle scribbled a note for her P.A. and welcomed the prospect of a rare leisurely evening, before flying to Paris next morning.

"And by the time the flowers are delivered Kate, I doubt if even your sharp old eyes could find anything overlooked. And I'm glad - and privileged, to have continued your success. Though Heaven help me if I hadn't!" she mused. She could almost hear Kate chuckling 'Junior Management eh? Our organisation should teach some of those upwardly mobile youngsters a thing or two if they have eyes to see.'

The lecturers and guest speakers arriving this afternoon, had been fulsome in their appreciation, claiming - as indeed was the intention - that much of their work had been done for them. That would please Kate inordinately, as would the news of solid bookings well into next spring.

Nearing the copse she turned, hearing hurrying footsteps on the gravel path from the west wing. Someone was trying to attract her attention. "Excuse me Miss er.... Sorry. I've forgotten your name. We met earlier - I wonder if you could help me."

Amused at the natural directness of the man who had literally just crossed her path, she said, "You're one of the guest speakers aren't you?"

"Yes. My slot isn't actually until Thursday but..."

"Looking after Overseas Agents."

"Good Lord. Why on earth should you have noted that?"

Danielle smiled, thinking to herself, 'And there's the difference Kate. You would also have remembered his name.'

"Is there something you'd like changed?" she asked.

"Absolutely not. Everything's tip top. No, nothing to do with the Centre - at least only tenuously. I came a day or so early because I'm looking for someone.... the reason I accepted the invitation to speak here actually. Lecturing isn't normally my line." Her brisk walk halted, Danielle shivered involuntarily. "You're cold. I'm sorry. Let's go back into the Centre .... or better still, come for a drink with me."

"Certainment pas! I don't even know your name!"

SAFE AS HOUSES

His grin was as open as his style, and he thrust out his hand. "Richard Heydon."

The name was somehow familiar. "And exactly who are you looking for?" she asked.

"Someone called Kate. I don't know much else about her - not even her surname. But she *did* have a fashion house in this area - in fact, right here on this site I believe. But no longer, obviously. Hardly surprising as she must be old by now, but I'd rather hoped there'd be some evidence of her - or perhaps family around to give me a lead."

He looked up and screwed his face as a disheartening drizzle began to settle in tiny droplets on her hair. And then she remembered. Heydon. A name first mentioned by Emmeline, and one that had surfaced intermittently, and intriguingly, throughout all the years she had known her employer - and for a long time before, from all accounts.

Resolutely moving forward she said, "I was just going home to make some supper. I think it would be a good idea if you joined me."

"Now that gives me a problem," he said, feigning gravity.

"Oh?"

"We haven't been introduced!" And he laughed with such an appealing spontaneity at her expression, and then as a sudden squall whipped at their faces, said, "Thanks. I'd like that."

A precipitate fall of autumn leaves speckled their path, and they crunched them delightedly in the manner of children. Before reaching the flat she stopped, and turning a key left in the shed nearby, said, "I adore a log fire, don't you?"

"Don't have much call for them in Kenya, but I could certainly appreciate one this evening. Here let me get that."

She held the door against the wind as he bent to pick up the basket of logs.

Some hours later as they washed the dishes together, she apologised for the simplicity of the meal, not having expected company.

"I can't remember when I enjoyed one more." He paused and then added, "But I must confess that I was so enthralled by the company, I can't now tell you what I ate." He wore a preoccupied smile. "Danielle - how do you think Kate would react to my going to Paris tomorrow too?"

It was difficult to concentrate on how Kate would react because - and it came as something of a shock to realise it - she wanted to yield to her own feelings, which disturbingly had refused for the past three hours to be anchored to common sense.

"May I think for a moment?"

"It was actually a rhetorical question. I intend to go."

She was relieved at the single-mindedness that would obviously brook no argument.

"If she's as sprightly as you say, she might even agree to a short visit to England. I can just imagine the old fella's face! It would buck him no end."

"You think she might still feel for him - at her age?"

"Do people stop loving when they are old?"

"No, that was a silly thing to say. But they haven't met in years. Surely if they'd wanted to be together they would have arranged it by now?"

"Not when my father, on his own admission, spent most of his life being a blind idiot. And I'm not so sure about their paths not having crossed for some time. He went to Paris last spring and I've a suspicion he saw her."

"Doesn't sound like him not to have followed it through."

"So you know him?"

"Of him. And then only sketchily. But meeting you makes sense of some of the things Kate said to me sometimes, when my English wasn't so good and she could pretend she had meant something other than the impression she'd given, - on the very rare occasions she allowed sentiment to surface! She insisted that some people - and I'm certain she meant your father - were like quicksilver; could be known, loved even, because that did not require their permission. But sometimes it was necessary to accept they couldn't be tied against their will without also destroying the chemistry and affinity. Which I suppose meant that real love was to let them go. And she *did* love him. Of that I haven't the slightest doubt."

Richard appeared suddenly withdrawn, recognising how near the brink he had been of setting something in motion solely in the interests of his father. Talking with Danielle made him realise he had entertained no feelings at all for the character central to his proposed initiative. Having now learned something of her - visualised her living here - conducting her business - he wished only to encounter the woman whose charm his father had described so avidly. Whatever followed now must be as a result of due regard for them both.

It was getting late. "I'll pick you up in the morning," he said. "We can leave my car at the airport."

"Crack of dawn?"

"I'll be here. Goodnight Danielle. And thanks for a perfect evening."

"Goodnight Richard."

SAFE AS HOUSES

And as the door closed behind him, it seemed as if the whole universe would leap for joy.

"So you think I'm too old to have stars in my eyes Richard?" Kate asked. Stars or not, they were twinkling with amusement at the situation in which all three were now a part. He shot a mock accusing glance at Danielle but was pleased he had had the tact to leave them on the pretext of sightseeing. After all Danielle had had her own purpose for coming before he had intruded so unexpectedly. In fact after she'd been given a progress report on the Centre, had assured herself of Danielle's well-being, and had the briefest explanation of Richard's need to see her, Kate had gone to bed only a little later than usual. As for their joint arrival, she was perfectly capable of recognising a woman in love.

"So Richard, being the object of your visit, am I as you imagined?"

"On meeting you Miss... Mrs.."

"Just Kate will do."

She's enjoying being in control, he thought. Later on when he could feel that he knew her a fraction as well as she appeared to understand him, he would ask why she hadn't been able to manipulate his father. "Kate, you are wonderful. I am frankly bewildered that my father can have been so intuitive in business, and yet unable to see what was under his nose as far as you were concerned. Why on earth did he let you go? I wouldn't have done! Why you could have been my mother!"

Again she laughed, but it was her eyes that were so expressive. They would, he thought, always reveal emotions that the rest of her body language might try to suppress.

"Hardly," she said, almost wistfully he thought, "but I know what you mean. And I would have enjoyed that. Coping with the two of you would have been the sort of challenge I thrive on!"

"You think I'm like him Kate?"

"Given that we are newly acquainted, the only apparent difference is your age. You certainly have all his charm - though I imagine you are less self centred."

She made the statement as though the defect in his father's character were of no importance, and the implication must be that her feelings for him were unconditional. She had obviously loved him as he was, and not as she would have him. Turning to Danielle she said, "Since it is I this gentleman has come to visit, I don't feel selfish - though perhaps a little bold, - in asking him to escort me to Les Halles. And perhaps he will tell me something of his life, since I shall not pretend I'm less than vitally interested."

"At your service Madame!" he replied. "And will you come too Danielle?"

"Thank you - no. I shall lock myself away for the morning." Hesitating only for a moment, she asked, "May I tell Richard?" Danielle glowed with a happiness that had taken Kate by surprise.

"Why not? Everything else seems to be out in the open!" And then she added mischievously, "At least, that which concerns *me*!"

"Kate has at last written the final chapters of a book she began some years ago. I pleaded with her to finish it but she claimed she had no heart for it, and that it must remain perhaps the only job she had never seen through to completion."

"So what was it that changed your mind Kate?" Richard's question was uncomfortably astute.

"Oh I couldn't break the habit of a lifetime, now could I?"

The attempt to be flippant failed, and watching her keenly, he asked, "It wouldn't have had anything to do with last spring?"

Her composure transiently deserted her and defensiveness was apparent as she looked from one to the other.

"So I was right! The two of you did meet!" he declared, and his laughter could have been Tom's.

"Just for an evening. Your father and I had cocktails together after a performance at the Opera House."

He smiled and took her arm. And to Danielle he said, "We shall turn a few heads in Montmartre this morning, don't you think."

"Sans doute! Au'voir mes amis!"

From his window, Armand Cardules watched them depart. The likeness was unmistakable. So the wretched man's son had come to take her back to England; home where she belonged now that she was old. In a matter of hours she would visit him to explain, announce her intention to return. And a bleak unwelcome chasm would replace the quiet zeal with which he now greeted each day he was privileged to share with her.... seeing life through her eyes.... sharing in the delight with which she observed human nature, insisting each had his story to tell. Oh God, he could not tolerate the anonymity of growing old without Kate to brighten each day.

SAFE AS HOUSES

Richard was astounded by her energy and the vivacious eagerness with which she greeted all they encountered, but when she put out a hand to steady herself after being separated from him by hurrying youngsters, he took command. "We'll stop for a coffee young lady. Meanwhile place your arm in mine. No matter if folk think you've got a toy boy!"

"We're in Paris," she retorted, "where people don't get hysterical about such human situations. And anyway, I shall enjoy the experience!"

She would indeed, for he had inherited every last scrap of his father's charisma.

He indicated a table on the sidewalk about to be vacated, and pulled out a chair for her. Sitting himself opposite, he took her hand, and asked, "If he didn't recognise what he had, why didn't you tell him? You were made for each other."

"It wasn't quite as straightforward as you imagine, Richard, There is. . . was, a vulnerability about being in love with someone you fear - know, may not reciprocate... too much at stake if you overplay your hand; the danger of causing someone to feel trapped." She paused. "I think I'd like that cup of coffee now."

He beckoned to the waiter, and then teased gently, "You didn't tell each other even over cocktails last spring?"

"The discovery that one is old brings with it an easy familiarity and disregard for convention. One accepts the futility of play-acting so I didn't have to pretend that when he took my hand again, it wasn't just as exciting as it had been all those years ago. But to be honest it was *because* I wasn't young any more and had convinced myself that the simple joy of holding hands was a thing of the past." She sipped her coffee, and smiled provocatively. "Passion on a pension does lose some of its fervour you know!"

For Tom she knew that nothing had changed, and with characteristic lack of preamble he had finally told her that he'd feared what he described as 'the silent ferocity of her love', despite her efforts to conceal it; that such commitment made him feel nervous, afraid of missing what might still be on the horizon. And she could live with that, for in a remarkable way, the frankness at last on the one issue he had always fudged, brought them closer. That the affinity was still intact, made her feel content.

"I was happy that I'd never encompassed him beyond his will," she said, "and we enjoyed the same thistledown magic that had brought us together in our twenties. He told me he'd visited Armand on previous occasions for news of my whereabouts, but Armand had been unhelpful. Your father loved to travel as you know, but loved also to find company on arrival. It was Armand's assumption that I was the object of his visit - and a guilty conscience - that gave the game away when he assumed Tom would have been angered by his repeated deception."

"So my father has a rival?"

"Not an unpleasant sensation for an old lady!" she laughed, and fearing he might attach credence to her pertness, added, "No! Armand is a very old friend who has spent a lifetime being captivated by young women. We discuss the world together, and share the times that might otherwise be pointlessly empty."

"A mutually agreeable arrangement?"

"One I value, for whilst I'm far from being a gregarious character, indeed need more solitude than most, I am on occasions easy prey for depression."

"That's difficult to believe."

"Because I'm in the company of someone with whom I'm very comfortable. Which rather proves my point!"

"You've not allowed his 'interests' to spoil your relationship?"

"No, because I've never been in love with him. For his wife it was a continual torment. That's the vulnerability to which I referred." She sipped her coffee. "Tell me Richard, does Tom know of your visit here?"

He considered his reply, knowing he had reached a point at which revelations could provoke damaging reactions. He explained his invitation to the Conference Centre, how the locality had evoked memories for his father who'd talked about his intermittent, but lifetime friendship, with one called Kate, suggesting that his son should, whilst there, seek news of her.

"You'll appreciate Kate that at that point I had no idea whether you were even alive. I was prepared to make such enquiries as time allowed, and then I met Danielle - and well here I am."

"Yes indeed." An almost irrepressible joy welled within her. That Tom's son should lecture in her Conference Centre; an echoing down the years that finally gave meaning to their encounter a lifetime ago. And then adjacent to such happiness came a sudden, terrible tightening in her chest. Her lip quivered slightly as she asked, "Is Tom ill, Richard?"

Stunned by her perspicacity, he lost the initiative. "Why do you ask?"

"Because otherwise he would have accompanied you."

He did not comment, but felt in his inside jacket pocket. "I've a letter for you Kate. I was to give it to you if, and when, I found you."

SAFE AS HOUSES

'My Kate,' she read, and the absence of the conventional opening imparted such a unique sense of him, that her efforts to restrain the trembling in her fingers was of no avail. Richard placed a solicitous hand on her arm. "I'll be back in a few minutes."

'So you are to meet my son!' she continued. 'I can just imagine the years rolling back, for you have to agree he is the proverbial chip off the old block. Not so handsome of course! But appearance is where similarity ends, as your intuition will doubtless have already enlightened you. He's thoughtful, introspective and lacks my conceit and egotism - which though a blessing, is surprising to me. I had to depend on a housekeeper to raise him in Kenya when his mother reached the conclusion that her decision to marry me had been nothing less than disastrous. (See what I spared you Kate!) Business necessitating my frequent absence did little to ensure a stable environment for the young chap.

Trouble was Kate, I was too young and arrogant to believe the world would not be littered with people like you. Even when, so long after, I met you again, I was too damn selfish to share you with Bob. I suppose I resented the time he couldn't help but demand of you. Guess I recognised that with his intuition, he'd soon realise how shallow was my capacity to love compared with his, and that would have created a conflict, not least for you.

And then years and years later, - was it only last spring - there you were at the Opera House, dainty, and oh so enchanting. And despite the selfish motive that had brought me to Paris, I finally matured, and during the evening we spent together, determined you would continue to have the freedom to go to the Opera, the Galleries.... take aperitifs with that damn Frenchman who guarded your whereabouts so jealously. I wouldn't allow you to spend your old age looking after mine. Do you know Kate, up 'til then I had never once thought what I could do for you. Well I'd do it now, I decided. I'd savour the image of my woman . . . imagine you taking your seat at the theatre, or walking in the Champs Elysées, elegant even with silver hair (I've practically none left); unburdened by the dictates of a man grown sick and irritable.

We shall probably never meet again. I'm desolate it's taken me a lifetime to realise how much I love you; have always loved you, my dearest Kate.

Yours ever, Tom.'

Richard was surprised, but relieved, for he was not sure how one dealt with emotional old ladies, to find her perfectly composed when he returned.

"Was that a rotten thing to have done?" he asked – "giving you Dad's letter in public? It seemed so natural after our conversation."

"On the contrary, I'm glad you did. Tell me, your father is not short of money?"

"He's a wealthy man - despite his professed ambition to go to his grave having enjoyed every cent of it! The illness has obviously put a brake on his jaunts, much to his chagrin. He's not a good patient Kate."

So he was having the necessary care. She had noted that the envelope, but not the letter, was written in his hand.

"His nurse would have taken his dictation. He hates the fact that his handwriting is no longer firm. Vanity of course," Richard chuckled.

"Yes he had a good hand - and turn of phrase too."

Her lack of further comment puzzled him, and finally he said, "It's been quite a morning. Shall we go and hear what Danielle thinks of your book?"

"Just one more visit! The Opera House. I shall ask if they could rout out a programme of the performance we saw. In the excitement of meeting, I dropped mine, and I think your father left his at the restaurant afterwards. I'd like you to give it to him, together with a programme I've kept since we were young."

He picked up her wrap that had slipped from the chair. "Don't be disappointed. I imagine - if they can find one at all - they'll have to send it on to you," he warned.

"I agree we may have to exercise a little persuasion. Shall we make that our objective?"

"Kate you're incorrigible!"

"Is that what I am? Fun anyway!"

Danielle was eager for their return. "Kate Benson, to think I beavered with you in worrying about a business, when you have such talent!"

"I know! Look!" Kate held aloft the programme from the Opera House. Richard sank into the nearest chair. "Would you believe, she had the poor chap ferret in the archives for that! Even offered to man his telephone whilst he searched!"

The characteristic determination was so instantly recognisable that Danielle merely shook her head in amusement, "And did he agree?"

"No but he did accept an invitation to dinner next week as compensation," Kate replied, removing her hat and gloves.

"Really Kate. And you know that wasn't what I meant. I shall take your book back to England and not rest until I've found a publisher for you."

Suppressing her delight - for it was seemly that being old, she should do so, Kate said phlegmatically, "I think I can help you there. On the second shelf of the cabinet, you'll find the card of a London agent. He also urged me to finish the book. Poor man, he stayed at the hotel with the intention of taking in several exhibitions, but managed to sprain his ankle, so read my book instead."

"That's what made you finish!"

"No. Richard was right. It was Tom's visit - and my acceptance of a truth I had refused to acknowledge all my life." She turned to him, and added softly, "One that your father's letter today endorsed. Thank you for coming to find me Richard." She announced that she would retire after a light supper, insisting that the two young people should go out to dine. "You must; you're in Paris. Sacrilege to do otherwise!"

"You won't join us?" Danielle invited.

"I have had the most wonderful day - a privilege to be alive. But I hope I'm not totally devoid of tact. Off you go and have a memorable evening. In any case my energy is spent. I shall take a cognac with Armand as usual, and then go to my room and write a letter for you to take to your father, Richard. Give him my love. Tell him that I'm too old to travel now."

"But Kate..." Danielle was perplexed as Richard left them to go and shower.

Kate silenced her, and as fatigue threatened to surface, whispered, "It's not always wisdom to tell the absolute truth, nor is honesty necessarily the most sensitive policy. Goodnight my dear. Amuses-toi bien."

Reading his letter again in the privacy of her room, she was surprised to feel so little. She could have written it for him. And not so long ago, neither age nor distance would have prevented her from rushing to his side to care for him. But hers had been a wholesome wanting; a simple healthy desire to love, and be loved. Nothing remotely connected with the sense of duty that had dictated so much of her life. Only now, when he was confined to a life bereft of itinerary and excitement, did he find her an attractive proposition; a useful, compliant companion who could lessen the tedium of growing old alone.

She replaced the letter in her bag. Far from being the emotional blackmail intended, his words had been almost a lancing, delivering her from the long carried burden of unreciprocated loving. But it was essential she did nothing to disillusion the son whose qualities gave credence to paternal pride, and of whom she had already become fond.

SAFE AS HOUSES

Sitting awhile by her window, she contemplated both the day, and the future. It would not be long now before Richard whisked Danielle away, leaving the Centre ripe for change and development, and surely it could only be a matter of time before her two nephews, finding themselves with sole responsibility, gave life to the idea that had crossed the threshold of their consciousness when they had visited the Centre some years ago when she was at its helm, and before Bob had died.

Armand rose to greet her when she tapped at his door, but lacked his usual effervescence. The suspense of waiting had resulted in a paranoia that intensified as his frustration was prolonged. Consumed with angry misery, he said without preamble, "I've missed you Kate. And if you have come to impart the news I have ze most feared, please do not prevaricate with pleasantries."

She placed a hand on his arm, not knowing whether it was to comfort him, or to draw strength for herself upon their amity and understanding. The merest suspicion of tethered tears made him fear the worst, and he drew up a chair beside his own, whilst retaining a grasp of the tiny hand that had reached out to him.

"Prevarication has not been a characteristic previously attributed to me, Armand. I'm flattered you consider me still capable of learning new tricks."

"The man with Danielle - he is ze son of your long-time acquaintance, yes?"

"An improvement on the old model! We can be so glad for Danielle. She's waited many years for such a liaison. I have such hopes for them."

He regarded her quizzically, a dull misery collecting in his throat and settling there. "Fond as I am of Danielle, it is your plans I would prefer to discuss Kate."

"Plans! Am I always to have plans? Was it not you who entreated me to 'let go', relinquish the striving? You don't approve of the result of your teaching Professor!"

"Kate I know - and understand - but you must tell me if you will go to him." His tone was imploring.

Appreciating only at that moment the gnawing anxiety within him, she drew her chair closer and said gently, "Armand, I have no plans - and indeed no longing, to go to England. With your permission I want only to remain here with the friend I have, over the years, grown to love." She paused awkwardly, having surprised herself. "There, you may now add boldness to the unfamiliar characteristics of Kate Benson."

SAFE AS HOUSES

They sat silently for some moments. Eventually he asked, "When did you decide Kate?"

"I confess, the moment of decision slipped by without my noticing - but it was today that I recognised I had made it. I feel safe here as if nothing can hurt anymore. Our togetherness is not conventional, nor part of a plan either of us made. Much more to do with your persuasion to turn circumstances to advantage for both of us." She had answered in simple truth, having no desire to complicate or to manoeuvre an advantage.

"Whilst you were out with le monsieur, Danielle she tell me that your book will be success énorme and ask me why it take so long when words flow so freely."

"And of course you were able to tell her." Kate smiled.

"I tell her zat many times it call out to you to finish. But it was of yourself, so must be denied in favour of other demands. For my part, I apologise Kate for asking your time so frequently when you had such inspired work to accomplish. But though I apologise, I am too selfish to regret, for we 'ave 'ad ze most wonderful days."

"Days I would not want to have missed either, Armand. But the book is finished, and I'm content to hear you say it is of myself; a part of me, for I know now what I can give to Danielle just as the Centre will be for Greg and Andy." He felt no compunction to interrupt her reverie. "Yes, finished now to my satisfaction."

She had striven to make it perfect in every detail, as she had approached all the other enterprises she had undertaken. But in this work, was the Kate who had, all her life, lived inside her and whom she had dragged out only with the greatest effort of will. From somewhere in her mind she had tapped the consent to acknowledge her own identity.

He poured their cognacs, touching her glass with his own. "To all our tomorrows Kate - mon amie vraiment précieuse."

"Was her book really that good?" Richard asked, sliding the blade of his knife with considerable relish through a steak au poivre placed before him.

"Incroyable. I feared she may not sustain the momentum after ze long lapse, but it is impossible to detect ze break. The final chapter will take ze reader by surprise, but it is expertly contrived. The only regret at ze end is that there are no more pages to turn. As soon as we get to Heathrow I shall telephone ze agent."

"She was obviously tickled pink, even though she tried to hide it!"

"Do you know Richard, I think publication might mean more than ze Centre - maybe even as much as Innovation. I shall speak wiz Greg and Andy - I can already imagine ze celebration we shall prepare.."

"You're very confident. I hope you're not disappointed."

"If not a potential success, it would have been in ze bin long before our arrival."

"If you say so. And talking of the Centre, I must dash off some notes. So much has happened, I'd almost forgotten about the Conference. Say, you don't think we could phone and fake a tummy bug?"

"Of course not!" she retorted, and it amused him to feel that it might have been Kate responding to such an outrageous suggestion.

In two days her world had changed perspective, and Danielle sought to commit to memory all that had occurred while it was still fresh in her mind, and before the special looks and words were diluted by commonplace affairs. So utterly enjoyable to be alive was it, nothing else seemed of consequence. It had come as a revelation, happened in seconds, and was recognised in an instant by her beloved Kate. Unversed in the language of love, she said only, "I wish I had your confidence - to be able to write notes at the last moment I mean."

He drew his napkin across his mouth. "Last moment! I've a whole twenty four hours! Besides, I shall be talking about things that are second nature to me - actions I take all the time. I'll tell them about reality; academia will have given them the theory."

She found him utterly engaging to watch, as unfettered by extraneous minutiae, he tossed his concentration back into enjoying the here and now. And for her part she could not but believe that a single moment of her life from this time forward, would be bent to any other purpose than that of loving him.

"I am intrigued why you did not persuade Kate to visit your father – that was your objective?" she said.

"It was a proposition I realised she'd already put to herself last spring, and for whatever reason, rejected. I merely respected that decision."

"I'm surprised. Looking after people comes naturally to Kate."

He nodded. "Exactly. It would have been all too easy to add another responsibility, and that's not what I came to do."

Signalling to the waiter for the bill, he said, "It's still a beautiful night - let's walk for a while before we go back. Unless you're tired?" Her radiance made a reply superfluous and taking her hand in his, he led her from the restaurant.

Other guests were also returning as they entered the hotel, but as the young man on Reception sighted Danielle, there was an arresting urgency in his expression. "Mademoiselle .... Monsieur......... Le maître, he asks you go immediately to his salon privé. Monsieur le médicin, he is also there."

"Monsieur Cardules est malade?"

"Non. Pas le monsieur....... c'est la Madame. ...la Madame anglais."

Ignoring the lift, they tore up the staircase. Armand stood at the doorway of his sitting room, his face contorted with agony.

"Monsieur Armand. Where is Kate? What 'as 'appened? She is ill.... elle doit aller à l'hôpital?" Danielle was frantic in her questioning. And then she felt Richard's arm around her shoulder, as instinct told him what the old man was about to impart.

"It is too late Danielle; Kate, she 'as gone." He moved towards his chair, the effort of standing, suddenly too much. "We 'ave our cognacs comme normal. She is so 'appy and tell me of a day ze most wonderful......... her meeting wiz you Monsieur..... your admiration of her book Danielle .... and a message very special from England. Then she depart me because she want to make reply to ze letter, and also prepare ze manuscript for you to take. I am content and do not detain her because we already make ze plans for our excursion tomorrow. She tell me zat she will not leave Paris after all! Tantôt, as every evening, I tap at ze door to wish her sleep well but zer is no reply...."

Richard shook his head in disbelief. "But she was so well - incredibly vivacious. Why I had to insist she came back this afternoon. Idiot. I should have done so much earlier."

"Then you would have been the first to persuade her to stop before completing what she had set her mind on," Danielle assured him, and turning to Armand who was nodding his agreement, said, "I would like to go to her please."

"Of course. Le médecin will be finished. I come again please after you."

The doctor was closing his bag having completed the necessary documents.

"You are family?" he asked cautiously.

"Yes." Danielle spoke without hesitation. "Kate est ma famille."

"It was heart failure, most benign. No pain. Please accept my condolences Mademoiselle, Monsieur. I will leave you. I must prescribe a sedative for Monsieur Cardules. He is in shock. Please see that he will take it."

"I'll do that." Richard assumed a sensitive control. As the doctor left them, Danielle picked up an envelope that lay on the coffee table, and passed it to Richard.

"It's addressed to my father."

"But unsealed, meaning she intended you to read it too. Kate was such a stickler for detail, she would not have forgotten to seal an envelope."

He withdrew two programmes; the one they had winkled out of the reservations clerk that afternoon at the Opera House, the other now yellowed with age, of the Margaret Rutherford play Kate and Tom had watched in London on the night they met, nearly half a century ago. The briefest of messages was slipped inside.

"No strings Tom; just thistledown spanning forty seven years. As ever. Kate."

"Not the forty eight he thought then," Richard mused aloud, and then, "That's the answer. Last spring was when it snapped."

"At least he won't know Kate refused to go to him," Danielle whispered, unaware of his thoughts. "I think I am glad about that. She loved him so much. I did not understand her ziz morning at all."

He did not reply. Was this, he wondered, the one decision Kate Benson couldn't live with, despite her resolve? He glanced up to see Danielle take Kate's lifeless hand in her own. "You want to be alone with her. I'll go to Armand."

Danielle stood for some while, silently grieving the woman who had been her teacher, mentor, friend and family. Eventually she walked over to the bureau where Kate had kept her manuscript. She had put it in a tough cardboard box, and with it was an envelope addressed to the agent Danielle was to visit in England. Lifting out the substantial bulk, she noticed that a crisp new sheet had been inserted to replace the previous first of several hundred pages, on which had originally been typed simply: 'For Tom.'

Richard entered the room again, supporting a distraught Armand who appeared so much more frail than when they had arrived yesterday. With tremulous smile, Danielle beckoned to him to join her at the window, and taking his arm, indicated the dedication Kate had so recently penned.

'In memory of Polly Smith, and with profound gratitude and affection for my dearest friend Armand Cardules, without whose support, companionship and philosophy, this book would not have been written, nor a lifelong ambition realised.' K.B.

By the same author:-

The Angel Within: 1994. Reprinted 2004

ISBN   0-9548598-0-4

A poignant, remarkable account of a young couple's struggle to accept that their first child has Downs Syndrome. 'The Angel Within' is an incredibly moving story, and one that lays bare the effects of mental handicap on family life.
Janet Wade has captured the frightening, loving, often lonely experience of living between the real, and a Peter Pan world. Honestly expressing everyday feelings and concerns, this is a book that tugs at the emotions.

Sensitively written, often humorous, it is best of all extremely readable.

'Read this book. Don't skim it. If you skim it you will miss the all-important moments that tell how a family with a disabled daughter missed out on all sorts of things they had expected, and indeed planned, but secured so many joys and satisfactions that were wholly unplanned.........Sometimes funny,   sometimes deeply moving.'

The Lord Rix, Kt CBE DL.
Chairman Mencap